The Birthright Chronicles

Lake
Elan
West
Branch
River
Mt. Nebal
Leborum
Forest
Temple
of Elohim
Saddun
Range
Pele
Feling
Orc
Gatlon
Reaumun Mountains
South
Leborum
rd
Accri
Forest
Dublack
Lef
East
Dublack

# Guardians
# of
# Magessa

# Peter Last

Published by:
Bluewater Publications
www.BluewaterPublications.com

# Credits

- ➢ Robert Rausch artist with Gas Studio of Tuscumbia, AL for his extraordinary work on the book's cover.

- ➢ Scott Campbell created illustration on the front cover

- ➢ David Walker graphic artist that designed the map

- ➢ Sheri Dee Developmental Editor

# Acknowledgements

I would like to express my sincere gratitude to everyone who helped make this book a reality. I would specifically like to thank the following individuals who made this book possible through their constant help, suggestions, and snide comments.

- ❖ My mom and dad for bearing through eleven years of this. A special thanks to my father for his impossibly thorough proofreading eye. When he was grading my papers in school, it was the "evil eye." Now it's just plain useful.

- ❖ My sister Rachel for her constant advice on revisions. Even the seven hundred and fifty thousandth time, when I bet she just wanted to strangle me with my own keyboard cord!

- ❖ My family for the trial runs, suggestions, and critiques of my book. They also offered many encouraging comments like, "This actually isn't too bad!"

- ❖ Ben for his suggested improvements to the story. Also for struggling through college alongside me while I wrote this. Your help with the book and in the classroom was invaluable.

- ❖ The other Ben, for believing my work was good enough to publish, even before he read it. If you're seeing this, it means you're finally starting to read the book!

- ❖ My girlfriend for sticking with me, even when I had to spend more time on the book than I had for her.

- ❖ Robert Womack for his first sketch of the illustration on the front cover. His ability to capture my vision was impressive.

- ❖ Tyler Yasaka for his work building my website. He also filmed and edited promotional pieces.

- ❖ Ben Broyles for promotional filming and marketing assistance.

- ❖ John Givens for allowing me access to his incredible medieval attire and battle accoutrements collection.

- ❖ Sheri Dee for her fantastic editorial and proofreading skills; also, for all the marketing guidance.

- ❖ Finally, and most importantly, God for giving me the ability and opportunity to do this. This book is all for you.

# Prologue

Jothnial brushed his shoulder-length, jet-black hair out of his eyes as he peered around the corner. At least the hair used to be jet-black; there were now strands of silver showing. He looked to be in his late forties or early fifties, but he had actually just turned forty-one. He still held his six-foot frame erect, but other signs of the stress of his job were evident in his looks and bearing. Even his elfish blood wasn't able to stave off the effects of the stress.

The hallway was clear, so he stepped into it and dashed to the next corner. He looked both ways before consulting a map from his pocket. In his mind, he could still clearly hear his commander laying out the plan.

"Jothnial, you will swim across the moat and enter the courtyard by means of the sewer grate. Our compatriot has removed it completely and replaced it with a weaker version; you should be able to break through it easily enough. You can't teleport in, due to a detection spell that has been woven over the castle. That also means that if you use magic while inside, you'll be lit up like a beacon. You'll have to do this old school, at least until you're ready to leave.

"Once inside the courtyard, you'll have to figure out a way to get into the castle. Our contact has suggested that you might try the eastern gate since the guards there are lax compared to the others. Given your abilities, you might also try scaling the walls. Once you get inside, make your way to the third floor. The entire south side is a laboratory for your target, Molkekk's head magician. Getting inside the laboratory will be difficult since it is guarded inside and out by fifty of Molkekk's best soldiers. Our contact has no advice for this part of the mission since no one is allowed near the laboratory except for a select few. Use whatever means necessary to get inside that laboratory and eliminate the magician.

"Once the job is completed, you will have a few options for ex-filtration. If you have managed to remain undetected, it may be possible for you to leave quietly the way that you entered. This would be the optimal approach. If things heat up and you require our assistance to extract you, the roof of the castle is the best option. It provides a flat landing area for the dragons, as well as giving us a height advantage over the castle guards. Other than that, I can't offer much advice. You'll have to play this by ear and hope for the best."

Jothnial thought that he had detected something in the commander's briefing, not in the words themselves, but in the tone that he used and the edge in his voice. It was almost as if this was personal for him. He didn't think that before a mission was the time to bring it up, but he wondered about it just the same. What connection could the elf that led the squad of magicians have to the wizard Molkekk?

Getting inside the castle had been easier than Jothnial had expected, but the halls were so confusing that he was having trouble just finding the stairs to the third floor.

*"Why they couldn't have one staircase going from the bottom to the top is beyond me,"* he thought. *"It's almost like it was designed to confuse people who don't belong here."* On second thought, that was probably not far from the truth. Wizards were notoriously suspicious and this was likely a precaution, one that was paying dividends right now. Absent-mindedly Jothnial fiddled with a pendant that hung from his neck. The silver bauble was circular in shape. Four, curved axe heads were equally spaced on a plain wreath, forming a sort of cross shape. Each axe head was emblazoned with an etching of a triangular, knotted rope. In the center of the pendant, a stylized dragon curled around itself so that it held its tail in its own mouth. The dragon's visible eye, a tiny ruby chip, glimmered with unnerving depth against the dull silver.

Jothnial tried once again to locate his position on the map but for naught. It appeared as though the scrap that he held had no real resemblance to the system of halls that confronted him. By turning the map ninety degrees, he was able to locate an area that looked somewhat like his current position, but it wasn't a perfect match. It looked like this diagram was of a different building entirely; the hall that he was currently standing in didn't actually exist according to it. He shook his head in confusion and glared at the map one last time before folding and placing it back into his pocket. If he was correct in his assumption that the confusion here was one of the wizard's defenses, it was probable that many, if not all, of the walls were magical in nature and probably rearranged periodically. Whatever the case, the map was useless to him. Jothnial flexed his left hand and rubbed the leather of his half-finger glove against the wall. He carefully sniffed each hall before choosing the one to the left.

After a quick look to make sure that the hall was clear, he dashed to the next corner and glanced around it. A group of twenty soldiers was coming straight toward him so noisily that he wondered how he could have possibly not heard them before. He ran back the way he had come, but came face to face with a group of soldiers as soon as he rounded the corner. For a moment they stared at each other, neither making a move. The elf recovered first and sprinted back down the hall.

Jothnial rushed around the corner and headed for one of the many doors that lined the hall. He dove inside and pulled the door closed after him, keeping it open a crack so as to be able to see through it. The soldiers who were chasing him rounded the corner, and he closed the door all the way to escape detection. The interior of the room was dark, and he bumped into things as he tried to find a suitable place to hide. A large unlit fireplace occupied most of one wall, and Jothnial lost no time in sliding into it and up the chimney. In this face down position, the blood rushed to his head, but he could keep an eye on the room this way. He pressed his thighs into the sides of the flue, shifting his weight to his legs.

Almost immediately the room's door opened and one of the groups of soldiers entered. Most of them stood by the door, while five of them continued toward the back wall, a torch lighting their way. At the back of the room, the small circle of light cast by the torch exposed a cradle containing a small baby girl. The baby was dressed in a simple white dress which the soldiers wasted no time in replacing with one of blood-red. One of them picked the baby up, and the soldiers left the room.

Jothnial waited for a few moments after they were gone before sliding out of the chimney and running to the door. The soldiers with the baby were just rounding a corner in the hall, but the other group was nowhere to be seen. After a careful check in both directions, Jothnial sprinted down the hall just catching the last soldier before he disappeared around the corner. He had to stop himself from using magic to dispatch the man, opting for a more conventional method. He covered the man's mouth with his left hand and stabbed a long, sharp dagger into his heart with the other. The soldier thrashed around frantically for a short time, trying to warn his comrades, but Jothnial's grip was too strong. He dragged the dispatched soldier into a nearby room, removed the dagger, and quickly cleaned it. Though it would have been a fantastic disguise, he didn't have time to strip the soldier and put on his armor; however, all of the castle guards wore large, billowy capes. Jothnial wasted no time in taking the oversized piece of cloth from the dead man and fastening it to his own shoulders. He also took the soldier's helmet and placed it on his own head. The fit wasn't perfect, but it would be good enough to disguise him from the back.

With the cape and helmet secured, Jothnial silently slipped back into the hall and sprinted back to the corner that he had caught the soldier going around. The hall branched several times to either side along its length, and Jothnial's sharp eyes saw the cloak of a soldier disappear around the corner of one of these branches. He sprinted down the hall, careful to keep his steps light and thankful for the soft leather boots on his feet. He hurried to the back of the procession and fell in step with the other soldiers; he didn't know where they were going, but hoped they would lead him somewhere useful.

The soldiers wound through the hallways of the castle following a long and confusing path that Jothnial couldn't have memorized, even if he had wanted to. They finally stopped in front of two massive doors and the group's leader provided a password to the two sentries. The doors swung inward, and the column of soldiers filed through them, entering a massive gothic-style room. The ceiling extended upward for at least fifty feet and grotesque statues filled the place; Jothnial's attention was drawn to the biggest object in the room: a large, stone altar located at the room's center. The structure was massive, standing at least twenty-five feet high and had been formed completely out of a solid block of some sort of black stone. Stairs were cut into all four sides and every available surface was covered in relief carvings. A smaller altar stood on top of the large one, and Jothnial guessed that it was here that the offerings would be placed. It was to here that the soldier carrying the baby walked.

Jothnial realized what was happening and slunk back into the shadows. He silently strung his bow and nocked an arrow. He watched as the soldier scaled the side of the stone edifice and placed the baby on the smaller altar. The soldier now retreated back to his companions while from the other side of the room, a man dressed in black and blood-red robes swooped up onto the altar. He was sharpening a knife on a whetstone, as he slowly climbed the many steps. Once on top, he placed the stone on the edge of the smaller altar and turned his gaze to the baby. He gave a ghastly, evil-looking smile and raised the knife.

Jothnial's arrow was already drawn and aimed, and without a moment's hesitation he let the barbed shaft fly. The arrow found its mark, burying itself in the throat of the priest. In the shocked silence that followed, the priest grabbed at his throat as he staggered around the altar. Jothnial sensed that he was trying to heal himself, but the arrow's tip had been silver. The priest staggered backwards, tripped over a carved gargoyle, and fell over the edge, plummeting the two and a half stories to the stone floor. Before anyone knew what was happening, Jothnial burst out of the shadows, scaled the altar's steps, and had the baby in one of his arms. With his free hand he drew a short sword and held it in a defensive position. It was clear that he was ready to take on anyone who approached, but the soldiers were still shaking off the shock of what had just happened. Jothnial backed off the altar and headed for the end of the room from which the priest had come. Before he had reached safety, the soldiers were after him. One of them loosed an arrow and with superhuman reflexes, Jothnial knocked it aside with his sword.

Jothnial came to a pair of doors that were every bit as big as the ones on the other side of the room and leaned into them, pushing with all of his strength. They didn't even budge. He looked over his shoulder and saw that the soldiers were in full pursuit now. He knew that using magic would light him up like a firefly under the castle's detection spells, but he didn't have any other options. There were too many guards for him to fight while holding a baby and the doors were too heavy. Regretting the action as he performed it, he pressed his hand up against one of the doors and extended a tendril of magic. With a groan, the door swung outward, and Jothnial rushed through. He spun around and shoved another spell at it to close it. The door slammed shut just as one of the soldiers tried to dive through. The sharp edge of the door cut completely through the soldier's body, but Jothnial was already moving forward. Now that he had tripped the detection spells, if he stopped moving, he would be dead in minutes. He spun on his heels and froze in his tracks.

What he saw directly in front of him was impossible he knew, even for a skilled magic user. A marsh lay before him blocking his way for as far as he could see in either direction. The only way across was a solitary, rickety-looking bridge. A blood-red moon hung low in the sky and cast a red light on everything for miles around. Nothing before Jothnial matched with reality; he had been on the second floor of the castle, so the door couldn't have taken him outside. Not to mention that the moon, which had been yellow when he entered the castle, was now red. The only thing that coincided with reality was that there had been a marsh outside the castle, but it was separated from the actual building by a wall and moat.

Jothnial knew what he was seeing and yet his brain told him that a spell of this magnitude would be impossible; but obviously it was magic that had somehow been used to make the inside of the castle bigger than it really was. The only way that he could think of for this to be possible was if the doors he had just entered had transported him to a different dimension; however, he hadn't noticed any shift in dimensions so he eliminated that option immediately. In any case, the marsh stank of magic, and Jothnial knew that he had a better chance of escaping if he went back through the doors by which he had gained access to the marsh. He turned and for the second time in as many minutes was shocked by what he saw. The doors he had passed through to get to the marsh had been massive, but the doors he saw now were at least a hundred times taller. In that moment he realized how a marsh could fit inside a castle and berated himself for not figuring it out earlier. Everything here, including himself, had been shrunk—everything except for the doors.

*"I should have expected something like that,"* Jothnial chided himself. *"After all, I'm infiltrating Molkekk's headquarters. This place was bound to stink of dark magic."*

He extended another tendril of magic toward the doors, but stayed several feet away from them. He knew what was on the other side of those doors and would gladly have left it there if it weren't for his current predicament. He slowly nudged one door open without any more effort than he had expended the first time. Clearly, being shrunk had not affected his ability to work magic. He waited for the soldiers to burst through the doors, but nothing happened. The seconds turned into minutes and still nothing. Jothnial slid his sword into the scabbard on his back, and using his free hand, formed a small ball of magic between his index finger and thumb and spread it on his eyes. Immediately, his surroundings took on a transparent form, showing all that was hidden. He looked toward the door and instead of seeing the temple on the other side he saw a hillside. With a snap of his fingers, his vision returned to normal. Moving cautiously, he walked toward the doors. He peeked through the open one and saw that his magic had not deceived him. On the other side was a sunny hillside with a stream running down it. A small cottage stood on top of the hill.

Jothnial was bewildered by the change, but more frightened by the fact that he had no idea where he was. He took a slow, deep breath and let it out before comparing his options. On one side of the door was a marsh that stank of evil. It could easily hide enemies and would be difficult for him to traverse. On the other side of the door was a brightly lit hill. It did not seem evil in the least and was very open. If Jothnial were attacked, he would have plenty of time to react. He went over the decision in his head hundreds of times, knowing quite well that the wrong choice could cost him his life.

He finally stood, turned his back on the door, and walked toward the marsh. He knew that he would choose this eventually. This was, after all, the headquarters of Molkekk. Nothing was pleasant here without a purpose, and even so, the hillside seemed *too* pleasant.

Jothnial made his way to the bridge that spanned the marsh. It appeared rickety and was broken down in many places, but somehow he knew it was the only way across. He carefully stepped onto the first plank of the structure and tested it before putting his whole weight on it. A splash sounded off to his right, and he jerked his head around. Ever-expanding rings rippled in the water, originating from a spot on the marsh only a dozen yards from him. He eyed the water suspiciously before taking another cautious step. As he continued to navigate the bridge, the conviction that he needed to reach the other side of the marsh grew.

Fifteen minutes passed as Jothnial hopped from plank to plank. The bridge was in a greater state of disrepair than he had thought, and he sometimes had to leap over gaps that spanned up to ten feet of empty space in order to reach the next plank. He had to stop to catch his breath, and he did so while leaning against one of the posts that supported the bridge. The gap he faced next was the largest yet, spanning possibly fifteen feet, but only a hundred yards beyond it was land.

He carefully sized up the gap, took a flying leap, and landed with only his toes on the plank. He was off balance and stood there for several long moments struggling to regain his footing. He might have had a chance if this were anywhere else, but here the wood was all slick with mold. His feet slid off of the board, and he tumbled backwards into the sticky mud of the marsh. His first thoughts were for the baby which he held up with one hand. The mud was so thick that he sank into it slowly, giving him time to reach for and find purchase on the slimy planks of the bridge. The baby was now about even with the bridge's surface, so he thrust her onto the timbers. Moments later his face submerged and for a moment he began to panic. This was no ordinary mud; he was almost overcome by the malicious magic that was behind it, trying to pull him down and suffocate him. Gripping the bridge with both hands, he pulled as if his life depended on it. After what seemed like an eternity under the mud, his head forced its way out and he took deep gasping breaths of the rancid marsh air.

Even in the small amount of time that he had ceased to pull his body upward, the mud had begun to suck him back downward. With a groan, Jothnial began to pull again causing every muscle in his body to scream at him. With unhappy squelching noises, the mud slowly gave him up. Hand by hand he clawed his way up onto the bridge, fighting the mud the whole way. Finally he was able to pull his feet free and crawl forward a few more feet just for good measure. Exhausted, he dropped face down on the bridge, gasping for breath.

It was several minutes before he trusted his limbs to hold his weight. When a small amount of strength had returned, he pushed himself to a sitting position and looked around for the baby. She was laying on the bridge a foot or so from the edge, unaware of what was going on around her. The bottom of her dress and her legs were covered in mud, but on the whole she was not hurt. Jothnial looked down at his clothes and as he had expected, saw that he was covered in the foul smelling mud of the swamp. It was already starting to dry on him, creating a hard shell on his skin that pulled at him when he moved, and it was time for him to move if he had any intentions of getting out of here alive. He had already spent a good amount of time here, and every second more was one closer to something that he couldn't deal with catching up to him. With a groan he picked up the baby and pushed himself to his feet.

The thought of dry land only a hundred yards away made Jothnial want to get there as quickly as possible, but he forced himself to proceed cautiously. After all, it was not only his life at stake, but the life of the baby in his arms as well. The next step was all that he focused on until, suddenly, he found himself standing on solid dirt. He looked up and saw for the first time a large, plain looking structure blocking his path. An observer might call it a house, though that description would have been generous. It was simply a large, white cube with a single door in the exact center of the wall facing him. Jothnial walked around the back of the house, examining the wall as he moved. He wasn't sure what material it was made out of, but it certainly wasn't wood.

The back of the house looked exactly as the front had: a solid wall with a single door cutting through it. Jothnial might have ignored the structure altogether if it had not been sitting on a small plot of land surrounded on all four sides by the marsh. It appeared as though the bridge was the only way to the island and the only way off. The magician decided that as long as he had made the dangerous and useless trip out here, he might as well see what was inside the building. Cautiously, he opened the door and peeked inside. The entire inside of the house was empty, so he stepped through the door. There were no furnishings or subdivisions of the house; it consisted of one large, empty room. No windows looked out of the house, and it had only two doors.

Jothnial stared in bewilderment. Previously, he had been certain that he needed to cross the marsh, but now he was positive that he had made a mistake. Behind him, the door creaked, and he spun around to face this new development. In the doorway stood what could only be described as massive, black, and ugly. It was at least fourteen feet tall, two feet taller than the tallest ogre Jothnial had ever seen, but didn't resemble one at all. It looked like a pile of mud with arms and legs. It didn't appear to have a head, and Jothnial didn't spend too much time looking for one. He figured that even if he took it off, the thing would not die.

The monster slowly advanced from the door and made its way toward Jothnial. By now the elf could tell that it reeked of magic. He reached for one of the silver throwing knives on his belt and flung it at the blob. The projectile hit the monster dead center and disappeared into it. For a second nothing happened, and Jothnial started to panic.

*"That thing has to be magic,"* he told himself, *"and the knife I threw was silver. Everyone knows that silver destroys magic."*

Before Jothnial had time to finish convincing himself, the blob exploded and threw him across the house. He almost lost the baby, but managed to keep hold of her. The warning bells in his brain were working overtime, and he landed on his feet and spun to face the front door of the house. A man with blood-red robes stood in the doorway. His eyes were completely white, and it was obvious that he was blind. He seemed to rely on his sense of smell to navigate, and it led him straight toward Jothnial. The magician reached over his shoulder, pulled his sword from its scabbard, and began to circle to the man's right.

The man seemed to immediately sense the change in Jothnial's behavior and withdrew a sword from the folds of his cloak. He approached Jothnial slowly and sank into a fighter's crouch. Jothnial wondered how the man could tell where everything was even though he was blind. He raised his sword to block a blow from the blind man and was surprised at how powerful it was. With a quick, twisting move, he thrust his blade at the blind man's stomach. The blade sank in up to the hilt, and Jothnial jerked it down and then up, causing the man to fall in half.

Jothnial started to turn away from his victim, but was stopped short. The man fell in two pieces, but not a drop of blood spilled onto the floor. Instead, the two halves of the man's body began to grow. In no time, two exact replicas of him stood in front of him. They both clenched swords in their fists and began to circle Jothnial. The elf began to turn in a circle, trying to keep both opponents in his sight, but they continued to circle further apart. Soon one of them would be behind him and ready to attack. Thoughts rushed through Jothnial's head as he tried to decide what to do. Could one of the men be an illusion? That was an easy trick for even an inexperienced magician. Then again, maybe the first attacker was an illusion as well. After all, he didn't bleed when he had been split in half.

There were too many options to consider and Jothnial knew that if he didn't move quickly, he was going to be vulnerable. Gripping the baby more tightly in his left arm, he turned and bolted toward the man who had maneuvered behind him. He went to his knees at the last second, sliding underneath the man's blade and past him. In one smooth motion, Jothnial rose to his feet and spun, bringing his sword in a wide, vertical slash toward the man's neck. The sword met next to no resistance as it cut, and the man's head fell to the floor. Again, no blood issued from the cut as the man's body quickly grew another head. Meanwhile, the head on the floor morphed shapes and grew into a tiger.

Jothnial looked at his three opponents, carefully sizing them up. It appeared as though wounding them would do nothing but create more enemies. This had to be magic.

*"What's happening?"* Jothnial wondered in panic. *"The silver in my sword appears to have no effect on them, and yet they have to be magic."*

The tiger waited for the two men to come even with it, and all three enemies started to surround Jothnial. He backed up in order to keep all three in his sight. In only a few steps he felt a wall against his back, so he slid sideways along the wall until he had moved into a corner. With his back now safe from attack, he waited for his assailants to move in. The men advanced together, but the tiger didn't wait. Magic shot from Jothnial's right fist and hit the tiger as it jumped, flinging it across the house and into the other wall. It immediately rose to its feet and began to bound back toward him.

The second that Jothnial threw the tiger with magic, he rammed his sword into the floor and reached for a silver throwing knife. With a flick of his wrist, he buried the knife in the shoulder of one of the identical men. The weapon began to glow and shake violently, and Jothnial watched, holding his breath. What happened next was something that he had never seen before, something that he had not thought was possible. The knife continued to glow brighter and shake more violently until it exploded into a thousand slivers, all flying directly at Jothnial. He had no time to avoid the missiles and was just able to block the baby with his body and raise his arm to defend his own face. The silver slivers hit him, stopping only where they met metal. In all the gaps of Jothnial's armor, they had a devastating effect, smashing into his skin and leaving a million tiny cuts. The blind man paused only momentarily as the skin of his shoulder grew back and hid the hole where moments ago a knife had been buried. When the healing was complete, the man removed a throwing knife of his own from his belt. With a motion so fast that his hand appeared as a blur, he hurled the weapon across the room.

A stream of magic blasted from Jothnial's fingers, making the air around it glow a faint green. This was a bit like killing a cockroach with a mace and chain, but Jothnial had had enough of this battle. The magic met the knife halfway between the combatants flipping it to the side and continuing straight toward the blind man. The man was oblivious to the stream of magic and it hit him in the chest. In that moment, the only thing that Jothnial could think of was his lessons in school about wave motion. The magic bounced off of the blind man and rebounded back like a wave hitting a wall. Before he had time to react, the pulse of power hit Jothnial and would have thrown him into the wall had he not already been pressed against it. He flew through it instead, landing outside on his butt and sliding several more feet on the packed dirt.

The magician rose to his feet, still gripping the baby in his left arm. She was crying now and he wondered why she had chosen right now to start. Or maybe she had been crying the whole time and he had just now noticed. He also wondered exactly how he had managed to keep a grip on her for so long and through so much. He had managed, but it was hindering his ability to fight; he would have to do something. Dropping to one knee, he laid the girl on the ground and yanked the cloak from his shoulders. While keeping one eye on the hole in the building's wall, he used a few deft twists of the cloth and some creative finagling to secure the bundle to his back with the baby facing outward. Now these unholy creatures would see exactly what he could do.

The tiger burst through the hole first and Jothnial rose to his full height. This beast might be faster and stronger than he was, but he could certainly out think it. He watched in a detached manner as the animal bounded towards him. He could see the saliva dangling off of its teeth and the look of pure evil in its eyes. There was a lot of rage focused behind this creature and not much else. The tiger came within striking distance and without missing a stride leaped at Jothnial. The elf held fast, spinning away and down at the last possible second. A well timed spell created a concussive force that threw the tiger a dozen feet off of the island and over the marsh. For a moment it seemed to be suspended in the air, then it fell into the mud below. Jothnial could have been imagining things, but it seemed as if the marsh gave gleeful sounding gurgles as it sucked the screaming tiger down to its demise.

Jothnial felt more than heard the whistling of the air to his left and spun just in time to catch the blind man's blow on his bracer. The blade skidded off of the hardened leather, and he leaped away from the attack. He pulled the last of his throwing knives from his belt and held it in his right fist, the blade pointed toward the ground. He brought his hands up towards his face in a fist fighter's defensive stance and shifted his weight forward to his toes. He might be facing an armed opponent when he had only a short knife, but it was something that he had been trained for. The next blow from the blind man was low, and Jothnial blocked it out with his left bracer. His right fist flashed forward, dealing a smashing blow to the man's jaw. The punch would have staggered the stoutest of fighters, but it didn't seem to affect the blind man who immediately countered with an over-handed slash. Jothnial stopped the blow with his knife and captured the sword blade with his leather clad left fist. In a movement faster than the eye could follow, he stabbed the man three times in the throat and face with the knife and stepped back. The man wasn't even shaken by the attack, but brought his sword up to deal another blow.

Jothnial's brain was working overtime. The man before him appeared to be indestructible and his twin had just stepped out of the building. It didn't appear as if there was any way to defeat them except for the mud. It had taken the tiger and might do the same for the men. He would have to get a better position for that to work, since he was currently between both of them and the swamp. All of his thoughts went to the wind and his instincts

15

took over when he saw his opponent's sword raise for another blow. Moving forward to crowd the blind man, he drove the dagger in his fist into the man's stomach while capturing his wrist with his left hand. He left the dagger buried where it was and used his right fist to concentrate a punch on the blind man's elbow. The arm buckled under the force and the sword dropped into Jothnial's waiting hand. He spun left and delivered a back kick to the man's chest, throwing him off balance. The magician pounced on his opponent and drove him to the ground. He lifted the sword high and slammed it down into the man's stomach and the dirt beyond.

Jothnial didn't know if the blade would keep the man pinned or for how long, but at least it gave him a slight head start. He turned back to the building and ran towards it. His gut told him that the structure held the way out of this god-forsaken marsh, but getting in would be a problem. The other blind man stood in the hole in the wall; he would have to go around to one of the doors or... Jothnial flung a spell at the wall about fifteen feet from where the blind man stood, blowing another hole through the thin barrier. He squeezed through the makeshift door and broke hard to the left to retrieve his sword from where it still stood, stuck into the floor. Out of the corner of his eye, he saw a section of the wall at what would have been second story level shimmering as though heat waves were rising in front of it. He grabbed his sword and sprinted toward the shimmering wall. He couldn't make the jump, but magic might be able to do the trick. Timing a concussion spell to throw you upward was dangerous, but he had done it successfully before. The timing had to be perfect, but perfection was nothing new to Jothnial. The blast somersaulted him up and through the shimmering wall so fast that he almost flew straight through it into whatever was beyond. As he catapulted toward the shimmering surface, vague images began to materialize on the other side of it though he was moving far too quickly to process them before he found himself flying through a window that hadn't been visible until now. He twisted around, clawing for something to grab onto and was just able to seize the window sill. He almost lost his grip as his momentum tried to tear his fingers loose, every tendon in his arm stretching. For a moment he was suspended horizontally, sticking straight out from the window, then time caught up with him and he swung down, slamming into a wall.

Jothnial immediately recognized that he was hanging from a second floor window of the castle that he had infiltrated almost an hour ago. He pulled himself up and peered through the window, not knowing what to expect. He saw nothing but an empty room and pulled himself through. He was prepared to find himself in the house that he had just left, but the room on the other side of the window remained the same when he tumbled inside. He had no time to figure out what had just happened because the doors on the far end of the room shook from a blow. Jothnial looked toward them just in time to see them burst open and a mob of soldiers rush through. Without a second's hesitation, Jothnial formed a large ball of magic in his right palm and used it to create a whirlwind. He clutched his sword to his chest and wrapped the other arm around his back to secure the baby as they shot upward. The whirlwind shattered each floor as they approached and in seconds they burst through the castle's roof. Jothnial killed the whirlwind and dropped back onto what remained of the castle roof.

*"Ebenezer!"* he shouted to his dragon. *"Get over here now! I've got a bunch of soldiers after me that really want to kill me!"*

Standing exposed as he was on the castle roof, the few minutes that followed were an eternity for Jothnial. The baby on his back was screaming again, but at least that meant that she was alive. The soldiers could be heard below, shouting to each other as they tried to work out a way to get onto the roof. For a moment the world stopped and nothing happened. Despite the baby's cries and the shouts of the soldiers, silence seemed to govern the night. The stars twinkled overhead and time stood still.

A ladder rose through the massive hole in the castle roof, breaking Jothnial's trance. He gripped his sword tightly in his fist and waited for the soldiers to climb. There were a lot of them, but at least they were only human. He could fight against those kinds of odds. The first soldier stuck his head up through the destroyed roof and looked straight at Jothnial. The elf stared back and let his sword's tip rest on the toe of his boot. His smile was genuine and there was a devious glint in his eye. A black dragon with gold tracing through his scales dropped out of the night and slammed onto the ladder's top. Jothnial rushed over to him and jumped into the saddle on his back.

With a roar, Ebenezer took off in a rush of wind and flew away from the tower as fast as he could. For a minute it looked like they might make a clean getaway. The tower was fading quickly into the distance and the night would provide Jothnial and his dragon with cover once they were away. Then, just when it seemed that everything would work out, a bellow reverberated across the plain. Jothnial looked back to see a dark shape rise to block the moon. Silhouetted as it was, it was easy to make out the shape of the dragon and the man riding on it.

Ebenezer pumped his wings faster, but the following dragon still gained on him. Jothnial stretched out his hand and pointed at the dragon, but his magic only bounced harmlessly off of a translucent shield that was surrounding the beast. Grimacing, Jothnial increased his attack and felt the shield slowly begin to give way under the barrage. Another force fought back, replenishing the shield's power. Jothnial continued to attack, but his strength was leaving him.

"Please help me, God," he screamed just before he passed out. "I can't hold out!"

******

"That can't be good."

Four figures sat in the shadow of a large cluster of rocks as they looked across the marsh at the castle that Jothnial had entered only an hour before. At first glance, they all appeared to be humans. The truth was that they were all *humanoid*; however, only one of them was actually a human. Two elves were on the west side of the boulder, distinguishable from the human only by their lack of facial hair. On the east side of the boulder was an orc, who also could easily be mistaken for a human. Thick hair on his arms and face was the only telltale sign that he was an orc. The four figures carefully studied the castle on the far side of the marsh. Nothing had happened since Jothnial had left; however, there was now a disturbance on the top of the tallest turret of the castle. One of the elves whispered a word, and the entire group could immediately see the turret as though it were only a few yards away. Planks of wood and other debris flew into the air, and on top of the tower's roof stood Jothnial.

"How come it seems like this always happens when we send him in?" one of the elves asked with a sigh.

"It doesn't happen *every* time, Commander," the human responded. "Remember that time last spring when we were infiltrating the stronghold in Gludog? He came off brilliantly that time, except that he got wounded."

A group of dragons stood behind the observers, and one of them leaped into the air, shot over the men's heads, and flew silently toward the castle in the distance. The men's vision normalized, and they looked up to see which dragon had left.

"Looks like Jothnial called for his dragon," the commander commented. "By the way, if you will recall, at Gludog we were not supposed to be seen at all. The mission completion was negated by the fact that we were discovered."

"It wasn't his fault, Commander. You saw that with your own eyes. He did everything by the book, but he was still seen."

"That one wasn't his fault, but what about the time before that? It should have been a simple snatch-and-grab, but he screwed it up. If it weren't for him, we wouldn't even be here in this situation."

"That was his second mission, so he was anxious to please and made some stupid mistakes. He did mess up on that mission, but he pulled off his first one without a single flaw."

"Yes, I remember that," the commander grumbled. "As I recall, that was the mission after which I accepted him into our squad. Now I almost wish that I hadn't."

"Now, Commander, you don't really mean that," the orc spoke up. "You know that he just..."

"Enemy magic in the area!" the human hissed. Then, after a moment, "There's a magical shield surrounding the dragon following Ebenezer. Who knows how much magic Jothnial's used in the last hour. We can't count on him to be able to take the dragon down."

"Then help him!" ordered the commander. "Jared and Scrogg, you attack the shield directly. Wellter and I will try to attack the magician that's sustaining it. With any luck, we'll be able to take it down."

"And it had better be fast," the human shouted. "Jothnial just passed out."

The four magicians became silent as they each concentrated on their tasks. Jared and Scrogg attacked the shield, but with no success. The magician behind it was very powerful. The commander and Wellter both sent out tendrils to determine the size and strength of the shield and found that it was small, surrounding only the dragon it was protecting. The commander knew that as a rule smaller shields were easier to sustain and consequently harder to attack. With the size of this particular one and the strength of the magician sustaining it, there was little chance of successfully attacking it directly.

"We have to get closer to that thing," the commander hissed to Wellter while tucking his pendant under his breastplate. "We're too far away to do any permanent damage. We need to set up a shield to protect Jothnial until we reach him."

The two magicians leaped onto their dragons and headed in the direction of Jothnial and Ebenezer. Together, they quickly produced a makeshift shield just in time to catch a blast of fire from the pursuing dragon. The fireball bounced harmlessly off of their shield and flew back at the dragon that had spewed it. It slapped against the enemy shield and was deflected downward to the ground below.

"Did you see that, Commander?" Wellter called. "That shield protects against both magic and physical threats."

"And the magician's sitting beneath it on that dragon's back," the commander called. "You sustain our shield, and I will take care of this man."

Without waiting for an answer, the commander directed his dragon to maneuver to a position directly above the enemy dragon. He crouched on his saddle and looked down into the eyes of the magician. Without another thought, he leaped from his saddle and, as he plunged toward his adversary, drew a silver knife from his belt and held it blade first below his body. As the silver passed through the shield, the magic barrier disappeared with a small explosion and a mass of fireworks. The commander hit the dragon hard, knocking the breath out of his lungs and jarring the knife from his grip. He recovered quickly, but even as he looked up, his opponent slashed at him with a knife. The commander jerked away from the wild move, but the blade slashed across his cheek, leaving a streak of blood. He clawed his way into a more maneuverable position and crouched to face the next attack. The magician again slashed with the knife, but the commander shot out a hand and grabbed the hilt of the weapon. With a sharp wrench, he twisted the magician's hand around and slammed the weapon into his stomach. He let go of the magician and watched him slip off the dragon then turned to face the head of the dragon. He composed a small spell, cast it at the dragon's head, and leaped from the back of the beast. As he reached the apex of his jump, he felt the claw of his dragon settle around his body, and he knew that he was safe. Below him, the enemy dragon plummeted toward the ground and landed with a large splash in the marsh below. The commander looked over at Jothnial and extended a tendril of magic toward him. His vital signs were strong, so the commander settled back for the journey to headquarters.

# One

Senndra used the shock from the blow to spin in a tight circle on her heels. As she finished the move, she ducked under the inevitable slash aimed at her upper torso. Jumping into a standing position, she parried a blow aimed at her legs and returned a slash at her opponent's head. Her attacker struck her blade near the hilt, partially jarring it from her grasp. She managed to hold onto the weapon, and her opponent lost no time in pressing his advantage. He swung at Senndra's head, and she wasn't able to get her sword up in time. Instead, she dove under the blade and rolled past him. She rolled onto her knees and spun around, swinging her sword at her opponent's knees. He easily jumped over the poorly-aimed swipe and brought his sword down at Senndra's head. Senndra used her sword to deflect the blow then brought the hilt around and slammed it into her aggressor's stomach. He avoided most of the force of the blow by leaning backwards; however, his breath was still knocked out of him. Senndra jumped to her feet and aimed a quick slash at him. Despite the fact that her opponent was on his back and that he hadn't even gotten his breath back, he was still able to block the blow and return one. The counter attack caught Senndra off guard, and she barely stopped the blow from smashing into her stomach. Her attacker's blade bounced down her sword, hopped over the hilt, and slashed across her hand. Senndra could tell that the injury was only a flesh wound, but the pain was still enough to cloud her reaction. She looked down just in time to see her opponent hook his sword into her pant leg and jerk. The motion threw Senndra off balance. As she toppled, she lost her sword, and the next thing she knew, she was on her face and could feel the cold steel of a sword on her neck.

"Do you yield?" he asked.

Senndra rolled her eyes. "As if I had a choice. You beat me again."

She rose slowly to her feet and finally raised her eyes to meet those of her opponent, Lemin, her sword fighting instructor. He had elf blood though how much no one knew for certain and it could hardly be discerned from his looks. He was about six feet tall, with short, cropped black hair and the beginning of a beard and mustache. Senndra knew that it would be gone before it got even a quarter of an inch long. As if its sole purpose was to mar his otherwise good looks, a scar of five or six inches, normally white but now red after the exertion of a sword fight, stood out on his left cheek. He held Senndra's sword out to her, and she took it and slid it into its scabbard.

"You're dismissed to have that cut taken care of," Lemin told Senndra. "It doesn't appear to be more than a flesh wound, so don't expect to get out of class tomorrow," he added with a twinkle in his eye. "I want you here bright and early so that I can beat you again."

"Not tomorrow, I'm afraid, sir," Senndra answered as she wrapped her hand in a cloth that Lemin handed to her.

"What do you mean?" Lemin asked as he glanced at Senndra quizzically. "Do you have something more important to do?"

"No, sir," Senndra answered. "Tomorrow I'm going to beat you." She waved to the rest of the class and turned to leave.

"Whatever you say," Lemin called after her as she started down the trail that led to the medical station. "Just be here tomorrow, and we'll see who beats who. And remember that the swordplay competition is tonight," he added.

Senndra grinned to herself as she broke into a jog. She really did like Lemin, though he seemed to take delight in beating his students every time he fought them in the ring. And he always did beat them, usually in under a minute. As usual, Senndra had held her own for more than three minutes, but had finally been bested by her instructor. Also as usual, she had been wounded in the fight and was dismissed early to take care of the wound.

The hospital came into sight, and Senndra slowed to a walk. The trails were deserted at this time since the academy students were in their classes and all of the instructors were teaching. As a result, there were no distractions, and Senndra loved the quiet. She could just sit for hours on end and observe nature, the plants and the animals interacting with each other. As she walked toward the hospital, her gaze strayed to the forest, down the mountain from where she was. She couldn't be certain, but she thought she could make out the shape of a deer on the outer edge of the trees. Suddenly, a red blur burst from the clouds above the forest and dove toward the deer. The deer broke into a sprint for the trees, but before it had gained safety, the dragon that was hunting the deer grabbed it in its claws and flew away.

Senndra let out a breath she didn't know she had been holding and continued to stare at the place where the dragon had disappeared. Just the sight of the creatures made her heart beat faster. Everything she knew about dragons pointed to their intelligence and grace. Even the way the dragon had killed the deer had been graceful.

Senndra shook herself from her thoughts and walked the rest of the distance to the hospital. She pushed open the door with her good hand and walked through the empty waiting room to the table that served as the receptionist's desk. The receptionist looked up from a book at the sound of the door opening and saw Senndra.

"How are you today, Senndra?" she asked as she used her finger to mark the book that she had been reading.

"Pretty good, Michal," Senndra answered. "Just got nicked sword fighting, and Lemin sent me down here."

"No one else is here, so you can go in," Michal said as she reopened her book.

Senndra walked past Michal and down the hall to the back of the building. Here, one of the only doors in the building separated the doctor's personal study from the rest of the office. The study was rather large and lighted by three large windows. It was basically empty, containing only a bookcase and a desk. Behind the desk was a small, balding man.

"Hello, Senndra," the man said as he set aside some papers. "What are you in for today?"

"Hello, Doctor Samuel," Senndra responded. "It's just a small cut from sword fighting."

"Don't miss a day, do you?" Samuel said as he rose from his desk. He led Senndra out of his office, down the hall, and into an operating room.

"I was thinking about preparing the equipment before you got here, but decided against it," Samuel said as he gathered supplies from several cabinets. "Now I'm beginning to wish I had done so."

"Like you said, I never miss a day," Senndra responded. She removed the cloth from her hand at Samuel's prompting and held it out for him to examine.

"Nothing more than a flesh wound," he said after examining the cut. "It shouldn't slow you down at all."

"Good," Senndra said. She watched as Samuel first cleaned out the cut then wrapped a bandage around her hand and fastened it.

"Thanks, Doctor Samuel," Senndra said when he finished. She left him in the room to put things away and walked back outside. The peace and quiet she had left only fifteen minutes ago had been replaced with the chatter of students as they left their classes. They followed the main path down the mountain toward the dorms, and Senndra joined them. She didn't see anyone she knew and continued in silence. She passed the mess hall and was just in view of her dorm when an unwelcome voice sounded behind her.

"Hey Senndra, wait up."

"What do you want, Vladimir?" asked Senndra, turning around to face him.

"Nothing," he said as he pulled up in front of Senndra. "Just wanted to say hi."

"Well, in that case, hi," Senndra said, her voice tight.

"So, what are you planning on doing this afternoon?" Vladimir asked. "I was wondering if you wanted to hang out."

"I don't think so, Vladimir," Senndra responded curtly. "Not right now."

"Then how about later?" he asked.

"I don't think so," Senndra answered. She spun on her heels and marched away from him to her dorm. She didn't look back until she reached the safety of her room. She opened the door and stepped inside and was met at once by the smiling face of her roommate, Rita. She was a pretty girl, with blond hair that hung down to her waist and blue eyes that seemed to attract every male cadet on the campus.

"What happened today?" she asked as she examined Senndra's bandage.

"Just a scratch from sword fighting," Senndra answered. "Nothing to worry about."

"You couldn't have at least waited until the last one healed?" Rita asked. "So, what has you so perturbed?"

"Who else…Vladimir," Senndra responded, disgust in her voice. She unstrapped her sword from her hip and threw it onto the top bunk. "One would think he could take a hint, but every time I turn around, I'm tripping over him."

"Vladimir isn't nearly as bad as you make him out to be," Rita said. She sat on the lower bunk, but kept her gaze on Senndra. "I think he's lonely and is just trying to make a friend. I mean, you remember what that's like, right? It was only what, two years ago that you ended up here?"

"Yeah, the same year that Daddy died," Senndra sighed. "I was only fourteen then, and it was really scary coming here. I don't know if I've ever told you this, but thank you for being my friend."

"All I'm saying is that you could try being a little nicer to him," Rita said. She climbed out of the bed. "Anyway, lunch is in ten minutes, so we need to head up to the mess hall."

Senndra rose and followed Rita out of the room.

******

Josiah grasped the javelin in his left hand and held it in front of him with the tip pointing at the ground. He eyed the target carefully and gauged its distance. This was the farthest one yet, with a distance of possibly fifty yards. That, combined with the fact that the target wasn't much bigger than a human torso, made this a very hard throw. The sun beat down on Josiah, causing sweat to drip down into his eyes and blur his vision. With a swipe of his hand, he wiped the sweat off his face and gauged the distance to the target again. At the signal from his instructor, Josiah pulled the javelin back and prepared to throw it. He kept his eyes on the small black circle that represented the center of the target, and when the call was given, he heaved his javelin. The spear shot through the air with only a shallow arc, and Josiah held his breath as it covered the fifty yards. It hit the bottom right corner of the target with a splintering of wood.

*"Not too bad,"* Josiah told himself. He glanced at the other cadets' targets and saw that half of the javelins hadn't even reached them. Of the ones that had flown far enough, all but two had hit their targets, mostly on the outer edges. The call to retrieve the javelins was given, and the cadets advanced down the range, chattering as they went.

"Nice shot, Josiah," called the cadet who was two stations to Josiah's left.

"Thanks, Cirro," Josiah responded, "but it really wasn't all that good. It barely hit the target at all."

"At least it made it far enough," Cirro said. "Mine was way too short, probably by fifteen feet."

Josiah shrugged and walked the rest of the way to his target. The javelin was more than four inches from the nearest edge and had hit with enough force to sink in at least six inches. Josiah braced his foot on the target, grabbed the shaft of his spear, and pulled the weapon from where it had lodged. Shifting his grip to the middle of the javelin, he rested it on his shoulder. He quickly walked back to the line that he had thrown from and spun around, ready to throw again.

"That's it for today," the instructor called to his students. All the cadets shifted their spears onto their shoulders and began to make their way to the northwest corner of the range. There a small door cut a hole through the hedge that ran all the way around the practice field. The cadets left in a single file line and made their way to the northeast corner of the hedge where the armory was located. Josiah waited patiently as the line crawled along at a snail's pace. When he finally reached the armory, he entered the building, put his spear on the rack, and went back outside to wait for Cirro.

Half a minute later, Cirro came out of the armory, and he and Josiah began to cross the city that was their campus. The fifteen minute walk back to the barracks took them past massive buildings with extraordinary architecture. Huge flights of stairs and pillars guarded the doors of the buildings, and large statues graced the lawns. At the north end of the campus, a wall stretched across a pass in a mountain range. The only break in the wall was a massive gate that opened onto a vast plain. The gate was currently shut against attacks from the soldiers of Molkekk.

Josiah shuddered even as he thought of the name. Molkekk was the ancient enemy of the men of Magessa. He had opposed Magessa because they worshiped Elohim, the creator and ruler of the world and all that was in it. Legends portrayed Molkekk as any of the original six races that inhabited Magessa and the surrounding lands. But on one thing they all agreed— Molkekk had allied himself with Oglemophin, a fallen angel that had once had the duty of leading the worship of Elohim. Oglemophin had become jealous of Elohim and sought to take away his throne. A bitter fight had followed. One-third of the angels followed Oglemophin, but they were defeated by those that remained faithful. In the end, they were thrown out of heaven.

Oglemophin took up residence in Hades, the fiery underworld, and from there assaulted the earth, trying to turn the races away from Elohim. After a damning covenant, Molkekk received his magical abilities from Oglemophin's extensive power. Even with his new might, Molkekk knew that he would have difficulty destroying Magessa and waited patiently, gathering more strength. Finally considering himself strong enough, he had waged war against Magessa only to be thwarted by a magician named Jothnial.

Jothnial was a young elf with a long life ahead of him, but he chose to give it up to defeat Molkekk. Just two years ago he had led an army of magicians to Molkekk's headquarters to confront the sorcerer face to face. The final confrontation took place in the door of Molkekk's base, a tower in the city of Volexa Temp. The battle was bitter, and according to the stories, had lasted for three days. At long last, Jothnial gained the upper hand and dealt Molkekk a fatal blow. As he turned away from his foe, Molkekk rose and delivered a strike to his back. Jothnial fell and died there along with the evil wizard.

Molkekk's body died from the wounds sustained in the fight, and in order to survive, he was forced to convert himself into a spirit and bind his powers to the tower that was his headquarters. Though his power was greatly stunted, Molkekk was still able to fulfill his wishes by taking control of the inhabitants of the surrounding lands. He also created a new race called the goblins, which had no will of their own, but were instead an extension of his consciousness. Since his defeat and confinement to his tower, he had lain dormant; nevertheless, the northern gate of Saddun was always guarded against his inevitable attack.

In contrast to the large, magnificent city gate, the barracks looked out of place. The building was only one story tall and about five hundred yards long. This one building was actually composed of a score of smaller ones all connected together and could house one thousand cadets, though it remained empty for most of the day.

"So what's with all the activity around campus?" Cirro asked Josiah as they walked.

"They're trying to make it look better—more presentable," Josiah responded. "You've been here less than a year so you don't know this, but every year the academy in Belvárd sends some of their students over here to visit. Don't ask me why. Maybe it's supposed to build unity in the army or something. Anyway, the people in authority around here find it necessary to make our campus look as nice as possible."

"So that's what's up," Cirro exclaimed. "Yesterday I had an altercation with a teacher and got put on a painting detail as punishment. We put new coats of paint on a dozen buildings. Now they look as good as new. You'd think the counsel was coming to visit from all the things that are happening."

"Which means that you had better be on extra good behavior," Josiah said. "If they catch you doing anything out of line, you'll probably be planting flowers along twenty miles of road or something like that."

"Yeah, not exactly something I want to do," Cirro responded, "especially not in this heat."

Josiah and Cirro entered the barracks and were immediately assaulted by the strong stench of body odor. It wasn't because the building had an inadequate ventilation system; there was just no way to decrease the smell of one thousand sweating men. Already the lunch bell was ringing, so Josiah and Cirro quickly changed into new clothes and headed for the mess hall.

The dining facility was crammed past its capacity as usual, but Josiah and Cirro had little trouble getting to their table. They sat down and began to ravenously devour their meal.

"There's never enough food at this place," Josiah grumbled to Cirro. "It's a wonder we haven't starved yet on these rations."

The hall was suddenly plunged into silence, and Josiah looked up to see what had caused it. A high-ranking instructor was standing on a table at the front of the hall and holding up his hands for silence. As soon as he got it, he began to speak.

"Thank you," he said. "I have an announcement. The time has come for the annual academy get-together. For those of you who are new here, that means that some of the cadets from the academy in Belvárd are coming to visit our campus in the next few days. As such, you are expected to be on your best behavior while they are here. Also, all of the cadets will be expected to help make our campus presentable. You will be assigned by companies to do different tasks; you will hear about that from your company leader."

"What does that mean?" Cirro asked after the instructor had gotten off the table.

"Exactly what he said," Josiah replied. Then he smirked and added, "Also, since we're having company, we'll be getting better meals."

"Well, you're the barracks leader; so what assignments do we have?" Cirro asked.

Josiah shrugged. "I haven't heard anything about them yet, though I'll probably find out pretty soon."

"This'll be fun," Cirro said sarcastically. "I always thought that I'd end up planting twenty miles of flowers, but I figured that it would be for something bad that I'd done."

"It's your dream to plant twenty miles of flowers?" Josiah asked as he rose from his seat. "I'll be sure that no one else steals that job from you."

******

The mess hall bustled with activity as those who had finished their meal left and those who were on KP cleaned up. Senndra sidestepped two of the cadets headed to the kitchen with massive stacks of dishes. She trotted across an open area and squeezed past two other cadets who were talking. She pushed her way out the mess hall doors and glanced around. Rita was nowhere in sight. Senndra figured that she would be in their dorm room since there were no classes for two hours after lunch and the morning classes always tired Rita out. She chose the correct path and headed toward her dorm. She made her way into the building and ascended the stairs to the second floor. As she reached her floor, she could tell immediately that something was out of the ordinary. Two guards stood by the door as though waiting for her. As she got closer, she was able to make out the design on their breastplates—a fire-breathing dragon.

"Senndra Felling?" one of the guards asked as she came to a stop at her door.

"Yes, what is it?" Senndra responded.

"Good news from the hatchery," the same guard answered. "Your dragon has hatched. We have been sent to escort you there."

"Very well," Senndra said. She kept her face emotionless, but inside she was ecstatic. "I need to grab some things from my room, but I'll be out in a second."

She entered the room and headed straight for the bunks. Rita was sleeping on the bottom one, so Senndra made sure not to disturb her as she retrieved her sword from the top bunk. She strapped it onto her left hip, grabbed her cloak from off the back of a chair, and left the room. She followed her two escorts down the hall and the stairs, and back outside. They took the same path Senndra had traveled only minutes before and walked at such a fast pace that Senndra had trouble keeping up. Soon they reached the mess hall and took another path that led toward the top of the mountain. The way grew steeper, and Senndra was panting before long. The guards' pace slowed down as they progressed; however, Senndra still had trouble matching their speed. After a long, grueling climb, the hatchery finally came into view.

Senndra followed the guards through the doors of the hatchery. One of them stayed with her while the other left. Senndra did her best to keep a calm look on her face and not make her panting too obvious. Gradually, her breathing slowed to normal and she was able to look around. The room was entirely empty, with no furniture at all. In contrast, the walls were covered with paintings, some of dragons and others of different military settings. Senndra was about to walk over to the wall to better examine the paintings when the guard who had left returned. Following him was a small woman with white hair. She wore a green, loose-fitting dress that had many pockets in it. With a flick of her wrist, she dismissed the guards.

"Senndra," she said when the guards left the room, "my name is Miss Farley. I am the superintendent of the hatchery. You have already been told by your escorts why you are here, so if you will follow me, I will take you to your dragon."

Miss Farley turned and walked back down the hallway she had emerged from only minutes ago with the guard. Senndra followed her to another large room. This one had chairs in it and a receptionist on the far side. Miss Farley crossed the room, unlocked a door with a long, bronze key, and entered another hallway. Senndra followed her to another door that was opened by a different key which Miss Farley drew from one of her pockets. The door opened to the top of a flight of stairs, and Miss Farley descended them with Senndra close behind. The stairs were almost pitch black, and emptied out into a dimly lit room. As Senndra's eyes grew accustomed to the dim light, the details of the room slowly became clear. It was very long and narrow with small alcoves covering the walls. Miss Farley was already walking across the room, and Senndra ran to catch up.

"Now I must ask you something," Miss Farley said after stopping in front of an alcove. "You do know what colors dragons can be, don't you?"

"Of course," Senndra responded immediately. "Dragons are most commonly red, orange, green, blue, silver, and black, though they can be any color."

"Do you know the significance of the different colors?" Miss Farley questioned.

"With one exception, the color of a dragon has no effect on its abilities," Senndra answered. "A black dragon, however, has increased abilities. Their scales are tougher, their claws are sharper, and their fire is hotter. As you know, black dragons are a result of Molkekk's attempt to mutate dragons to form a better and more loyal army. The mutations were only marginally effective; the black dragon's abilities were enhanced, but not enough to give them a distinct advantage over other dragons.

Also, the mutation did not increase loyalty to Molkekk whatsoever. Of course, the side effect of the mutation was that the dragons scales turned black, a trait that they pass onto their offspring."

"This, of course, is a bit of an anomaly," Miss Farley said, "since there is no known factor that determines the color of a dragon. The black dragons are the only color that will have children the same color as the parents one hundred percent of the time. "You were correct in stating the colors of dragons, Senndra, but your situation is rather unique. You see, the color of your dragon has not been seen for over five hundred years. It is not a mutant as the black dragons are, but a natural variety; however, it is different from other dragons."

"What do you mean?" Senndra asked with a puzzled tone in her voice.

"Your dragon's color is mud brown, a color only seen once before. As I mentioned earlier, that sighting was over five hundred years ago. The dragon was killed in the Battle of Fire Water Marsh before he was fully developed. In that time, he differed from other dragons in the fact that he had no scales but only tough skin and that he could not breathe fire, only very hot air. The one normal characteristic was the length and sharpness of his claws. It is difficult to tell at this time, but it appears as though your dragon has these same characteristics. Because of these disabilities, you will have to take special care of him. Also when you begin to fight, you will have to make sure that he does not become over-confident."

Senndra was speechless and could only watch in silence as Miss Farley stepped to the side, giving Senndra a line of sight into the alcove. The little dragon inside raised his head and looked at Senndra with tiny eyes. In that moment, Senndra knew that she had fallen in love with the little creature.

******

"You ready to fight, Josiah?"

"Go away, Cirro," Josiah said without even opening his eyes. "I don't want to do anything right now except sleep."

"Come on. It's been an hour since lunch," Cirro said. "Besides, if you don't exercise, you'll get fat."

"When I get fat, I'll come to you for help," Josiah answered. He swung his feet over the side of his bunk and dropped to the floor. Except for an empty bunk here and there, the entire barracks was filled with sleeping cadets. "I guess at least the training field will be empty," Josiah grunted.

"Exactly," Cirro said.

The two friends walked outside and crossed the campus to the training field. Josiah was still not completely awake when they entered the building by the field to retrieve their weapons. With clumsy moves, Josiah pulled a key from his pocket and unlocked his locker. He reached inside and withdrew a sword and scabbard. He slipped the sword belt around his waist, buckled it, then closed and relocked the door of his locker. He walked to the door of the building, but before stepping out into the open, dunked his head in a basin of water standing there. The water was hot, but it still woke him up a little more. He wiped his face on his sleeve and stepped outside.

Cirro was in the middle of the field swinging his sword in several defensive and offensive maneuvers. Josiah gripped the hilt of his sword and pulled it out of the scabbard. The sound of metal on metal jolted him completely awake. He held the weapon in a defensive position and watched Cirro carefully. The two combatants circled each other slowly, drawing closer with each step. When they were finally within striking distance, Josiah struck without hesitation. Cirro jerked his sword down to block the blow then snapped it up in a strike at Josiah. Josiah stepped back, letting the sword whistle by in front of him, then he stepped up to attack.

The two friends continued to exchange blows, using standard attacks and defenses they had been taught. They always did this, remembering their lessons and warming up before the real fight. This was the ultimate competition, coming as close to fighting to the death as possible without actually hurting anyone. Not that it was likely that a fatal injury would occur with the blunted practice weapons, but the heavy metal blades could still do damage. Josiah had a nasty scar on the knuckles of his right hand that attested to the fact.

After about fifteen minutes, the feel of the fight changed. As if on unspoken consensus, the fight had begun in earnest. Cirro led with a jab aimed at Josiah's shoulder. Josiah moved his sword up to block the swipe, but Cirro jerked his sword down in a slash at the back of Josiah's knees. Josiah lunged forward and planted his shoulder in Cirro's chest, taking him to the ground. He rolled off of his fallen opponent, jumped to his feet, and spun around. Cirro was still on the ground, so Josiah dashed toward him and tried to place his sword's point at Cirro's neck. Cirro spun around and raised his foot, blocking Josiah's blade with his boot. He rolled backwards, grabbed his sword from the ground, and rose to his feet. Josiah leaped toward Cirro with his sword extended, but Cirro had more than enough time to react. Instead of blocking the blow, he simply let it slide off his blade. As Josiah's momentum brought him past Cirro, Cirro brought the hilt of his sword around and slammed it into the side of Josiah's head. The blow stunned Josiah and knocked him to the ground.

"You are vanquished, foul fiend," Cirro said, placing the tip of his sword against Josiah's throat.

"So I'm a foul fiend today?" Josiah asked. He got to his feet as he rubbed his head. "How long did it take you to come up with that one?" He slid his sword back into its scabbard and began again to massage the side of his head. "Tell me again why I fight with you? We both know that you're going to beat me every time."

"Don't despair, Josiah," Cirro said. "Today you withstood my onslaught for a full minute. If you keep this up, pretty soon you'll be able to hold out for all of a minute and five seconds. And if that isn't a good enough reason for you, then how about this one: it's just so much fun to beat you time and time again! I believe I've sold the idea sufficiently, so would you like to try again?"

"That was the shortest minute I've ever experienced," Josiah snorted. Then he added, "Of course, I'll try again; otherwise, you'll never leave me alone."

The two friends fought several more times, with Cirro gaining a decisive victory each time. They finally quit and headed for the building next to the training field. They quickly placed their weapons in their lockers, splashed water from the basin by the door on their faces, and headed back toward the barracks. The whole period of exercise had taken about an hour, and as they walked, they met several groups of cadets heading toward the training grounds. They exchanged pleasantries with all of the newcomers, joking with them as they passed. When they reached the barracks, they headed out back to the showers to cool off.

******

Senndra tucked the dragon into its bed and stepped back to watch it sleep. She had only recently come up with a name for him—Feddir. He had a ridge of spikes trailing from the top of his head to the tip of his tail. There was a single spike on his nose that had a strange orange tint to it. His mouth didn't have any teeth yet, since he was a newborn, but he would get them in the next few weeks. His wings were folded around his body, making him look like he was wrapped in a blanket.

"You ready to go?" Rita asked from the other side of the room. She crossed to where Senndra stood and looked at Feddir. "He sure is cute," she commented.

"I'll be ready in a second," Senndra said. Her leather armor creaked as she crossed the room to her bunk. She grabbed her quiver from the top bunk and strapped it on. Normally the quiver contained twenty razor-sharp arrows and her unstrung bow as well as the sheath for her short sword, but tonight it would only hold the sword. Though it was bulky to use only as a sheath, Senndra had grown use to the feel of it on her back and always wore it when she expected to fight.

Senndra grabbed her sword belt from the bunk, slid the blade from its scabbard, and threw the sheath back onto the bed. With a quick move, she slid the weapon into the scabbard on her back and then tightened the straps that held the assemblage in place. She retrieved her cloak and helmet from a chair and headed out the door, with Rita right behind her.

The two girls left their dorm and took the path that led up the mountain to the mess hall. After only a few hundred yards, they branched off the path onto a wider one. They were soon surrounded by cadets who were all heading in the same direction. It took them ten minutes moving at a good clip to reach their destination, the sword fighting ring. Already, the stands surrounding the ring were beginning to fill, and Senndra knew that before the event started they would be full beyond capacity. This was not only because the sword play competition was a mandatory affair, but also because it was the most exciting academy event of the year.

Twenty of the best sword fighters would face off. Each contestant had to get a recommendation from their instructor, which Senndra had obtained easily. On competition night, they participated in a tournament in which the twenty contestants fought each other in a series of one-on-one matches. It was single elimination, meaning that when a contestant lost, they were ejected from the tournament.

Senndra walked to her place in the contestant box. Once in her seat, she slid her helmet under her chair and scanned the crowd for Rita. She didn't find her, but instead caught sight of Vladimir. He had clearly gotten to the arena quite early since he had a seat very near the front. Although there were people on all four sides of him, it appeared as though they were ignoring him and he kept to himself.

Senndra again tried to spot Rita, but as she looked, the contest officiator appeared. He walked with long, slow strides to the middle of the arena where he mounted a platform. By the time he got there, the whole stadium was silent.

"Welcome to the academy's twenty-third annual sword fighting contest," he began. "I will not spend too much time talking since I know that you are all ready for the contest to begin; however, I would like to recognize a few people before we start. First, I would like to thank the entire group of sword fighting instructors that recommended the contestants. I would also like to introduce Jason Devlon and Marcus Arillion. They will act as the referees of today's contest to ensure that the rules are abided by and that no one gets hurt. So without further ado, let the competition begin."

Cheers erupted as the man left the arena and another came to take his place. This man was the grand admiral of the academy, and his presence quickly quieted the arena down once again. Senndra barely noticed as he gave his speech. The butterflies in her stomach wouldn't go away no matter what she did, and the wait only made them worse. She watched as the color guard brought various flags out and posted them at certain intervals around the arena. Next, four dragons dropped out of the sky and took their places at the four corners of the arena. Finally, the first man took the platform again. The crowd applauded as he announced that the contest would begin, starting with a fight between two cadets whose names Senndra couldn't remember.

The two combatants stepped into the arena and walked to the platform in the middle. The first cadet ascended the structure and saluted the crowd, bringing a thunderous cheer. After the applause had died down, the second cadet copied the motions of his opponent. Again the crowd yelled their approval. The two opponents climbed off the platform and moved to opposite sides of it. An officiator climbed onto the structure and raised a flag. When he dropped the flag and backed away, the two opponents began to circle toward each other.

Senndra knew that focusing on the two fighting cadets would probably distract her more than it would help. Instead, she began to inventory her body, checking all of her joints and other body parts for mobility and pain. All of her joints appeared to be in working order, though her left knee was a little bit stiff from her bout with Lemin earlier in the day. Her limbs were free of pain and would not present any problem in the contest. Senndra looked up and saw that both contestants in the ring were holding up well. Sighing, she tried to come up with something to think about in order to pass the time. Vladimir came into her mind, and though she tried to push the thought away, it remained. She couldn't figure out what it was about him that made her so uncomfortable. She wasn't normally outgoing, but her behavior regarding Vladimir was very strange even for her. She was so lost in thought that she missed the name of her opponent and almost missed her own name. Looking up, she saw a different set of cadets leaving the arena and wondered how many matches she had missed. She shrugged off the thought as she grabbed her helmet and entered the arena. Her opponent was already several yards ahead of her. She fastened her helmet as her opponent scaled the platform and saluted the crowd, bringing a roar of applause. After the cheering had subsided, Senndra climbed onto the platform and saluted the crowd. She didn't even wait for the applause to subside before she drew her sword from her back scabbard and jumped off the platform onto the ground. She circled to one corner of the stage and watched, as an officiator ascended the stage and raised a flag. He let the flag fall and quickly left the stage.

Senndra had seen these fights for several years now, and all but one of them had started with the combatants circling the stage toward each other. In only one fight had a contestant started by leaping onto the platform in order to give himself a height advantage against his opponent. This opening move had ended in disaster, and no one had tried it since. But Senndra was not one to do things the accepted way. Besides, she had a plan that would utilize the stage for more than just height advantage. As soon as the flag dropped to start the match, she took a step forward and leapt up onto the stage and looked down at her opponent. He looked up at her in astonishment, but took very little time to adjust to her new position. Senndra watched as he stepped forward and jumped up onto the platform. She vaulted over him, landing in a crouch and instantly spun, straightening as she did so to aim a blow at his ankles. He jumped over the blow, landed, and brought his sword down on Senndra from above. She lifted her arm so that the leather armor there only received a glancing blow, and the blade slid off. Jumping straight up in the air, she landed on the platform in front of her opponent and brought her elbow up into his face. He fell senseless onto the platform, clearly beaten.

The whole fight had taken less than half a minute, and it seemed as though the crowd was not ready to cheer yet. Silence reigned in the stands for a full second before the cadets realized that the bout was over and the arena was filled with shouting. Senndra raised her sword in a salute, slid it into her scabbard, and headed to the contestant box. She walked back to her seat and sat down, ignoring everything around her. She knew that if she paid attention, she might lose her concentration.

"Senndra."

Senndra looked up and saw Lemin crouching beside her. He extended his hand, and she shook it.

"A brilliant move," he said. "That's the first time I have seen an opening move like that actually work. I don't think anyone has ever finished off a match in so little time, especially against someone that much larger."

Senndra glanced across the field to the platform and saw two officiators placing her unconscious opponent on a stretcher. Now that she had time to look at him, she could see how big he truly was. He was somewhere between six and six and a half feet tall and had to weigh at least two hundred and fifty pounds, with no fat on his frame. His sword, which lay beside him on the stretcher, was twice as long as hers.

"That was a very smart move," Lemin commented. "The way you put him away, you hardly exerted yourself at all. And because of that, you'll have a slight advantage over your next opponent."

"Thanks for the tip," Senndra said as Lemin rose to his feet. She closed her eyes and mentally went through each move she had been taught. Some of her competitors would be better sword fighters than her recently dispatched opponent, and she needed to be ready for them when they came.

******

Senndra drew her sword and saluted the crowd. This time, she continued the salute, soaking up the excitement of the spectators. She could hardly believe that she had gotten this far, to her fifth and final fight of the night. This one would decide the winner of the tournament. The cheers of the crowd were subsiding, so she jumped lightly off the platform and headed to a corner. She took several deep breaths to calm her nerves. She needed to be in the best condition for this fight. She glanced across the platform at her opponent and wondered if she had any chance at all. He was massive and, concealed as he was by his armor, looked a lot like her first opponent. Her only hope would be to outmaneuver him with the sword and not take a direct attack. But she had seen him fight his other opponents and knew that he was at least as good as she was with a blade.

The officiator climbed the platform and raised his flag. He then lowered it and backed away. Senndra's opponent immediately jumped up onto the platform, ready to confront her, but she stayed where she was. She slowly backed away from the platform so that her opponent couldn't attack her from above.

The other combatant seemed at a loss for what to do. In every previous fight, Senndra had started out by jumping onto the platform, and her lack of aggression clearly flustered him. He recovered quickly and jumped off the platform to meet her. He landed several feet in front of Senndra and advanced quickly, aiming a swipe at her head. Senndra dodged left and ran back several steps. Her opponent attacked again, swinging hard toward her torso. Senndra was able to catch the blow on her sword and let it slide to the side. She ducked as her attacker brought the hilt of his sword around and came up as the blow passed. He was wide open, so she aimed a blow at his shoulder; he stepped backward to avoid injury.

Senndra retreated a handful of steps and tried to catch her breath. The onslaught of the other cadet couldn't have taken more than a minute, but it was extremely ferocious and had left her gasping. Her training kicked in, and she launched herself across the area that separated her from her foe. She acted on one principle that Lemin had drilled into her head time and time again: never let the enemy act first; make the first move. She spun as she flew through the air, moving from left to right so that her sword came at her adversary from his right side. He saw the move just in time and jerked his sword up to block the blow, but was too slow. The parry rotated Senndra's blade so that it hit her opponent's head with the blunt side, smashing against his helmet with a ringing sound. The blow threw him sideways, but he maintained enough of his wits to turn the uncontrolled fall into a roll.

Senndra watched as he got to his feet, unwilling to strike while he was down. His stance was unsteady and it was clear that the blow had rattled him. Senndra made sure he saw her advancing and then attacked with vigor. At first, the other cadet fell back from her blows, using his sword only to block. However, as time passed, he began to counter her attacks. The pair delivered and blocked strike and jabs for no more than a few minutes, but to Senndra it seemed like an eternity. Both combatants moved constantly as they circled each other, trying to gain the advantage in the fight. Finally, when Senndra thought it would never end, her opponent pulled a move she never suspected. As she made a move that had most of her body weight behind it, the other cadet moved as if to block the blow, but stepped out of the way at the last second, allowing Senndra's momentum to carry her forward. With all of her weight forward, she hit the ground hard, rolling over just in time to evade a strike. She rolled to her right to avoid the next attack and came to her feet, instantly assuming a defensive position.

Senndra expected that her opponent would be thrown off by her evasive maneuver, but she immediately found herself being pressed by him. As she began to gain control of the attack and return blows, she tried to think about some way to beat him. His defense was almost too good to penetrate, and he was too fast to surprise. He landed a jab to her shoulder, and it gouged into her armor, though it didn't penetrate to her skin. She brought the hilt of her sword up toward his face, but found her wrist trapped in a vise-like grip. Her opponent jerked his sword from her armor and, with a twist of his wrist, sent her flying to the side. She rolled several times before coming to a stop face down and unconscious.

Senndra felt herself jerked back to consciousness by the prick of a sword tip on her throat and knew that it was all over. The sword tip was removed and she rolled over. As she prepared to make her way back to the contestant box in defeat, she saw something that surprised her. Her opponent had withdrawn his sword and was now holding it over his shoulder. She scrambled to her feet and grabbed her sword from where it lay on the ground. Holding it in a defensive position, she waited for an attack. It didn't come; the other cadet advanced with his hand, not his sword, extended.

"The name is Timothy," he said. His voice was muffled by the helmet, and yet Senndra heard something in it that made her believe Timothy wouldn't attack. She extended her hand as well, and the two leather gloves clasped in a handshake.

"I just wanted you to know," Timothy said, "that no matter who wins this match, I'm glad I have had the honor of battling you. Though you are at a disadvantage in size, you still fight better than anyone I know. In addition, the fact that you did not take the easy way out and attack when I was down shows that you have honor in your heart. Therefore, even if I do fall to your superior skill, I will be honored to do so." Timothy backed away to his previous position and raised his sword in salute.

Senndra's mind began to race as she considered what had just happened. She had come to this contest to win and had defeated all of her opponents. Part of what had enabled her to do that was hating them enough to beat them. Her hatred for her current adversary had grown throughout the fight, giving her strength. Now, the simple action of telling her that he would be willing to accept defeat had dissipated it. Senndra wondered how she would be able to go on fighting someone such as this. Granted, she didn't hate Lemin and was still proficient against him, but that seemed different somehow. She didn't think she could return this attitude, but when she looked and saw that his sword was still raised in salute, she realized how self-centered she had been. She had wanted to get into the contest so that *she* could win. She hadn't even considered the fact that there were nineteen other contestants that wanted to win just as much. And now, here was a young man that had the skill to win and it didn't matter to him. Whether or not he won made so little difference that he didn't care if he got beat by a girl. Slowly, Senndra raised her sword in salute and stood there for several seconds. She finally pulled her sword back down into a defensive position and prepared for an attack. Now that she had nothing to prove, she began to actually enjoy the fight. Her opponent lunged at her, and she sidestepped him. He spun on his heels, bringing his sword back around toward her, and she was able to block it with her sword. Again the two cadets began to exchange blows, neither of them moving so much as a foot. Suddenly, with a move that Senndra couldn't quite see, her rival swung toward her chest, but pulled his blade down at the last minute. Senndra was unable to drop her blade in time and felt his blade contact the back of her knee. The joint buckled, sending her to the ground. When she felt the sword point at her throat this time, she knew it was to finish the match.

Senndra rolled over once the pressure was relieved and climbed to her feet. With a deft move, she pushed her sword into its scabbard, took off her helmet, and turned to face the only person who had been able to defeat her. He had also taken off his helmet and revealed his features. Though Senndra had estimated him to be at least eighteen, she took one look at his face and decided that he couldn't be more than fifteen. He had short, red hair, but the thing that held her gaze the most were his eyes. He had red eyes—not as though he hadn't gotten enough sleep or what would come from crying, but truly red eyes. A red circle, instead of a blue, green, or brown one, stretched around his pupil, making his eyes quite unnerving. Senndra shook his hand again then pulled her sword out and saluted the crowd. Timothy did so as well, and the cadets in the stands went wild. Senndra and Timothy slowly let their salutes fall and headed back for the contestant box. In that moment, Senndra knew that she had gained a friend for life.

****** 

Josiah stood out in front of the ranks of his soldiers. One thousand cadets were in perfect formation, waiting for inspection. Josiah could tell that the sun was already bothering them, but they were doing their best not to show it. A commotion came from behind, so he turned around. Approaching him was the grand admiral of the academy, along with several other high ranking officers.

Josiah turned to his troops. "Attention!" he called, and immediately the cadets became even straighter than they had been before. Josiah spun around to face the approaching officers and saluted them. The officers lost no time covering the remaining distance. They returned Josiah's salute, and as they passed, Josiah fell in behind them. The officers came to a halt only a few yards from the first rank of cadets, and their eyes slowly traveled up and down the rows looking for flaws. Several minutes passed as they scrutinized the cadets before them, then the grand admiral turned to Josiah.

"Your troops are again in perfect order, Commander Pondran," he told Josiah. "You will receive your instructions in short order, so don't let your men get too comfortable." Without another word, he turned and began to walk away. One of the officers following the grand admiral paused when he reached Josiah. He pulled several pages from a binder and handed them to Josiah.

"Here are your orders, Commander Pondran." Though the words were nothing out of the ordinary, the tone revealed that the speaker would have been happy if Josiah had dropped dead where he stood.

"Thank you, Superior Officer," Josiah responded in a monotone. For the life of him, he could not figure out why the man hated him so much, but he wanted no trouble.

"And you had better have the barracks ready by inspection," the superior officer said in a threatening tone. "If I find so much as a splinter out of place, I'll have you busted down to a basic infantryman in no time."

"Yes sir, Superior Officer," Josiah answered, though he had to bite back several angry retorts. He had serious doubts that the officer could bust him down, especially that low, but he didn't want to test the theory. The superior officer stalked off, and Josiah turned back to his soldiers.

"At ease," he ordered. He waited for the soldiers to relax a little before continuing. "You heard the grand admiral. We have a list of things we need to do between now and when the students from the academy in Belvárd come, which is…" he looked down at the paper in his hands, "…in two days. Actually less than that," he corrected himself. "They are supposed to be arriving sometime tomorrow. Your captains will instruct you as to what your duties will be. You are dismissed for now."

The cadets began to break formation and head into the barracks to change from their uniforms. Five of the cadets, one for every two hundred, approached Josiah, and he led them into a small office at the front of the building. He slid into a chair behind a small, battered desk, and the five captains entered the room and stood in front of the desk, the last one closing the door as he entered.

Josiah looked down at the list of assignments and sighed. He was almost positive the officer had given his cadets the most work, but he wasn't going to complain. Instead, he began to mentally divide it up between his five captains.

*"Well, looks like Cirro really is going to get to plant flowers along twenty miles of road,"* he thought sourly. He grabbed some paper from a lower drawer of his desk and began to write on five sheets. Divided up into five parts, the work load appeared lighter, but the cadets would still have to work hard in order to finish it. He finished transferring the assignments and handed the five sheets to his captains. The men saluted, then turned and left.

Josiah sighed and rose to his feet. He would have to supervise the men and would probably put in a good amount of work himself. He waited for four groups of the cadets to leave the barracks then left his office. The captain in charge of the men who remained in the barracks approached Josiah.

"Well, Terza, let's get this show on the road," Josiah told the captain. "To start, remake all the beds with military precision. After that, I want every single bed checked to make sure it is perfect. Next, I want you to get some sandpaper and rub down all of the bedframes. I don't know if that commander can actually do what he threatens, but I'm not planning on finding out. After you do that, I want every inch of this barracks swept, dusted, and polished. Wash down the walls and everything else that isn't perfectly clean. Once you have all that done, let me know, and I'll come look at it and see if there is anything else I want done. Oh yeah, one other thing—work well, but quickly. This barracks needs to be done for inspection; that should happen shortly after lunch. It wouldn't hurt to have it done before that because, knowing my superior, he will drop in early."

50

"Yes sir, Commander Pondran," the captain said and saluted. "Everything will be done as you ordered."

"Good. I'll be back in a few hours to see how things are progressing."

Josiah turned and walked out of the barracks and headed for the buildings on the north side of the campus. Cadets swarmed the streets as they hurried to prepare the grounds for the arrival of the cadets from the academy in Belvárd. Several hundred cadets, all obviously under the same captain, washed and painted several buildings and tried to bring them to perfection by the following day. Cadets also swarmed the roads, planting flowers and pruning the shrubs that already existed. Several trees that had been judged to be too closely spaced were dug out and new trees had been planted. As Josiah watched, the old trees were cut up into pieces and taken to the campus wood pile. Through the windows of several buildings, Josiah could see cadets sweeping, mopping, dusting, and painting the insides of the buildings. Josiah shook his head and again wondered why the campus officials found it necessary to wait until the day before the Belvárd cadets' arrival to do everything. He finally found his troops and stopped to examine their work. One squad was working on the outsides of seven buildings. They had constructed some temporary scaffolding and were crawling all over it in order to wash the outside of the buildings and repaint them. Another squad of cadets had been divided into several smaller groups, each of which was responsible for cleaning the inside of a building. Josiah approached the working cadets and began to look for his captains. He saw one examining the paint on one of the buildings and made his way toward him.

"Morning, Stanslaw," Josiah greeted the agitated captain. Stanslaw turned and saluted, and Josiah returned the salute.

"Good morning, Commander Pondran," Stanslaw responded.

"How's everything coming along?" Josiah asked as his eyes roamed the buildings.

"Pretty good so far, Commander," Stanslaw answered. "We started off with some problems, but they have been taken care of, and we're working quite well and efficiently now. I estimate that we'll be done with our assigned work by the end of today at the latest."

"Good," Josiah answered. "Keep that schedule if possible, and if you get done early, tell me. I'll probably have something else for you to do."

Stanslaw saluted and, after Josiah returned the salute, he turned back to supervising the work. Josiah turned and walked toward the east end of the campus. Along the main road, a squad of his troops was planting flowers, pruning bushes and trees, and replacing trees when necessary. Josiah headed straight for the captain, who saluted him, and he returned the salute.

"What's the situation, Yugart?" he asked.

"We're coming along great so far, Commander," Yugart answered. "I split my squad up into several smaller groups and each is covering a road. This group," Yugart gestured to the cadets in front of him, "is one of the larger ones, so they're covering the main road. I've got messengers going to each of the other groups to bring reports, and so far they're all making good time."

"Commander Pondran?" The call came from down the road to the west, so Josiah turned to see a group of several officers making their way toward him.

"Yes?" Josiah answered. "What is it?"

"More orders, Commander," a superior officer from the group answered. "These are jobs that never got assigned to anyone." An officer advanced and handed a sheet of paper to Josiah.

"Yes, sir, I'll see to this immediately," Josiah said as he glanced across the sheet. The officers saluted, then turned and left. Josiah saluted their backs and turned to Yugart.

"I'm going to need about five men, Yugart."

"Very good, sir," Yugart said. "It will probably be best for you to pick five from this group so that you can be off to do what needs to be done."

"Very well; I think I will." Josiah saw that Yugart forwent the salute, but didn't argue the fact. The morning was already getting tedious with all the salutes. Instead, he turned to the west and headed down the road.

"Cadet Cirro," he called as he passed a group of cadets pruning some trees. "Bring your tools and choose four more cadets." When Cirro and his detail reached him he added, "Let's go. We've got a lot of work to do and time's wasting."

\*\*\*\*\*\*

Senndra groaned and rolled out of bed. Her body throbbed and ached with every movement, and she knew that she would regret last night's tournament for quite a while. Still rubbing the sleep out of her eyes, she grabbed her uniform and stumbled down the hall to the showers. She found only one stall open and took it. For some unknown reason, the thought of first-year cadets popped into her head. They were the ones that had to get up before everyone else and pump water up to the top of the building. That way, when the cadets used the showers, they simply controlled the flow of water from a tank down to the showers.

The water was cold, so Senndra didn't linger. After she finished, she headed down to her room. The only thing scheduled for today was an awards ceremony, during which several people would be recognized, including cadet of the year, best swordsman of the year, and many others. There were no classes today, so Senndra planned to relax in her room and read a book. She pushed the door of her room open and glanced at Rita. She was still sleeping in her bed, and it looked like it would take quite a bit to wake her. Senndra switched her gaze to Feddir and saw that he was still asleep as well. She grabbed a bag from the cupboard and poured a small amount of the contents into a bowl that sat next to her sleeping dragon. According to Miss Farley, this was the best thing to feed young dragons, but Senndra still grimaced as she saw what looked like dried beetles and meat. She placed the bag back in the cupboard and turned to the single bookshelf in the room. As she did so, she caught sight of her weapons hanging on the back of a chair.

"Lemin's class!" she gasped. In the excitement of last night, she had forgotten that Lemin was planning on having class today. Quickly, she grabbed her sword from the quiver, slid it into its regular sheath, and headed out the door. She strapped on the weapon as she ran down the hall and burst into the stairwell at a sprint. She took the stairs two at a time, and exploded out of the dorm at full speed. Glancing at the sun, she guessed that Lemin's class was probably only half over, so she might not get in too much trouble. Actually, if she knew Lemin correctly, she wouldn't get in any trouble at all, but she didn't want to disappoint her teacher. After all, he seemed to have his heart set on fighting her today.

Senndra sprinted up the path that led to the fighting arena and didn't slow down until she had almost reached it. With one more bend to go, she slowed to a walk and strode into the arena. Lemin was sparring with another cadet, so she entered the stands and sat with the other cadets that were there. The crowd was much larger than normal, and for some reason, it felt to Senndra that everyone was looking straight at her. She tried to shake the feeling and watched the cadet that was currently in the arena with Lemin. She noticed that while he guarded himself well, he was clearly outclassed by the instructor. The fight lasted another twenty seconds, in which time Lemin managed to successfully strip the sword from his opponent. The cadet retrieved his sword and left the arena even as the next one entered. This cadet carried himself better than his predecessor, but when he moved to engage Lemin, Senndra saw that he, too, was severely outclassed by the instructor. As the battle began, another cadet moved to sit by Senndra. She turned to see Timothy and was again unnerved by his eyes. She wondered exactly what had caused that phenomenon.

"I never found out last night…so, what's your name?" Timothy asked.

"Senndra," she stammered. Despite the fact that his eyes were unusual, Timothy was quite handsome. She had never been good around other people, much less good-looking men, and now her tongue seemed to tie itself in knots.

"You did well yesterday," Timothy commented, glancing at the two combatants in the arena. Lemin was toying with the cadet, and they both knew it. As a result, the cadet was getting increasingly frustrated.

"Thank you," Senndra responded. "Apparently you did better," she added with a laugh.

"I may have won the contest," Timothy said, "but I'm not the one that everyone is talking about. The fact that you beat your first opponent in under a minute is amazing. You even broke a record by defeating him in less than forty-seven seconds, but that isn't what people are talking about. You finished the bout in exactly eighteen seconds, which is phenomenal. I don't even think Lemin has beaten someone that quickly before. Anyway, a lot of the cadets," Timothy gestured to the crowd in the stands, "including myself, showed up today to watch you spar with Lemin. You're the person with the best chance of beating him, and they want to be here to see it happen."

"Well, it's very nice of them to think that," Senndra stammered, "and I want to believe them, but I don't think they're correct. Besides, aren't you the one with the best chance of beating Lemin? After all, you did win the contest."

"Doesn't matter to them," Timothy answered. "They think you'll beat him, and the only way they'll believe otherwise is if you get out there and lose to him. Besides that, you definitely have some advantages that I do not. After all, you consistently beat your opponents in very little time. I have never before beaten anyone as quickly as you have. Who knows, perhaps that will give you the edge that you need to win today.

"Oh, and one other thing," Timothy said. "You had me on the ground last night and didn't press the advantage. Why not?"

"That was only fair," Senndra argued. "Anyone with any decency would have done the same."

"Well then, a lot of people I know and a lot that I don't know have no decency. They openly admit that they would have taken advantage of the situation and ended the fight," Timothy answered.

The statement left Senndra speechless, and she turned back to watch the activity in the arena. There was a new cadet fighting Lemin now, and he was faring no better than any of the other cadets that Senndra had seen previously. With a well-aimed slash, Lemin swung at the cadet's legs, but pulled his blade up at the end of the stroke and pressed the point against the cadet's throat. As the cadet left the arena, Lemin scanned the crowd until his gaze fell on Senndra. Lifting his hand, he beckoned for her to come. Slowly, she got to her feet and began to descend toward the battlefield. Out of the corner of her eye, she could see Rita arriving at the arena. She appeared breathless, as though she had run the whole way, but Senndra didn't think about it. Instead, she focused on Lemin and carefully scanned his body. He didn't appear to be exhausted in the least, nor was he even sweating. That was good; Senndra didn't want to beat him and then have it attributed to the fact that he was tired. She laughed to herself; now *she* actually thought that she had a chance against the elf? It was amazing the thoughts that a lot of delusional spectators could put into her head. She reached the ground and hopped over the fence that enclosed the arena. She crossed the distance between herself and her instructor and slid her sword from its scabbard.

"Amazing what a lot of people will convince themselves of," she said and gestured to the cadets in the stands.

"It's nothing special," Lemin responded. "Every year they do the same for the cadet who wins the tournament, but this year it's different. I guess they think you really have a chance of beating me. Not that I'm worried," he added with a grin.

"I don't need to let you rest or anything, do I?" Senndra asked. "I'd hate to beat you and then have it brushed aside due to a technicality."

"*If* you beat me," Lemin said, "then I will give you full credit. As it is, I'm not even winded." He raised his sword. "On guard."

Senndra raised her sword and began to slowly circle Lemin. As she watched him move, the first principle of sword fighting popped into her head. Always attack first. Without warning, she leaped forward, with her sword held out, and caught Lemin's blade on her own. She brought the hilt of her sword up in order to hit Lemin's head with it, but he dove sideways away from her. He jumped to his feet and attacked so suddenly that Senndra barely had time to duck. She waited for him to fly over her head before she stood and swung around, her sword extended. The flat end hit him on the shoulder and sent him spinning away. Senndra quickly capitalized on her advantage and crowded Lemin. She raised her sword and brought it down for a stroke that was meant to end the match, but the instructor managed to get his weapon up just in time. He blocked Senndra's blow and returned with one of his own. She spun away from the strike and ended up backwards to her opponent. Instinctively, she guessed what his next move would be and swung her sword around behind her back. She heard the sound of metal on metal as she spun around. Lemin raised his sword for another blow, and Senndra raised her sword in a defensive gesture. The blow came down with such force that it slammed Senndra's sword sideways, almost wrenching it from her grip. Pain stabbed through Senndra's wrist, and she knew right away that her right arm was practically useless. Lemin swung another blow, but this time Senndra had no weapon to stop it. Instead, she raised her arm and grabbed her opponent's wrist. His sword stopped mere inches from her face, and she ducked backwards before he could force it any further.

Senndra stepped away from her opponent and slowed her breathing. She tossed her sword from her right hand to her left. She knew that her skill with that hand was much less, but it was better than fighting with a sprained wrist. She swung the sword through the air several times and listened as it whistled, then prepared to meet her instructor. He attacked first, faking a blow to her head, but finishing with a blow to her midriff. Senndra had seen that move more times than she could remember and deftly met his sword with hers before spinning away. She knew that if she tried to withstand a full force attack, she would not stand a chance with her right arm out of commission. She raised her sword and attacked Lemin, putting all of her weight behind the blow. He appeared ready to block the strike, so Senndra faked it toward his head. She switched to a jab to his knees, but it never contacted. Lemin sidestepped Senndra's sword and allowed her to fall forward into the dirt.

Senndra rolled over and watched as her opponent approached. He extended his sword as though to press its point against her throat, but she wrenched her weapon out from underneath herself and batted his sword away. He attacked again, this time bringing a blow down from above. Senndra knew that she could not block Lemin's sword, so she swung at his knees. He had to pull back his blade to hop over Senndra's sword, but it only bought her a few extra seconds. One last time, the instructor raised his sword for a victory blow. As he brought his weapon down, Senndra raised her sword and slammed the flat of its blade against Lemin's wrist. The force of the blow snapped his wrist down and flung his weapon several yards away.

Taking advantage of her disarmed opponent, Senndra rolled to her feet and swung her sword at him. For a moment she could see Lemin's face clearly, and the smile on his face told her that she had underestimated him. Ducking the blow, he spun to her left side, capturing her wrist and twisting it around behind her back. The movement jarred the sword from Senndra's grip and moments later, she felt her own steel at her throat. The fight was over.

"Well, it looks like the cadets will have to wait to see me get beaten," Lemin said as he released Senndra's arm and returned her sword. Senndra slid the weapon into her scabbard. She turned to look at the cadets in the stands and saw that many of them were starting to leave.

"Is your wrist okay?" Lemin asked Senndra. "I saw you take a good hit early on. Maybe you should have the doctor look at it."

"It's not bad," Senndra said. "I've been there pretty much every day since I started sword fighting. I think I'll give the doctor the day off."

Lemin had to be told several times that everything was fine, before he finally dismissed Senndra and called for another student. Senndra jogged to where Rita sat in the stands.

"It was a good fight," Senndra's friend said. "Better luck next time, I guess."

"Better luck? Against Lemin?" Senndra said. "It's nice of you to say so, but I seriously doubt it. I would wager that there are only a handful of people in the world who could beat that elf."

"You're right, but one of those people is here right now."

Senndra gave a surprised exclamation and jumped in her seat. Vladimir had snuck up on her without a sound.

"Really? Rita said in a voice of disbelief. "Who here could beat Lemin in a sword fight?"

"That's easy; the best sword fighter here," Vladimir responded.

"Timothy?" Senndra asked incredulously. Here was finally something that she and Vladimir could talk about. "There's no way that he has a chance. Lemin's far too good."

"He's good to be sure," Vladimir agreed. "Better than most people in the world, in fact, but you can tell that he is a dragon rider at heart. He prefers to shoot arrows from the back of a dragon, not swing a sword in hand to hand combat."

"So what about Timothy?" Rita asked. "What's he like?"

"He was born to fight with a sword," Vladimir answered. "He has the build and proficiency for it. I wager that given a few more years of training, you will be hard pressed to find anybody who could beat him."

"You talk like you know Timothy," Senndra said. The question was implied.

"Somewhat, yes," Vladimir answered, "but what I said doesn't have to do with that. All you have to do is watch them fight. Actually, here's your chance."

Senndra looked toward the arena and watched as Timothy walked out to face Lemin. The two barely exchanged pleasantries before beginning to fight. It was clear that today was about the tournament champion facing off against the best instructor at the academy.

"Watch the motion of the feet," Vladimir said almost as soon as the fight commenced. "Timothy has excellent range of motion, and while Lemin is also moving well, it's almost as if he doesn't want to take any steps."

"That would make sense if what you said earlier is true," Rita commented. "If he's used to fighting on a dragon, he would have learned to keep his feet locked into the stirrups at all times."

"Look at his arm motion," Senndra countered. "He's constantly moving his sword back and forth, trying to find an opening."

"Agreed, but his style is for close fighting," Vladimir countered. "He prefers a short sword or a knife, and it shows. Timothy uses a hand-and-a-half sword, which gives him the advantage of length. If he can utilize it properly, that could almost win the match for him."

"Almost?" Senndra asked.

"Lemin has obviously fought against long swords before, and he has more experience," Vladimir explained.

"You're not making it sound like much of a contest," Rita said. "I guess you think Lemin has a wrap on this match?"

"Timothy was practically born with a sword in his hand," Vladimir said. "Just watch the fight. It'll be exciting if nothing else."

Timothy and Lemin had moved constantly during the course of the short conversation, but without drastically changing position. They were still in approximately the same location that they had started the fight, and continued to exchange blows for another minute. Timothy was the first to break contact though Lemin didn't press the advantage. Both of the combatants looked winded but continued to circle each other, looking for a good opening. There were a few weak thrusts exchanged, an attempt by each fighter to keep the other on the defensive, but nothing even resembling the original energy level. Then, in an instant, the tempo of the fight changed again.

Lemin blocked a thrust from Timothy and retaliated with an overhand slash. The younger man sidestepped to avoid the attack and circled counterclockwise. The clash of metal again filled the place as the combatants slashed, thrust, blocked, and parried. Though there had been argument over the fact last night, there was no uncertainty now as to who the best cadet at sword fighting was. For the moment, the outcome of this match, cadet against legendary instructor, seemed to be in doubt. The fight continued to rage, and the cadets watching were on the edge of their seats. Was this finally their chance to see Lemin beaten?

Something about Lemin's carriage changed, a change that Senndra had seem many times before when the elf was not in clear control of a bout. Something was about to change, though what it would be was uncertain. She didn't have to wait long to find out. Ducking his head to avoid a blow, Lemin stepped quickly toward Timothy, striking him in the stomach with his fist. Timothy staggered backwards, but the elf was on top of him already. Capturing the younger man's sword arm under his arm, Lemin struck the wrist, causing his opponent to drop his weapon.

Timothy had been taken off guard by the new strategy implemented by Lemin, but had adjusted quickly. The elf was faster than he was, but he was larger and stronger. Ripping his sword arm free, he delivered an open handed strike with his left hand. The blow contacted Lemin on his breastplate, thrusting him backwards and putting space between the two combatants.

"This is where it falls apart, I guess," Rita commented. "Unarmed, he doesn't stand a chance, right?"

"No," Vladimir agreed. "He's toast at this point."

"Don't count him out yet," Senndra said. She didn't know why, but she really wanted to see Timothy win. Maybe it was just that she wanted to see Lemin beaten like every other cadet here.

Timothy threw his fists up in front of his face in a typical fighter's pose. Lemin dashed forward, stabbing as he came within range of his opponent. Timothy used the palms of both hands to block the blade away and spun, kicking Lemin in the chest. The elf staggered backwards and circled clockwise. Timothy stooped and picked up a handful of dirt from the ground. As the elf charged, the younger man flung the dirt at his face, but the move was futile. Lemin spun right, avoiding the dirt and kicking Timothy in the side. Timothy was knocked off balance and fell, and Lemin followed up with a strike. Timothy rolled sideways as the blade descended, then back on top of the sword. The weight of his body pulled the hilt toward the ground, ripping it from his opponent's grip. He rolled off of the sword and retrieved it from the ground. Now the tables were turned; he had the weapon and his opponent did not.

Dodging blows from Timothy, Lemin ran backwards toward where the younger man's weapon had fallen a few minutes earlier. Diving to avoid a swipe, he slid past the sword, grabbing it as he passed and rotating his body to end the slide on his knees. Timothy pressed what was left of his advantage, raining a series of blows down on Lemin, but the elf was too skilled. Blocking every strike, he rose to his feet and swung wide at his opponent. Timothy jumped back, barely avoiding the strike.

"It's a short sword, dummy," Vladimir said to himself. "You can't fight like you're used to fighting."

With both of the combatants armed again, they backed away from each other momentarily to catch their breaths. This was a short reprieve; Lemin knew that Timothy had very little practice with short swords and was clearly at a disadvantage, one that the elf was not going to squander. He stepped forward, striking as he moved. Timothy caught the first strike on his blade and tried to return the blow, but his blade missed Lemin by a foot and a half. The younger man just wasn't used to the short weapon in his hands.

Lemin clearly had the advantage now, and he chased Timothy around the arena, constantly swinging his weapon. The outcome of the fight was all but determined, but Timothy either didn't realize how outclassed he was or didn't care. He continued to run away from his instructor, looking for opportunities to strike, but not finding any. It was a simple task for Lemin to finish the fight. Staying out of range of Timothy's sword, he rained blows on his defenses. The young man was weakening, and it was beginning to show. Lemin thrust his sword forward, but Timothy batted it to the side. The next attack was the final one, the one to finish the battle. Lemin swung hard overhand at Timothy. The blow smashed through the tired man's defense, and Lemin pulled it back under control before it hit Timothy's shoulder. Though the blade of the sword was blunted and Lemin had softened the blow, it was still enough to knock Timothy to the ground. Lemin placed the tip of sword momentarily at Timothy's throat before removing it and allowing him to stand.

"Well, now I feel like he was toying with me during the sword fighting competition," Senndra said.

"That seems unlikely," Vladimir countered. "Timothy isn't the sort of person to toy with an opponent. He finishes them off quickly if he can."

"Then he must have been off his game yesterday," Senndra persisted. "He is certainly a lot better of a fighter than I am."

"It's true, he is," Rita agreed.

"Rita!" Senndra exclaimed, looking at her friend in disbelief. "You're supposed to be on my side."

"I am," Rita said, "but he's better than you are."

"Which isn't to say that you're a poor fighter," Vladimir pointed out. "You made it to the last match and deserved to be there. There just aren't very many people in the world who can fight as well as Timothy. Give him a few years and he'll be able to take down Lemin without a problem."

"Not without a problem," Senndra disagreed. "Lemin's got too many tricks up his sleeve for that."

She watched as Timothy and the elf shook hands. It was crazy to think that anyone would be able to beat Lemin without a problem. He had seen more action in his life than all of the cadets in the academy combined. No, she decided, dismissing Vladimir's comment, Lemin was not someone to be trifled with, no matter your skill with a sword.

\*\*\*\*\*\*

Five hours later, Senndra was again seated in the stands of the arena. Rita sat on one side of her, and Timothy was seated on the other. They had arrived at the arena an hour before and had talked to pass the time. Now, however, they grew silent as they waited for the ceremony to begin. All around them, the sound of several thousand cadets was deafening. Rita sat on Senndra's right, looking around in awe. She was a vision if there ever was one. She wore a very becoming blue dress that fell to the middle of her calves, but the real eye-catcher was her hair. She had worked on it for several hours and, with Senndra's help, had made it perfect. With her beautiful features and the halo of golden curls that surrounded her face, there didn't seem to be a single male in the area that wasn't staring at her or at least sneaking glances. The single exception was seated to Senndra's left. Timothy sat with his chin on his palm as he looked out into the arena, seemingly oblivious to Rita. Vladimir, seated on the far side of Timothy, was another story. Senndra had decided to give him a chance in light of their almost normal conversation at the sword fighting arena earlier in the day. She didn't mind that Timothy had invited his friend to sit with them; as it turned out, he was nice enough even if he wasn't exactly normal. On the other hand he might be a bit *too* normal, Senndra realized, noting the way he was practically gawking at Rita. Oh well, given enough time, he would get used to her.

The ceremony started abruptly when an old man ascended the stage. Senndra immediately knew by his robes that he was a priest of Elohim. He lifted his hands for silence and gradually got his wish. He looked to the sky, closed his eyes, and stood thus for several minutes. All of the cadets stood, closed their eyes, and waited for the priest to begin speaking.

"Almighty, magnificent God," he began when he finally broke the silence, "we praise and thank you for your wondrous works. We thank you each day for what you have given to us. We ask you for forgiveness for our sins and pray that you will help us to obey your commands and edicts in the following days.

"I now thank you for all of the cadets gathered here today. I thank you for the commitment they have made to serve their country in the military and pray for your protection over them. I ask that you be with the ones that are completing their training, as well as the ones that will continue their training. Protect those who will be going into danger and help them to use what they have learned here to serve you by protecting their country.

"I also ask for your blessing on the ceremony today. May everything go as planned as the extraordinary cadets of this academy are recognized for their achievements. In your name I pray, amen."

Senndra opened her eyes and looked at the stage again. The priest climbed down, and another man took his place. He waited for the priest to leave the arena before he began.

"Welcome to the one hundred and seventy-fifth annual awards ceremony of the Academy of Belvárd. Please stand and recite with me the pledge to the nation of Magessa." All of the cadets rose to their feet, saluted their country's flag, and following the lead of the man on the stage, recited the pledge to Magessa.

Once the final words were spoken, the man stepped off the stage and another came to take his place.

"I think you all know what I'm going to be doing," he said once he reached the top of the stage. This man was a skilled orator and instantly had everyone on the edge of their seats. "It's time for this year's Extraordinary Performance awards! We'll recognize the top ten percent of the cadets currently enrolled here as well as bestow the coveted 'Cadet of the Year' award. The awards are based on physical and academic performance as well as leadership ability. The cadets that you will see tonight are truly the best of the best and will be leaving tomorrow to visit Saddun, the academy in Gatlon. Though we are the best there is,"- there were mild laughs of agreement across the crowd - "there is much to be learned from the cadets at Saddun. Oh, and it's going to be really fun! So without further ado, I'd like to present the winners of this year's awards. Please come forward when I call your name."

"The Cadet of the Year goes to..." the man looked down at his paper, flipped it over, and then began to go through his pockets. There were groans across the audience; this wasn't the first year that he had made this show. "Here we go!" he said as he pulled a sheet of paper from a pocket. "The 'Cadet of the Year' goes to Senndra Felling, for excellent show of physical and mental strength!"

The man continued down his list of the top ten percent of the students at the academy as Senndra descended the steps toward the arena. All she remembered was that Timothy and Rita were also listed. She was not surprised that Timothy was selected, though she had been uncertain about Rita. She was glad that her friends would be going with her to visit Saddun.

Senndra reached the arena and, directed by helpers there, walked to her station in front of the stage. She reached her spot and turned around to face the stands. As she watched, cadets from every corner began to stream down the stands as they were called. The names seemed to go on forever, and Senndra recognized several. It appeared as though all of her friends would be going on this trip that promised to be a fun and welcome break from classes. If there was a better way to get to know Timothy and Vladimir, she couldn't think of it. A great experience with low stress and fun activities awaited them in Gatlon, and she couldn't wait to begin.

# Two

The buildings steadily shrank as Senndra rose into the air. From her vantage point, she could see the entirety of the mountain on which the academy was built. The campus sat on the top third of the mountain, with the hatchery at the top of the campus and the dorms at the bottom. In between these two points were the mess hall, sword fighting arena, archery range, medical building, classrooms, an armory, and a store.

Senndra was riding astride a bright red dragon, which was about eighty-five feet long from his nose to the tip of his tail. The tail composed roughly one third of this length. A ridge of blunt bumps ran from the top of his head and grew sharper as they progressed toward the end of his tail, culminating in a double set of two spikes. A saddle was fastened between two bumps near the dragon's neck. His wing span was twice his body length, and the wings beat effortlessly, propelling him upward in ever-widening spirals.

As the dragon rose higher, the temperature steadily dropped, and Senndra was glad for the bulky clothing that she had complained about having to wear earlier that morning. A dull blue dragon crossed just in front of Senndra's, enabling her to identify the rider as Lemin. He seemed relaxed as he sat in the saddle. The only things that kept him from plummeting to his death were straps fastening each leg to the saddle, leaving his hands free.

Lemin passed and another dragon crossed Senndra's line of sight. This one was dark green and carried Vladimir. He had apparently taken to riding a dragon better than Senndra and had even been able to lose himself in a book. Senndra glanced around and saw the cloud of dragons and their riders. There were ninety-eight cadets and twelve instructors, making for a total of one hundred and ten dragons of all colors and shades. The dragons continued to circle the mountain until they reached an acceptable height for flying. Then they turned east and began their journey toward Saddun.

The land looked like a map lain out on a table. Belvárd was directly below Senndra and stretched out in all directions. She could see mountains to the west which marked the edge of Belvárd, and she knew that mountains also bordered the east and north sides. Sulmon was across the mountains to the west, and Gatlon those to the east. Plains covered the land to the north of Belvárd. As the dragons traveled east, Senndra could gradually make out more physical features on the horizon. Slowly, the Pelé River came into view. Branches from the river stretched all the way to the mountains. The agriculture of the region was centered on the river, the sides of which were lined with farms. Docks bustling with activity were stationed periodically along the waterway to aid in the transport of goods. In about the middle of the river was a large dock around which most of the river trade took place. The dock stretched over the river, with places for boats to moor underneath it. It doubled as a bridge, and farmers with wagons loaded with produce could be seen moving over it toward the market just west of the river.

The next building to come into view could be identified by the large flags that flew from it. The crest on them was circular with four axe heads equally spaced on a plain wreath, forming a sort of cross shape. Each axe head was emblazoned with a triangular, knotted rope of burnished silver. In the center of the wreath was a more intricate knot resembling a four leaf clover. The whole figure, also known as the cross of Elohim, was set on a green field and marked the structure as the temple. This was also the symbol and flag of Magessa, but it had not always been so. Nor had the humans always lived in and controlled the country. The nation had started out as a single family living in Magessa. At this time, a famine struck the land, so Meander, the king who ruled the country of Volexa Temp, approached Derek, the patriarch of the family. At one point in time, Derek had helped Meander by gathering an army and attacking Meander's enemies. If it had not been for Derek, the country of Volexa Temp would not exist, so Meander offered to return the favor. Since his country had not been touched by the famine, he said that he would feed Derek and his family until the famine passed, at which time he would give them land to farm. Derek accepted, and he and his family moved to Volexa Temp, where they lived in peace for many years. Several generations lived and died and Heflik, a king who knew not the works of Derek, came to the throne. He saw in Derek's descendants the threat that they might become greater than his people, rise up and overthrow him. To repress them, he took away their land and made them slaves. From sunup to sundown, they were forced to work on Heflik's building projects and to work in his fields; yet the nation, being blessed by Elohim, grew larger and stronger than ever. Heflik saw that his plan to weaken the children of Derek was not working, so he ordered that all of their baby boys be killed at birth. The children of Derek cried to their God to help them escape the clutches of Heflik, so He sent to them a man named Benjamin.

The children of Derek would not allow their sons to be killed, and it was only a short time before Heflik discovered that his orders were not being followed. The Derekite mothers were forced to hide their babies so that they would not be found and killed by Heflik's soldiers. It was at this time that Benjamin was born. His mother hid him for several months in her house until he was too big to conceal. She smuggled him to some of her friends that worked in Heflik's palace. These people promised that they would keep Benjamin safe and put him in the royal nursery among the other children. There were so many royal babies that the addition of one more child went unnoticed, and Benjamin was brought up in the palace as one of the sons of Heflik.

Sometime after his twentieth birthday, he was surveying one of the building projects of Heflik when he saw a task master strike a Derekite. He had seen this happen many times, but this time a strange feeling came over him and he struck out at the task master. The man died from the blow, so Benjamin buried him. The next day, as he was going about his own business, he heard two servants gossiping. One told the other that Benjamin had killed one of Heflik's men, and Benjamin knew that his secret was out. He quickly gathered together a few possessions and fled from Volexa Temp.

Benjamin traveled north into a great desert called the Sea of Sand. For seven days he pressed on until he ran out of water. Thirst overcame him, and just as he was about to give up all hope, he saw trees in the distance. At first he thought his mind was playing tricks on him, but he trudged toward the trees anyway. Finally, his strength gave out and he fainted. He was awakened that night by his thirst. The sun was not beating down on him anymore, and he found the strength to rise to his feet and trudge toward the trees again. When he was still quite a distance away, he saw that the trees were not the only sign of life in the vast sea of sand. Shrubs and grass covered the ground surrounding the trees. He staggered into the oasis and found a stone well at its center. Water from the well refreshed him, and he was now able to examine his surroundings. Trees encompassed the perimeter of the oasis, and the shrubs that Benjamin had seen were actual crops. He was standing in a field of ripe grain.

He quickly became acquainted with the people that lived in the oasis. They were known as Sea People because they originally lived by an ocean that was several hundred miles to the northwest. Benjamin lived with the Sea People for twenty years, following them wherever they went and watching their flocks of sheep.

One day while performing his duties, Benjamin came upon a circular-shaped mountain range. The tribe that he lived with had noticed it as soon as it came into sight, and although they tried to climb it, they were never able to make it all the way to the top. They could make it about halfway up, but even though they continued to climb, they never covered any more distance. Because of this, the Sea People regarded the range as holy and rarely went near it except in extenuating circumstances. Today, however, the sheep brought Benjamin to its slopes. Under normal circumstances, he would have stayed with his sheep, but the mountains held some unknown attraction to him. Not even knowing why he did it, he worked his way up the slope of the mountains. He reached the peak much sooner than he had expected and looked down into the bowl that was formed by the mountains. What he saw would be etched in his memory for the rest of his life. The mountains surrounded a large hole in the ground out of which columns of fire and lava spewed into the sky. Benjamin stared at the fire fountain, fascinated by what he saw. In fact, the sight before him was one that few people had or would ever see. After a moment of staring, he made his way down the mountain to the edge of the fiery hole. When he had reached his destination, an especially-large fountain of fire shot out of the ground and Benjamin thought he heard a voice.

"Benjamin," the voice said.

"Who is there?" Benjamin responded.

"It is I, the Lord God of heaven and earth."

"Where are you?" Benjamin asked, searching the rocks around him. It almost seemed as if...but that couldn't be. The voice couldn't be coming from the fire. And yet it was. The hole belched forth another fountain of fire, and the voice spoke again.

"Benjamin, take off your shoes, for you are on holy

ground."

Benjamin obeyed the voice. Although he had never been taught about Elohim, he miraculously knew who He was. "Here I am, Lord," he said. "What would you tell your servant?"

"My people are in bondage in the country of Volexa Temp. For years they have cried out to me to save them, and I have heard their cries. I am sending you to Heflik, king of Volexa Temp, and you will tell him to free my people, the Derekites."

"But Lord, I am an outcast from that place. If I show my face there, they will kill me."

"Do not be afraid. I, the same God who has sent you to Volexa Temp, will bring you out of it again. You have nothing to fear from Heflik or his armies. You will enter the country and go first to my people. Tell them that their salvation is near if they will but turn away from their sin."

"What am I to tell them if they ask who has sent me?" Benjamin interrupted the voice.

"Tell them that Elohim has sent you. Tell them that Elohim has heard their cries, and He will lift them out of bondage. Now I lift them from the bondage of slavery, but I will soon lift them from the bondage of sin."

"And how will I prove that you sent me?" Benjamin argued. "Without proof, they will not believe."

"I will give you two signs so that my people may know that I have sent you. First, take that rod over there."

Benjamin looked around him and saw a stout wooden rod laying only a few feet from him. He could have sworn it had not been there a short time ago, but he concealed his surprise. He lifted it in his hands and was surprised at how light it was.

"Take the rod and break it in two," the voice commanded.

Benjamin grasped the ends of the rod in his hands and brought it down over his knee, snapping it as though it were a dry twig.

"Now, fit the two ends of the rod together and hold it so that your hand covers the crack."

Benjamin did as he was commanded. He fitted the rod together and held his hands over the crack. When he peeled them away, he gasped at what he saw. The rod was whole again.

"It may seem impossible to you," the voice told Benjamin, "but with God all things are possible. Here is the second sign. Circle your hands around the rod at the top and slide them toward the ground."

Benjamin did this and as his hands passed over the stick, it changed from its brown color into a bright white—so white that light almost seemed to be shining from it.

"Do what you have done again," the voice commanded. Benjamin did so, and the rod returned to its normal color. "These are the two signs that I give you so that my people will know that I have sent you. After you have convinced my people that you are sent by me, you will approach king Heflik and command him to let my people go. He will not listen to you, but do not be discouraged. Every time he refuses, I will send a plague on Volexa Temp so that the world may know that I am God. Now, go and do as I have commanded you."

Benjamin turned around and scaled the slope that he had recently descended. When he reached the top, he looked down on the desert that spread out before him. Turning left, he could see the city of Volexa Temp in the distance. He now knew where his mission would lead. He had only to get down the mountain and begin. He began the descent and again completed his trip much quicker than he had expected he would. His sheep had scattered to look for food, so he rounded them up and headed back to the Sea People's camp.

******

Night had fallen by the time Benjamin entered the

74

outskirts of Volexa Temp. He had been traveling for three days and was exhausted, but he had a mission to fulfill. Fields of wheat and other crops were located on the east side of the city. The settlement of the Derekites was located here. Benjamin entered the town and wandered the streets, wondering where he would find the elders of the town. To his surprise, he stumbled on them by accident as he rounded a corner. A group of men were standing around a fire and talking in low voices. Immediately, Benjamin knew in his heart that these were the men to whom he was supposed to speak, so he strode into their midst. Finding an overturned barrel to stand on, he got the attention of the men.

"Elders of the Derekites," Benjamin began and then faltered. In all the time that he had been traveling, he had not given the slightest thought to what he was going to say, and now he found himself in an uncomfortable position. But words jumped into his head, and he thanked Elohim for them.

"Elders of the Derekites your salvation has come. Your God has sent me to free you from slavery, and in time, He will send another to free you from your sin."

That was as far as he got before he was interrupted by one of the elders. "You were sent by our God? What is his name? How are we to know that you are from Him?"

"Elohim has sent me to lead you out of the land of Volexa Temp and has given me two signs to show you that He has sent me."

Benjamin preformed his two signs and then spoke to the stunned crowd. "Elohim has sent me to lead you out of Volexa Temp," he repeated. "He alone will save you from your slavery, but I will lead you to the land that He will give you after you have left Volexa Temp."

"What about Heflik?" one of the elders objected. "He won't let us just walk out of here."

"No, he will not," Benjamin responded. "Every time I ask

Heflik to free you he will refuse. But..." Benjamin held up his hand to silence the questions of the elders, "Elohim will send signs and wonders to Heflik. By these the king will know that Elohim is the only true God. In the end, Heflik will have to bow to Elohim and set you free."

The elders were finally convinced that Benjamin was indeed sent by God, so they gave him a place to stay. The next day Benjamin arose and went into the court of Heflik. The throne room was filled with people, and it appeared as if there was some sort of party in progress. Entertainers and musicians were performing before the king, but they stopped when they saw Benjamin pushing his way through the crowd. By the time he reached the foot of the stairs that led to Heflik's throne, the whole room was as silent as a tomb. For several minutes, Benjamin stared at Heflik, waiting for the king to break the silence.

"And who might you be?" Heflik finally asked.

"Who I am is not important," Benjamin answered. "Who I represent is the question you should be asking."

"Very well then," Heflik said with a yawn. "Who do you represent?"

"I was sent by the God of the Derekites, and he commands you, 'Let my people go.'"

"He commands *me*?" Heflik laughed. He plucked a grape from a dish sitting by his throne before continuing. "And why should I listen to this god? I have my own gods, the *true* gods, and they tell me to do no such thing."

"The God of the Derekites is the one true God who made heaven and earth and everything in them. This is the God that commands you to let His people go."

"I still think that my gods are the true gods. Why should I think otherwise? Prove to me that the one that you speak of is the true God."

Benjamin said nothing, but instead raised his staff in his

hands and pulled both ends in toward the middle. Just as had happened in the desert, the rod broke in two as easily as a twig. Heflik started to speak, but Benjamin cut him off with a hard stare. Then he fit the two ends of the rod back together, with his hands covering the crack. When he removed them, the stick was whole.

"A clever magic trick," Heflik mused. "But what is that supposed to prove? I myself am something of a magician and could do that paltry bit of magic." So saying, he took his scepter in both his hands and broke it over his knee. Then he fit it back together, and when he pulled his hands away, the scepter was complete. Benjamin faltered for only a second. He hadn't counted on Heflik being a magician, but the magic that Heflik could do was only a small thing compared to Elohim's capabilities. Benjamin again took his staff in his hands, this time circling them around the wood. He slid his hands down the staff, and as they passed it became pure white. Heflik cowered back in his throne, trying to shield the brightness of the stick with one hand. After several moments, Benjamin circled his hands around the stick again and slid them down the rod. The whiteness immediately left.

"And what does that prove?" Heflik roared at Benjamin. "Again, just another bit of magic. Get out of here before I have my guards throw you in the dungeon. I will not be persuaded that your god is the true God."

Without another word, Benjamin made his way out of the throne room.

The following day, Heflik was strolling in his gardens when a voice called out to him. He looked up to see Benjamin walking toward him. Heflik had recovered from his tirade of the previous day and received Benjamin civilly.

"Hail, messenger of the nonexistent god. What message do you have for me today? Or have you come to send a punishment on me for disgracing you yesterday?"

"The Lord God says, 'Let my people go,'" Benjamin said, ignoring Heflik's taunt.

"I already told you yesterday that I will not let my slaves go. You might as well give up and go away. Or better yet, have your God take his best shot at me."

"That is exactly what will happen since you have refused to obey His commands. All of the water in and around the land of Volexa Temp, including its main wells and springs, will turn to blood." Without saying anything else, Benjamin turned around and left.

Just as Benjamin had said, all of the water of Volexa Temp turned to blood. Heflik called for all his magicians and wizards, but though they worked night and day to reverse the curse on the water, they could not. After a week, Heflik begged Benjamin to return the water to its former state and promised that he would do as Elohim had commanded; however, once the water was restored, he refused to obey. Another plague was brought on the land of Volexa Temp. This time frogs covered the country. After several days, the frogs miraculously disappeared, and Benjamin approached Heflik again. Heflik again refused to set the Derekites free, and a plague of lice struck the land. Six plagues followed the plague of lice. Flies afflicted the country, the cattle were infected with disease, boils covered every living thing, hail ruined the crops, locusts ate the remaining crops, and darkness covered the land for three days. After each plague, Heflik refused to obey Elohim.

"Thus says the Lord God of the Derekites, 'Let My people go,'" Benjamin said to Heflik after the ninth plague had been lifted. Heflik sat on his throne with his face in his hands. He was trying not to show it, but the plagues were wearing him down.

"Your God still commands me to let his people go?" Heflik asked, raising his head. His voice rose to a shout, "Well, I don't care what your God says," he swore. Then he added, "And if I see you again, you will surely die."

"You have said it," Benjamin answered quietly. "You will not see my face again. But the God of the Derekites will send one last plague on you. The angel of the Lord will smite every firstborn in the land, and they will all die."

It happened just as Benjamin had said. Every firstborn of every household in Volexa Temp died except for those in the houses of the Derekites. They smeared the blood of a lamb on their doorposts, as Benjamin commanded them, and the angel of death passed over them. The next morning, cries of grief and anger arose from the houses of Volexa Temp as mothers found their children dead in their beds. Heflik himself was not exempt from the curse; his son died at the hand of the angel as well. When he woke to find that his son was indeed dead as Benjamin had said would happen, he sent word to Benjamin, telling him to take the Derekites out of Volexa Temp. Benjamin had spread the word the night before that the Derekites would be leaving, so they were ready to move as soon as they were told by the king to leave.

Benjamin led them out of Volexa Temp to the south. He was heading to the land that Derek had originally lived in before he moved to Volexa Temp-the land that the Derekites would take back. The whole nation marched out of the city with much singing and rejoicing. Today was the day of their salvation! They were finally free from slavery. But, as Heflik sat sulking in his palace, a thought occurred to him. All of his slaves were leaving; who was going to work his fields and build his buildings? At once he gathered his army and set out after his slaves.

The sons of Derek were only a few miles from the city when Heflik's army set out after them. Panic immediately spread through their ranks, and chaos filled the camp. Just when it seemed like all hope was lost, Benjamin walked out to stand between the army of Heflik and the people of Elohim. He raised his rod and pointed it at the army. Then, pronouncing the curse of

Elohim over the enemy, he turned around to again lead the people south. The nation began to crawl forward again, wondering what was going to happen to them. Heflik and his army were steadily gaining ground. However, as they approached the fleeing nation, the ground underneath them became soft and sucked them downward. The wheels of the chariots stuck, so the soldiers leaped out to chase their quarry on foot. The weight of their armor pulled them into the marsh, never to be seen again. The land behind the Derekites continued to turn into marsh until one seventy-five miles of the unstable, swampy soil lay between them and Volexa Temp. This would forever be a barrier that protected them from their enemies to the north.

The Derekites entered the land of Magessa and wiped out all of its inhabitants that did not serve Elohim. Because the elves and ogres of the forest and the orcs in the mountains all served Elohim, they were allowed to stay. After Magessa had been conquered, it was split into three districts called Rampön, Belvárd, and Gatlon. A temple to Elohim was built in the center of the country to remind the people who had brought them out of slavery and who they served.

******

By the time Senndra came back to reality, the temple had vanished from sight. The plains on the ground had been replaced by mountains that were covered with forest. The thick trees masked from view what Senndra knew was there: orc cities. These cities were a somewhat unusual occurrence because many orcs still lived amongst the humans in Magessa. With only a few exceptions, this was something that the elves and ogres of the region would never consider. They traded and interacted with the humans on a regular basis, but they lived entirely separately in their own cities.

Legend said that orcs were very messy and brutal creatures that looked immensely different from humans. The legends were very wrong. In fact when orcs lived amongst the humans in their cities, they did not draw much attention because of their incredible similarities. They looked almost exactly the same as humans, except their hair was thicker and their bodies were typically more muscular. Due to the similarities of humans and orcs, when individuals of the two races married, their offspring could be mistaken for either race.

The forest flew underneath Senndra and soon Saddun came into view. It was easy to mistake it for a city because that, in effect, was what it amounted to. The academy was arranged in a very sensible order, not meant for beauty, but efficiency. The dragons circled over a large field in the middle of the campus, and Senndra could see that a large group of cadets was gathered there.

"It looks like the entire academy turned out to meet us," she thought. "There's several thousand of them down there all lined up in nice little rows."

The dragons circled lower, and gradually, Senndra was able to make out the features of the people on the ground. She heard a command come from below, and the entire army came to attention as the dragons landed.

\*\*\*\*\*\*

Josiah stood several paces in front of his soldiers and watched the approaching dragons as they circled toward the parade field. His men were arranged in five groups with the captain of each group standing in front of his squad. All of them were standing ramrod straight, keeping the strictest military bearing. The sun was out again in full brilliance, and Josiah could see sweat on the faces of several of the closer cadets. They had worked until midnight the previous day and had risen at six in the morning to finish their work. They had labored hard, and despite the fact that more tasks had been added, they had finished an hour and a half before lunch. Josiah had allowed them to nap until the noon day meal, staying awake himself so that he could rouse them. Of course he hadn't stayed up by himself, but had the company of Cirro. Again they fought, and again Cirro beat him.

The dragons came in toward the field in single file, landing in rows that stretched from one side of the field to the other. There were at least one hundred dragons in the group, each with one rider, and they lined up in five rows. Several of the dragon riders remained aloft on their steeds, and it became evident that they would not stay, but accompany the dragons back to the academy in Belvárd.

Josiah had seen a dragon each year since he joined the academy, but the sight of the huge beasts still amazed him. The dragons ranged in size from eighty to one hundred feet long and were every color imaginable, most of the colors being represented by several shades. Their claws and teeth, Josiah knew, were razor sharp and could cut a horse in half with ease. As they stood in rows, with the sun glinting off their scales, they looked intimidating. The riders dismounted, unstrapped their saddle bags, and formed several rows. One of the instructors advanced from the group and approached the grand admiral of Saddun. The two men saluted each other and began to converse in voices that Josiah could not hear. When they finished, they made their way back to the cadets that had just dismounted their dragons, and the grand admiral began to speak. Josiah couldn't make out any of the words, but he had a good idea of what was being said. It was most likely something to the effect of how glad they were to have visitors and how accommodating the people would be. Finally he finished and made a motion to Josiah. Josiah stayed where he was, and ninety-seven of his soldiers lined up behind him. Since he had gotten stuck with the job of escorting the visiting cadets around the campus, he had decided to make it a one-on-one thing. There was one guide for every visiting cadet, and this guide would show their charge around the campus for the first day.

The grand admiral said some more things that Josiah couldn't hear, and a girl detached herself from the group of cadets and made her way toward the group of guides. It was decided beforehand that Josiah was to escort the first cadet called, so he went out to meet her.

"My name is Josiah Pondran," Josiah said and extended his hand.

"Senndra Felling," the girl responded and shook his hand.

"Let me get those," Josiah said, gesturing to Senndra's saddle bags. She relinquished them gratefully, and the two cadets left the parade field. In silence, Josiah led Senndra across the campus toward an antiquated dorm that was reserved for visitors. He pushed open the door and allowed her to enter a hall on the first floor. The two cadets walked about halfway down the hall before stopping in front of a door labeled with the number twenty-three. Josiah fished a key out of his pocket and handed it to Senndra. She unlocked the door and entered the room, gasping at the sight of it. Despite the fact that the room was small, it was one of the most luxurious rooms in the entire academy. It had carpet instead of the standard hardwood floors of the barracks, wood paneling instead of rough boards for walls, and even its own bathroom. Josiah slipped past Senndra and dropped her bags over the back of a chair. Then he retreated from the room and sat out in the hall, waiting for his charge to emerge. As he waited, other guides and their cadets entered the dorm. Each of them followed the same procedure as Josiah, showing the cadets their rooms and then waiting outside. Cirro entered with a young man in tow, and Josiah looked up to see what he looked like. From his first glance, Josiah was shocked. The cadet had red eyes.

"Pretty strange, huh?" Cirro commented when his charge entered his room and closed the door. "The eyes really unnerved me at first, but he's a great guy. I think I'm going to enjoy showing him around."

"Lucky you," Josiah responded. "I got stuck with a girl that is a little too…" he searched for a word, "…feminine for my taste."

The cadet with the red eyes emerged from his room, and Cirro led him out of the dorm. The two chatted about what they were going to see next, and Josiah wished that he had gotten someone like the red-eyed cadet.

The door behind Josiah opened, and he jumped to his feet. Senndra had changed from her bulky flying clothes and now wore the uniform of the cadets of the Academy of Belvárd. Her hair hung down past her shoulders, and Josiah thought she looked very pretty. He suddenly decided that maybe he didn't mind having a feminine charge.

"Well, what would you like to see first?" he asked when he had found his voice.

"I don't know," Senndra answered. "You know the place better than me. Why don't you take me somewhere interesting?"

"You like history?" Josiah asked. "We have a museum that is dedicated to the war against Molkekk, curse his name."

"I think I might like that," Senndra answered. "Let's go see that."

Senndra followed Josiah out of the dorm and down a path that was lined on both sides by trees that had been perfectly arranged and trimmed less than twenty-four hours before. The path led to a fancy building that was surrounded by a twelve foot stone wall. Josiah escorted Senndra to the gate of the wall, and they entered the museum. The interior of the building was dim, and Josiah was forced to blink several times to allow his eyes to adjust. When he was able to see, he led Senndra down row after row of relics. The shelves and display cases held armor, scrolls, books, weapons, banners, and many other artifacts that had been used in the war against the dark lord, Molkekk.

It took the two cadets several hours to work their way through the entire museum, but they finally found themselves at the end. Only one more door was left to open, and in an attempt to surprise his guest, Josiah opened it with a quick movement. Behind the door was another dim room that was lit by periodic torches. Against the far wall, in a sort of shrine, was a set of armor with a banner above it.

"And this," Josiah said with as much flourish as he could muster, "is the armor of none other than the elvin magician that confined the spirit of Molkekk to his tower in Volexa Temp. Above the armor is the banner of Magessa. It is a tribute to the fact that he is one of the last elves who willingly lived among humans in this country."

"You don't mean..." Senndra stopped short and floundered for words. "Are you saying that this is the armor of the elf Jothnial?" she finally asked.

"Yes, I'm glad you know his name," Josiah said. "Few in this country do, despite what he did."

"Well I should certainly hope that I know his name," Senndra retorted. "After all, he was my father."

Josiah's mouth dropped open and he turned to look at Senndra. He carefully scanned her from head to foot before turning to the portrait of Jothnial.

"You can't be his daughter," he stammered. "You don't look anything like him. Besides," he added with another glance at Senndra, "you aren't even an elf."

"Be that as it may," Senndra said with a shrug. "I am still legally his daughter. Of course I don't resemble him. He rescued me on one of his missions when I was still a baby, and he brought me up as his own."

"I'm sorry for showing you this," Josiah said after a short silence. "I guess seeing it probably stirs up memories that aren't too pleasant."

"On the contrary, thank you," Senndra replied. "This brings back all kinds of memories, some bad, but many more good. Also, it is nice to see the tribute that was made to him."

"Oh yes, he was a great warrior," Josiah said quickly. "But even greater than his ability to fight was his faith in Elohim. Because of it, he was able to be a much better magician than many others."

A bell sounded outside.

"That would be the dinner bell, right?" Senndra asked. She turned away from the armor and left the room. "It sounds exactly like the bell at my academy. And dinner couldn't come at a better time. I'm starved."

# Three

Josiah lay on his bed, his sheets at the foot, having fallen off as he thrashed in his sleep. The nightmare that he was experiencing plagued him greatly, and he longed only for consciousness; but it would not come. In his dream, he stood on the northern wall of Saddun. Before him stretched a host of dwarves, too many to count, and they were sieging the wall. He had a bow in his hand, and he loosed scores of arrows at the enemy until he had exhausted his supply. He turned to throwing javelins but in no time the dwarves were placing ladders against the wall. Josiah drew his sword and raced down the wall to where he saw a dwarf scaling it. He knew that he could never defeat the entire host of dwarves, but he would die trying.

A hand reached out and shook Josiah from his sleep. He jerked to consciousness and reached for his weapons, but he did not have them. It took him a second to realize where he was and recognize the person who had awakened him as an officer. He swung his feet over the side of his bed and stretched before standing.

"Sir," the officer said with urgency in his voice. "The grand admiral requests your presence immediately."

"The grand admiral?" Josiah asked. Sleep still clouded his mind, and he wondered if he had heard correctly. "What on earth would he want with me at this hour?" he said while stifling a yawn.

"I do not know, sir," the officer said. "I was only instructed by my superior to escort you to a meeting with the grand admiral."

The officer seemed worried, so Josiah threw on his uniform and followed him out of the barracks. They crossed the campus, and Josiah in his half-awake state could barely discern that they were headed to the largest building in the area, the headquarters of all the important officers of the academy. They passed through the doorway after the officer had given a password to the guard stationed there and walked quickly down several halls, up a flight of stairs, and finally to a room at the end of a hall. The officer pushed open the door, announced Josiah, and left.

Josiah found himself in the room with six other men. Four of them he recognized as his fellow commanders, one he saw was the grand admiral, and the other was the general of the academy. They were surrounding a desk, but turned as Josiah entered the room. Josiah crossed the room to the desk and saw that a map of Magessa and the surrounding areas was lying there alongside a map of the city.

"Now that you're all here, I will begin," the grand admiral said. His audience of six looked at him as he took a position at the bottom of the maps. "Approximately twenty minutes ago, a soldier entered the city. No one knew who he was or what business he had outside of Magessa, but he insisted that he had news for me, so I was awakened. He told me that his name was Tarlex and that he had one purpose: to inform me that an army of dwarves, while still quite a distance from the city, was approaching and would be here by sunrise. I asked him how he knew this, and he answered that he himself had seen the dwarves and had perceived that they were ready for war and heading in this direction. I immediately sent out scouts to confirm the report and bring information on the size of the force. When I turned back to question Tarlex, he had vanished. I commenced a search for him, but so far it has turned up empty.

"Since the danger of an attack from the dwarves has been hanging over our heads for some time, I have chosen to take the man at his word. In any case, we will know for certain if there is an attack force when my scouts return; but right now, I am thinking of defensive measures. I do not wish to alarm anyone until we have all of the facts, but if what Tarlex said is correct, the enemy has substantially more men than we do. I have already dispatched messengers to nearby cities, so we can expect reinforcements. In the meantime, however, we need to concern ourselves with defending the city."

The five commanders and the general were silent for several seconds after the speech ended, but soon gained their voices and all began to talk at once. The grand admiral called for silence, and the room quieted.

"General Uriah, what do you have to say?" the grand admiral asked.

"Well, it seems to me, sir," Uriah began, "that since we will most likely be heavily outnumbered, we need to take advantage of our defensive position. Indeed, if the attacking army has no siege equipment, though I think they will, we would be able to hold them off indefinitely. I believe we need to take precautions to prevent that siege equipment from reaching the wall. For instance, if we dug a ditch in front of the wall, at least around the gate, it may prevent rams from reaching the gate."

"What about you, Commander Pondran?" the grand admiral asked.

"I think we should have every intention of defending the wall," Josiah said, "but we also need to take precautions in case it is breached. This stream," he pointed to the map, "runs down the middle of the city and provides the best chance of defense if we lose the wall. If we destroy the bridge that crosses it, the enemy would be forced to enter the water. If we then pour oil into the stream, we can light it when they try to cross. The fire should kill some of them and hold off the others at least for a while. I also think it would be prudent to set up other defensive structures, either improvised walls or ditches, in order to slow the enemy if they breach our walls."

"We also need to secure the buildings," one of the other commanders spoke up without being called upon. "If the enemy is given the opportunity, they will use the buildings for cover if they should break into the city. Therefore, I suggest that we lock and block the doors of most of the buildings, leaving only a few open for us to use for defensive cover. Choose the buildings so that if we lose them, the enemy can't use them effectively for cover. That way, if the enemy should drive us back and take up positions in the buildings, we will be able to hit them."

"I think that all of these ideas have merit," the grand admiral said. "Smether and Pakerd, take your men outside the north wall and dig a ditch to protect it. General Uriah will go with you to supervise the work. The rest of you will remain here to talk about other defensive measures. Uriah, send for the captains of these men and have them come here."

Uriah left the room to oversee the work and the grand admiral and remaining three commanders turned back to the maps on the desk.

"If we could do as Commander Pondran suggested with the stream that runs through the middle of the city, it would be a temporary barrier. It could kill a few soldiers, but we'll need some more substantial barriers, possibly walls and trenches. I think five on either side of the stream will be sufficient. Pondran, take your men and construct the ones on the north of the stream; and Fridle, you take your men and do the same to the south of the stream. Velikogo, you will take your men and do as you suggested, boarding up certain buildings and leaving only a select few open. That's all for now, gentlemen. May the city hold firm."

"May the city hold firm," the commanders responded and left the room. Josiah met his captains in the hall outside the room, and they fell in behind him as he walked quickly out of the building.

"Terza," Josiah said, and his captain came alongside him. "I need the map of the city from my office in the barracks. It's in the bottom drawer of the desk, on top of everything else. Get it, wake the soldiers, and then meet us at the bridge that crosses the stream in the middle of the city."

Terza saluted, spun on his heel, and headed back toward the barracks. Josiah led his company of captains to the bridge. When they reached it, he sat in the middle and waited in silence. His captains, sensing that there was something important afoot, kept quiet as well. It was ten minutes before Terza arrived at the bridge. He had awoken the soldiers, and by now they would be on their way to the bridge.

"Thank you, Terza," Josiah said as his captain handed him the map he had requested. He spread it out on the bridge, and his captains gathered around it. "The Grand Admiral has been warned of an imminent attack on the city and has required us to make five makeshift barriers to the north of this stream," Josiah gestured to the water that ran under the bridge they crouched on. "If each of you has your men create one barrier, we will have five. Each barrier should stretch all the way across the city and prevent the enemy from crossing in one way or another. I don't care if it's a wall or a trench or both; I just want the barriers. And by the way, it wouldn't hurt if there were several stages to each one." Josiah paused for a moment and drew five lines across the city on his map. "I've decided that we will make each barrier at roughly equal distance from each other, so there will be one at each of the lines that I have marked on this map. Each of you choose one and get to work. We only have a few hours until the enemy arrives, so be sure to work quickly."

The five captains crossed the bridge to their troops and led them across to the north side. Josiah also crossed to the north side. He wanted to make sure that his soldiers did good work. It wasn't that he didn't trust them, but this was his first encounter with real-life battle, and he wanted to survive.

****** 

Senndra's dreams were interspersed with images of dragons, academies, castles, and Josiah. The handsome young cadet who had showed her around the campus had snuck into her dreams. From the moment that she saw him, she had liked him and not just for his looks, though they certainly helped. The way that he carried himself indicated that he had confidence, and the way that he had treated Senndra showed that he was a gentleman. It was something that Senndra would never have admitted to herself, but that she couldn't hide from her subconscious. Even though she had just met him, she liked Josiah Pondran.

On the other hand, there was also Timothy. The red eyed cadet who had beaten her in the sword fighting competition had also been sneaking into her dreams of late. She appreciated him as a friend and yet, she couldn't help thinking of him in romantic terms as well. He was so handsome with his clean cut features and his eyes. Obviously they were very different than those of anyone else she knew, but something besides their color had captured her attention, something that intrigued her. Timothy was fun to be around and not nearly as much a gentleman as Josiah. That wasn't to say that he was rude, but he lacked many of the niceties that Josiah had. Senndra didn't know if she liked that about him or not.

Even inside her dream, Senndra chided herself for being such a flake. How much more cliché could she get than liking two boys at once? She liked each of them for who they were and while she could control her thoughts while she was awake, she couldn't stop from comparing them in her dreams. She despised herself for it and yet couldn't help it. This was a matter of her emotions and not something that her brain could control.

Senndra sat straight up in bed, awakened by the ringing of the campus's chapel bell. It was still dark outside, and she was reluctant to get out of bed. She knew that the bell was telling of some emergency, so she forced herself to get up. As an afterthought, she grabbed her weapons from the back of the chair and strapped them on before opening her door and stepping into the dorm hall. Cadets had already filled the hall and were heading outside to see what was causing all of the commotion. Senndra glanced down the hall and saw that Timothy was just emerging from his room. His weapons were strapped on his back, and he had a breastplate strapped on over his leather armor. He spotted Senndra and pushed his way through the crowd to her.

"You're going to want your armor," he shouted above the noise when he had reached her. "The only reason we would be getting up at this time of night is either for a fire or for an attack. I already looked out my window, and there is no fire."

"An attack?" Senndra asked. There was concern in her voice, and she already had the door of her room open.

"We're on the edge of Magessa," Timothy answered. "That is the reason this city was originally founded, to provide a defense against attacks."

Senndra dashed inside her room, closing the door as she entered. She quickly unstrapped her weapons from her back and began to put on her leather armor. A leather shirt and pair of pants were the majority of the armor. Senndra strapped on a pair of leather boots. A metal breastplate covered her torso in the front and back, and a pair of leather gloves completed the outfit. Senndra returned the weapons to her back and exited the room again. By this time, a large number of the cadets had exited the building, leaving only a few stragglers behind. Timothy waiting for her, and together they headed out of the building and made their way to the chapel.

By the time they got there, the rest of the cadets from Belvárd were there, and Lemin was standing on the porch. He gestured for the throng to quiet down, and they eventually did.

"Intelligence of the grand admiral of this academy has reported that a large army of dwarves is headed this way. Reinforcements have been sent for, but they will not arrive until midday while the attacking army will arrive around sunrise. If they gain the city, they will have the upper hand when our reinforcements come; therefore, we need to hold this city until our help arrives. As soldiers of the country of Magessa, it is your *duty* to fight the enemies of the country and prevent invasion or die trying. We will swell the ranks of the cadets of this academy and fight beside them, giving our lives if necessary to maintain the freedom of Magessa.

"This group of soldiers is so small that I will be the only one in command. We do not fall under Saddun's chain of command, so you will take your orders from me and the other instructors. With that said, we will dismiss to the north wall of the city. The enemy will be here in about an hour, so prepare for the coming battle."

The group of cadets scattered and headed for the northern wall. Some were silent as they walked, while others talked among themselves. They all shared one thing in common—this was their first battle and they were scared spitless. Senndra heard metal rasping on metal and turned to see Timothy draw his sword. He tested the edge on his finger and then slid it back into the scabbard on his back. Senndra started to ask Timothy something, but thought better of it. Instead, she drew her own sword and tested its edge. She had sharpened it right before she had left the academy of Belvárd, and the blade was quite sharp. She slid the weapon back into its scabbard and headed toward the north wall. Timothy followed, and in fifteen minutes they had reached their destination.

"Do you see Rita?" Senndra asked Timothy as she craned her neck and looked around.

"Over there," Timothy said and pointed. "She's on top of that wall, just at the top of the stairs."

Senndra looked and spotted her friend before going to meet her. She pushed her way through the crowd of cadets from both academies until she had reached the stairs that led to the top of the wall. She dashed up the stairs and greeted her friend. They had hardly started to talk, when an officer approached them.

"Clear the area," he ordered. Another officer was doing the same at the bottom of the stairs, so Senndra, Rita, and Timothy headed down the wall to a tower that appeared vacant except for a few sentries. Senndra noticed that officers were clearing the areas around the other stairs to the walls of the city and wondered what was happening. As she watched, a group of cadets approached the stairs that she had just ascended and began to tear them apart with picks. Within ten minutes, they had rendered the stairs useless.

"Brilliant," Timothy said to himself, but loud enough that Senndra was able to hear. "They're taking out the stairs so that if the enemy gains the city, they will not be able to get onto the wall."

"That may be brilliant," Rita said as she entered the tower, "but it also shows that the powers that be think there is a pretty good chance that we will lose the city."

"That is always a possibility," Timothy countered.

"And yet, the stairs to a city wall are rarely removed before a battle. We have a less than average chance of surviving," Rita answered.

"Do you think we even have a chance of holding the city, much less preventing the enemy from breaching it?" Timothy asked. "You're right that we have a less than average chance of surviving. If what I have heard is correct, it isn't a matter of whether or not the dwarves have as many soldiers as us. The question is what the odds are going to be. Will we be outnumbered five to one or will it be more like ten or twenty to one? One thing is for sure, they'll outnumber us badly. If we do not use some impeccable tactics, we'll be crushed before our reinforcements are halfway here."

"You're so cheery," Senndra muttered. "You don't have to be so depressing."

"It's only depressing because you know it's the truth," Timothy answered. "I myself am not worried about how badly we are outnumbered. We have a strong city, and we are fighting for our homes and country, while they are fighting for nothing but more land. Most important of all, they are not fighting for Elohim, and we are. He will not let His people fall."

"Do you ever doubt Elohim?" Rita asked suddenly. "If He is going to protect us, why did He even allow us to fall into this situation?"

"To answer your first question," Timothy answered, "I have doubted Elohim for most of my past. It was not until recently that I began to follow Him, but He has always proven Himself faithful. The answer to your second question, I think, is that the people of Magessa have failed to garrison an army in this city as they have done in the past. This may not be against the orders of Elohim, but the action has consequences. I think there is a more important reason, however. My opinion is that the dwarves are acting under orders of Molkekk. I have nothing to back that idea up with, but that is my opinion. We, as the people of Elohim, stand in Molkekk's way, and he will stop at nothing to crush us. Such is the way of life for a follower of Elohim. There is always someone trying to make life hard for you, even to the extent of exterminating you.

"But even in the face of this opposition, we still have the upper hand. Elohim will not abandon us, especially to His enemies, and He has the power to save us. To Him, the dwarf army outside of the city is no more than a bothersome fly that He could squish between His thumb and forefinger."

"Then why doesn't He do that?" Rita asked. She was close to tears.

"You know He doesn't work like that," Timothy answered. "He prefers to have His followers fight the battles for Him. He will enable us to complete the tasks that He sets before us, but He wants us to do them so that we might show our love for Him."

"There is another not so pleasant reason that we're in this position," Senndra spoke up. She had been silent for the entire conversation, but she felt that it was necessary to say what she had in mind. "You said that Elohim's enemies will always attack us since we are His people. I agree with that, but you also said that He will never allow us to fall into their hands. By saying this, you are forgetting the story of Benjamin when he led the Derekites from the land of Volexa Temp. In the end, they were victorious. But before that, they were in captivity by the enemies of Elohim. I believe that if Magessa turns away from Elohim, He might let our enemies capture us so that we turn back to Him. Besides that, I think the country is about ripe for such a punishment. You have to admit that the people of the country have been slowly turning away from Elohim. Sure, the superficial worship of Him still goes on, but the majority of the country has been turning from Him."

"You are right, of course," Timothy said with a sigh. "I know that such a judgment may hit us, but I haven't wanted to believe that. Now that we are faced with this, I think it may be the judgment that has been a long time in the making."

\*\*\*\*\*\*

Josiah surveyed the work that his soldiers had done. He ran his eyes down the entire length of the barrier and nodded his consent. This was the last barrier that he was going to examine, and it was by far the best. It consisted first of a shallow trench that had pointed wooden stakes driven into the bottom. Next, the dirt from the trench had been piled up into a three foot wall that had more pointed stakes on top. Another trench had been dug into the ground directly after the dirt wall, and the bottom of this trench was covered with shards of pottery and other sharp objects. Finally, there was a wall built on the far side of the second trench. This wall was composed partially of dirt but had plenty of bricks, rocks, wood, and other things mixed into it.

The men had done a good job and had even had time to collect weapons from the armory. These were not the dull practice weapons that they had trained with, but sharp ones, deadly in their purpose and ability. Looking around, Josiah could see that there was a variety of weapons present, each man having retrieved one that he was experienced with. Swords were by far the most common, but spears were also a popular choice. Pikes were also scattered through the company of soldiers, but they were few and far between.

"It looks good, men," Josiah said after thoroughly examining the barrier. He had tried as hard as he could to come up with reasons why the barrier wouldn't hold up, but had not been able to find any. Again he cast his gaze across the barrier and nodded in assent. It would work quite well. Josiah looked east and saw that the sun was just beginning to push above the horizon.

"Very good work," Josiah said, "now adjourn to the north wall. We're expecting an attack any time now, and we're not going to give up the city without one heck of a fight."

The soldiers scattered and quickly made their way to the north wall. All of the stairs to the wall had been demolished, making it necessary for the cadets to go through the gatehouse in order to gain the top of the wall. Josiah sighed and followed his men. He knew that their training had been extensive and that they were, for the most part, ready for the coming battle. Even though they had been deprived of their needed sleep, he knew that the dwarf army had also been up for a long time and had not gotten sufficient sleep either. All said, the coming battle would be a tough one, and no matter which way it ended, there would be a lot of bloodshed.

Josiah reached the gatehouse and waited as scores of soldiers used the same building to get onto the wall. Finally his turn came, and he entered the side door of the stone building. He quickly ascended a spiral staircase that passed several doors before coming out on the top of the wall. To his left, his men had gathered into their squads of roughly two hundred men apiece, and when he came out of the gatehouse, his captains approached.

"Commander Pondran," Terza addressed him, and all five captains saluted. Josiah returned the salute and waited for his captain to continue. After several seconds, Josiah realized that his captain didn't have anything to say, so he took over.

"Do we have any orders from higher up yet?" he asked as he walked down the wall toward his men. Even from this far away he could see that they were aligned in straight lines of military precision and were at attention.

"There were orders, sir," Terza answered. "They were simply that your men were to defend the area of the wall they now cover."

"Good," Josiah said as he cast his eyes over his troops again. "In that case, I can set things up like I want. You have a good order, but you need to pull the men closer together, shoulder to shoulder. Have half of the archers in front and a row of pike men behind them. Then I want the other half of the archers on the ground back there," Josiah said and pointed to the ground just inside the city wall.

"Already done, sir," Terza responded. Josiah looked and saw that there were three hundred of his soldiers on the ground behind him. They were split into two groups and were surrounded by a thin line of swordsmen for protection in case the enemy breached the walls.

"Very good," Josiah said after he had again surveyed the entire setup. "I guess there's not much else we can do. Except," he added hurriedly when he saw a look of reproof from Cirro, "we still have yet to pray and ask Elohim for protection and victory." Josiah heard a snort from somewhere among his soldiers, but a glare silenced the offender. After his men had become silent, he bowed his head and began.

"Dear Almighty God, thank you for your protection today in all of the activities we have participated in so far. Thank you that no one was physically hurt as they constructed barriers throughout the city. Thank you that we heard about the enemy in enough time to be able to send for reinforcements.

"Now, dear God, please protect us as we battle the dwarves that are at this moment en route to our city. Lord, you know that they have turned from you and are now following the evil lord Molkekk. We know that it is because we follow you that we are now being attacked, and we ask that you be with us in the upcoming battle. Help us to overcome the enemy, that Magessa may remain a free nation, and that we might worship you in peace. Amen."

******

Senndra gripped her bow in her left hand and an arrow in her right. The sun was just starting to rise off to her right, and as if on cue, the dwarf army appeared out of a fog that lingered on the plain outside the city. Senndra could see no siege equipment amongst the ranks of dwarves, but that didn't mean it wasn't there. She averted her eyes and looked down the wall of the city. Archers stood shoulder to shoulder for as far as Senndra could see. As she looked at those about her, she could see fear in their eyes. Almost none of them had ever been in a battle before, and they were just as worried as she was.

Senndra took a deep breath and tried to settle her nerves. *"Just do what you're supposed to do and leave the rest to Elohim,"* she told herself. Turning her gaze back to the dwarves just outside of bow range, she saw that they were changing position, and catapults were coming out of the fog. The engineers who were running them set them up well out of range of the defenders' weapons and began to prepare them for their first salvo. Out of the corner of her eye, Senndra could see an officer make a motion with his sword. Almost half a minute passed before he made a motion that Senndra recognized as the command to prepare to fire. She turned her attention to Lemin, but he was motionless, his sword at his side. Senndra turned and saw that the commander who was motioning with his sword was facing someone behind the wall. Her gaze drifted backward until it came to rest on six trebuchets.

A loud report from over the wall brought her gaze back around to the dwarf army. The catapults had fired, and their missiles were headed for the wall. As the boulders approached the wall, their targets became obvious, and the soldiers in those areas began to scatter. But it was to no avail. Two of the shots dug into the ground before they reached the wall and bounced harmlessly off its base, but the other ten boulders reached their targets. Five of them hit about halfway up the wall; four of those did little damage; the last one, however, knocked loose a part of the wall. The wall creaked but did not fall. A few of the catapult shots hit the gatehouse and bounced harmlessly off. The most damaging shots hit, with precision, a tower to Senndra's left. The boulders punched through the relatively thin wall of the tower, and the whole structure collapsed. Thankfully, it fell in such a way that left no breach in the wall.

An audible command was heard from down the wall, and the trebuchets fired a return salvo. Most of the missiles landed in front of the army and rolled into it, killing the soldiers in their paths. Two of the shots hit the catapults they were aimed at. Debris flew in all directions as the boulders hit, but the other catapults were already preparing for their next attack. The trebuchets were ready first, and another salvo was fired. This one destroyed another catapult, which in turn fired its shot haywire into the army behind it. The remaining catapults, however, fired with deadly accuracy and punched a hole in another tower. Again there was no breach, but Senndra knew that it was only a matter of time before one was opened. Several of the other shots hit the wall where it had been previously damaged, and although it gave a tremendous groan, it still did not collapse. There was another burst from behind the wall, but no more catapults were destroyed.

"Griffins!"

Senndra immediately turned to see a flock of the magical creatures that she had only heard about in stories approaching her position from the west. The origin of the first griffins was unknown, but many people suggested that they had been created by Molkekk in his early attempts to create a race of warriors for himself. They were a fusion of a lion and an eagle. The front half of the beast was that of an eagle, complete with wings, talons, and a beak, while the rear half had the back legs and tail of a lion. The legendary ferocity of these beasts, along with their ability to fly, made them a living nightmare for soldiers. Though they could not individually meet a dragon in battle, in flocks they could certainly hunt them. And now, at least a hundred of these terrifying creatures were closing in on the trebuchets from the west behind the wall.

"Fire at will," Lemin commanded in a stone-cold voice. Senndra immediately turned, nocked her arrow, and targeted an incoming griffin. She released her arrow, and it sped straight and true, slamming into the griffin's neck. Senndra immediately nocked another arrow and took aim again. Just as she was about to fire, a shot from one of the catapults hit the wall off to her right, and chips of stone rained down on her. Her shot went wild but still managed to pierce the wing of a griffin. By the time the griffins reached the trebuchets, their numbers had been cut in half. Nevertheless, they were able to destroy four of the siege machines before retreating. Senndra glanced over her shoulder and saw that only three of the enemy catapults remained. The dwarves were charging now, with several hundred ladders leading the army.

"Front line, about face," Lemin called. Senndra spun and faced the oncoming dwarves.

"Prepare to fire," Lemin called. His voice was still calm and controlled. Senndra drew an arrow and nocked it.

"Fire," Lemin commanded, and Senndra released her arrow. Even as she drew another arrow and placed it on the string, she watched her first as it sped toward the army. She lost sight of it before it hit and turned her attention to her next arrow. Another command to fire was given, and again a wall of arrows flew out to meet the enemy. Senndra saw several hundred of their number fall, but they were hardly noticeable as the other soldiers trampled them beneath their feet.

By now the dwarves had reached the wall and were leaning their ladders up against it. One was directly in front of Senndra and others were close on either side.

"First and second lines, draw swords," Lemin called. Senndra slung her bow over her quiver and grabbed her sword from its scabbard. All around her, her comrades were following suit. Lemin's short sword was still fastened to his back along with his bow, and in his hands he held a massive two-handed sword from Saddun's armory. "Don't let them take the wall," he commanded and brought his weapon down on the top rung of the ladder near him. Just before the blade contacted, a hand reached up to grab the rung. Lemin's sword cut the fingers off the hand and rang as it bounced off the top rung of the metal ladder. The hand disappeared, but was instantly replaced by a dwarf body. Lemin ran the attacker through with his sword, but even as he shoved the deceased dwarf off the ladder, another rose to take its place. Senndra swung her sword and took the head off of the first dwarf that ascended the ladder that was in front of her. Seconds later, a pike man used his weapon to shove the ladder away from the wall. As he retracted his weapon, he convulsed and turned just enough for Senndra to see the black feathers of a crossbow bolt protruding from his plate mail. He fell from the wall, and Senndra ducked below the crenellations just in time to avoid a barrage of deadly crossbow fire. Dozens of archers dropped, some dead and some fatally wounded. The remaining archers immediately began to return fire. Senndra sheathed her sword, grabbed her bow, and stood up. She placed an arrow on the string and targeted an enemy archer. She let the arrow fly and in seconds had another arrow on the string. More arrows flew upward at the defenders, and more archers perished. Senndra continued to let the arrows fly from her string even as archers all around her fell. Immediately to her right, Timothy fired on the enemy below, but his arrows seemed to do little against the enemy horde. Up and down the wall, the remaining pike men scurried around trying to shove off as many ladders as possible. But as soon as they dispatched one, several more rose to take its place.

"Retreat to the first barrier!"

Senndra looked toward Lemin and saw that he was already rallying together the remaining cadets from the academy of Belvárd. She fired one last shot and hurried to join her friends. She glanced behind the wall and saw that the trebuchets had turned to fire on the walls to either side of the area where the ladders had been raised. They were cutting the enemy off from the rest of the wall. Senndra reached Lemin and looked around. Of the one hundred and six soldiers from Belvárd, only fifty-three remained. Senndra tried to find Rita and Timothy in the throng, but couldn't locate either. Everyone looked the same, dressed as they were in battle attire.

"Retreat to the gatehouse," Lemin ordered. "Anyone who volunteers will stay with me and cover the retreat."

Without another word, Lemin turned and stood on the wall, facing away from the gatehouse. One of the other instructors led the cadets in an orderly retreat down the wall, but Senndra didn't follow. She slowly turned and looked down the wall to where the enemy was chasing an army of cadets toward her.

"Senndra, what are you waiting for? Let's go," a voice called from behind her. She ignored it and took her place beside

Lemin. He glanced over at her with a look of appreciation. He turned back to the charging enemy and raised his sword.

Senndra glanced sideways and saw that Timothy had come up beside her. His sword was still in its sheath, but he had his bow out, and an arrow was on the string. The arrow flew down the wall, past the retreating cadets, and into the dwarf army, felling one of the soldiers. Within seconds he fired again, and another enemy fell. He exhausted the remaining arrows in his quiver, slung his bow over his shoulder, and drew his sword.

"Let the cadets pass, but do not permit the enemy to get through," Lemin ordered.

Senndra watched as the cadets reached her and streamed around either side as she stood her ground. All too soon they had passed, and there was nothing between her and the enemy. A glance to either side showed that Lemin was doing his best to loosen up, while Timothy seemed to be concentrating on something. Senndra turned her attention back to the enemy, who by now were no more than twenty yards away. Suddenly, with an incredible groan, a section of the wall in the middle of the dwarf ranks gave way and collapsed. Dwarf bodies and chunks of stone dropped out of sight; perhaps a hundred enemy soldiers had been destroyed, but more important was the fact that most of the survivors were on the other side of the hole. Only about thirty soldiers were left for the defenders to face.

They closed the distance quickly, and in seconds, Senndra was bringing her sword up to block the blow of an ax. A blur shot past her through the air, and the head tumbled off a dwarf. Out of the corner of her eye, she could see that Josiah had returned with a handful of soldiers and was now staging a defense on the wall.

The soldier that had saved Senndra spun on his heels and engaged three enemies at once. His skill with a blade was quite evident, but Senndra could see that he was outnumbered. Running forward two steps, she thrust her sword into the heart of one of the dwarves. Another was approaching her from the side, so she spun and slashed at his torso. Her blade scraped off his armor, and she found herself wide open to his attack. Air whistled past her ear, and a dagger buried itself in the dwarf's neck.

As quickly as the fighting had begun, it ended with complete annihilation of the enemy force. Timothy stepped past Senndra and retrieved his knife from the body of the dwarf that he had killed. With a quick move, he wiped the blade on the tunic of the dead enemy and returned it to its sheath. Then, by unspoken agreement, all of the defenders sprinted down the wall toward the gatehouse.

A barrage of crossbow bolts whistled over their heads, coming from the front of the wall, but they were too high to do any damage. They reached the gatehouse and descended its now empty stairwell. To the west, dwarves were pouring into the city through the hole that had saved the defenders on the wall. Already, a clear route to the first barrier was blocked off, so Josiah led the small group to the east. They headed for the interior of the city and a section that had not been overrun with enemies. Josiah led them between the buildings, through a maze of alleys that only a native of the city would be able to navigate. Taking a roundabout path to avoid the enemy troops, they slowly made their way south and east until they finally came in sight of the first barrier. Suddenly Josiah stopped and motioned for the others to do so as well.

"What's up, Commander?" Cirro asked Josiah.

"Take a look for yourself, Cirro," Josiah said, motioning toward the open area between them and the barrier. Cirro looked out and swore under his breath. Only a hundred yards to the west, a group that contained at least several hundred dwarves was parked just under the cover of the buildings. Every so often, they would send out an attack party that would be driven back by archers from the other side of the barrier.

"We can't cross to the barrier yet," Josiah said. "Those dwarves are just too close for us to be able to do it safely. That's without even mentioning what our friends on the other side of the barrier might do to us. After all, they could very easily mistake us for dwarves. I guess all we can do is wait it out. Once we get to the other side of the barrier, I know of a way to get behind our lines. But not from where we are now."

Cirro started to swear again, but stopped himself.

"So you're saying that we should just sit here and wait? Do you have any idea what you're saying? We'll be sitting ducks. We won't have any cover and not even an ideal spot to defend in a hand-to-hand fight."

"I know that, Cirro," Josiah answered, "but we don't have much of a…"

Josiah was interrupted by a shout from the back of the group. He and Cirro spun around and saw that dwarves were entering their alley from the north. The cadets drew themselves up into a battle formation, but it was doubtful that they would be able to hold out against the dwarves. Two arrows whistled from out of the group of cadets and dropped two dwarves, but then they were too close for another shot. The first line of cadets was engaged, and the sounds of battle filled the alley. The dwarves cut through the first line but were held back as more cadets came to fill in their fallen comrades' places.

"Josiah, over there!"

Josiah turned to see Senndra looking at him and pointing to the south end of the alley. Dwarves flooded in this end as well, preparing to attack the undefended flank of the cadets. Quickly Josiah drew his sword, and Cirro came up alongside him. They were joined by Senndra, Timothy, and Lemin. All held their swords in various stances, but the same look of determination was on all of their faces.

Josiah seemed to enter a dream world as the dwarves drew nearer. He felt as though this was not real, but he knew that it was. The closest dwarves came into focus when they were only a few yards away, and yet they seemed to take an eternity to cover the distance. The sound of metal shod boots striking the ground pounded in Josiah's brain, and his sword dropped a fraction of an inch. The faces of the enemy, many showing expressions of fear and anguish, came into focus. Josiah knew they must be feeling many of the same things that he was.

In the next moment, time seemed to snap back to normal speed. The dwarves crashed into the defenders and drove them back a step or two, but they could not break through. Josiah parried a blow from an axe and swept his own blade across the shoulders of the enemy, cleaving his head from his body. Another dwarf took the dispatched one's place, and when Josiah killed him, another took his place. Josiah couldn't tell how long the encounter lasted, but no matter how many enemies he killed, more entered the alley and continued the attack. He knew that the end would come sooner or later. He was sure he would make one mistake that would allow an attacker to land a fatal blow, and that would be the end. The mistake came, and Josiah looked in shock as the axe of his opponent swung toward him in slow motion. He heard running feet behind him and was thrown out of the way just in time. He watched, unable to move, as the axe swung straight toward where he had been moments before, only now that space was occupied by Terza. He didn't even have time to shout as he watched Terza try to block the blow. The axe knocked his sword to the side and slammed into his stomach, splitting his torso nearly in half.

Josiah stared as the dwarf jerked his axe from Terza and turned to face another enemy. He recovered himself and began to charge with a guttural roar, but before he had reached the dwarf, his enemy dropped with a knife in his neck. Timothy pushed in front of Josiah and blocked his charge.

"Don't be stupid, Josiah," he shouted over the clamor of battle. "The men need you to lead them, so don't go off and get yourself killed. If you do, everyone here will probably die." Timothy turned and took Josiah's place in the line of defenders.

Josiah stooped over to pant for breath and for the first time realized how tired he was. He straightened up and looked around, taking in the situation. While the dwarves to the south had not made any headway at all, the dwarves to the north had killed at least half of the defenders and were steadily working their way forward. The cadets were fighting in an alley with nowhere to go but up the walls or through a door that had been nailed and locked shut. Without a second thought, Josiah launched himself at the door. He hit the solid wood and bounced off, rolling away. He rose to his feet and looked at the door again. As he allowed himself to relax, his mind slowly cleared, and he was able to think more clearly. He turned and grabbed the sleeve of a massive cadet who was not engaged in the fighting.

"Open that door!" he shouted. It took the cadet several seconds to comprehend who was ordering him around, but after he realized, he immediately went to work. He planted his shoulder on the door and pushed inward with all of his might. Nothing happened for several seconds, but then the door gave way a fraction of an inch. Josiah planted his hands on the door as well and began to push. The nails that were holding the door slowly slipped loose until they slid completely out of the wood, and the door swung open. Josiah and the cadet who had opened the door both tumbled inside, but were back on their feet in no time.

"Stay here and block the door against the enemy," Josiah ordered. "I'm going to get the others in. Let the cadets pass, but stop the dwarves."

Without waiting for an answer, Josiah ran out the door and commanded a retreat. Slowly the defenders pulled back into the open building until the dwarves were almost to the door.

Lemin and Timothy stood side-by-side, blocking the doorway as the dwarves tried to force their way in.

"Pull back inside!" Josiah shouted at them, but they paid no attention. Josiah shrugged and motioned to the cadet who had opened the door. The cadet slid his sword into its scabbard and reached out and grabbed both Lemin and Timothy by their collars. With a snap of his wrists, he sent them flying into the building. He spun back to the door and slammed it shut just as the first dwarf was trying to enter. The door caught the body of the dwarf almost at the waist, preventing the door from closing. The cadet punched the dwarf in the face, dislodging his body from the door, and slammed the entrance shut.

"The bolts—now," Josiah ordered uselessly. Already there were men sliding them into place. "Check the inside of the building," Josiah said next. "Make sure all the doors are fastened and see what kind of a defense we have in this place. Also see if there is any way to get from here to any of the adjacent buildings."

As Josiah's cadets spread out to obey the command, Lemin began to count the cadets under his command. Only twenty-six remained, and of those, three were wounded. Of the twenty-three that were suitable for fighting, more than half were exhausted.

"Attention!" Lemin ordered, and the cadets assumed orderly ranks as quickly as possible. Senndra could tell that despite their speed, they were all too tired to face another attack. She could see Lemin's eyes roaming over the cadets and knew that he would arrive at the same conclusion.

"I believe that, due to the state of our soldiers and the size of the building, it will be easier if we move to the second floor and defend it," he said to Josiah.

"We'll wait for the report from my men," Josiah answered sharply. Senndra could see that he was panting hard from the recent fight.

"We must ascend at least to the second level," Lemin argued. "There are dozens of ways to enter the first floor of this building, but probably only a handful of ways to reach the second floor; at any rate, being one level up will give our archers better range and line of sight."

"I said that we wait until my men come back with a report!" Josiah shouted.

Lemin glanced at Senndra and raised an eyebrow. He motioned her over, and she crossed the room to where he stood.

"What was Josiah normally like in your dealings with him?" he asked.

"He was quite nice and polite," she answered, "and not at all like he's acting now."

"Or you were just too enamored with his good looks to notice that he was rude," Timothy joked from his position at the end of the ranks closest to Lemin. Senndra glared at him.

"He's probably just scared and doesn't know how to react to what is happening around him," Lemin decided. "I mean, giving a cadet command of soldiers is fine until you encounter a battle. Then, those who were otherwise good leaders may fail miserably. I'll give him until his men get back from their reconnaissance mission to make a decision. If at that point he makes a bad choice, I will pull rank and take command of his men."

"How do you like that?" Timothy asked when Lemin left. "I knew that he had seen combat before, but who would have guessed that he was this good. I'll tell you what, if he ordered me to march off of a cliff, I believe that I'd do it."

"So, what about Josiah?" Senndra asked. "You think that he'll be able to pull it together?"

"Well, he has until his men get back," Timothy said. Both cadets jumped at a pounding on the door. "And then again, he may not have that much time."

"Stations!" Lemin called from across the room. Immediately the cadets jumped to their feet and drew their swords. Lemin directed the freshest soldiers to the front of the group and took his place with them. Again the door was battered from the outside, and the cadets tensed. Every eye was on the door, and every nerve was on edge, so everyone jumped when Josiah shouted from the back of the room.

"Dwarves have breached the building!" he said. "Retreat to the second floor!"

"Commence retreat!" Lemin called, and the cadets under his command scurried to obey. Mustering their remaining energy, they ran through the confusing rooms of the building until they arrived at a staircase. From every direction, the sound of dwarves crashing through the rooms was heard, spurring the cadets to move faster. The stairs seemed to spiral upward forever, but Senndra finally reached the top and stopped to catch her breath. Lemin and his cadets stayed to defend the area while Josiah led his soldiers down a hall a short distance to barricade another set of stairs.

"Block the stairs," Lemin ordered before she had time to inhale deeply even once. "Get whatever you can find—tables, chairs, whatever. I don't care what you get as long as it will stop those infernal dwarves."

By this time, Senndra could barely walk straight. Timothy, however, seemed to have an eternal supply of energy. He dashed into a room that was close by and returned with a chair in either hand. He carried them to the stairs, flung them down, and returned for two more. From down the stairs, Senndra could hear the sound of dwarf boots running upward. Adrenaline coursed through her veins, and she dashed into a room that was near the stairs. She spotted another cadet trying to single-handedly move a table and helped him carry it from the room. They dragged it to the top of the stairs and, with a mighty heave, threw it down. It slid down the stairs and passed out of sight, but Senndra could still hear it sliding. Finally she heard it slam into a wall followed by a dwarfish curse. Senndra could only imagine the damage the table had caused and went to grab a couple of chairs to add to it. She pulled them to the top of the stairs and flung them down. This time they hit other debris and came to a stop even before they had passed out of sight.

Several cadets had come across a rich supply of nice heavy objects like books, dishes, and other odds and ends, and were stacking them up by the stairs for use as weapons. Senndra only watched them for a split second before dashing to another room and grabbing a small end table. She hefted it onto her shoulder and carried it to the stairs. By this time, there was a visible barrier of chairs, tables, and other furniture extending up the stairs and into view. As Senndra watched, a dwarf struggled into view, walking on the furniture. Without thinking, Senndra heaved her table down the stairs at him. It connected solidly and threw the dwarf out of sight.

"Nice shot, Senndra," Timothy said as he walked passed her and heaved two chairs down at the growing barrier. After him came Vladimir carrying several large quilts. He dropped them all at the top of the stairs and, one by one, unfolded them and threw them at the furniture.

"I found a large table," he said, turning to Senndra and Timothy. "I think it's big enough to cover the bottom half of this doorway."

Timothy and Senndra followed Vladimir into a room where there was a long table that would seat at least twenty men. Together they struggled to drag the thing to the stairs, where they stood it on its side and blocked the bottom half of the doorway at the top of the stairs. Then they gathered with Lemin and the rest of their comrades behind the makeshift wall.

They didn't have to wait long for a small group of dwarves to come into view. Immediately the cadets rained a barrage of heavy articles on them, and they retreated back down the stairs. Senndra saw that Vladimir was not throwing things like the rest of the cadets, but instead appeared to be deep in thought. Suddenly he rose to his feet and made his way to where Lemin peered over the upturned table.

"If I may have a minute, sir, I would like to talk to you," he told Lemin. Lemin turned around and took in the cadet that stood before him. Apparently the intense look on Vladimir's face convinced Lemin to grant the request.

"Certainly. And who am I speaking to, may I ask?"

"I am Cadet Vladimir Peterson. I was wondering what you intend to do now that we have successfully barricaded ourselves in?"

"Do we have to do anything?" Lemin asked. "It seems that we have the upper hand for the moment, and I think we will be able to hold them off for quite a while."

"But in fact our position is not secure, sir," Vladimir said. "All that has to happen is for the dwarves to get wise and destroy our barricade from the bottom. My guess is that if a few choice parts are taken out, it will all slide down the stairs. Even if it does stop the dwarves from getting up here, when they try to attack several times and are defeated they'll withdraw."

"Exactly. And we will have done what we intended," Lemin said as he nodded.

"You didn't let me finish, sir," Vladimir said. "There is more than one way to skin a cat. They will realize that they can't kill us by attacking, so they'll set fire to the building and burn it down around us."

Lemin stood silent for several moments as he thought. He paced back and forth in front of the stairs for some time before turning his attention back to Vladimir.

"And what would you have us do then?" he asked. His countenance was downcast, and it was apparent that he had already tried to formulate an excuse for why what Vladimir said was false and came up empty. "I don't suppose you would have any brilliant ideas as to how to get out of here?"

"Well," Vladimir began, "It occurred to me that the gaps between the buildings in this city are so narrow that the table we are using to block the stairwell would probably be able to serve as a bridge to another building. All we would have to do is find a balcony or window with a corresponding one on the adjacent building. Then we could lay the table across the gap."

"Let me think about that for a while," Lemin said and turned away from Vladimir.

"I would make a decision quickly," Vladimir responded. Lemin turned around, and Vladimir motioned to the makeshift barricade that had been erected. Smoke was already beginning to drift up the stairwell.

"Go and find what you're looking for," Lemin said with some urgency in his voice. "I'll send a message to Pondran and tell him what the situation is."

Vladimir didn't immediately begin his task, but first crossed to where Senndra was sitting against a wall, her legs pulled up and her head on her knees.

"Senndra," Vladimir said, and Senndra slowly lifted her head. "I need your help in order to find a way out of here." Senndra raised her head, and Vladimir held her gaze for a moment before looking further down the hall.

"Timothy," Vladimir called out, and Timothy turned toward him. Vladimir motioned for him to come over, and he did so immediately. When Timothy got close enough for his eyes to become visible, Senndra felt a feeling of security travel up her spine at the familiar oddity. Vladimir waited for Timothy to join them before beginning.

"Here's the plan," he said. "If we sit here, we're going to get roasted by the fire the dwarves have started downstairs." He glanced at the stairwell and saw that the amount of smoke had noticeably increased. "If we want to survive, we have to get out of here, and the only way to do that is to reach another building from this one. I've already talked to Lemin, and he approved my plan to find coinciding windows or balconies from this building to an adjacent one. Then we can bridge the gap with a table and cross to the other building. Basically what we need to do now is spread out and search for a pair of windows that will work. You two work together, and I'll find another cadet to come with me."

Vladimir rose to his feet and began to search for a willing helper. Timothy turned to look at Senndra. With a shrug of his shoulders, he reached out a hand to help her up. She gratefully took it and let him pull her to her feet. Timothy took the lead and moved down the hall. But before they had gone more than a couple of yards, Vladimir was back at their side, this time with another cadet.

"Lemin is moving the rest of the cadets to the other staircase that Pondran was defending, so if you find what you're looking for, report to him there."

Vladimir was gone once again, so Timothy and Senndra began to quickly work their way down each hall, looking in every room along the perimeter of the building. There were a few windows that would work as a last resort, but none that were exceptionally suited to their purpose. As they neared the front of the building, they finally came upon a room with an escape route that would suit their needs perfectly. It had a balcony that was directly across from a balcony on the adjacent building. As soon as they had confirmed that the setup would work, they rushed back into the halls, making their way to where Josiah and Lemin had their soldiers. By this time, the fire was eating its way through several portions of the second floor, which they were forced to avoid. Because of this, it took them close to five minutes to reach the other soldiers. By this time, the fire was quite extensive, and Timothy had to shout to be heard above the sound.

"We found what we're looking for," he shouted at Lemin. "There's a balcony that is directly across from one on the adjacent building. If we tear a plank off of the table blocking the stairs, we can use it to bridge the gap."

"Good," Lemin shouted in reply. "Let's get a plank and head there immediately."

In no time Timothy and Senndra had torn a long plank loose and carried it between them as they headed back the way they had just come. Behind them, they could hear Lemin and Josiah ordering their soldiers, now a small group of just over sixty, to move. They quickly maneuvered their way through the building to the exit that Senndra and Timothy had found. Upon entering the room, they positioned the plank and stepped to the side and allowed the soldiers to file across. Near the end of the line, they met Lemin and Josiah.

"They're making the move to the next building well, I guess," Senndra said.

"At least the line keeps moving. The important thing is to make sure that the enemy doesn't realize we are there once we get across."

"Well, let's go then," Josiah said and started for the door. Lemin followed, but stopped and turned when neither Senndra nor Timothy followed him.

"You heard the man; let's go," Lemin said.

"Where's Vladimir?" Senndra asked suddenly.

Timothy cursed loudly. "He and his friend are still in the building somewhere! We need to find them before we get out of this death trap."

"The 'no man left behind' idea, huh?" Lemin muttered. "Maybe I taught them a little too well." In a louder voice he said, "Well, let's get moving." In response to the looks on their faces he added, "What? You didn't expect me *not* to come, did you? After all, three is safer than two."

"We can't spend time arguing, so I'll agree," Timothy said. "But if you're coming, we need to get moving right now. This building isn't going to last very much longer."

"Josiah," Lemin yelled through the door of the room with the balcony. "I'm leaving for the time being and putting you in charge of my troops." He pulled his head out of the room. "Okay, let's go."

Together, the three companions started back into the burning building in pursuit of their missing comrades. The building was burning hot by now, and sweat ran down the faces of all three. The integrity of the building had been breached quite a while ago, and with every step, the floor and ceiling creaked, threatening to collapse at any moment. To add to these dangers, smoke filled the air, making it hard to breathe or see more than an arm's length in any direction.

As the three moved through the building, they called out Vladimir's name, but never received any response. They skirted the outside wall of the building with no luck and then moved their search toward the rooms in the middle. As they moved toward the center of the structure, the smoke lessened and they were able to see more clearly. They searched for what seemed like hours until they convinced themselves that they would never find their comrades. They turned and headed back for the outer edge of the building, but suddenly a section of floor caved in. They headed back the way they had come only to have another section collapse almost underneath their feet. Weaving their way through the halls of the building, they tried desperately to find a way out. The smoke was so thick now that they could not see more than a few inches, and they had resorted to feeling their way through the building. Senndra stumbled and fell. She called out to Lemin and Timothy who immediately moved in her direction. Even using the sound of her voice for direction, the navigation was still difficult.

"What is it?" Timothy asked when he found Senndra. He had tied a cloth over his mouth to help filter some of the smoke.

"I tripped over something here," Senndra responded.

"Probably just some fallen furniture or something," Lemin said irritably. "Let's get going."

"It's not just some furniture," Senndra responded indignantly. "It felt soft, almost like a body." She groped with her hands through the thick smoke until she found the body over which she had stumbled. "Over here," she called. "I think it's Vladimir!"

"Where's his friend?" Timothy said. He was suddenly on his hands and knees beside her and groping about. Lemin joined the search, and together they explored the surrounding area. After several minutes of hunting, they turned up nothing.

"We need to get going or we're not going to get out of here ourselves," Timothy finally shouted over the roar of the fire. "We haven't found him yet, so I doubt he's around here."

"You're probably right," Lemin said. He walked in a stooped posture to where Senndra sat on the floor next to the prone body of Vladimir, his head in her lap. Lemin hefted the unconscious body onto his shoulders and started down the hall as fast as he could move. Senndra scrambled to her feet and followed quickly after him, though it was hard for her to concentrate due to the vast amounts of smoke she was inhaling. She was lightheaded and unable to keep track of time. It felt as if she was dreaming, and her brain couldn't process anything. Suddenly she bumped into Lemin, who had abruptly stopped moving. Through blurry eyes, she could see the elf heave Vladimir through the air toward a wall that appeared out of the smoke. He turned around and grabbed her arm and shoved her toward where Vladimir was lying, and she stumbled and fell to the ground. A loud cracking noise startled her, and she jerked her head around just in time to see a massive beam falling toward Lemin and Timothy. Smoke rolled in, blocking her view of the two men. Suddenly Timothy came flying out of the smoke and rolled to a stop at Senndra's feet. He sprang to his feet as soon as he came to a stop and turned back toward where Lemin still was. The smoke hid any view of what was happening, and then Lemin broke through the screen. He hurried to where the others were and began to feel along the wall.

"What are you looking for?" Timothy shouted.

"A fireplace," Lemin shouted back. "We should be able to climb up it and onto the roof of this building. The walls and roof are made of stone, so we will be safe from fire up there."

Timothy wasted no time in searching for the fireplace as well. Lemin crossed from where he was searching and headed for the wall on the other side of Senndra. On the way past, he tossed a rope to Senndra.

"Take this and tie it under Vladimir's armpits," he explained slowly. "That way I will be able to pull him up the chimney."

Lemin hurried off, and Senndra struggled against her lightheadedness as she tried to tie a decent knot under Vladimir's armpits. Her eyelids became extremely heavy, trying to lure her to sleep, but she struggled to keep them open. She knew that closing her eyes could mean death, but she was unable to help herself. She had managed to tie the rope under Vladimir's arms, but by that time, she couldn't manage to keep her eyes open any longer, and she slipped into unconsciousness.

# Four

Senndra felt a drop of cold water hit her face and roll off. She coughed and sat up, fighting lightheadedness as she did so. She could feel the patter of raindrops on her cheeks and arms, and the chill jolted her to complete consciousness. Slowly the things around her came into view, and she immediately spotted Timothy and Lemin a few feet away from her. Both were on their knees in the posture that many assumed when they prayed to Elohim. Senndra struggled to her feet and saw that they were on the roof of the building they had just escaped. Vladimir was at her feet, apparently much worse off than she was.

Senndra looked out over the city and saw that, despite the stone walls, the fire had spread to several other buildings. However, as she watched, the sprinkling of rain increased to a light shower, then to a hard shower, and finally became a downpour. The rain poured out of the sky, preventing the spread of the fire and putting out many of the lesser blazes. The larger fires continued to burn despite the rain, though they did so less ferociously than before.

To the south, the dwarves had penetrated the first two barriers and were working on the third. They were pressing the defenders hard, and it was obvious that they were meeting very little resistance. Suddenly a section of the army broke through the barrier and began to attack the defenders, who succeeded in repelling them. Another section of the barrier was breached, and this time the dwarves were able to gain a secure foothold. Quickly the dwarves rushed through the breach and pushed the defenders back to the fourth barrier.

Senndra looked away from the fighting and back toward her comrades. Lemin and Timothy had finished praying, and Timothy was now checking Vladimir for vital signs. He shook the unconscious boy, and after a few moments Vladimir's eyes fluttered open.

"Where am I?" he asked as his eyes searched the area around him.

"On top of the building that we were trapped in only a few minutes ago," Timothy answered. "We were able to escape up a chimney and onto the roof. Luckily it's made of stone so it can't be burned."

"Fire," Vladimir mumbled. "Yes, now I remember. The house was on fire, right? And we were finding a way out, and…" he stopped talking.

"And what happened next?" Timothy prompted.

"I don't know," Vladimir shrugged. "The last thing I remember is starting to look for a way out of the building. After that my mind is blank."

"Well, to make a long story short, we got out okay," Timothy said as he helped Vladimir to his feet. "Now we need to meet up with Josiah and the other cadets. Then, if we can get back around to the correct side of the dwarves, we can help hold the city."

"It's never going to happen, you know," Vladimir said as he looked out toward the fighting. "The dwarves will push our men all the way to the south wall. After that, they will be able to kill our army with ease, and they will have access to Magessa."

"We won't let that happen then, will we, buddy?" Timothy said.

"And if we don't have a choice?" Vladimir countered.

"You always have a choice," Timothy said forcefully. "*Always.* Right now we have the choice to give up the city for lost and give the enemy access to our country or to defend both the city and our country. Yes we might die in the endeavor, heck we might not even succeed, but that does not remove the choice."

Vladimir shrugged. "Well in that case, we might as well attack them right now."

"Hold on, Vladimir," Lemin said, coming into the conversation. "I want to attack just as much as you, but I also want to come out of this alive. What do you have in mind?"

"We pull a left flank attack," Vladimir said. "The left flank is the weakest part of the army, and if we can hit them there, it will throw their army into confusion, at least temporarily. That will give us a chance to get across the next barrier."

"Well," Timothy said shrugging, "it's as good as any other plan, I guess." He looked at Lemin. "We might as well try it."

"What about our other options?" Lemin asked.

"What other options?" Timothy countered. "I've already gone over hundreds of ideas in my head, and none of them will work."

Lemin scratched his head and looked at the sky. He rose to his feet and paced back and forth for several minutes before deciding that they would follow the plan.

******

Josiah and his men crouched in the building, careful to give no indication to their enemies as to their location. The clouds overhead made the room almost pitch black, and the recent rain made wearing armor extremely uncomfortable. Sweat trickled down the faces of the soldiers as they waited in complete silence, hoping they would remain undetected.

A lookout crawled back toward Josiah, carefully avoiding the windows. He had stripped off his armor in order to move quickly and without noise.

"Commander, the dwarves have left the immediate area and have pushed the defenders back to the fourth barrier," the lookout said once he had reached Josiah. "There are a few straggling dwarves, but I don't think they should present a problem."

"Troops, the danger has passed. You can get off the ground now," Josiah said. The cadets rose from their bellies and heaved sighs of relief as they were able to stretch their aching muscles. They slid their drawn weapons into their sheaths and began to talk in low voices.

"Well, what kind of a position are we in now?" Josiah asked the lookout at his side.

"I don't really know, sir," the lookout responded. "I couldn't see the south end of the city very well from where I was."

"Then go round up the lookouts that can see that portion of the city," Josiah ordered. "Take a station where they were so that you can see the largest area possible."

The lookout saluted and moved away, and Josiah sat down to think. There was a possibility, now that the dwarves had moved to the fourth barrier, that he would be able to lead his troops back to the fighting. A tunnel ran from the museum, which sat between the second and third barriers, to a building near the training grounds. If he could get his men safely through the tunnel before the dwarves progressed too far through the city, they would be on the right side of the approaching enemy and could again draw swords against them. That would be much better than lying in a building, sweating and doing nothing.

Josiah was pulled from his pondering by the approach of three cadets who had been on lookout duty. They saluted him, and he saluted back.

"What's our position in the city?" he asked them. "How far have the dwarves pushed our army back?"

"Well," the middle cadet responded. He knelt down on the floor, and Josiah and the other two lookouts crouched down in a circle around a map that he was scratching in the floor. "If we're here," he made an X, "and the northern wall is here," he scraped a line, "then the dwarf army is fairly close to the middle of the campus." He dragged a long, weaving line that represented the stream through the middle of the campus.

"What about the museum? Can we get there?" Josiah asked anxiously.

"Well, I suppose we could get that far," the scout responded slowly, "but the whole building is crawling with dwarves. They're working on tearing the blockades off the doors now, but they should gain entrance in a short time."

"Then we have no time to lose," Josiah said and rose to his feet. "Stanslaw, gather all of the men together and get them ready to move out. Keep the lookouts at their posts and tell them to give the alarm if anyone comes close."

Josiah pushed his way through the crowd of cadets and made his way to the stairs. The room at the bottom was so dark that he could see nothing down below. He shrugged and looked over his shoulder. Stanslaw had the cadets in neat, orderly ranks and had switched out the tired lookouts.

"Draw swords," Josiah said in an undertone. The room was filled with the sound of sixty swords being drawn all at once, and Josiah immediately wondered if his order had been a good idea. He shrugged and headed down the stairs; there was nothing he could do about it now.

The first floor of the building was almost pitch black, with light entering only through the cracks of boards that had been nailed across the windows. The cadets were walking as quietly as possible, but the sound of sixty cadets in armor was hard to hide. Josiah gave up worrying and told himself that the enemy would see them soon anyhow. He felt his way through another dark room until he found the doorway that led out. From the far side of the next room, he could see light filtering through the bottom of a door and headed for it.

"Stanslaw," Josiah called, and his captain was at his side in an instant. "That door is going to be nailed shut, so I will have some cadets open it. Now listen closely. When we get out of here, I will take the first half of the cadets and you take the other half. Make your way to the museum and fall on the right flank of the dwarves there. I will do the same thing, but to their left flank. Once we have gained access to the museum, take your men inside and I will regroup with you in the room that contains the armor of Jothnial. There is a tunnel there hidden under a large rug near the back of the room. The tunnel runs from the museum to a building that should be behind the barrier that the dwarves are attacking now. If I don't regroup with you in five minutes, take your men through."

"Yes sir," Stanslaw responded. He moved away and began to pass the orders down the line. The first four cadets in Josiah's ranks moved forward to the door. They were burly men and immediately threw themselves into opening the door. The door was nailed from the outside, so the cadets used their swords and whatever else they could find to pry it open. Finally, after several minutes of work, the door gave an inch, and light streamed in through the newly opened crack. The cadets didn't slack their assault on the door, and less than a minute later had succeeded in opening it.

Josiah dashed past the cadets that had opened the door and burst outside. His brain seemed to register everything at once. Ahead of him he could see a group of perhaps one hundred dwarves assaulting the museum. In front of them was the bulk of the dwarf army still attacking the fourth barrier. Josiah could hear his soldiers following behind him, and off to his right, he could see Stanslaw leading his men at a rapid pace toward the right flank of the dwarves at the museum. Josiah raised his sword and sprinted the last few feet to the unsuspecting dwarves. He swung twice and dispatched two of the enemy. He swung again and continued to press his way to the museum, but his soldiers were faster. Seeing their commander facing the dwarves so bravely, they were filled with a surge of heroism and smashed into the dwarves, crushing all in their path. Suddenly the charge was over; access to the museum had been gained. Now they needed to defend it from the rest of the dwarf horde.

******

"There they go," Vladimir said. He was looking out over the city from his perch on the balcony. "Looks like Josiah is trying to gain the museum, but to what purpose? He'll be easily surrounded and killed there."

"*Why* he's there is not the point," Lemin answered. "The point is that we need to meet up with him and his soldiers." He jumped over the balcony railing, spun around, and grabbed onto it as he fell. He let go and landed on the ground some twelve feet below. Vladimir followed suit, leaving Timothy and Senndra on the balcony.

"Can you make that jump?" Timothy asked. Senndra could sense some concern in his voice and would normally have enjoyed it, but now that she was tired and cranky, she merely resented it. Without a word, she followed Lemin and Vladimir over the railing and landed on the ground beside them. Timothy watched as she took her bow from where it was slung on her back. He shrugged and jumped to the ground.

"What now?" Senndra asked. "Josiah's men have killed about half of the dwarves, but that still leaves fifty. How are we supposed to get through that many enemies?" She had been watching the dwarves while trying to nock an arrow on her bowstring. Now she looked down and saw, to her dismay, that her bow was ruined, probably in the fire. Lemin did not notice but answered Senndra's question instead.

"I'm counting on the fact that the dwarves will be unnerved by their recent massacre," Lemin explained. "If that is the case, we will have a decent chance at penetrating their ranks."

He took off running, drawing his sword. Senndra slid her arrow back into her quiver and flung her bow away in disgust. She took off after Lemin at a dead sprint, reaching over her shoulder as she ran to draw her sword. She gripped the handle with both hands and let out a battle cry. The dwarves were startled by the sound and swung around to find its source. By the time they recognized the diminutive size of the attacking force, Lemin had already led his small group into the museum. The building, however, was devoid of friendly faces.

Lemin ran toward a door, flung it open, and dashed inside. The other three soldiers followed, taking cover just as a barrage of dwarf crossbow bolts whistled past the door and dug into its frame. Lemin led the way into the interior of the museum, always following the noise made by Josiah's soldiers. He finally burst into the room that contained the armor of Jothnial. It was a dead end. Lemin prayed for safety as he motioned for the others to hide. With a wall in front of them and a horde of angry dwarves behind, they would need it.

In the next room, the dwarves were searching for their prey. They were slowly making their way toward where Lemin and the others were hiding. As the dwarves got closer, they sensed that their query was near and began to run. Senndra, following Lemin's lead, readied herself for an attack. Suddenly Lemin's favorite phrase jumped into her head: *"Always attack first."* Just as the foremost dwarf was about to enter the armor room, she jumped from her hiding place and slammed her weapon up to the hilt in the dwarf's chest. She tried to yank it free, but as she braced herself, a hand grabbed the back of her shirt and flung her backwards just as the ceiling of the adjoining room collapsed on the dwarf and her sword.

"What the heck was that?" Lemin said from the ground where he dove just as the ceiling collapsed

"I don't know," Vladimir said with a sideways glance at Timothy, "but whatever it was, it weakened the supports for this ceiling. If we don't get out of here fast, we're going to be in trouble."

"Over here," Timothy called from the back of the room. He was using the blade of his knife to pry at the floor, and before long, a trapdoor opened. Without a second thought, Lemin and Senndra hurried to the trapdoor.

Vladimir followed Timothy through the hole, and Senndra was about to when Lemin stopped her. "You'll need weapons, Senndra," he yelled. Senndra turned to see that he was holding the sword and bow from Jothnial's armor. She gratefully took the weapons from his hand to replace her lost ones. She turned back to the trapdoor but felt Lemin's hand on her shoulder.

"You'll want this as well," he said, handing her a pendant. The cross of Elohim hung from a thin golden chain. At its center was a stylized figure of a dragon. The pendant was made entirely of silver except for the dragon's single visible eye which was a small ruby chip.

Senndra draped the chain around her neck and tucked the dragon figure into her shirt. She quickly slid through the trapdoor, her boots landing on a hard-packed dirt path. Although it was dark, she quickly moved further into the tunnel. She heard Lemin land behind her, and the trapdoor above him thudded into place just in time.

The sound was absorbed by the dirt walls of the tunnel, so the only way Senndra knew that the building above had collapsed was by the way it shook the ground. Dirt rained from the walls and ceiling of the tunnel, and for a second, Senndra thought it would cave in and kill them. By some miracle, it did not.

"Let's move," Lemin ordered. "I don't know how long this tunnel is going to hold up, but I don't want to be in it when it decides to fall down."

The cadets followed their instructor down the tunnel. There was no light, so they had to each keep their hand on the person in front of them. They traveled for no more than a minute before their progress stopped.

"This tunnel is a dead end," Lemin said after a few seconds. "It feels like it caved in when the building collapsed. There doesn't appear to be any way through... no, wait. There is some sort of stone pipe here that might run through the collapsed section of tunnel. At least, I can feel a breeze coming through it. It's going to be a little tight, but I think we can manage."

By this time, Senndra's eyes had adjusted to the gloom of the tunnel and she saw a bit of light from where Lemin felt the breeze. Either that or she was just imagining it. In either case, she watched as Lemin disappeared into the hole in the wall. His head vanished first, but was quickly followed by his waist and his feet. As he disappeared completely into the hole, some dirt slid to the floor. The integrity of the tunnel didn't seem to have been damaged, so Vladimir entered next. He quickly slid through the hole, and all too soon it was Senndra's turn. She was terrified by the prospect of crawling into a small hole that ended in an unknown place. She had always been a bit claustrophobic, but had learned to control it. Now that fear came flooding back with such force that she physically shuddered at the thought of entering the hole.

"Hurry up, Senndra," Timothy urged. "We can't stay here; we have to keep moving." He looked at her, saw that she was shivering, and realized what was plaguing her. "It's going to be fine," he told her, taking one of her hands. "Lemin and Vladimir went in front of you, and I'll be directly behind you. Besides that, Elohim is looking out for us. Nothing is going to happen to you."

"You really think that Elohim has time to look out for me?" Senndra asked. "There's a battle going on up there. No doubt there are plenty of other people more important than me that He's looking out for. He probably doesn't have time for me."

"You know that isn't true," Timothy said. "Elohim is interested in the well-being of all His people no matter where they are or what they are doing."

Senndra nodded and turned toward the hole. She took a deep breath and plunged in. She pulled herself through the stone pipe by the tips of her fingers for several minutes. Many times she felt herself begin to panic, but the thought of Elohim looking out for her comforted her and enabled her to keep the emotion under control. Suddenly the tunnel ended and she fell through another wall of dirt and hit the floor. Instantly Lemin and Vladimir were at her side, helping her to stand.

"How far behind you is Timothy?" Lemin asked.

"He said he was going to be directly behind me," Senndra answered.

A body fell through the hole in the wall and landed with a crash. Lemin and Senndra hurried to lift him to his feet. A spark flashed behind them, and they spun around, their weapons already out of their sheaths.

"Whoa! It's just some flint and steel," Vladimir's voice said from the darkness. "I never go anywhere without it. We should be able to use this to light something. It will burn out fairly quickly, but if we move fast, we can cover a lot of distance in that time."

"Well, let's get moving then," Lemin said and shoved his sword back into its sheath. "Vladimir, you'll be in front with your torch. I'll come directly after, followed by Senndra and then Timothy."

"With your permission, sir," Timothy spoke up, "I'll collapse the tunnel so that no one can come up behind us."

"Can you do that?" Lemin asked.

"Yes sir, I believe I can," Timothy answered.

"Then do so and catch up with us when you're finished," Lemin ordered. Then, to Vladimir, he said, "Okay, let's move out."

There was the sound of flint striking steel, but this time the light didn't fade. A cloak that Vladimir had wrapped around a splintered plank from the surrounding rubble was now burning. The tunnel was bathed with light, and Vladimir immediately took off running. Lemin was close behind him, and Senndra sprinted in order to keep up with them. Behind them she could feel more than hear the sound of the tunnel caving in, and she forced herself to run faster. Finally the light died and flickered out. But even as it did, she could tell that Lemin and Vladimir were still running. She heard them say something about light up ahead and then there was the sound of them drawing their weapons. She reached for the sword on her back and did the same. Enough light filtered through the end of the tunnel so that she was able to see where the stairs began. Panting slightly, she took them two at a time and burst into the open. Behind her she could hear the noise of running and turned around to see Timothy appear out of the tunnel.

"What's going on?" he gasped when he reached her. He turned and glanced over the field of battle. The dwarves had just broken through the barrier that was directly to the north of the stream that ran through the middle of the city, and the defenders were fleeing across the stream on planks laid across its width. Senndra had heard from Lemin that pitch had been poured into the stream, and she expected someone to light it, but nothing happened.

"Something's wrong," she told Timothy in a worried tone. "Nobody has lit the stream."

"What do you mean?" Timothy asked. He looked up and surveyed the battle field in front of him.

"Before the attack, our people poured pitch into the stream," Senndra explained. "They planned on lighting it when the dwarves crossed. But now that they're crossing, nothing's happening."

"There's always the possibility that they're waiting for a few more dwarves to enter the stream," Timothy said. "But judging by how many have already crossed, I would say that is not the case. Follow me."

Timothy took off at a fast run to where Lemin stood behind the sixth barrier, preparing for an attack from the dwarves. The defenders had expected someone to light the pitch and had not retreated to the next barrier immediately. Now they realized that there was a problem and were running as quickly as possible to the relative safety of the sixth barrier.

Timothy reached Lemin and slid to a sitting position with his back to the barrier. Senndra was close behind him and was seated beside him only seconds later. Lemin dropped to one knee, and while keeping his bow ready and one eye on the approaching enemy, he turned his attention to Timothy.

"Commander," Timothy yelled above the ruckus, "wasn't the pitch in the stream supposed to be lighted when the dwarves started to cross?"

"Something's wrong!" Lemin shouted back. "The archer that was supposed to do it was stationed in that tower over there."

Lemin pointed to a rickety wooden platform a couple hundred yards east. The platform was almost on the bank of the stream and had an ideal vantage point. But it had very few defensive structures incorporated into it. Even from where she stood, Senndra could see that there were several dead soldiers in it.

"The dwarves are butchering our men out there," Timothy shouted.

"And what can we do about that?" Lemin asked as he loosed an arrow into the enemy.

"I have an idea," Timothy said. "Do you have any oil?"

"No," Lemin responded and loosed another arrow, "but I see a torch to the west; and wherever there is a torch, there is fuel."

Timothy rose to his feet and sprinted down the wall, avoiding the soldiers that were pouring over it and taking defensive positions. Senndra followed behind him, sprinting as fast as possible, but she was left behind. As she ran, she could see Timothy searching for a torch that was not lit. She dropped to a safe position when she reached him, and he carried a torch to where she sat. With a quick motion, he reached under his shirt and tore off the sleeve. He rubbed the piece of cloth vigorously against the end of the torch until it was coated in pitch and then wrapped it around the tip of an arrow, which he handed to Senndra.

"You're a much better marksman than me," he said. "It's at least a hundred yards to the stream, and I can't arc an arrow to hit the water, but I know you can."

Senndra took the arrow and weighed it carefully in her hand. She wanted to argue that she couldn't make the shot either, but she knew that would be a lie. She laid the arrow on the ground and reached back for her bow. Instead she touched the bow of her father, Jothnial. She strung it quickly and laid the arrow on the string. Legend said that the bow had magical powers that would enable the user to hit any mark at any distance. Senndra hoped it was true. She would need all the help she could get. She peeked over the barrier and gauged the distance to the stream. Already, the expanse between it and the barrier was swarming with dwarves, making estimation difficult. She figured that it couldn't be more than two hundred yards or less than one hundred. She looked down and inhaled deeply, trying to let the tension out of her body.

*"God,"* she prayed silently as she crouched. *"I know that I can make this shot, but it's going to be difficult with only an estimated distance and with people shooting at me. Please be with me as I fire. Guide my arrow and help it fly true to its target."*

Senndra opened her eyes and saw that Timothy was taking his hands away from the arrow, which was now blazing. He had two rocks in his hands that Senndra guessed were flint and steel. She stayed crouched for one more moment then rose to her full height and drew the arrow back. She pointed the arrow up to what she guessed was the right elevation and let it fly. She dropped down to a crouch and watched with anxiety as the arrow arched over the enemy army. It reached its apex and began to drop back toward the earth, sparks flaking off of it and floating in its wake. Senndra held her breath as it approached its target. It hit the mass of dwarf soldiers and disappeared into their midst. For several seconds nothing happened, but Senndra kept her eyes on the stream. Suddenly it exploded with a burst of fire that spread quickly down the entire length of the city. Dwarves screamed in pain as they were consumed by the flames, and others scrambled to get away from the inferno.

A shout sounded at the barrier and the defenders poured from behind it at their enemies. The dwarves panicked as they found themselves trapped between fire on one side and charging soldiers on the other. Some tried to escape through the fire and were burned, while others were slaughtered by the advancing soldiers. Soon, the south side of the stream was clear of dwarves.

Senndra and Timothy ran to where they saw Lemin and Vladimir returning from the carnage.

"How was that, commander?" Timothy asked. "Don't you think that was an admirable shot?"

"It could have been better," Lemin grumbled. It was obvious that he thought Timothy was complimenting himself.

"Well, you can think what you want," Timothy said, "but I think Senndra made an excellent shot. In fact, I would even say that it was a brilliant shot."

Vladimir saved Lemin from embarrassment by speaking. "The shot wasn't bad," he said, "Let's just say that it did its job, and that's good enough for me. At least for the time being we have a wall of fire between us and them, and we're safe."

"That's true," Lemin said, "but in only a couple minutes, that fire will die down, and we will have to face the full fury of the dwarf army. You had better rest as much as you can while I go speak to the other commanders here."

Lemin strode off in the direction of a gathering of soldiers, leaving his three cadets at the barrier. Senndra looked over at her two comrades and saw that Timothy had already fallen asleep with his head resting against a barrel. Vladimir was making himself comfortable, and he was soon motionless as well. Senndra sighed and propped herself up so that she could see over the barrier. She knew that someone needed to stay awake to warn the others when the dwarves renewed their attack. Soon the monotony of the task overtook Senndra, and her mind began to wander. She thought of Feddir, who she had left at the academy of Belvárd. When she had last seen him, he was not much bigger than a large cat. But she knew that when she saw him again, he would probably have at least doubled in size. She tried to remember all that she could about him—the color of his skin, his exact dimensions, even how many teeth he had. She gradually found herself longing to have the little creature with her, and she began to despair over the possibility of never seeing him again.

Yet even as she despaired, she thanked Elohim for the opportunity that she had had to know Feddir at all. She also prayed for protection for herself and for all of the defenders of the city.

******

A shout jolted Senndra from her sleep, and she jerked her head up. One glance told her that the dwarves were preparing themselves for another attack, so she jumped to her feet. She glanced at Timothy and Vladimir and saw that they were yawning and rubbing their eyes. Turning back to the battle, she nocked an arrow and drew it back to her ear. From the remaining flames of the stream, a single dwarf carrying a white flag approached the defenders. Senndra held her fire at the sight of the white flag and slowly released the tension on the bowstring. The dwarf walked to within shouting distance of the defenders and began to speak.

"Citizens of Magessa, the enemy of the dark lord Molkekk, lend me your ears. You are being pressed from the front by more than one hundred thousand soldiers. We are certain that no reinforcements will come and we know that you are lacking in numbers. But the dark lord has ordered us to offer you terms of peace. If you will but lay down your weapons and surrender yourselves to our army, we will spare all of you. You will be made subjects of lord Molkekk, but you will be treated well. You will find yourselves just as well off as you were before. We do not want to needlessly slaughter you here. What say you to these terms of peace?"

No one answered for a few seconds. They had not expected an offer of peace from Molkekk, and it stunned them into silence. Finally someone spoke up.

"You lie!" he shouted at the dwarf. "You said that you do not want to needlessly slaughter us here, but I know that you would much rather do that than spare us. Now leave before you are shot where you stand."

"It is true that we used to be a violent people that would rather kill than take prisoners," the dwarf answered, "but the lord Molkekk has changed us. Now we would rather offer you mercy at the order of our lord."

"And what about Elohim?" the same defender shouted. "Why have you forsaken him for an inferior lord? We all know that Elohim could squish Molkekk between his thumb and forefinger if he wanted."

"Then why hasn't he?" the dwarf asked. "It is because Elohim is nonexistent. He is a myth that was invented to frighten small children into doing what they were told and to give the people of Magessa hope. Give me one example of when he has shown that he lives. You cannot, for there is none.

"The lord Molkekk, on the other hand, is quite alive. He has been seen by thousands of people and has even fought against you in times past. He has a lineage traceable back to the earliest times, and he will last for eternity. He is the true ruler of Magessa, and none will stand in his way. You can either move aside and surrender, or be crushed into oblivion."

"He is shaking the confidence of our people," Timothy noted to Senndra. "Shoot him before he does any more damage."

Without waiting for another command, Senndra drew back her arrow and let it fly at the dwarf. It approached him from the side, and he never even saw it before it slammed into his head, penetrating his brain. He slumped sideways, his white flag crumpled beneath him.

"Well, get ready for all hell to break loose," Vladimir said. "You can bet that after that we won't get another offer of peace."

Within minutes, Vladimir's prediction came true. The dwarves formed themselves into a solid wall and rushed at the defenders. Three volleys of arrows hit the dwarves before they reached the ranks of Magessa. But for every dwarf that fell, another stepped up to take his place. The attack fell back slightly under the rain of arrows, but eventually the defenders grew tired and the arrows faltered. Again the dwarves attacked, but this time they were being covered by their own crossbow men. The soldiers that tried to fire at the attackers were cut down by the deadly hail of enemy arrows.

"There's no chance that we can hold them here," Vladimir yelled over the ruckus of battle. "There's too many of them even if we were able to shoot at them."

"Well, we're not leaving until we get the order," Timothy shouted back. "We're not abandoning our post."

"We'll get cut down once the enemy reaches us," Vladimir commented. He peeked over the barricade to check the dwarves' advancement.

"The enemy cross bows will cut us down if we try to run," Timothy countered. "At least we'll be safe from arrows once we get among the dwarves."

"That's a small comfort," Senndra muttered as she slid her sword from the scabbard on her back. She ran her finger down the blade, feeling every imperfection. Just touching the blade instilled courage in her. Her father had wielded this very sword in battle many times and never once shrank from his duty. Not even when it cost him his life in a battle with Molkekk did he run, and Senndra promised herself that she would wield the sword with equal valor. The enemies of Elohim would learn to fear it again.

"Get ready," Timothy said. He peeked over the top of the barricade. "They're almost here," he said and sat down again.

"How close?" Vladimir asked. A dwarf vaulted over the barricade and Timothy leaped to his feet and took off his head with a single swipe.

"They're pretty blasted close," he said and turned to hold back the flood of dwarves flowing over the barricade. Vladimir and Senndra sprang to their feet and pressed their backs against Timothy's, forming a triangle. The three companions battled the vicious dwarves with all of their energy, swinging and parrying until their arms ached. Still they knew that if they let down their guard, not only would they die, but it would mean the death of their friends as well.

The dwarves didn't know how to handle the presence of three seemingly unbeatable enemies. They threw themselves at the three warriors time and time again, but nothing could break past their flashing swords. After what seemed like an eternity, the dwarves fell back and allowed a circle of empty ground around the defenders. Senndra dropped her sword point to the ground, but kept her eyes on the enemy. She could sense that something was about to happen, and she didn't think it was going to be good. To the north, the dwarves' crossbow men were moving toward where the defenders were entrenched behind the seventh barrier. A dozen of them stopped when they reached the empty ground, loaded their bows, and prepared to fire.

Timothy swore and covered his face with his hand. Vladimir was focused intently on something in front of him, and Senndra was the only one to act. She stabbed her sword into the ground and grabbed her bow from where she had slung it on her back. A skill that was largely considered useless, but that she had learned at the academy came to mind. She turned the bow horizontal, grabbed two arrows from her quiver, and with skill that could only be acquired from hours of practice, placed them both on the string. She pulled back the string and, without waiting to aim, let the arrows fly. One of them missed the archers entirely, but the other buried itself in the arm of one of them. A split second later, Senndra had three arrows on the string and let them fly again. This time one of them hit a dwarf full in the face, dropping him instantly. The remaining two glanced off the armor of other archers. Senndra reached back for more arrows, but her quiver was exhausted. With an air of dejection, she turned toward the archers and watched as the remaining ones lifted their crossbows and took aim.

"Fire!"

The command came from behind Senndra, and she glanced back in time to see several dozen arrows streak past her and her friends. The deadly barrage knifed through the dwarf archers, dropping them like flies. Senndra grabbed her sword, and she and her friends turned and fled back toward the safety of the barricade; however, they found their way blocked by a group of dwarves that had turned to face them. Timothy and Vladimir looked at each other, shrugged, and each jerked a knife from his belt and threw it at the dwarves. Both projectiles hit their targets, opening a hole in the dwarf line. Within seconds, Timothy, Vladimir, and Senndra had taken advantage of it. With drawn swords, they hacked their way through the dwarf army to where the defenders were trying desperately to hold the barricade. Their task was made easier by the fact that most of the dwarves were facing the defenders and were unable to protect themselves. In less than a minute, the companions had gained the relative safety of the barricade and immediately turned around and helped to hold the dwarves back. Time seemed to disappear as they swung, parried, and killed. Senndra slowly felt herself relax, and her learned reflexes took over. She tried to imagine that she was not battling for her life, but that she was fighting her friends in friendly combat. As she did, her movements became more fluid and she was able to gain the upper hand. Previously, she had been trying simply to survive; now she was able to hold her own against the dwarves much more easily. A dwarf approached Timothy from the back and raised his ax to strike, but he never had a chance. Senndra disemboweled him with a swift stroke then brought the blade around and plunged it into a dwarf that was threatening her.

Slowly the attack began to lessen, and finally the dwarves pulled back from the barricade. The defenders knew that to follow would be suicide, so they stayed where it was safe. As the archers peppered the dwarves until they were out of range, Senndra searched for arrows and found the quiver of a deceased dwarf. She took it from the body, brought it back to the wall, and laid an arrow on the string. By this time, the defending archers had turned their attention to the advancing line of crossbow dwarves. Commanders rushed up and down the barricade, forming the archers into groups. As one would fire, another was reloading so as to keep up a constant barrage of arrows. The crossbow dwarves marched steadily toward the defenders until they were within range of the bowmen. Every crossbowman had an arrow on his string, but still the command to fire was withheld; and still the dwarves drew nearer. Senndra bit her lip and tried to hold her emotions in check, but the calmness she had recently experienced when fighting hand-to-hand was now replaced by tension and impatience. The dwarves were finally able to fire on the defenders and raised their crossbows and took aim.

"Duck!" Vladimir hissed and dropped behind the barricade. Timothy and Senndra followed suit and saw that, along the length of the barrier, the other defenders were doing the same. The sound of bow strings snapping was heard, and a barrage of deadly sharp arrows flew at the barricade. Most of them passed harmlessly over the top or buried themselves in the barrier, but out of the corner of her eye, Senndra saw one smash through the wall and impale Timothy's right shoulder. Timothy was flung to the ground, where he writhed in pain and grabbed at his shoulder. His actions induced more pain, and he desisted. Vladimir crawled over to him and began to examine the arrow.

From down the barricade, the call to fire was given, and Senndra jumped to her feet and took aim. The dwarf archers had fired their loaded bolts and were now desperately trying to reload in time to fire on the defending archers. Arrows rained down on the dwarves, and they began to drop; however, the impact was minimal. For every dwarf that fell, at least ten were unharmed and hurried to reload their crossbows. Before Senndra could get another arrow on her bow string, the dwarves fired. She ducked, barely escaping death. She glanced over at her friends and saw that Vladimir had succeeded in getting the arrow out of Timothy's shoulder, and they were in the process of bandaging it. Senndra peeked over the wall and saw that the dwarf infantry was again charging toward the defenders. She and several hundred other archers rose to their feet and sent a swarm of arrows at the enemy. The dwarves' progress halted as if they had hit a wall, and in seconds they were scrambling back out of range of the enemy archers. Again the dwarf archers fired and again Senndra ducked behind the barricade just in time. By this time, Timothy's shoulder was bandaged, and he had his sword gripped in his left hand. Vladimir turned back to Senndra and mouthed something to her that she could not determine, so she shrugged and turned to look over the barricade. This time, unlike the previously unorganized attempts, the dwarves were advancing in an orderly fashion, with the infantry in front and crossbow men behind them. The defending archers rose from behind the barricade and fired again. This time, however, most of their arrows hit the infantry and didn't even penetrate to the archers. In response, the dwarf archers rained a hail of crossbow bolts on the defenders, wreaking havoc among their ranks. Senndra dropped behind the wall and crawled to where Timothy and Vladimir sat with their backs against the barricade.

"They're advancing again," she said. "They're taking it nice and slow, but even so, I would say they'll be here in less than a minute." She turned to Timothy. "Perhaps you should get back behind the next barricade before they reach us."

"And perhaps you should consider what you just said," Timothy retorted. "The enemy has archers, so anyone that leaves cover will be shot down in no time. Besides," he added with a grin, "I placed first in the sword-play contest at the academy. I think I can kill a few of these brutes—even if it is left-handed."

"As you wish," Senndra said. She pulled the sword on her back from its sheath and laid it across her knees. Her fingers traced the blade from hilt to tip and back. Unlike many swords of its era, it had no runes or sketches on it, but was composed entirely of unmarked silver. Even in the brief time that she had used it, she had succeeded in giving it several notches and hundreds of scratches. Again she remembered how her father had wielded the very same sword without shrinking from his duty, even in the face of death, and her resolve was strengthened. Under no circumstance would she fail him. She would stand and fight to the death.

She gripped the hilt of the sword with both hands and held it so that the point extended in front of her.

"Get ready," Vladimir called over his shoulder. "They're coming. And when they get here, it is not going to be pretty."

"Of course not," Timothy said grimly. "Everyone knows that dwarves are ugly."

Senndra snorted at the attempt at humor and then allowed herself to relax. Even as she curled her feet underneath her body, she released the tension in her muscles and allowed her nerves to relax. At a shout from Vladimir, she jumped to her feet and spun around, her sword ready to kill. The first dwarf seemed surprised at her sudden appearance, and she dispatched him before he could even attempt to defend himself. The next dwarf had time to think before he reached her and attacked with his ax swinging. Senndra found the feeble attempt funny and laughed as she hopped lightly over the blow and stabbed her sword into the enemy. The dwarves attacked on every side, trying to breach the barrier. But all along the wall, the defenders were determined to hold back the attack. For almost a quarter of an hour, the fighting continued without either side gaining the advantage. In an instant, however, the dwarves found the hole they needed. Several hundred yards from Senndra, a defender fell at the hands of a dwarf, and there was no one to take his place. Instantly, the dwarves pushed through the opening and swarmed along the barricade, killing the unsuspecting defenders.

"Heads up!" Senndra yelled to her companions. Her cry saved dozens of cadets to her left and right as they looked up and saw the dwarves had breached the defending line. The defenders began to gather into circles, with soldiers facing out from all sides. As the dwarves surged forward, they were hindered by these knots of resistance. With one last swipe that took a dwarf's head off, Senndra jumped off the wall and hurried to take her place in a circle.

"Fall back!" The order was issued from the south, behind the next barricade.

"You heard the man," Senndra yelled at those around her. "Let's move that way," and she gestured to the south. "I'll stay to cover your retreat." She absorbed herself in attacking the dwarves, slashing and stabbing at them if they got within her range. Beside her, she could sense two cadets that she knew would be Vladimir and Timothy. Together the three friends did their best to hold back the tide of attackers, but there were too many dwarves. They pushed around the small group, forcing them to change their formation into a circle. But even as they did so, an explosion rocked the city off to the east. It was followed shortly by another to the west, which was much closer than the first. The blasts threw the enemy into disarray. Dwarves scattered everywhere, trying to get away from the detonation areas. Another explosion shook the city, this time less than a hundred yards to the east. Dwarves were thrown in all directions, raining bodies and gear down on those below. Senndra raised her arm to shield herself from the falling debris, but she took a blow to the head from the shaft of an ax. She sank to the ground, and all she could see were stars. She tried to pull herself from her stupor but was unable to do so. She didn't hear Timothy saying that the explosions would cover their retreat, and neither he nor Vladimir noticed that she did not follow them to the next barricade. Instead, she slumped to the ground with her head on her hands. The last thing she remembered was the reality that the warm sticky fluid all over her face was blood. Then she blacked out.

# Five

Lemin saw Timothy and Vladimir coming toward the barricade. He could not tell through the dust thrown up by the recent explosions whether or not Senndra was with them, but he had a bad feeling. An eastern wind blew a cloud of dust across the battlefield, obscuring his view entirely. But when Timothy and Vladimir burst out of the cloud, he instantly realized that Senndra was not there. Timothy and Vladimir covered the last hundred feet to the barricade and leaped over it. They slumped against it and tried to catch their breath from the sprint they had just made. Lemin quickly made his way over to them and knelt down beside them.

"What happened to Senndra?" he asked with urgency in his voice.

"What do you mean?" Vladimir asked with a gasp. "She was right behind us, wasn't she?"

"No she wasn't," Lemin said. "I didn't see any sign of her. But you're saying that as far as you know, she's still out there alive?"

"As far as I know," Timothy said.

"Then I'm going out after her," Lemin said and stood to his feet.

"I'll come with you," Timothy said and rose unsteadily to his feet.

"You're too tired to keep up with me," Lemin said. "Even if you could, you would be more of a liability than a help with that shoulder wound. You stay here and get some rest. That's an order."

Lemin turned and bounded over the barricade and made his way into the smoke. As he ran, he drew his sword and held it out in an aggressive position. He couldn't see anything through the dust in the air, and he hoped that he wasn't going in circles. He staggered through the cloud for several minutes, trying to find his way out, and when he did, it was so sudden that he was not prepared for it. One second he was in the cloud and the next he was through it and in the open air. He threw a quick glance in both directions looking for Senndra, but so many bodies dotted the ground that he doubted he would be able to spot her from a distance. Without a moment's hesitation, he started running, keeping an eye on the bodies on the ground, but also keeping watch for any hostile troops. Ahead he could see a group of dwarves surrounding a body, and he quickened his stride. The dwarves would not waste time on a dead body, which meant the one that held their attention was clearly alive. Lemin had a feeling it was the person he was seeking. His pace increased to a sprint, and he covered the last dozen yards in less than a second. With a thunderous roar, he leaped through the air and landed in the middle of the dwarves. His sword swung hard, decapitating two dwarves and forcing the others to back up. With a quick glance, he saw that he was greatly outnumbered, facing as many as twenty enemies. A sideways look confirmed that this was Senndra; the dragon pendant that he had given to her earlier had come loose and was lying on her chest.

Lemin suddenly felt as though he was being drawn out of himself and that he was watching from a distance. He felt a presence that he had not felt for years begin to seep into his consciousness. He did not push it away as he normally did, but allowed it to remain and grow. For how long this continued, he could never remember, but as it spread, images of his past began to flash through his mind. He saw himself as a young man at the temple of Elohim beginning his training as a magician. He was struggling to raise a small stone, but in a moment years had passed and he was effortlessly making the stones disappear and reappear. Next, he was commissioned into a secret organization that was composed entirely of magicians. Then the ogres attacked, and he tried to cover his face, but nothing could blot out the sight that had caused him to turn his back on Elohim. He and the group of magicians under his command were surprised by hostile ogres in a narrow canyon. He was running down the rocky canyon, trying to escape the death that was behind him. He tripped and rolled down a small hill, then jumped back to his feet and was running again. He was safe now and made his way back to the site of the ambush. There was no sign of the ogres; the only bodies in sight were those of his companions. There was no sign of life in any of the bodies; all of them were dead, with gaping wounds. Pictures of his dead companions flashed past his eyes in succession, each more hideous than the last.

Such was the sight that had caused Lemin to turn from Elohim. He did not understand how He could let such atrocities happen if He was indeed an all-powerful God. Why would he let so many magicians, all in His service, be ambushed and killed? Lemin had had no answers when the event had occurred, and he had none now; however, he had seen enough since then to know that Elohim had a purpose for everything, even something as awful as he had been through. Until this point, Lemin had been unwilling to accept this reality, but now he believed it without reservation. As he thought about it, it was the slaughter of his men that had caused him to take a teaching job at the academy of Belvárd where he had been able to mentor many of the country's best warriors, including Senndra, Timothy, and Vladimir. Lemin knew that Senndra was destined for great things, but Timothy and

Vladimir were different altogether. They were trying to keep their respective secrets, but Lemin had guessed what they were from the first days that he had seen them. It was hard to hide secrets from a magician, even if he was out of practice in the arts.

*"If I wish for them to be able to accomplish great things,"* Lemin thought to himself, *"I'll have to keep them alive long enough for that to happen. With the help of Elohim, I'll make sure that happens, even if it means my death."*

Lemin felt himself being pulled back into his body and glanced around to see what had happened in his absence. Nothing seemed different, and the dwarves appeared as Lemin had last seen them. Lemin pushed the thoughts from his mind as the first dwarf attacked. He blocked the blow and slashed back, but the dwarf danced just out of his reach. Lemin's mind was now aware of the magic lacing the city in an intricate pattern. As he kept the dwarves at bay, he began to work out a way to defeat them. With his mind he began to pull magic together into an invisible fist-sized ball. Though the pattern was rather simple and took him the lesser part of a second to construct, its effects were incredible. At detonation, it created a blast of energy that threw the surrounding dwarves several yards; he could hear the snapping of bones as they landed. Using the time he had just bought, he pulled the pendant from around Senndra's neck and put it around his own, tucking it into his shirt and out of the way.

Lemin was slightly winded from the use of magic, but that did not decrease his exhilaration. The last time he had used magic had been more than a decade ago, and he had expected to not be very proficient in his use of it now; however, the effects of his spell put new courage into his soul. He stooped to pick up Senndra and straightened again, ready to run back to the barricade. As he turned, however, a hidden dwarf let loose an arrow at him. He scrambled to put together a spell that would block the missile, but he was too slow and succeeded only in slowing down the arrow so that it bounced off the armor on his back. The razor-sharp edge of the weapon bounced sideways and slid across his arm, slicing through his leather armor and cutting him to the bone. Lemin roared in pain, but he knew that locating the dwarf and killing him would be a bad idea. Instead, he turned and headed south and back to safety.

He was depending on the dust that covered the battle field to mask his retreat, but it was already beginning to settle. He increased his pace to a dead sprint, and the ground flew beneath his feet. His arm began to throb, but it would have to wait until he had reached safety. The distance between him and the barricade steadily decreased, but it was still too far for him to assume that he was going to make it. The dust blew from the field, and Lemin could now see the defenders crouched behind the wall, all with their bows trained on him. Before he had a chance to react, the call to fire was given, and a multitude of arrows flew toward him. He scrambled to gather the magic that surrounded him to construct a shield. Were he not out of practice, the task would have been laughably easy, but in his current state, there was just not enough time. As he tried to weave the pattern with magic, the arrows closed in on him, and he ducked to try to dodge them. They didn't hit him, but they didn't pass over him either. He glanced up hesitantly and a puzzling sight met his eyes. The arrows were suspended in the air above his head, and as he watched, they fell to the ground. Lemin knew that he hadn't had time to weave the spell necessary to protect himself, and he wondered what had just happened. He didn't take the time to think about it too much now, however, and with Senndra in his arms, he sprinted the last hundred yards to the barricade. Apparently, the defenders had determined that he was an ally because they did not fire on him again. When he reached the barricade, he passed Senndra's motionless body to Timothy and Vladimir then climbed over it himself. He dropped onto the other side and stooped to catch his breath.

"She's not seriously hurt," Timothy said after examining Senndra. "She's got a nasty gash on her forehead, but the bleeding has almost stopped."

Lemin looked up and saw Timothy staring at Senndra intently. His hands were traveling up and down her body without touching her. This, coupled with the fact that Timothy's shoulder was as good as new, led Lemin to believe that his deduction about the boy had been correct. But there was just no time to address the issue now.

"Take her to the rear of the army and give her time to recover," he ordered Timothy. As Timothy left, Lemin turned to Vladimir. "Go get Commander Pondran and tell him to meet me here. I need to speak with him."

Vladimir hurried off to do Lemin's bidding, and Lemin turned his focus to his wounds. The worst one was the gash on his arm from the arrow, and it was taken care of with a relatively simple spell. The thing that he needed most now was rest to allow his body to recuperate. He sat down and leaned against a barrel so that he could look across the barrier at the enemy. The dust had cleared almost completely, allowing a view straight to the opposing army. The dwarves had recovered from the explosions and were regrouping for another charge on the barricade that the defenders now hid behind. Despite the heavy casualties that the defending army had inflicted, there appeared to be just as many dwarves as when the battle had started.

Lemin glanced to the south and saw that only two more barricades stood between the south wall of the city and the enemy army. He looked up at the sky and noticed for the first time that the rain that had stopped, though he didn't know when that had happened. The clouds had passed and from the position of the sun, he estimated that there were perhaps two hours until midday. *"Two hours until reinforcements arrive,"* he thought to himself. *"If we can hold out that long, we might have a chance of surviving."* He slid his sword from its scabbard and laid it across his knees. Next he turned his mind to remembering the patterns of various spells that might come in handy in the coming battle. As he recalled, destruction spells, such as the one that he had used when rescuing Senndra, were very physically draining; however, spells that did not take very much energy could be just as lethal. If, for instance, a spell was used to trip an enemy, that enemy could then be killed more easily. In the same way, relatively little energy was used to drain a specific area of air, rendering the soldiers there unconscious. If used effectively, magic often did not kill enemies, but it changed the environment to render them helpless. Lemin turned to remembering how various simple spells could be used to a great effect. He concentrated on this until Vladimir returned.

"Here is Commander Pondran," Vladimir said. "You wouldn't believe the time I had trying to…"

"Thank you, Vladimir," Lemin responded, cutting him off. "And now you can turn around and watch the enemy so that we will have warning when they decide to attack." He switched his attention to Josiah. "A brilliant kid, but he can ramble on sometimes. Now, what I wanted to talk to you about, as you have probably guessed, is our situation. Here's the deal; we have only two barriers left between us and the south wall of the city and around two hours before we're supposed to get reinforcements. We've already given up seven barriers in three hours, so we need to make these last ones count. The problem is that the barriers cover the length of the entire city, and when the dwarves breach one point, they can attack our backs. We don't have enough men to defend the entire barrier, so we need to change our strategy. Who is the highest-ranking officer? Actually, who's in charge here?"

"Last I heard, General Uriah is still alive," Josiah said, "so that puts him in command. Technically, the grand admiral is in charge, but he leaves the running of the army up to the general."

"In that case, I need to talk to Uriah," Lemin said. "Tell him that the highest-ranking officer from the academy of Belvárd wishes to speak to him before the dwarves put together another attack. If he wants to keep me waiting, tell him that I outrank him; I'm an admiral."

"Yes sir, right away sir." Josiah said. He moved away and motioned for one of his officers to join him. After a brief discussion, the officer took off down the wall, and Josiah rejoined Lemin.

"That is taken care of," he said. "Now, is there any other reason that you wish to speak to me?"

"Not right now," Lemin said. "Get back to your men and keep them ready. It looks like the dwarves may attack before the general gets here. Other than that, stand by for further orders."

Josiah nodded and left in the direction from which he had come, his entourage in tow. Lemin turned his attention back to the dwarf army and saw that they still did not appear as though they were about to attack. He wondered what was taking them so long, but welcomed the reprieve.

"Vladimir," He called to his cadet. When Vladimir reached him, he said, "I want you to round up as many of our cadets as you can find and bring them here. There may not be many left alive, but I need our cadets reunited. Keep an eye on the dwarf army, and when they attack, defend where you are. If you don't get back here by the time the dwarves overrun this barrier, look for me at the next one."

Vladimir jogged down the defenders' lines, looking at the faces of as many soldiers as possible and gathering those from Belvárd. Lemin sighed and looked back at the dwarf army. The fact that they were still not even getting ready to attack made him uneasy. With a snap of his fingers, he wove three strands of magic together and looked through them down the length of the city. What he saw wasn't a surprise to him, but even so, a curse jumped unbidden into his mind. A large group of the dwarves had marched to the end of the city where there were no defenders. They had crossed the barrier there, and they were now heading back toward the defenders. Lemin waved away the magic that covered his eyes and turned to see Josiah coming toward him with another man in tow. The second man was a large brute with a full head of red hair and a dull red beard. By all appearances, he was just another ordinary soldier, but Lemin could tell from the intelligent glint in his eyes that he had better than normal military genius. *"After all, that is all that separates the regular soldiers from their commanders,"* he told himself, *"intelligence."*

"You wanted to speak with me?" the large man asked.

"Yes," Lemin replied. "You must be General Uriah. Josiah told me that you are in charge of the soldiers from this academy."

"That is true," Uriah answered.

"Well, in that case, I need to speak to you." Lemin pointed to the east. "What can you see in that direction?" he asked.

"Nothing," Uriah answered. "There's so much dust in the air that I can hardly see a hundred yards."

Lemin deftly wove three more strands of magic in the same manner that he had only minutes ago. He spread the spell over Uriah's eyes and stepped back.

"Elohim, protect us!" Uriah almost shouted. "What on earth am I seeing?"

Lemin wiped the spell away and faced Uriah. "I just used magic to allow you to see through the dust and smoke to the east end of the city. You saw exactly what you thought you saw and what I saw only minutes ago. The dwarves have bypassed our defenses and are marching up from the side. They'll end up between us and the gate, and we'll be pressed from both the front and the back. If that happens, we won't have a chance of surviving."

"And I suppose you have a plan for making sure that this won't occur," Uriah said, "or you wouldn't have sent for me."

"Indeed, I have an idea," Lemin said. "No doubt, with enough time, you would have thought of something similar, but

154

this is my plan. We no longer have enough men to defend the entire length of the city. The most important thing at this point is that we hold the south wall and gate so that when our reinforcements arrive, they will be able to join the fight and not get slaughtered."

Lemin was interrupted by a shout from the dwarves to the north, and the army began to advance. "We have an advantage here," he said quickly. "The dwarves to the north are attacking too soon. We may be able to repel them because they will be counting on us being surprised by the dwarves to the east. We still have about five minutes before they reach us, so if we work quickly, we can repel the enemy to the north without putting ourselves in danger. After that, we need to form our soldiers into a box that surrounds the gate. Our archers and half of our swordsmen need to be on the wall to protect the stairs leading up to it."

"I have a better idea," Uriah said. He pulled a horn from his belt and blew two blasts on it. "That is the signal for the engineers to destroy the stairs leading up to the south wall. Now all we will have to defend is the gatehouse."

"Good idea," Lemin called over his shoulder. "If your men can drive back the dwarves to the north, I will see what I can do to stall the ones to the east."

"How…" Uriah began, but Lemin cut him off.

"Don't worry about that. You do your part and I'll do mine."

\*\*\*\*\*\*

Senndra groaned and rolled onto her back. It felt like there was a herd of horses stampeding around inside her head, and when she opened her eyes, the sudden assault of light hurt. She groaned again and, despite her body's complaints, pulled herself to a sitting position. She dropped her head into her hands, and on the right side felt a large spot of dried blood. She explored the area thoroughly with her hand and found that it wasn't very bad, so shrugging off the pain, she pulled herself to her feet. Her vision was blurry for a few moments, but it soon cleared, and she was able to look around. She was in a tower that she recognized as one on the wall of the city. Where she was in the city, she couldn't tell, so she headed for the door of the tower. She stepped out onto the wall. The strong sunshine blinded her so that she could not see for several seconds. Finally her vision adjusted, and she noted that she was on the south wall of the city. The sun was directly in front of her to the east, but it was still fairly low.

It would have been a beautiful day if the circumstances had been different. As it was, the sound of fighting coming from the north interrupted the serenity of the morning. Senndra turned to take in the battle, and as she did, she spotted Timothy on the wall to the east. She knew that he wanted to be in the middle of the fighting, and she could only guess what he must be feeling at the moment. She walked down the wall to join him. As she drew closer to him, he turned to face her. The look on his face was grim, and she questioned him with her looks. He motioned with his head to where a lone figure was making his way to the east of the army. Senndra could just make out that an army of dwarves was approaching him. She squinted to try to distinguish his features more clearly and gave a start.

"Is that Lemin?" she asked Timothy. He nodded and she continued, the words tumbling out of her mouth. "What does he think he's doing out there? He'll get himself killed."

"Not exactly," Timothy answered. His voice was low, and he added in a whisper that Senndra could not hear, "He has rejoined our ranks."

"You think he can take on all of those dwarves single-handedly?" she asked. "That's impossible, even for someone of his skill in fighting."

"Just watch and see," Timothy answered.

Senndra started to answer, but his look silenced her. Instead, she turned her attention back to Lemin. The dwarves were closing the distance to him quickly, and Senndra estimated that they would reach him in about three minutes. As the dwarves drew closer, she began to pray to Elohim.

*"Please be with Lemin as he faces the dwarves,"* she prayed. *"Let no harm befall him though his enemies outnumber him greatly. Be with him as he faces death and bring him through this alive, amen."*

Senndra turned her attention back to Lemin, but even as she did so, she heard a small voice. She knew it was not herself that spoke. The voice was much kinder and more glorious than she could imagine, but it spoke to her clearly. She turned toward Timothy, who had also turned to look at her.

"You heard him too," he said, not as a question, but as a statement. Senndra nodded, and together they turned and ran down the wall to the east. Senndra grabbed her bow and an arrow from her quiver. With a smooth motion, she placed the arrow on the string of the bow and began to gauge the distance of the dwarves even as she ran.

"Get ready," Timothy told her. She barely had time to wonder what he meant before they were flying through the air, off of the wall. Senndra screamed at the unexpected danger, but Timothy seemed unalarmed. As they approached the ground, their speed of descent decreased until their feet touched down; a slight bending of the knees was all that was necessary to absorb the shock of the landing. Senndra glanced over at Timothy for an explanation, but he was facing in the direction of Lemin and had already started to sprint toward him. Senndra followed, but she steadily fell farther and farther behind. She clutched her arrow in one hand and her bow in the other and increased her speed. Slowly she began to gain ground on Timothy and was only a few seconds behind him when he reached Lemin.

"What are you doing down here?" he asked them. "You're supposed to be in a safe place."

"Elohim commanded us to come to your aid," Timothy explained. He looked toward the advancing dwarves and added, "And it looks like you'll need all the help you can get."

"In that case," Lemin said, "I'm working on weakening the supports of the buildings between us and them so that they will fall and form a wall. I know that Senndra won't be able to help with this, but you should be able to, Timothy."

"So you knew all along, just as I suspected," Timothy said. He turned his attention to the buildings Lemin had indicated and began to concentrate. His hands made slight motions, as though he was weaving invisible threads, and Senndra was confused as to what she was seeing.

"It's magic," Timothy answered her unspoken question without even looking at her. "I'm not exactly what you would call a normal person. I'm a magician. I can work magic. Just as Lemin can. Now prepare yourself; the dwarves are coming."

Senndra was stunned by what she had just heard. And Timothy wanted her to get ready to fight? *"He expects me to just turn around with a cool head and fight after what he just said,"* she growled to herself. Without taking her eyes off of the dwarves, she placed the arrow in her hand on her bowstring. *"I guess I'll just have to make him tell me all about his being a magician later,"* she decided. She loosed several arrows at the approaching enemies then slung her bow on her back and drew her sword. The dwarves broke into a run and charged toward her between two buildings.

"Now," Lemin said calmly, and suddenly, the buildings gave a mighty groan and collapsed inward on the dwarves. Buildings across the city, all the way to the south wall, began to collapse, one after the other, until a wall separated the dwarves from the defenders.

"That will stall them for a while," Lemin said, "but not forever. We need to get back to the main army and help them stave off the dwarves from the north." He broke into a run, and Timothy and Senndra followed. They tore across the city to where they could see a vicious fight in progress. The cadets and soldiers of Magessa were holding the dwarves back, but just barely. Every instant it seemed as though the mass of enemies would break through the line and crush the resistance, and yet they never quite managed it.

"They're holding the dwarves back, but we need to repel them entirely," Lemin gasped to his companions. "Get into the fight and rally the troops. If we can't push the dwarves back, we will fall in short order." He sprinted to a point along the defenders' line where the dwarves were especially thick and began to hack his way through them. A small explosion rocked the enemies around him, sending them flying in all directions.

Timothy sprinted to another point on the line of defense and began to attack with renewed vigor. Senndra followed close behind and saw him engage the enemy. His sword swung wildly, but in such a way that it blocked the blows aimed at him. The dwarves around him tried again and again to push him back, but to no avail. From the ranks of the dwarves, a dwarf giant came out to challenge him. The giant was six feet tall and was well-muscled. In his hands he carried a battle ax that had to weigh at least fifty pounds, yet he held it as though it was a toy. He approached Timothy from the side so that he did not see him coming. With a roar, he swung his ax at Timothy, aiming for his waist. But Timothy heard the roar and, with superhuman reflexes, jumped over the blade and landed on his heel, spinning to face his attacker. With his free hand, he began to make strange motions that ended with a thrust toward his opponent. Blue lightning shot from his fingers and hit the dwarf giant in the chest. The blow knocked the soldier to the ground, and he lay there twitching as sparks continued to spider web across his body. Timothy ended his suffering with a quick thrust of his sword. He turned to face the dwarf horde again, but they had retreated just far enough to get out of the range of his sword. He thought he could detect fright on the faces of some of his enemies, but he knew that he needed to drive the stake of fear deeper into their hearts. With a slight motion of his hand, he sent a fire ball careening into the enemy soldiers, causing them to turn in panic and scramble to get away.

Timothy wiped his sword blade on the cloak of one of his fallen foes. He rose to his feet and replaced it in its sheath before returning to the defenders' line. He walked over to Senndra and just looked at her.

"Now, why don't you tell me what you forgot to tell me before?" she said, a slight edge of irritation in her voice.

"And what do you think there is to tell?" Timothy responded. "I already told you everything. I am a magician as is Lemin."

"You don't have anything else to say for yourself?" Senndra shot back.

"What do you want me to say?" Timothy questioned. "There's nothing to explain."

"How about telling me why you…" But Senndra was cut off by Lemin, who had just approached the two cadets. In the battle, the pendant had come loose from his shirt and was now resting on his breastplate.

"Timothy, nice show of power out there," he commended. "If it weren't for you, I would never have been able to collapse the buildings on time. You also used your power admirably while fighting. Remember, however, that you must only use it as Elohim commands; never use it for your own gain. If you are confused at all on the point of whether you are to use magic or not, don't use it."

Senndra had been sputtering throughout this whole speech, but now found her voice.

"And you!" she said turning to Lemin. "You're a magician too? Why did I not know this? And isn't that my father's pendant?"

"I would like nothing more than to explain this to you," Lemin said, "but it's a long story that would take a lot of time to tell."

"I've got time," Senndra said.

"We need to prepare for the next dwarf attack," Lemin countered. "I don't have the time right now."

"Then make time," Senndra said and crossed her arms.

Lemin glanced over his shoulder at the retreating dwarves, then back to Senndra. She was glaring at him, and it was evident that she would not be put off. Also, in a way, he owed her an explanation.

"Alright, I'll try to keep this short," he said. "I don't remember all of it and there are some parts that I do not wish to repeat, but in a nutshell this is the account you're looking for. I don't tell anyone that I'm a magician because I don't like magic." He gave a humorless laugh and amended, "More correctly, magic doesn't like me."

"What do you mean?" Senndra asked.

"I've used magic many times in my life and every time I do it seems to lead to something terrible," Lemin said. "As a child I had a run-in with some very bad wizards and it's followed me for the rest of my life. It seems a curse that I cannot shake is following me. Anyway, when the dwarves attacked, I suspected that I would need to use my magic again, but I wasn't ready to accept it. That's why I gave you the pendant and did not keep it for myself. I now understand that all available resources need to be brought to bear against our foe, which is why I have reclaimed the pendant. I am resolved to use my magic no matter the consequences; if I do not, we may all die."

"I still don't get it," Senndra said. "Is the pendant magical? Why do you need it?"

"The pendant is hard to explain," Lemin said. "It is not magical, do not make that mistake, but I still require it to use my power. Let's just say that it keeps the curse at bay."

"The curse from your childhood?" Senndra asked. Lemin nodded.

"Look Senndra," Timothy said after a pause, "I know that you're not happy right now, even I'm a little miffed at Lemin right now, but we have bigger problems at the moment. Like now that we have driven the dwarves back, what are our plans?"

"I have conferred with the general of the army of Saddun," Lemin answered. "All of the stairs to the southern wall have been destroyed, so the only way up is by the gatehouse. We were originally planning to protect the gatehouse from the ground, but we have decided that we don't have enough time. Instead we're going to get everyone onto the wall and defend it from on top. You had better get moving. We need everyone on the wall before the dwarves put together another attack."

"Well, I have at least until we get on top of the wall to talk," Timothy told Senndra. "I can answer any questions that you have and I'm sure that there are a lot."

"That's okay," Senndra answered. "I don't really want to talk to you right now."

"Oh come on," Timothy said. "I just met you. Did you really think that I was going to tell you every last deep dark secret about myself? I try to get to know people before I give them a reason to mistrust me."

"You're a *magician*," Senndra retorted. "What's not to trust?"

"Molkekk's a magician," Timothy pointed out.

"Even so," Senndra said. "I would have thought that with something this big you would have told me."

"And all of the while your response is justifying my actions," Timothy countered.

"I'm done with this conversation," Senndra said and stalked toward the wall. Timothy rolled his eyes and started walking, making sure to stay a few steps behind. In battle and in dealings with others he knew when to attack and when to fall back. This was definitely the time for a strategic withdrawal. He'd give her time to cool down before he attempted to speak with her again.

******

Josiah looked down from the tower in which he and his men had taken refuge. Two hours had passed since the army had moved onto the wall, and in those two hours, the advance of the dwarves had come to a complete standstill. At first they had tried to force their way up the stairs of the gatehouse, but to no avail. Next they had tried battering the gate down, but these efforts were met with a barrage of arrows and rocks on the rams that were being used. The dwarves had even brought siege engines up to destroy the wall, but the defenders' ballistae were able to foil this attempt. After being defeated for the third time, the dwarves had fallen back to the middle of the city, which was where Josiah saw them now. They had set up field hospitals and were caring for their wounded. They appeared to be happy, at least for the moment, to wait out the defenders. They knew that there were probably no provisions on the wall, and they would gladly starve out the defenders. What they didn't know was that reinforcements would soon be coming to the aid of their enemies. Josiah looked toward the south and saw a small cloud of dust rising from the plain outside of the city. He motioned for one of his captains, and Stanslaw approached him.

"Take a look at that and tell me what you think it is," Josiah said and pointed to the cloud of dust.

163

"It's definitely a rider," Stanslaw commented. "If I had to guess, I would say it is the advanced messenger of our reinforcements."

"That's what I was thinking as well," Josiah said. Together the two cadets watched as the horseman covered the distance to the city. Within thirty minutes of the first sighting, the man was at the foot of the wall, and Josiah ordered a rope to be lowered to him. The man nimbly climbed the rope and was hauled over the wall's crenellations.

"Get this man some water," Josiah ordered one of his men. To the messenger he asked, "What news do you bear?"

The man looked Josiah straight in the eye and said nothing for a while. A soldier arrived with water, and the messenger drank it before responding. "Only this news," he finally said, "our governor at Feling has decided not to send any reinforcements to help. There will be no army from him."

"What do you mean?" Josiah exploded. "You are telling me that the elders of Gatlon have laughed at our request for help? Don't they know that if this city falls, the enemy will almost definitely overrun Magessa?" He turned away from the messenger and stalked down the wall.

"It was not my decision," the man tried to explain. "If it was up to me, the whole army of Magessa would be coming to your aid. As it is, there seems to be some treachery in the ranks of Gatlon's authority."

"After this is all over, you can be sure that someone will look into that," Josiah said, turning back to the messenger. "For right now, though, there are more pressing matters at hand. I'll arrange for food to be brought to you before you leave."

"I'm not leaving, sir," the man replied. "I said that if it were up to me the whole army of Magessa would be coming this way, and I meant what I said. I don't have that power, but I'll be staying here to fight."

"So be it," Josiah answered. "If you will come with me and repeat what you have told me to the general, you can be finished with that and start preparing for battle. By the way," he added, "I don't know your name."

"My name is Petrarch Bentinck, but I am called Petra by my friends. I am curious, however. Why do you think the dwarves won't attack again for a while?" he asked as the two men started down the wall together.

"When we retreated to the wall, they attempted attacking us several times," Josiah explained. "We were able to repel them, and they sustained such great losses that they have not attempted to attack us since. We will still keep our guard up, of course, but now our plans are focusing more toward attacking them."

"Was I informed correctly when I was told that this battle only started this morning?" Petra asked. When Josiah nodded, he continued. "Why are you already thinking about a plan of attack? I mean, it never hurts to be aggressive, but I have never heard of an aggressive attack so soon into a siege."

"But this isn't your normal siege," Josiah answered. "The battle may have started only this morning, but the enemy has already taken the city. Normally, the siege would be over at this point and we would all be dead, but then again, I have never put too much stock in *normal* warfare. Anyway, the reason we're thinking of a counter attack already is that we have no supplies. We had most of our resources in the city, and we were pushed back too quickly to take many of them with us, so we have less than three days' worth of food. We are in control of the gatehouse, so we control the gate; but that doesn't mean that we can use it. Any attempt to bring anything in that way would result in a dwarf attack. If we had to, we could always resort to lifting stuff up the wall by ropes. But as it is, we have nothing to lift. We were supposed to get supplies with our reinforcements, but…" Josiah sighed. "Well, you know better than I what our support is."

"Yes," Petra said after a few moments. "The situation is indeed grave and calls for drastic action. Perhaps an immediate counter attack would be best."

Josiah stopped in front of the door to another tower, and Petra halted behind him. Josiah stepped up to one of the guards and spoke a few words in an undertone to him, and the guard led him and Petra through the door and into the tower. The interior was pitch black, but the guard quickly lit a lantern and placed it on a table in the middle of the room. Without a word, he left the tower, closing the door securely behind him.

"You might as well make yourself comfortable," Josiah told Petra. "Apparently the general is attending to other matters at the moment, so the guard is going to get him. If I have learned anything in my academy years, it is that the general rarely hurries. We could be here for a while."

As Petra took a seat at the table, Josiah took the lantern and used it to explore the interior of the tower. He found a tinder box and proceeded to light several more lanterns that were scattered about the room. When he had finished, there was a fair amount of light, so he returned to the table and took a seat across from Petra. As had become his habit in the last several hours, he sat almost perfectly still and began to pray to Elohim. He was so caught up in his prayer that he was startled when the door opened and the general entered. Josiah and Petra jumped to their feet and saluted the officer, holding the salute until he returned it. The officer walked across the room to the table and took a seat behind it as Josiah moved to stand beside Petra.

"And what is the purpose of this meeting?" he asked when he was comfortably seated.

"This is a messenger from Gatlon, sir," Josiah answered. "He has some news that I thought you should hear."

"From Gatlon," the general muttered to himself. "You may speak," he said out loud to Petra.

166

"There will be no reinforcements from Gatlon," Petra responded curtly. He waited for an outbreak from the general, but none came, so he continued. "I believe there is some treachery among the ranks of the authority of Gatlon. I only heard about your plight because I am the doorkeeper of the elders' council chambers.

"As soon as the meeting adjourned, I went home as quickly as possible and told my brothers and father about it. Immediately we set off, each in a different direction. My father, who is quite old, stayed at home, while my brothers left to take the news of the attack to Belvárd, Rampön, the ogres, and the elves. I came here to warn you that no help is coming unless my brothers succeed in bringing it."

"The news is grave indeed; however, you have softened it sufficiently," the general said. "The hope of any help at all is enough to keep us fighting until we drop dead one way or another. Even if there was no help coming, we would still give our lives to protect the country, and even the slightest chance of help is enough to keep us going." He turned to Josiah and said, "Commander Pondran, make sure this man gets on his way without anything hindering him."

"If it's all the same to you, I will stay and fight alongside your men," Petra spoke up, cutting off General Uriah. "This is my country as much as it is anyone else's, and I intend to do everything in my power to keep it free."

"Very well. It matters not to me whether you leave or stay to die with us. Do what you wish. Commander Pondran will attend to your needs and will be your commander if you wish to stay." The general opened the door of the tower and was gone.

"Well, let's get back to where my men have taken up residence, and I'll get you settled in and suited up," Josiah said. He led Petra out of the tower, extinguishing the lanterns on the way. The two men headed down the wall, talking as they went. Suddenly Petra pulled up short and pointed out into the city.

"You don't have any sentries out there, do you?" he asked.

"Of course not," Josiah answered. "That would be suicide."

"Exactly," Petra answered. "Then those moving forms out there are the enemy, and they're heading this way."

"Where?" Josiah asked as he lifted a hand to protect his eyes from the sun.

"Between those two buildings," Petra said and pointed to two storehouses near the southern gate. He turned back to Josiah for a comment, but Josiah was already moving, sprinting down the wall. He shouted to everyone as he went that another attack was coming.

"Well, I guess he saw them too," Petra muttered to himself and headed after Josiah. He caught up to him and stopped when he saw that Josiah was talking to several other men.

"Right over there, Timothy," Josiah said and pointed to the buildings that the dwarves had been between only moments ago. "I don't know what happened to them. I can't see them anymore, but you probably can."

"Actually, it doesn't work like that," Timothy said. "I can only work destruction magic and not much else."

"I can affirm that there were dwarves gathering out there," Petra broke in. "If I had a guess, I'd say that they were getting ready for another attack, given that they'll have the cover of darkness. That is an obvious strategy."

"I'll send word to the general and Lemin," Josiah said and headed back the way that he had come. But Timothy stopped him.

"You take care of the general and then get ready for the attack," the magician said. "I'll tell Lemin."

"Very well," Josiah replied. "Then I will get back to my men. Come, Petra."

The two men ran down the wall, but not so fast as to tire themselves. They passed several groups of soldiers, and Josiah stopped for each of them and told them the news of the attack. Within several minutes, Josiah and Petra had reached Josiah's company of men and informed them of the impending attack. There was a flurry of activity as the soldiers readied themselves for the fight. Josiah led Petra to a nearby tower. Weapons and armor were carefully stacked inside, so it took Josiah only a few minutes to find armor that fit the new soldier. He then turned to fetch a weapon as well, but Petra stopped him.

"I have my own weapon," he said and drew a brilliant sword from the sheath on his belt. "This sword has been passed down from generation to generation in our family, and I intend to use it just as my ancestors used it before me."

"Suit yourself," Josiah shrugged. He strapped on his armor, grabbed his helmet from the rack where he had left it, and stepped out of the tower and onto the wall. His two remaining captains, Stanslaw and Yugart, approached him. All of their armor was firmly in place, and their weapons were ready to be drawn at a moment's notice. The only thing that was missing from their battle uniforms was the helmet, which each of them held under one arm. They waited for Josiah to walk past and fell in behind him on either side. Josiah scanned the crowd of his soldiers that had taken less than five minutes to prepare for battle. He looked down the wall at several other groups who, even though they had received news of the attack earlier, were still not ready.

"They'll be heading for the gatehouse, so we need to get there," Josiah said. "The people down there aren't ready for the attack, and it could come at any moment. Stanslaw, take your soldiers and cover the east side of the gatehouse. Yugart, get your soldiers and cover the west side. I'll take the remaining men and plug up the stairs in the actual structure. I don't want any ladders on the wall, so take them down if they get set up."

Both captains hurried off to obey Josiah's orders, and Josiah turned to face his men. Many had been cut down in battle, and several of those that remained were injured; but the fear that had been in their eyes at the beginning of the day was gone. In its place, there was a look of determination to defeat the dwarf horde and save Magessa.

"Companies one, three, and four please step out," Josiah called. Two thirds of the soldiers stepped forward to distinguish themselves from those behind them. "Form ranks," Josiah called, and in next to no time, the soldiers were in orderly lines. "You are now called company one. The rest of you will form groups of three, and your task will be to keep the walls clear of ladders. Company one, follow me."

The company moved down the wall at a fast clip, passing soldiers who were struggling into their armor. They had soon gained the gatehouse and found another company of soldiers waiting there who were obviously ready to defend the stairs in the gatehouse.

"Company, halt," Josiah ordered. The soldiers stopped marching simultaneously, and every soldier stood at attention. "Left face," Josiah ordered, and each soldier spun on his left heel so that he now faced the city. "Draw swords and prepare for battle," Josiah ordered before approaching the commander of the other company of soldiers. The sound of weapons being drawn followed him as he crossed to the other company. He quickly identified the commander and moved to stand in front of him. The other man saluted first, so Josiah returned the salute.

"I am Commander Pondran," Josiah introduced himself. "I can see that you are a captain."

"My name is Markus," the captain replied.

"Do you have any previous orders from any of your superiors?" Josiah questioned. Markus shook his head, so Josiah continued. "How many men do you have at your disposal?"

"Around three hundred."

"Excellent." A shout from the city startled Josiah, and he quickly finished talking. "That should be more than enough to block one of the staircases of the gatehouse. I'll block the other, and two companies of my men will protect our sides."

Markus nodded and turned to his men to give commands. Josiah spun on his heel and headed back toward his troops. When he reached them, he looked out over the city and saw that the dwarves were already halfway to the gatehouse.

"Company one, close ranks," he called, and his men moved so that they stood shoulder to shoulder. Josiah motioned with his hand, and the soldiers moved forward so that the front line was mere inches from the top of the gatehouse staircases. The front line lowered their swords so that no dwarf could get past them, and the second line prepared their weapons in case any of the first line should fall. Josiah looked out over the city again. The dwarves had almost gained the gatehouse, when a shower of arrows from the left and right cut down the front lines. Before another barrage could be attempted, the next line of dwarves reached the safety of the gatehouse and darted into the stairwells.

"They are coming," Josiah called to his front line. "Be ready for them."

Already, the sound of dwarf boots striking the stairs could be heard in the stairwell, and in less than a minute, the first dwarf stuck his head around the corner. He could not stop his forward momentum and rushed headlong onto the sword blades of the first line of defenders. His companions could have stopped themselves in time had they wished, but they continued their headlong charge, swinging their axes wildly. They met the same fate as the first dwarf. It seemed as though the dwarves would be easily repelled, until a swarm of crossbow bolts hit the defenders'

171

ranks, cutting down half of the first line and several of the other soldiers. More men stepped up to fill the places of their fallen comrades, and the dwarves were still unable to gain access to the wall.

From two towers, one on either side of the gatehouse, archers pelted the dwarf archers, driving them back to the relative safety of the buildings. While the missiles cut down less than a tenth of the enemy archers, they did drive them out of bow range. The archers were gone; however, their purpose had been accomplished. Their covering fire had allowed ladder men, ax men, and archers to gain the foot of the wall, where they could not be easily hit by the defenders. All along the wall, ladders were pushed up, and enemy infantry began to climb them. Pike men immediately rushed to shove them off, but the archers at the foot of the wall shot them as soon as they tried. The infantry on the wall prepared for the enemy to reach the top of the ladders, and all too soon, the dwarves were climbing up over the edge. The defenders hit the dwarves with a shout, shoving many of them off the wall and engaging the others. The ascending dwarves were outnumbered, but more reinforcements piled onto the wall every second. The defenders stoically held the dwarves back; however, the sheer number of dwarves began to overwhelm them. Slowly the dwarves pushed the defenders away from the edge of the wall, making room for more enemies to ascend.

The length of wall that the dwarves had placed ladders on was relatively small, so the defenders were able to retreat down the wall to the east and west, but this split them into two groups. Slowly the dwarves pushed the defenders further down the wall, making more room. Josiah and his soldiers bravely held their ground against the onslaught, but they were still being slowly forced backward. Timothy, who found himself beside Josiah, was using every trick he knew to vanquish his foes, but there was no way that he could prevent them from taking more ground.

Josiah took a particularly rough blow from a dwarf and staggered backwards. Another cadet immediately took his place, leaving him free to observe the battle. Quickly his mind took in all of the details, and he struggled to come up with a prudent plan of action. He quickly searched the cadets around him and chose one that was nursing an injured arm.

"Go to the towers that have archers and tell them to fire on the dwarves on the wall," he ordered the cadet. "If we don't get these blivits off the wall soon, we'll be in trouble."

The cadet turned and ran toward the towers to carry out Josiah's order. Josiah watched him push through the crowd and out of sight before turning his attention back to the battle. Another idea came to him, and he began to issue orders, rearranging his men into a new formation. On his command, an overload of cadets charged down the south edge of the wall. The wall was crenellated on this side, so the cadets did not fall off. Instead, the excess of cadets drove a wedge to the side of the dwarves that began to force them off the wall. The dwarves immediately saw what was happening and started a counter attack. They charged the cadets in front of them, but as soon as they left the edge of the wall, Josiah ordered another group of cadets around the north side of the dwarves, sandwiching them between two groups. The cadets closed the trap immediately, taking the dwarves by surprise and killing them quickly.

The cadets were intoxicated with their success; however, they had only crushed a very small group of dwarves. Several hundred more enemies still fought on the wall, and more climbed onto it every moment. Josiah glanced toward the towers with the archers. They were still firing toward the city, so he turned back to the fight before him. He located Timothy and pushed his way over to him.

"Is there any way that you can use magic to get the ladders off the wall?" he shouted over the ruckus of the battle. Timothy relinquished his spot in the action to another cadet and paused to think. After several moments, he headed toward the section of wall where the dwarves were still clambering up the ladders. When he had almost reached the front line of the fighting, he sheathed his sword and began to make strange motions with his hands, almost as if he were forming an invisible ball of something. From what little he knew, Josiah understood that Timothy was working his magic, so he plunged headlong into the fighting. He fought furiously for almost half a minute before he heard the fruit of that magic.

Starting near the west edge of the dwarves, a series of explosions began to work their way across the edge of the wall, splintering the ladders and flinging them back into the city. Concussive waves spread out from the blasts, flinging dwarves caught in their paths off of the wall.

Josiah raised his sword in victory and plunged into the dwarves that had been stunned by this use of magic. Seconds later, arrows began to rain down on the attacking dwarves, so the cadets fell back, attacking only to contain the dwarves to an area that made it easy for the archers to see them. Within five minutes, the last remnant of dwarves had been squashed.

******

Josiah leaned his head back against the wall of the tower and closed his eyes. It was night now, and his body, tired as it was from all of the fighting, desperately needed sleep. The events of the day had not been ideal, but they had ended on a somewhat victorious note for the defenders of Saddun.

After the dwarves had been driven off the south wall, they had ceased their attacks. Their casualties had been heavy, and they realized that they were up against a magician so powerful that none of their minor magic workers could challenge him alone. Had they known that there were actually two magicians, they probably would have left. But as it was, they were most likely trying to figure out how to draw out and kill Timothy.

Despite the fact that there had been no more attacks, Josiah was still physically drained. The fighting at the beginning of the day had exhausted all of the soldiers. Just standing lookout on the wall as the sun beat down in full force was grueling, and several soldiers had already dropped from heat exhaustion.

Josiah knew that if he fell asleep, he would not wake up until the next morning, so he forced his eyes open and got to his feet. In front of him, Lemin and Timothy sat playing a game that, according to them, was the magician's equivalent to chess. When Josiah asked about it, Lemin tried to explain, but Josiah only caught bits and pieces of what was said. In theory, an infinite number of magicians could play it, but games were normally limited to no more than eight players. Games at official tournaments were restricted to two alliances, each with as many magicians as necessary. Each magician used a very small amount of magic to create an army, the size of which was determined beforehand. When the army was completed, it consisted of small soldiers made of magic, each of which was an example of an ideal soldier. They would react like real people; however, it was up to the magician to direct them in general battle formations and tactics. When both magicians had completed their armies, they would engage, each trying to outmaneuver the other. The name of the game, Josiah recalled, was Lex Tanna.

Josiah was very interested in the game, but it created a paradox in his mind. According to Lemin, a magician was to use his power only at the direction of Elohim, and Josiah could not believe that Elohim would direct someone to use magic to play a game. It was not until Lemin offered an explanation that Josiah finally understood.

"There are two kinds of magic in this respect," Lemin had said. "There is magic that you never use unless directed to do so, and there is magic that you use unless directed not to do so. The magic that is not used unless directed to do so is normally impressive magic like causing a city to rise out of the ground. Most magic, however, is of the other kind; that is, you use it unless otherwise directed. For instance, magic can always be used for things that Elohim would approve of, like protecting yourself and your companions in battle. In this case, playing this game is

175

keeping us sharp in our magical skills and military tactics, which definitely wins Elohim's approval."

Josiah enjoyed watching the two magicians competing against each other, so he concentrated on it in order to stay awake. Lemin was clearly much more skilled at the game than Timothy, and though he had an army that was only one-fifth the size of Timothy's, he still had the upper hand. It took him another five minutes to dismantle his opponent's army, but he did it with very little damage to his own. Lemin immediately launched into a detailed explanation of what Timothy had done correctly and poorly. Josiah moved to the window of the tower and looked south, searching for any sign of movement. Black, rolling fields met his gaze, and he turned away discouraged. He stepped out of the tower for a breath of fresh air, and the night chill hit him like a blow. He pulled his cloak about himself and started down the wall toward the section where his men were sleeping. As he went, he had to be careful to avoid sleeping soldiers that lay on the wall in a seemingly haphazard fashion; however, upon closer scrutiny, he could see that a path had been left for people to traverse the wall. As he neared the first lookout station, a familiar figure became visible: Petra Bentinck.

"Have you seen anything?" Josiah asked after the pleasantries had been given and received. "Not the slightest movement," Petra answered, keeping his eyes on the city. "And that goes for both directions. There's nothing to the north. Hold on a second," he said. "Is that a light over by the north gate?" he asked, pointing in that general direction.

"It could be," Josiah answered. "Why? Do you think you see something?"

"It could be nothing," Petra answered, "but it looks like there are some dwarves leaving the city. I can't be sure at this distance, though."

"I'll get Timothy and Lemin and see if they can help," Josiah said, and in minutes they were at the lookout post, staring at the spot that Petra pointed out. Lemin snapped his fingers, and suddenly the sky grew lighter until it was almost as bright as day.

"Is it dawn already?" asked Josiah in surprise.

"No," Timothy answered. "Lemin has simply cast a spell that allows us to see as though it were day. Look well and tell me what you see." Lemin waved his hand, and suddenly the north side of the city rushed toward the group until it appeared as though they viewed it from only a hundred feet away. Immediately Petra's concerns were confirmed. Dwarves were streaming out of the northern gate in an exodus and turned west to march along the Apathy Range, leaving only enough dwarves to maintain a half-hearted siege for the defenders to fight against. The sound of fingers snapping returned the observers' vision back to normal.

"What in heaven's name is happening?" Petra asked.

"The bulk of their army, at least fifty thousand strong, is moving west toward Belmoth," Josiah explained. "Belmoth has fewer soldiers than we do, and they'll have no warning. There's practically no way they'll be able to withstand the attack."

"We need to send them a message then," Petra exclaimed.

"If we send one through Magessa, they'll get there much too late to be of any help," Timothy answered. The only way that we can possibly get to Belmoth before the dwarves is if we take the same route they are taking; however, we can't do that until we destroy the dwarf army that is still in the city."

"And the dwarves left enough soldiers to keep us from being able to easily destroy them," Lemin finished.

"Exactly," Timothy said. "Of course we have to try to get past them, but it will be very difficult, if not entirely impossible."

"It's not impossible," Petra said.

"You're correct," Lemin said. "Given the correct strategy, we could destroy them."

"That's not exactly what I meant," Petra tried to explain, but Timothy interrupted him.

"We actually wouldn't need to destroy the whole army. We would only have to get a messenger past them."

"True," Lemin conceded, "but with as few men as we have…"

"Guys," Petra interrupted, and Timothy and Lemin looked at him. Petra gestured toward the fields to the south of the city. The magicians gasped as they saw where Petra was pointing. The moon was hidden behind a cloud, but even in the dim light, the soldiers could see that the field was crowded with ranks upon ranks of men for as far as they could see. Suddenly a soldier further down the wall began to shout.

"Idiot!" Lemin hissed. "What does he want to do? Just tell the enemy what's happening?"

"Make a sound-absorbing spell," Timothy suggested, and the two magicians immediately lapsed into silence as they struggled to weave a web of magic over the wall. Though Timothy was unable to construct something outside of his area of expertise, he was able to help the older magician with the task.

"I don't care what you have to do, but shut that man up," Lemin gasped to Josiah. Josiah turned and ran down to the agitated soldier. Petra, at a loss for what to do, followed him telling everyone they passed to keep silent. Less than a minute later, he saw in the distance that Josiah had reached the man that was shouting in ecstasy. As Petra drew closer, he could hear Josiah reasoning with the man to be silent.

"But look out there!" the man shouted. "It's a lot of…" Josiah brought his elbow up into the man's face, cutting off his shout. The man slumped to the wall unconscious.

"I never liked that guy anyway," Josiah muttered to Petra as he ran up, "and Lemin did say to shut him up no matter what I had to do." Petra gave a dry laugh and turned with Josiah to look out at the approaching army of reinforcements.

"How many men would you say are out there?" Josiah asked as he leaned on the crenellation.

"Well, it's pretty dark," Petra said, "but I would say there are anywhere between ten and fifteen thousand soldiers, and most of them are veterans. My guess is that the majority of them are elves. Probably only a fourth or a fifth of them are human with no more than a few hundred orcs in the ranks."

"I suppose the grand admiral will want to have all of the officers with him when he meets the leader of this force, so I'd better go find him," Josiah said. Petra followed him down the wall to the nearest group of soldiers.

"There's no place for us to keep all of them," Petra commented, gesturing to the approaching army.

"I'm sure we'll think of something," Josiah said. "Though they'll probably have to sleep at the foot of the wall," he added.

"If they get any sleep at all," Petra said. "My guess is that it will take the majority of the night to get them up onto the wall, after which they will be positioned in a way to maximize the effect of their attack. By the time all of that is done, it will almost be sunrise, and the fight will begin."

As the two men neared a group of soldiers, Josiah held up a hand to silence Petra and turned his attention to the warriors who were leaning up against the wall's crenellation.

"Do any of you know where the grand admiral is?" he asked.

"At his headquarters with his officers," one of the soldiers spoke up. "He's getting ready to meet the leader of our reinforcements and is gathering all of his commanders together to be there when he does."

"He always did like his ceremonies," Josiah commented, positioning himself so that his rank was visible to the men. The soldiers jumped to attention and saluted Josiah, who returned their salute.

"At ease, men, and thank you for the information," he said. Without another word, he spun on his heels and headed for the grand admiral's headquarters.

"I guess those guys didn't expect you to be a commander," Petra commented.

"The other commanders go about flaunting their rank and using it to get what they want," Josiah answered. "Since I don't do that, I am a bit of an anomaly, and many people do not suspect my rank."

"I'm wondering if people respect you for your humility," Petra said thoughtfully, "or if they prefer the other commanders. At least with the other ones, they know who they are dealing with all of the time. With you, they can't immediately tell what you're like."

Josiah suddenly stopped and spun to face Petra, moving in so that he was only inches away. "I do things the way that I do because I think it is best for my men," he said with a touch of hostility in his voice. "If you ever question who the men respect more, you should ask them. I'm confident that they will give me a good report." Without another word, Josiah whirled around and headed toward the grand admiral's headquarters.

"Whoa!" Petra said. He ran after Josiah, talking as he moved. "Sorry, Commander. I didn't mean to insult you; I was just asking a question." Josiah paid him no heed so he discontinued talking and lengthened his stride to keep up.

When they had almost reached the headquarters of the grand admiral, Josiah stopped and turned around. He started to talk, but Petra cut him off. "Look, Josiah, I'm sorry if I insulted you back there. I was just asking a question and didn't know what I was saying. I mean…."

Josiah stopped him with a hand. "Petra, there's nothing more you need to say. I need to apologize to you for becoming angry with you. You see, I have had quite a bit of criticism over the past years concerning the way I hold my positions of authority. When I heard what you said, I immediately thought you were attacking me, and I retaliated. It was not until afterward that I thought better of it."

"That's okay, Josiah," Petra said. "If I had known, I wouldn't have said anything."

"And I'm sure you wouldn't have, but I'm just telling you this so that we don't part on bad terms."

"Why? Where are you going?"

Josiah sighed. "The grand admiral really likes his ceremonies, which means that he'll want all of his officers to be with him when he receives the one in command of the army outside our walls. He wants to make the correct impression, which means that you'll not get to be there, seeing that you have no rank of importance."

"I guess that makes sense," Petra responded. "So when will I see you again?"

"Whenever this meeting is over," Josiah called over his shoulder. He turned his head forward and muttered, "And who knows when that will be."

Petra watched Josiah for several seconds before turning away to go find something to do. *"After all,"* he said to himself, *"there has to be something I can do in an army that's preparing for battle."*

******

181

Petra ran the whet stone over the blade of his sword again and gazed out to where he had last seen the grand admiral and his group of officers. He sat with his back against a water barrel that was positioned on the wall and, for the hundredth time, ran his hand up and down the smooth blade of his sword, searching for scratches and chips. He found none, of course, since he had already worked them all out more than half an hour ago. Turning his attention back to the sword blade, he ran the whet stone across it twice more before testing it on his finger. It was razor sharp, so he laid it across his knees. He leaned his head back against the barrel and looked up at the dark sky, wondering what the outcome of the next day's battle would be. Inadvertently, his thoughts turned into prayers as he asked Elohim for protection on him and the entire army. As he prayed, his nerves slowly calmed, and he opened his eyes and looked about himself. The same soldiers still stood on the wall at regular intervals, and they still possessed the same weapons. The same dwarf army was still encamped in the city, yet everything seemed just a little brighter.

With another glance toward the south, Petra rose to his feet. Swiftly he slid his sword back into its sheath and belted it around his waist. After checking the straps on his equipment, he walked down the wall toward the nearest tower. As he stepped through the doorway, everything suddenly changed. Outside, clouds had covered the sky, making the darkness almost oppressive. It was broken only at intervals by torches. The interior of the tower, however, was brightly lit in order to accommodate the soldiers inside who were getting ready for the battle the next day. The light also caused the activity in the tower to be more spirited than that outside. Swordsmen passed around handheld whet stones to sharpen their weapons, while others operated large ones that spun in a circle so as to more quickly sharpen weapons. Archers tested the strings of their bows and checked their arrows to make sure that they were razor sharp.

As Petra scanned the people inside the tower, his gaze lit on one person—a girl who couldn't be more than sixteen. He thought he recognized her from someplace, but he couldn't figure out where. After trying in vain to recall where he had seen her, he decided to go and introduce himself. *"Perhaps her name will jog my memory,"* he decided. He crossed the tower to where she was inspecting her bow for any imperfections. He cleared his throat, and she looked up at him.

"Hello," he began, "my name is Petra Bentinck, and I was wondering…"

"Did you say Petra?" the girl cut him off to ask. Petra nodded with excitement, but his hope that she recognized him was dashed when she turned back to her bow and said, "So you must be the messenger from Gatlon."

"Well, yes I am, but that's not why I came over to talk to you," he said. "I came to ask you a question."

"A question?" the girl repeated. She looked back at Petra with a look of interest on her face. "Well, have at it. If I can answer, I will."

"Do I know you from somewhere?" Petra asked. The girl's face quickly took on a look of confusion, so he explained himself. "You look really familiar to me, as if I know you from somewhere, but I can't place you."

"I don't know you from anywhere," the girl said. "Not that I can remember anyway."

She turned back to her bow and left Petra standing awkwardly in front of her. Just as he was about to turn away, another cadet came up. He was tall and well built, with short cropped brown hair. In his hand he held a sword that had runes etched along its entire length.

"Senndra, do you have a whet stone?" he asked.

Senndra. The name rattled around in Petra's head, yet no matter how many times he said it to himself, it still had no effect except to irritate him. How could he recognize someone and yet not recognize them? He was pulled from his thoughts by the cadet who had asked for the whet stone.

"Do you have one?" the cadet asked, making a motion as though trying to remember a name.

"Petra," Petra answered, sticking his hand out automatically. "And your name is?"

"Cirro," the cadet answered, taking Petra's outstretched hand. "You're the messenger from Gatlon, aren't you?" he asked. "You don't happen to have a whet stone on you, do you?"

"Actually, I do," Petra answered and withdrew the rock from his pocket. "By the way, how did you know my name?"

"I heard it from Josiah," Cirro said as he ran the stone over his sword blade.

"Then you know Josiah?" Petra asked.

"Yep, sure do," Cirro answered as he sighted down his sword blade. "I'm under his command, so I hear lots from him. News of you spread pretty quickly through the ranks. I have to say that I admire you for staying to fight. We're going to need all the help we can get tomorrow."

"Hear, oh Magessa, you are going to battle against your enemies, but do not be apprehensive or afraid," Petra said. "Do not be terrified or give way before the enemy. For Elohim goes into battle before you, and it is He who will fight for you to give you the victory." Cirro gave him a quizzical look, so he explained, "Those are the words given by Elohim Himself that are to be spoken to embolden the armies of Magessa. They are in the holy book in the fifth section of the law."

"Yes, I know," Cirro answered. He slid his sword into its sheath. "I am only surprised because there are very few nowadays who can quote the word of Elohim. To me it seems that it is all but forgotten."

"Sadly, that is true," Petra said, "and without the help of Elohim, this country is lost, not only physically, but also spiritually. If the people do not turn back to Elohim soon, I

184

wonder if it wouldn't be better for the country to be overrun; for indeed, the spiritual deadness of the country is appalling."

"True, and yet all we can do now is stand against the enemies of Magessa and hope that they are not a judgment sent upon us for our sins," Cirro responded. "Indeed, if this is another punishment of the country, I know we shall fail to defend this city."

"But I do not think this is judgment," Petra said. "I can't help but believe that Elohim would warn us of the coming of His wrath as He has in the past. No, I believe that this is simply an effort by the enemies of Elohim to destroy His chosen people."

"If that is so," Cirro said "I am not afraid to stand between the dwarves and my country. If this is not from Him, that means He is on our side. And if He be for us, who can be against us?"

"Agreed," Petra stated and lapsed into silence. He turned to examine Senndra again. He could tell that the silence was making her uneasy, and she soon broke it.

"Petra," she began, "you quoted the holy book not that long ago, so I was wondering if there are any other verses that you know, maybe a verse of comfort?"

"Indeed there is," Petra answered. "As one of the prophets said, 'The Lord is gracious, a steady rock in the troubled day; and He keeps watch over those who put their trust in Him.'"

Senndra was silent for several moments before she responded.

"Thanks, Petra," she finally said. "I really needed that."

An elf entered the tower, followed by countless more, all of whom moved through it and down the wall.

"Well, finally," Cirro said. "Maybe we can finally get this show on the road."

# Six

Lemin, Timothy, Vladimir, Senndra, and the rest of the cadets from the academy in Belvárd watched as rank after rank of soldiers flowed over the wall and into the city. There was already a small army inside, and not even all of the humans were inside. The last of them scaled the wall using ropes and makeshift ladders and used the gatehouse stairs to descend to the ground. For a moment all was silent on the wall then, from inside one of the towers, the elves marched in ranks down the wall. At the head of the column walked a solitary elf. He was clean-shaven and wore no helmet, so it could be seen that he had short, blond hair. His breastplate was not decorated with the same insignia as those of the men from Gatlon; instead, a picture of a sword crossed with a palm leaf graced his armor. The metal bracers on his arms could not hide the huge muscles underneath, and his greaves had a hard time containing the elf's highly muscled legs. A short sword hung at his side, and an elegant battle ax was slung on his back. He approached the grand admiral of Saddun.

"I am Grand Admiral Wellter of the city of Lêf, at your service," he said, making a fist with his right hand and hitting the left side of his chest with it. He left the fist on his chest for a second before allowing it to drop.

186

"It is I who am at your service," the grand admiral of Saddun replied, imitating the elf's gesture. "Indeed, if not for you, we would be lost. Your coming has saved us."

"Wellter?" Lemin blurted suddenly, a question on his face.

"Lemin?" the elfin grand admiral said, staring at the magician. Suddenly he was running across the wall, and then the two elves were embracing and slapping each other on the back.

"What have you been up to, you old hooligan?" Lemin asked, releasing Wellter. "A grand admiral? You must have done something with your life after I left."

"Just normal military promotion," Wellter tried to explain. But Lemin wouldn't accept that answer.

"Yeah right; I've been in the military a lot longer than you, and I never made it that high."

"I pulled off some important victories in a war in..." Wellter glanced at the nearby humans, "the land over the sea. I actually brought about the final victory which is, after all, a big deal."

"Sure, that's 'just normal military promotion,'" Lemin snorted. "I should have known that you would have been at the front of the war."

"So you have heard of it, then?" Wellter asked.

"Only bits and pieces, but I did gather that the..." Lemin coughed as he caught himself. "I did gather that *those in the north* were advancing on the city between the rivers."

"Indeed," Wellter responded. "They were trying to wipe out all of those that worship Elohim. Actually, their plan was to pass us by and attack another tribe to the south; however, that tribe was our brother in the religious sense. This, combined with the fact that they would be a threat until we confronted them, led us to attack them as they passed. This brought on a full-scale war which, thanks to Elohim, we won."

"You always have to be in the thick of things, don't you?" Lemin said with a laugh. "We can catch up later, I guess," he added. "Right now we have a battle to fight."

"You are right," Wellter said and returned to the grand admiral of Saddun. Lemin took his place among his cadets.

"So who is he?" Timothy asked in a whisper, as the formalities took place between the two grand admirals.

"In another life, I commanded a task force that was composed entirely of magicians," Lemin explained. "He was one of the magicians on my team, as was Senndra's father."

"I didn't know that you knew her father," Timothy said.

"Neither does she, and I would like to keep it that way," Lemin said. "I have my reasons for not wanting her to know, and I ask that you not tell her what you know."

"Whatever you say, sir," Timothy replied and turned his attention back to the army of elves. The formalities had been hastily completed, and the elves were now marching down the gatehouse stairs to take their place in the battle lines in the city. When the last of the army had descended from the wall, the cadets left their formation and put the finishing touches on their weapons and battle gear. Seconds later Josiah, followed by Petra and four other men, approached Lemin. Timothy recognized the other men as the commanders of the cadets from Saddun, but he would not have guessed it from their looks or the way they carried themselves. They had the rough look of men who had seen their fair share of battles, and their bearing also seemed to imply that they were much more experienced than they actually were. A map was in Josiah's hand, and when he reached the magician, he knelt down and unrolled it. Lemin and the other commanders knelt down beside him and began to point to different spots on the map and make gestures with their hands.

Timothy got close enough so that he could see what they were pointing at and overhear their conversation.

"Since you have been given additional men," Lemin was saying, "our forces combined will number around forty-five hundred. When the battle starts, we will begin to quietly work our way around to the dwarves' left flank. They shouldn't notice that our troops are not present, because as far as we know, they still think that our lines are thin. At a prearranged signal, we'll attack them on their left flank, and Grand Admiral Wellter will attack their right flank with several thousand elves. The first attack should damage them heavily, but that isn't our primary objective. If any dwarves escape from this battle and warn the main dwarf army about what has happened, it could bring their full might on our heads. Therefore, our first task when we attack is to form a line with Wellter's elves to prevent any dwarves from escaping."

"In that case, we should use a three-line containment method," Josiah said. "We have six groups of soldiers, so if we put two in each line it will give us three lines of defense as a safeguard."

"That would have the same men doing the majority of the fighting," Lemin objected. "If the battle was going to be short, that might work, but it could go on for some time."

"Josiah is right," Smether said. "The way the three-line containment is taught here is that when the first line has to rest, the second line steps up directly behind them. The first line then falls back through the second line, drops to the back of the formation, and forms the third line. Every time the first line needs a replacement we do this, so that we can hold out for as long as possible."

The five cadet commanders looked at Lemin as he thought the idea over. Finally he looked at them.

"I'll send a message to Wellter telling him of this strategy. We need to have the whole line on the same page, or the enemy will find a way through our ranks.

"Now, this is the second part of the plan. Some of the best magicians in the elf army are in Wellter's legions, and they will be weaving an invisible spell over themselves so the enemy will not be able to see them. When the signal is given to attack, we will attack first so that the enemies look toward us. This will give the elves the backs of the dwarves to attack. The effort of sustaining their invisibility spell will consume a large amount of energy, so they will have to drop it before they charge. This means that we need to have the dwarves looking solely at us by the time the elves move forward."

Timothy had heard enough, so he drifted away from the collaborating officers. Vladimir, Senndra, Rita, and several other cadets were standing in a group talking, but their conversation ceased when Timothy neared. He took a place in their group and looked at Vladimir as he began talking.

"So what did you hear over there?" he asked. The cadets waited expectantly, so Timothy answered as best he could.

"Just the battle plan for tomorrow. Actually, the one for today," he corrected himself and gestured toward the horizon. A glimmer of light was beginning to show to the east, and soldiers from the army of Magessa were scurrying to take their positions in the battle lines.

"So what's the plan? A head-on attack? "Senndra asked. Apparently she had gotten over her anger enough to talk to him again.

"No, the grand admirals are worried about some dwarves escaping and telling the main army about the defeat. So some elves and we cadets are going to be flanking them and forming a wall to keep them from escaping. As near as I can figure, this will put roughly half our men behind them and half in front. And given the number of dwarves that remain in the city, we should have a relatively simple time of eradicating them."

"So what is the estimate of enemies left in the city?" Vladimir asked.

"Somewhere between five and ten thousand," Timothy answered.

The order to form battle lines was quietly passed down the wall, and the cadets began to file off the wall to where Lemin awaited them on the ground. As Timothy got in line, a smile broke across his face—a stark contrast to the grim looks of the other soldiers.

"What are you so happy about?" Vladimir asked.

"It seems like this battle has taken a lifetime," Timothy answered. "And for that lifetime, I have always feared for my life, wondering when the dwarves would attack next and if they would kill us on their next onslaught. But things have changed now. For the first time, we actually have a good chance of beating these blivits, and that has my spirits very high."

******

The sun was just peaking over the hills to the east, its rays glinting on the armor of the army arrayed at the south end of the city. The dwarves were just stirring. All of their sentries were asleep or had simply not spotted the army as of yet. To the east and west of the dwarf army, legions of soldiers were moving into position on either flank. Soon all would be ready for attack.

The remainder of the cadet army moved through the abandoned city and congregated at the ambush position. Josiah's men were already in position, waiting only for the signal to spring from their hiding place and attack. Josiah stood at the head of his legion, now a little less than eight hundred strong. Cirro stood at his side, a large battle ax clasped in his hands. He was muttering to himself, clearly anxious to get past the waiting and start the fighting. Josiah glanced backwards and saw his men standing rank upon rank in perfect order. A fierce glint shown in their eyes, reflecting the past fighting; they were ready to finish the battle.

A shout sounded from the dwarf camp; they had finally spotted the enemy army. Josiah glanced at the camp and saw dwarves scurrying from their tents, half-dressed and trying to form some military semblance. He shifted his gaze to Lemin just in time to see the grand admiral give the signal to attack. In one fluid motion, he jerked his sword from its scabbard and thrust it toward the enemy, all while shouting a battle cry. Battle frenzy was suddenly upon him and he charged toward the enemy, not even looking to make sure that his men were following him. To him, it appeared as though everything was in exaggerated detail. As he burst from the buildings and into the open, the dwarves looked his way. He could see their startled and terrified expressions, but he didn't think about them or anything else. He could see Wellter's elves charging from across the city, but the dwarves were as yet oblivious to them. The army to the south was waiting for the other two armies to form a wall behind the dwarves before attacking.

Josiah hit the army with the fury of a madman. His sword flashed through the air, killing and maiming enemies in droves. Beside him, Cirro whirled his ax furiously, swinging the weapon every which way to ward off the dwarves. Josiah's men were hot on his heels, their numbers crushing many dwarves on impact. As they engaged the enemy, elves and cadets met to form a wall, blocking the dwarves' only escape route. The trap was finally complete, and the army to the south began to charge, pressing the dwarves on a new front. The dwarves quickly found themselves overextended. They tried to fall away from the onslaught of the army to the south, but the line of defenders to the north held them in the city. In less than fifteen minutes, their numbers were cut in half. Finally they were able to pull themselves into a military formation, but by this time, the army of Magessa had completely surrounded them, forcing them to form a circle with all sides facing outward. Then the second stage of the battle began. Archers had scaled the northern walls of the city and began to pelt the dwarves with a hail of missiles, decreasing their numbers greatly. The infantry had only to contain them to an area, as the archers steadily cut them down to only a few hundred dwarves. Finally, the rain of arrows ceased, and Wellter approached the dwarf lines. "Surrender and we will spare you," he said. "Throw down your weapons and you shall live; fight on and you will surely die."

The dwarves were silent, though fear showed clearly on their faces. Slowly, a murmur spread through their ranks, followed by a nervous shuffling. Then, hesitantly at first, they began to lay down their weapons until almost half their number had disarmed themselves; the other dwarves, however, clung stubbornly to their weapons. The unarmed dwarves began to quickly separate themselves from their armed comrades, knowing that the humans and elves would attack them. Almost before anyone knew what was happening, the dwarves were clearly split, and the soldiers of Magessa looked to their leaders.

"Only those who have refused to surrender will die," Wellter shouted. "Forward, and may Elohim be with us!"

The soldiers surrounding the dwarves pushed inward with a mighty shout. They parted as they reached the unarmed enemies, leaving soldiers to guard them; then they hit the remnant of the dwarf army. Though they were few in number, the dwarves fought fiercely, bringing the charge to a halt. They knew that this was life or death, and this fear fueled them.

Josiah saw the assault grind to a halt. Before him, soldiers threw themselves at the dwarf line, trying to break through, but nobody was able to succeed. He glanced around and saw his legion broken apart, fighting in a confused fashion. Soldiers darted this way and that with no strategy to their movements. Solitary men charged the dwarves, trying to force their way through the wall of stout men. Soldiers without comrades to watch their backs rushed into the fighting and were killed almost instantly. The army was falling apart, and Josiah knew that if something was not done soon, even a victory would be costly. He leaped onto a pile of dead dwarves and waved his sword in the air.

"To me!" he shouted to the soldiers. He noticed a standard of Magessa lying on the ground. It was torn and had blood splattered on it, but the silver cross showed clearly through the grime. Retrieving it from where it was being trampled underfoot, he clambered on top of an abandoned crate from the dwarf camp. He raised the banner in the air and again gave the rallying cry. This time the soldiers took notice and began to gather around him. In only a few minutes, several hundred soldiers, both human and elfish, had congregated. Absentmindedly, he wished that he could lead a truly organized assault, but he knew that the group of men around him attacking as one body just might be enough to destroy the dwarves. With the standard still in his hand, he gave a shout, leaped from the crate, and rushed at the dwarf line. With his left hand, he pulled his sword from its sheath, and raised it above his head. When he hit the dwarf line, he blocked an ax with the banner and smashed through the dwarves, his sword flashing. To either side of him, he could see soldiers hitting the seemingly solid line of dwarves, forcing them to give way. The soldiers swept forward, a wave impervious to any attempt to stop it, and soon the fight was over.

Josiah raised the banner of Magessa in triumph. Then he rammed the pole into the ground, marking the site of victory. He slowly wiped and sheathed his sword, slightly dejected, but also very relieved that the battle was over. His eyes swept the city that had been the field of battle. Once it had been the proud center of training for army officers, but now it was the scene of carnage and misery. The northern wall was largely destroyed, and many of the buildings had been burned or knocked down. Dead soldiers littered the ground, their weapons lying beside them and their armor torn and dirty. The wounded cried out in pain, and the dying gasped out their final breaths. Josiah's jubilance slowly drained out as he took in the other side of winning a battle. Death and agony were the companions of both the victors and the vanquished. Josiah heard a cry for water and wasted no time in heading for a well that was in the center of the city. He couldn't take away the agony of his comrades, but he could at least try to ease it.

****** 

Senndra sat with her back against a broken wall. Her weapons lay on the ground beside her where she had dropped them when the fighting had stopped. Her clothes were torn, and her armor was dented. The left leg of her pants had been cut and rolled back to reveal a nasty-looking gash that extended from just above her knee all the way down to her ankle. She tore off a piece of her sleeve and painfully bent over to apply it to her wound. Blood quickly soaked the make-shift bandage, so she placed the other sleeve of her uniform over the first. The flow of blood, which had not been too fast at first, eventually slowed to a stop, and Senndra tied her bandage in place with strips of her ruined pant leg. Before rising, she retrieved her weapons and replaced them on her back. Slowly she got to her feet and looked around at the soldiers nearest her, hoping to see a familiar face. She didn't see any, so she started to hobble across the city, asking the soldiers she met if they knew if there was a hospital set up yet. A man of about thirty years told her that there was a hospital in one of the old barracks and offered to help her there, but she declined the offer, assuring him that she could make it on her own. The short distance to the hospital took her more than half an hour to cover. She struggled on, gritting her teeth against the pain. Her vision blurred, and she stumbled frequently, but she stubbornly continued forward. Finally she met another man who offered to help her to the hospital. Again she refused the offer. The man ignored her protest, put her arm over his shoulder, and half-carried her the rest of the distance. At the door of the hospital, the man released her, and she entered the building. Suddenly having to bear her own weight again threw her off balance, and she staggered. She couldn't think through the buzzing sound that filled her head, but she knew that she was falling and couldn't catch herself. She heard a sound that seemed very distant and felt arms catching her. Slowly her vision cleared and she found herself looking at a cadet she thought she knew.

"Cirro?" she asked slowly.

"Yes," Cirro replied. "Don't worry. I've got you. Here, sit down against the wall."

He helped Senndra to the ground and carefully examined her leg. Slowly he peeled the bandage away from the wound, trying to cause as little pain as possible. Even so, Senndra's leg jerked weakly, and she slumped forward in a faint. Cirro removed the bandage from the laceration and grimaced as he looked at it. The cut was very deep, even reaching the bone at one point. Dirt and grime covered it, so Cirro reached for his water skin and washed it out.

*"At least it looks as though the weapon that cut her wasn't poisoned,"* he thought. *"That's a reason to be thankful."*

He dug some thread and a needle out of one of the pouches on his belt and turned back to Senndra. He carefully threaded the needle and then sized up her wound. Though it was deep, it was bleeding only a little and appeared as though the two sides would sew back together cleanly. He started the operation, knotting the end of his thread and systematically piercing the skin on either side of the gash with the needle. The tear in the flesh closed steadily until Cirro put in the last stitch, expertly tied off the thread, and cut it. He put the materials back into his belt pouch, lifted Senndra from the ground, and carried her into the barracks in search of an empty bed. Already the building was filling with casualties, but there were perhaps several hundred beds left. Cirro left Senndra in one of them and headed back out to the battle field.

\*\*\*\*\*\*

Vladimir rolled a dead dwarf off of his legs and left arm and wiped his sword on its tunic. He slid the weapon back into its sheath and started to rise to his feet. Pain shot through his right leg, and he slumped to the ground again. He tried to pull himself to a nearby barrel, but when he put weight on his left arm, pain coursed through it. This time he fell on his face. Carefully he worked himself into a sitting position and looked at his arm. A knife handle protruded from the rear side of the upper part of the limb. Vladimir carefully gripped the weapon, but he accidentally bumped his elbow against his knee, jarring the knife. Pain swept up and down his arm, paralyzing his movement for several seconds. The pain cleared and he gripped the weapon again, but released it as he remembered the pain of upsetting the wound. Steeling his nerve, he slowly wrapped his fingers around the handle again and took a deep breath. Slowly he drew the knife out of his arm, fighting the pain that shot through his body like fire. When he had extracted the weapon, he flung it to the side and began to gently examine the wound.

"Vladimir, what do you think you're doing?"

Vladimir looked up to see Timothy approaching. He didn't look at all the worse for wear despite the recent battle. But Vladimir speculated that he had probably just healed himself with magic.

"I was taking that knife out of my arm," he said and pointed at the discarded weapon. "It hurt like hellfire, but I did get it out."

"You should have waited until someone could help you," Timothy reprimanded Vladimir. He knelt down to examine the wound. "I probably could have gotten it out with magic."

"Nope," Vladimir answered confidently. "It was made out of silver. You know how silver is very, um, explosive when it comes in contact with magic. If you had tried to take that knife out with magic, my arm probably would have blown up. Which," he added with a pain-filled grin, "would have been pretty cool to see, but I think that I would have regretted it later."

The blank expression on Timothy's face changed to a smile. Then, with a shake of his head, he turned back to the wound and placed his hand over it while concentrating. A tingling sensation traveled from Timothy into Vladimir's arm, and when Timothy took his hand away a second later, there was only the faintest scar to show where the wound had been. Vladimir flexed his arm and twisted it around, looking at it from all sides.

"Well," he said with a shake of his head, "that sure beats having it stitched up and waiting several weeks for it to heal."

"You're as good as new," Timothy said and slapped Vladimir on the back. "Now let's see about helping the rest of the wounded out there."

"I can hardly walk," Vladimir answered. "I think my leg may be broken." Timothy made a move to heal his leg, but Vladimir stopped him. "Don't waste your energy on that," he said. "There are a lot more life-threatening conditions out there, and until all of them are taken care of, I don't want to see you wasting energy on a mere broken leg."

"Very well," Timothy said. "A hospital is being organized in the barracks, so if you head over there, someone can probably fix you up the old fashioned way. Good luck."

"Don't slow yourself down too much thinking about me," Vladimir called and began the painful trek to the barracks.

"Slow down thinking about you?" Timothy said over his shoulder. "What makes you think that I care that much?"

Vladimir smiled at the lame attempt at humor and hobbled toward the barracks with the aid of a broken pole that had once held a standard. Every time he took a step, pain shot through his body attesting to the many aches and pains he had received in the battle. Absentmindedly wishing that magic could cure everything, he rounded a corner, and the barracks were finally in sight. Someone had taken a cloth and nailed a large red cross over the door of the middle building. As Vladimir neared the building, he made out the form of a soldier that had fallen only a few yards from the entrance. He hobbled over to the man and painfully knelt down next to him. As he searched for a wound, he felt for a pulse on the man's neck. He could find no pulse and rolled the man onto his stomach, looking for the cause of death. The sight that met his eyes made him vomit; the blade of a dwarfish ax had carved an ugly gash from the right shoulder of the soldier down to his left hip. In the middle of the wound, Vladimir could see the man's spinal cord had been smashed. There were hundreds of shards of bone attesting to its previous existence. Vladimir vomited again and leaned against the wall of the barracks, turning his eyes away from this gruesome sight of death. He slowly pulled himself to his feet and staggered toward the entrance of the makeshift hospital. Even as he moved, the moan of a wounded man floated to his ears, and he turned to look out into the city. With a sigh, he began again his slow trek into the hospital. Heaven knew that if he had had the strength to help the wounded, he would have; but his own wounds had weakened him to the extent that he could hardly stand. Moving toward the back of the barracks, he collapsed in the first empty bed that he came to.

# Seven

Josiah rubbed his eyes, trying very hard not to fall asleep before he undressed. The day had dragged on as he had helped countless wounded, both friends and enemies. By the time all of the wounded had been moved into one of the barracks, the sun had set. And at the moment, Josiah wanted nothing more than to crawl into a tent and fall asleep. Just after he had pulled off his boots, however, Cirro stuck his head into the tent.

"What?" Josiah asked groggily. He rubbed his eyes again and then stared at Cirro through blurry eyes.

"The grand admiral wants you at his headquarters right away," Cirro stated.

Josiah sighed heavily and began to pull his boots back on. The thought of spending even more time awake didn't appeal to him, not to mention the fact that the grand admiral would probably want him to be able to think.

"Do you have any idea what he wants?" Josiah asked as he rose to his feet.

"Not officially," Cirro answered.

"If I thought you knew officially, I would have asked you what he wanted, not if you had any *idea* what he wanted," Josiah responded. "What's the latest rumor going around?"

"Most people think he is going to discuss what to do about the dwarves that are headed toward Belmoth," Cirro said.

"Oh joy," Josiah groaned with a shake of his head. "That's just what I need. We'll be making decisions that could cost people their lives, and we haven't had a decent night's sleep in more than three days."

"I suppose that's the way this business goes, Commander," Cirro answered. He held the tent flap open as Josiah stepped out into the open.

"When I come back, I'll probably have bad news for you, Cirro," Josiah called over his shoulder as he left. "You'd better get your weapons ready; my guess is that we'll be chasing those blasted dwarves."

He heaved another sigh as he headed toward the grand admiral's office just to let anyone within hearing distance know that he was not pleased.

"Not that there's anybody out here," he said out loud. "Everyone with half a brain in his head is already in bed."

"Thanks for the compliment," a voice close by said, startling Josiah. He spun around and saw Lemin emerge from an alley.

"Well, with all due respect, Admiral, what in heaven's name are you doing still awake?" Josiah asked.

"Probably the same thing you're doing," Lemin replied. "The grand admiral of the academy asked for my attendance in his office."

"Yeah, that's where I'm going," Josiah replied. "I just hope that we make the right decision," he added as he started walking again. "I mean, none of us has had a real night's sleep in several days. And I don't know about the others, but I think it's beginning to affect my thinking."

"You may be right," Lemin answered. The two companions were silent until they reached the headquarters of the grand admiral. As they passed through the doors of the building, Lemin said, "Yes, you are correct in saying that sleep deprivation might affect our thinking. But one thing is certain, if we are to defend Magessa as we have sworn to do, we have to decide what to do immediately. All we can do at the moment is what we think is right, and may Elohim help us."

"Amen," Josiah responded and came to a halt in front of the door to the grand admiral's office. "Speaking of which, I suppose that we should ask Elohim for guidance before we go into this meeting."

"You are right," Lemin said. He bowed his head and began to pray. "Almighty God, we thank you for providing deliverance from the dwarves, but now we are faced with another dilemma. Please give us your guidance and wisdom as we go into this meeting. Help us to come to a conclusion that is from you. Amen."

Josiah raised his head and saw that Lemin was already entering the grand admiral's office, so he quickly followed. Inside, seated or standing around a large, round table were the grand admiral of Saddun, Grand Admiral Wellter, General Uriah, various generals of the army from Gatlon, and the other four commanders of the Saddun army. Of these four, Josiah recognized two—Velikogo and Smether. Josiah had heard that the other two had fallen in battle, and he figured that these new faces were their replacements. Other men that he didn't recognize were also present, bringing the number of those present to just over twenty.

"I don't think we can give chase to the army at the moment," was the first thing that Josiah heard as he entered the room. This comment came from a man who was standing on the far side of the room.

"I didn't realize that whether or not we chase the enemy was the question at hand," Lemin shot back. Every head in the room turned to face the newcomers who had apparently entered the room quietly enough to prevent earlier detection. Lemin stepped up to the table that filled a large portion of the room and leaned his hands on it.

"I know, General," he said, addressing the man who had spoken, "that you took an oath to protect Magessa; is that not correct?"

"That is correct, sir," the man answered shortly.

"Then it would seem to me that it is your duty to plan how you are going to counter this threat to the country, not to cower inside your castle and hope that others will do the work that is appointed to you." Lemin glared at the general until the other's eyes dropped in shame.

"In my opinion," Lemin said as he straightened and clasped his hands behind his back, "we were put here in this position at this time so that we can help defend Magessa. While others might make the decision to ignore the threat due to personal safety, we have the chance to make the decision that is hard to make: the decision to do what is right. Indeed, what is right is almost always hard to do."

"You said that we were put here for a reason," another general from the army of Gatlon spoke up. "Put here by whom?" Lemin looked the man straight in the eyes.

"Put here by Elohim," Josiah answered before Lemin could speak. The general who had posed the question snorted.

"Well, it looks like someone here still believes in bedtime stories. Don't tell me that you actually believe in Elohim. If he's real, where's your proof that he exists?"

"Look around you, man," Lemin almost shouted. "The trees, the hills, the animals, all of the races; who do you think made all of these? If you do not believe in Elohim, then how did all of this come into existence? And if that isn't enough proof for you," Lemin snapped his fingers, and flames sprang to life on their tips. With an upward motion, Lemin sent the flames floating toward the ceiling, changing shapes as they went. When they reached the ceiling, they changed into a single column that shot downwards and was absorbed by Lemin's hand.

"Then again," Lemin said as he finished his display, "we aren't here to discuss Elohim. We're here to discuss what to do about the dwarf army that remains." He reached for a map that was rolled up on the table and unrolled it to reveal Magessa and the surrounding lands. "The dwarves left the city and are traveling west, probably staying very close to the Apathy range. If we leave a small force here to protect the city, we can take the rest of the army after the dwarves. A messenger can take a horse further north, pass the dwarves, and take a warning to Belmoth."

"Better yet," Wellter said as he rose to his feet. "We can split our army into two parts. The human part can follow the dwarves along the range, and the elves can go further north, pass the dwarves, and come up in front of them. This way, we might be able to force them to fight on the plain where all of their siege equipment will be useless. Of course, either way…"

"We're in trouble if we don't get dragon support," one of the new commanders of Saddun's army finished. Wellter nodded and sat back down.

"There's a station of dragons somewhere in the southern end of the Orc range," someone offered.

"Yes, there is," Lemin acknowledged, "but by the time our messenger finds the station and the dragons fly up to the battle, it could be too late. No, I think the Belvárd academy is our best bet."

"One problem there," Josiah objected. "There's no pass across the range, so the messengers will have to go around. They'll never make it in time."

"The two cadets that I have in mind for this task are exceptional," Lemin answered. "They'll cross the range, and if they can get to the academy in record time, this crazy plan might actually work."

The grand admiral of Saddun looked at those around him as though searching for advice. He leaned his elbow on the table and rubbed his face with his hand. His gaze drifted around the room again and finally came to rest on Grand Admiral Wellter. Wellter gave a shrug and spoke up.

"Personally, I think this plan is our best bet for defeating those dwarves. Of course, our numbers are rather thin, but there are still enough men to work with. Obviously we want to have a strong force to strike the rear of the enemy. But on the other hand, we don't want too small of a force at their head. I'll take maybe eight thousand elves around to the front of the dwarf army, while the rest of the soldiers will strike at the rear."

"But that leaves no one to defend Saddun," a general objected.

"True," Wellter admitted.

"On the contrary," the grand admiral of Saddun interjected. "That messenger said that one of his brothers had been sent to the ogres." He turned to Wellter. "Do you know if they are coming to our aid?"

"I should have thought of that," Wellter said. "They are only a day's march away."

"How do you know that?" a general asked.

"We elves have our ways of knowing these things," Wellter said. "You can rest assured that the ogres are coming."

"The ogres would be a great advantage in the battle," Lemin put in. "Perhaps we should leave some humans to defend Saddun and take the ogres to the battle."

"Two problems there," Josiah spoke up. "First, the ogres are a day's march away. We'll have to leave now if we hope to catch the dwarves before they reach Belmoth. Second, while the ogres were willing to come and help to defend Saddun, they may not want to march out against the dwarves with us." A contemplating silence followed, but was finally broken by Wellter.

"The fact that the ogres are a day away is no problem," he countered. "They are quick and can catch up to us easily. In respect to the other worry, though you humans do not have the best relationship with the ogres, we elves are very friendly with them. I think that if I leave an elf here to voice the request, they will follow."

"In that case, you should take all of the elves to the front of the dwarf army," the grand admiral of Saddun said to Wellter. "If the ogres bring two or three thousand soldiers to swell our numbers at their flank, that will more than make up for the elves."

"Quite so," Wellter laughed. "Considering that I will only be taking about a thousand elves from the rear. Besides that, I would count on between four and five thousand ogres. They may be a small nation, but when they turn out to fight, their numbers are surprising."

"That will put nine thousand elves at the army's head and six thousand humans plus the ogres and a few orcs at their rear," Lemin confirmed. "Make that three thousand humans plus the ogres and orcs," he corrected himself. "We're going to have to leave someone to defend this city.

"The enemy has an unknown number of soldiers, but our estimates are that they could have anywhere from fifty to seventy-five thousand. No matter which way you look at it, this battle is going to go badly unless we get dragon support."

"What about additional support from the elves?" Josiah asked Wellter.

"The forest across the mountains is sending an army that has probably three or four times the number of elves that we have now, but they won't get here for days. It could take as long as two weeks for them to arrive."

The Grand Admiral of Saddun finally spoke, commanding the attention of every man in the room.

"There's only one thing that worries me. Why did the dwarves discontinue their attack against this city? They could have crushed us if they continued the offensive."

"Their plan depended on speed and surprise," Lemin responded instantly. "I assure you that I have thought over these same events many times, and that is the only reasonable explanation. They expected to take the city so quickly that we would not be able to send messengers to the rest of Magessa. When we held them off, they made the most of their situation by leaving a token attack force here to trick us into thinking that they were still here. Our messengers would bring the armies of Magessa to this place, while the main body of the dwarf army would attack Belmoth and take it quickly since they would not be expecting the attack. With all of Magessa's armies here, they would be free to attack the rest of the country."

"How in heaven's name could the dwarves think that this would work?" the Grand Admiral of Saddun asked. "You're trying to tell me that they evacuated 75,000 soldiers from the city and hoped that we wouldn't notice? That seems unlikely."

"We wouldn't have noticed if it wasn't for the magicians here," Lemin countered. "Sure, we would have noticed tomorrow, but they think that damage is already done. With the armies of the country headed to Saddun, we would have to send messengers to find them once we realized what was happening, a process that would take days. As I said, their plan is all about speed and surprise, and in this case, misdirection."

"So, let's say that I subscribe to your theory," the Grand Admiral of Saddun said. "What then?"

"If that is indeed the case, we won't have to worry about the city," Josiah commented. "We could probably take all of the soldiers here with us without concern of a repeat attack."

"That is not a good idea," an elfin general said. "The three thousand men will be sorely missed at the battle; however, if any renegade dwarves wander back this way, we need to have a force here, however small, to beat them off."

"In either case," Lemin said, "the messengers will have the academy send dragons here as well as to the battle."

"So let me get this straight," Wellter interrupted. "I will take my soldiers around to the front of the dwarf army while the humans here and the ogres that are coming will attack at the rear of their army, leaving only a force of three thousand to defend Saddun. While we are moving into position, two messengers will be racing to the academy in Belvárd to get us air support. The academy will send dragons to both the battle and here to Saddun. We can attack the dwarves while they are sandwiched between the marsh and the mountains. The terrain will compress their battle lines and prevent them from circling around us. Two large armies, one elfin and the other from Magessa, are coming to this city, so when we defeat the dwarves, we should move to Belmoth to defend it against any attacks. This position will assure Magessa's defense for the moment until we can sort out the situation."

The next hour was spent ironing out the details of the campaign. Josiah found most of this very boring and wished that he was in bed. Only one part of the entire meeting interested him—the point when it was decided who would go to the battle and who would stay in Saddun. Lemin volunteered his cadets to guard the city. There were no people enthusiastic enough to undertake the responsibility so several companies of soldiers were ordered to join Lemin's cadets. It was suggested that Josiah's soldiers should also stay in the city, but Grand Admiral Wellter would not hear of it. The cadets' performance in the last battle had been so exemplary that the idea of them staying behind was quickly discarded. The discussion turned to other details, and Josiah listened, but did not participate. The only other detail that he caught was when the army was supposed to leave the city. Everything after that was a blur. He vaguely remembered walking from the grand admiral's headquarters to his tent and telling the legion's watchman what time he wanted to be awakened. The last thing he remembered was falling into bed.

The next morning came much too early for Josiah. He was awoken by one of his men, and as he sat pulling on his boots, he realized that he had only gotten a couple hours of sleep. Slowly he stood to his feet, stretched, and stepped out of the tent. His four remaining captains were lined up in front of him, and to their extreme right was Cirro. He was holding Josiah's sword and armor, as was his custom. He approached Josiah quickly and started to help him into the equipment, but Josiah silently refused the help and performed the task himself. When he had finished, he took the sword from Cirro and strapped it around his waist, straightened, and looked at his captains. His attention was immediately drawn to the fifth empty spot.

"Yesterday's battle was brutal to us," he said after a moment of consideration. "Our ranks have been diminished to such an extent that we no longer have enough soldiers for five companies. The soldiers from Captain Terza's company will be redistributed to replenish your ranks. Keep in mind that we will be fighting alongside soldiers of the highest caliber so be sure to control your soldiers in such a way that would bring honor to Gatlon and Magessa. The army will be leaving in an hour. You are dismissed."

\*\*\*\*\*\*

Senndra yawned and raised her head from her pillow. Pain immediately flooded her skull, and she fell back onto the bed. Shaking her head to clear the mental fog, she slowly slid her feet over the edge of the bed and sat up. Every bone in her body ached, but she wasn't about to let that stop her from getting up.

"You okay?"

Senndra slowly raised her head to see Vladimir sitting on the bed opposite hers. He was dressed in his cadet uniform, and though it was a little tattered, he looked fairly presentable. Senndra looked down at her own clothes and realized for the first time since she had awoken that she was dressed in her battle uniform. Though her armor and weapons lay on the floor at the foot of her bed, the rest of the outfit was as she imagined it should be. Her clothes were torn and dirty, and the left leg of her pants was split up to the knee. She remembered the wound in her leg, but strangely she felt no pain there. Painfully she bent at the waist and used her hands to probe the skin on her leg for the wound.

"You won't find it," Vladimir said.

"What?" Senndra asked as she sat up.

"The wound on your leg," Vladimir answered. "Some of the elfin magicians came through here before they left this morning and healed many of the major wounds. I used to have a broken leg, but they fixed it up just fine," he finished and gave his leg a pat.

"So the elves came in here before they left," Senndra repeated. Suddenly her eyes flew open in realization. "They came here before they *left*? Where did they go?"

"After the dwarf army," another voice answered. Senndra turned to see Timothy approaching. "What are you doing, Vladimir? Telling her just enough to answer the questions? If I were you, she would have already known all about that."

"Then tell me about it," Senndra said.

"The majority of the army is chasing down the dwarves before they get to Belmoth," Timothy began, but Senndra interrupted him.

"Belmoth?" she said. "Because that would give them an easier entrance into the country!"

"That's what we think," Timothy agreed. "Since Belmoth has not received news of our attack yet, the dwarves will be able to take them by surprise. Plus, all of the armies of Magessa are probably rushing here in answer to our messengers, so Belmoth will be a prime target for the dwarves."

"So who's chasing them?" Senndra asked. She slid down to the foot of her bed and began to strap her greaves on.

"The elves and some three or four thousand men," Timothy answered. "Rumor has it that an army of ogres will arrive here tonight, and they will be sent to aid in the battle. Speaking of which," Timothy said, directing his next statement to Vladimir, "we just got a part in this battle."

"Yes!" Vladimir yelled as he jumped up from the bed on which he was seated. "It's about time. So what are we doing?"

"You and I are going to be messengers," Timothy answered.

"Messengers?" Vladimir spat in disgust. "What kind of a job is that?"

"A better one than you might think," Timothy answered. "The alternative is to stay here in Saddun in case of another attack. Besides, there's a reason they need a magician on this assignment."

"You're starting to make it sound exciting," Vladimir said. "So where are we going, and what message are we carrying?"

"You might want to sit down again before I tell you," Timothy said. "We are going back to the academy and taking a message for help."

"*The* academy? As in the one in Belvárd?" Vladimir asked in disbelief. "And what help do we need now? We already won the battle."

"If you would stop interrupting, you would find out sooner," Timothy answered. "We have to get to the academy and tell them to send dragons to reinforce our armies in the upcoming battle with the dwarves."

Vladimir nodded then suddenly froze.

"How long do we have to make the journey?" he asked. "That battle is going to happen a long time before we can reach the academy, unless...don't tell me that we're going over the mountains."

"And running the whole way too, so you'd better leave most of your things here," Timothy said.

"Why running?" Vladimir asked. "We have horses; why not ride them? Wouldn't we travel faster?"

"Horses can't cross the mountains," Timothy answered. "If we rode, we would have to go around the bottom of the range, making the journey almost three times as long. Running will be slower to be sure, but we'll get there sooner this way."

"You know, I think that I might want to stay here instead," Vladimir said.

"Okay," Timothy responded. "I should be able to make the journey by myself." He turned and started to walk away, but Vladimir ran after him.

"You know what? I just changed my mind. I think that I want to come with you."

"Then get ready," Timothy said. "We leave in an hour."

"Right," Vladimir said and dashed out of the barracks, presumably to pack some belongings. Timothy waited for Vladimir to disappear through the door before turning back to Senndra.

"So I found these laying on the ground somewhere," Timothy said. He handed Senndra her sword and bow which she laid on the bed beside her.

"Thank you," she said, but he didn't move. "Was there something else?"

"Do you want to talk yet?"

"About what?" Senndra looked up at Timothy. As tall as he was already, this was definitely not a dominant position, something that she would need if this was the argument that she thought was coming.

"You know what I'm talking about," Timothy said. Senndra rose to her feet, but a wave of pain shot through her skull in protest. Timothy's next statement was cut short as he reached forward to keep her from falling.

"Are you alright?" he asked as he helped her sit back on the bed.

"Yes," Senndra answered. "Just a little light-headed from lying down for so long."

"Well," Timothy said. "I know you're probably feeling like the back end of a horse right about now, but I'm not sure when I'll see you again, so I'm not leaving until I've said what I have to say."

"That's fine," Senndra answered. "Just say it down here where I can actually see you."

Timothy crouched in front of Senndra, but to her annoyance, he was still taller. The bed that she was sitting on had to be as short as possible without actually resting on the floor. She shook her head and motioned down again.

"Really?" Timothy asked. "You want me to get on my knees."

Senndra shrugged.

"Whatever it takes to bring you to my eye level."

"Fine," Timothy said, a slight smile playing across his lips. He sank to one knee and looked straight into Senndra's eyes. "Is this low enough?"

"I suppose so," Senndra conceded.

"Good," Timothy said. "I know that you're mad at me for not telling you about my being a magician. Even though I had my reasons, I understand if you're angry and don't want to talk to me. I only ask that you listen to what I have to say.

"I never intended to hurt you or anyone else by keeping this secret. I don't know, maybe I should have been more up front about it. Whatever the case, if you still want to be friends, you need to know right now that I have more secrets than just being a magician. I have good reasons for keeping them, but that doesn't make it any easier. I might tell you what they are eventually, but as of now, they aren't things that I want to share.

"In light of this, I'll understand if you don't trust me anymore, but I wanted to let you know that I never meant to upset you or anyone else. I hope we can still be friends."

Timothy waited on his knee for several seconds, hoping for a response. Senndra was silent, so he stood and was about to leave the barracks when she spoke.

"Of course I still want to be your friend, Timothy," Senndra said. "Under one condition."

"That depends, what is it?" Timothy asked warily. He assumed that all hard feelings had been dispensed with, but that was no reason to agree to something blindly.

"You have to help me stand up without falling on my face or passing out," Senndra said. "I've been down here for so long I think I'll do one or the other if I try to stand by myself."

"You've got yourself a deal," Timothy said. He offered Senndra his hand and pulled her to her feet, maintaining the grip long enough to make sure that she wouldn't fall.

"Well, you have a mission to prepare for, don't you?" Senndra asked. "You'd better get to it."

"You're going to be alright now?" Timothy asked.

"As long as I take it slow," Senndra assured him. "Those elves might have fixed me up, but I'm still ridiculously sore."

"And we're good?" Timothy asked. He was backing toward the barrack's door now.

"Yes, we're good," Senndra laughed. The small motion made her ribs ache. "Go get ready for your thing."

Timothy jogged out of the barracks, and Senndra followed at a leisurely pace. She squinted as her eyes adjusted to the sunshine and was about to start walking when she realized that she was all alone. She didn't know where any of her friends were except for Vladimir and Timothy and they were going to be leaving soon. As she looked around, her gaze came to rest on another cadet that was coming her way. The long, flowing blond hair gave the cadet away immediately, and Senndra walked out to meet Rita. When the two friends met, they embraced each other.

"I wondered what happened to you," Senndra said over Rita's shoulder. "I haven't seen you since the beginning of this battle. Where have you been?"

"Probably doing the same thing as you," Rita said, releasing Senndra. "I did my part to hold back the dwarves and defeat them."

"You did all of that without a scratch?" Senndra asked. "That's better than I did. You should have seen what a mess I was yesterday. I thought that I was supposed to be the better sword fighter."

"Apparently skill isn't everything," Rita responded. "Sometimes it's better to be lucky than good. So tell me everything that happened since we last saw each other, and I'll show you the way to our tent."

"There's almost too much to tell," Senndra said as the girls walked off. "In fact, I don't think that you would believe half of the things that I've been through."

\*\*\*\*\*\*

Timothy, Vladimir, and Lemin stood at the gate of the south wall of Saddun saying their last farewells. There were no idle words wasted as the cadets received last-minute directions from their instructor. With a firm handshake from both boys, Lemin said good-bye, and the two cadets were off. The ground sloped gently upward, but it was maybe a mile to the real mountains. They ran, knowing that this was some of the easiest terrain they would encounter on their journey. Since speed was of the essence, they had packed very little. They brought only water, food for five days, and the clothes on their backs. The two cadets were very physically fit, but this journey would still push them to their limits. They had more than two hundred miles to traverse, and the first twenty-five miles were through the mountains. But they were still confident that they could make it to the academy before the battle with the dwarves began. The first mile passed quickly, and the boys were moving into the real mountains. The trail, such as it was, seemed to seek out the steepest, most treacherous slopes to scale, and the boys had trouble just avoiding injury as they ran. To make matters worse, a forest began shortly after the mountain did, and they had to deal with the underbrush and tree branches. They reached the peak of the first mountain and took the path downward. The going was faster now, but the trails were even more treacherous going down. At the bottom of the mountain, the trail disappeared, so Timothy and Vladimir took a gully that ran between two mountains. The gully seemed to be a dried creek bed, and they were able to make relatively good time as they ran up it. They granted themselves a rest at the head of the creek, and estimated that they had come close to seven or eight miles so far. After a short break, they continued at a more relaxed pace. The urgency of their mission never left their minds though, and at the peak of the next mountain, they began to run again.

The scenery rushed by too quickly for the cadets to see, but if they had had more time, they might have observed that the forest abounded with all kinds of animals. Deer ran through the trees, and birds flew through the treetops. The streams that flowed down several of the mountains were filled with fish of every variety. Even the plants were pleasing to the eye. Thousands of flowers filled the dirt between trees and grew on shrubs, filling the air with a pleasant aroma.

At the bottom of the mountain, the boys followed a game trail that ran alongside a creek. They stopped for a few minutes to replenish their water bottles and were off again. The path became more stony and rough until it burst out of the forest and into a short plain of rock. To the west was a rock wall a hundred feet tall over which a creek cascaded, creating a beautiful waterfall. They halted and took stock of their surroundings. The massive stone wall blocking their way extended to the left and right for farther than they could see. There appeared to be no way to the top, and they had not brought any climbing equipment.

"So what do we do now?" Vladimir asked. "We certainly can't climb that cliff, and who knows how far it will be before we find a way to the top."

"I told you there was a reason that I came on this journey," Timothy said. "Relax. I'll take care of everything."

"Not even you can get us to the top of that cliff," Vladimir objected. "You're not strong enough to get us up there."

"No, I can't," Timothy said with a glance at Vladimir. "But if we work together, we can do it."

"What do you mean?" Vladimir said. "What can I do to help you? Heaven knows I'll do what I can, but I'm just a regular person."

"First of all, you can stop the charade," Timothy said, fixing his gaze on his companion. "You know what I'm talking about," he added when Vladimir gave him a quizzical look.

"No, I don't think I do," Vladimir said. "Wait. You don't think that I'm some sort of magician, do you?"

"I said cut the charade," Timothy retorted. "We both know that you're lying. I know just as well as you that you're a magician, so you can stop pretending and help me."

"But…how do you know that?" Vladimir asked.

"I guess you thought you were pretty clever in hiding the fact, didn't you?" Timothy said. "And you did a good job of it too, but there were too many instances that you knew things that you shouldn't have. None of them were obvious, but remember that I am also a magician. I know what to look for, and I can practically smell the magic in you."

"Okay, you're right," Vladimir conceded with a roll of his eyes. "I am a magician, but I have my reasons for not wanting people to know, so don't tell anyone."

"Fine, just help me get us to the top of this cliff. Though it's outside my area of expertise, I did learn how to levitate. I'm not strong enough to lift both of us, so I'll need you to lift yourself."

Vladimir nodded, and the two magicians fell to their respective tasks. To an outside observer, it would appear as though the boys were simply standing there. Eventually, however, they began to slowly rise into the air. They floated upward until they were even with the top of the cliff. Drifting sideways until they were not suspended over empty space, they fell the six inches to the ground and collapsed onto the rocky soil.

"Good work there," Timothy said. He was slightly winded from the magical exertion and was having trouble catching his breath.

"Thanks," Vladimir gasped. "You know, it just occurred to me that we probably could have done that an easier way and exerted less energy," he commented when he had recovered enough breath to speak.

"Oh, I know you're right," Timothy agreed, "I just wanted to test your strength."

"Well, I don't think now is the best time to do that," Vladimir said. "We're supposed to be moving double time, not wearing ourselves out for stupid purposes." He climbed to his feet and looked down at Timothy.

"Come on, it's time to go," he said and offered his hand to Timothy.

The two boys broke into a jog and worked their way westward through the forest, which began again at the top of the cliff. As they ran, they noticed a marked difference in their surroundings. While the forest had been relatively easy to traverse and pleasant to be in at the bottom of the cliff, at the top it was overgrown with no beaten path to follow. There were no visible flowers or other pleasant sights, and the air was filled with the smell of decay. Though the boys were soon forced to slow to a walk, they still managed to keep up a fairly good pace and didn't stop for several more miles. In fact, their next break was again forced as their way was blocked by another tall cliff. This time, however, they were at the top of the cliff instead of the bottom.

"The good news is that this time we'll be going down, so it will be less taxing on us magically," Timothy commented.

"That's the wrong way to look at it," Vladimir chided. "Look at this cliff. It's not as steep as the other and has a lot of character. If we play this right, we should be able to get down without using any magic at all."

Timothy walked to the edge and looked down again, this time searching for more than the height. He saw that Vladimir was correct in what he had said; the cliff was quite a bit less steep than the other and had plenty of rocks jutting from its surface that could be used as foot- and handholds. He shrugged and figured that there was no sense in waiting around, so he turned around and carefully let himself over the edge. He searched with his feet for a rock, which he found and used as a foothold. Looking to the left, he spotted a rock that was within reach of his hand and grabbed it. He repeated the process with his right hand and found himself completely off the top of the cliff and hanging onto its face for dear life.

"Mix magic with the physical," Vladimir called from Timothy's left. Timothy looked in that direction to see that his companion was at least ten feet below him.

"What do you mean?" he called.

In response, Vladimir braced his feet on a rock and jumped to another one five feet to his left and three feet below him. He stepped off of this rock backwards and grabbed onto a handhold a few feet lower. Timothy shook his head in amazement as he watched Vladimir move. How the boy could use so little magic so effectively was beyond him. With a shrug, he decided that he might as well try the same thing, so he let go of his handholds simultaneously and fell. Reaching out with magic, he detected a rock just below him, which he grabbed. His shoulders jarred painfully as he jolted to a stop, and his fingers barely managed to maintain their hold on the rock. Shaking his head, he shoved away the pain and focused on the task at hand. He sensed a rock jutting two feet below him, so he dropped onto it. His feet had barely touched down before he jumped off the rock sideways and grabbed onto another. He let go of the rock and fell down to another one that was three feet below him. This time he used magic to slow himself slightly before he grabbed onto the rock, saving his arms from another jarring. He let go and fell several feet before propelling himself off of the wall and into the branches of a tree that grew nearby. With a deft move, he slid down the trunk to the ground.

"See how easy it is to get things done when you combine physical and magical?" Vladimir commented.

"Yes," Timothy answered. "I don't know why I never thought of that myself. I always worked entirely with magic or in the physical sense. When you combine the two, it seems to work much more efficiently."

"Oh yeah, it's a lot more efficient," Vladimir said as he started to weave his way among the trees. "If you physically do what is physically easy and use magic to do what is physically difficult, you can accomplish much more than by working exclusively in either reality."

"I don't get it," Timothy said. "If you're so good at this sort of thing, why do you hide it?"

"I have my reasons," Vladimir said vaguely.

"That's not an answer," Timothy said. "What reasons?"

"It's a long, boring story," Vladimir said. "You wouldn't want to hear it."

"Well, we've got the time now and it can't be as boring as running through the forest for hours straight," Timothy said. "Here's an idea: you start telling it and when I get bored I'll stop you."

"I don't suppose you're going to let me hear the end of this until I tell you?" Vladimir asked.

"Not unless you tell me why you don't want to tell me," Timothy answered. "Though, that would probably require telling me the story anyway."

"Fine," Vladimir conceded. "Because you're being an unmitigated pain in the butt, I'll tell you. You'll probably think that I'm an idiot for this, but here's the reason. Actually, let me start back a few years so that you understand where I'm coming from.

"My family, no, my whole *town* has to be the most uneducated place in all of Magessa when it comes to magic. They do not understand how it works or any of its limitations. There have been no magicians born there in all of recorded history and the view of magic wielders is less than superb. Nevertheless, when my talents became known, my father saw their advantage almost immediately.

"As with most families, we had a business that pretty much everyone was employed in. The problem was that *my* family's business happened to be less than legal. Counterfeiting, swindling, and burglary were how we made our living. As I said before, as soon as my father found out that I could use magic, he saw the advantages that such a skill could have for him. The problem was, he had no idea how magic worked or about any of its limitations. He assumed that because I could use magic, I could do anything.

"My specialty is defensive magic. Physical shields, magical shields, mental shields are what I can do best. I can even directly combat what another magician is doing if I have enough warning. What my father wanted me to do had nothing to do with my skills; rather, he was focused on talents that would allow me to conjure money for him or at least help me burgle houses more efficiently. Given that I was raised by a bunch of thieves, I had few scruples about doing wrong, and was eager to please my father. I tried to do the things that he wanted, but without much luck.

"I had always been the black sheep of the family and saw this as my chance to earn my place. I set about learning magic and getting power in ways that were not good. I was soon bound up in a lot of terrible things but getting better results than I had ever hoped for. While the family business was booming, I was on a serious decline. I never actually let them indwell me, but I was consorting with demons and other dark magicians on a regular basis. Though they were constantly after me to participate with them in their wrong doings, I was content with my own. Eventually, their promises of more power seduced me, and I went with them one night to see what their activities were all about.

"I'll spare you the details, I'm sure you know them if you've heard anything about dark magic, but I'll say that it was horrifying. The worst part though was that I didn't really care. As long as it got me more power, I didn't care what the process was. As providence would have it, this particular ring of wizards had for some time been under the scrutiny of a band of magicians, and this was the night that they made their move. I didn't know what was going on around me; I was way out of my depth. So, I did the only thing that I knew how, I threw up a shield to protect myself and sat in a corner, waiting for the confrontation to end. Eventually it did, the result being that all of the wizards were dead.

"The magicians began to scour the area for any more threats and came upon me in my protective bubble. Somehow they knew that I was not a lost cause and put me in a school for young magicians. There I learned about Elohim, about right and wrong, about magic. Within a few years I had made enough progress that I was released from the school and was relocated at the academy in Belvárd.

"Though the school of magicians had taught me a lot, I am still not as strong as I should be. I keep my magical abilities a secret so that I will not be pressured into the dark arts again, for though I have turned my back on them, they are always lurking there, waiting to draw me back in."

"Well, you were wrong," Timothy said after a few minutes of silence. "That wasn't boring at all."

"Boring is just an excuse," Vladimir said. "I simply don't like talking about my life, especially that part. It's a very sore subject."

"It's something that you'll have to face if you ever want to rise to your full potential," Timothy said. "Always remember that Lemin and I are here to help you."

The two boys started to run again, tearing through the underbrush as quickly as possible. The leading position was very tiring, so the boys switched places often. They crossed two more mountains and followed three more streams along the way. The sun was setting when they finally burst out of the forest and onto a plain. Still they pressed on well after it dipped below the horizon. They ran for several miles before slowing to a walk and eating a meager dinner.

"Timothy, can I ask you a question?" Vladimir said when he had finished eating. The two cadets were walking at an easy pace through a large field, making for a stand of trees in which they planned to spend the night.

"Sure, Vladimir, ask anything that you like," Timothy answered.

"What do you think about women fighting? You know, like in a battle," Vladimir asked.

"What do you mean?" Timothy asked with a quizzical look.

"You know, we have been living at an academy for the past several years where, in essence, we have been taught that women can fight just as well as men," Vladimir said. "In fact, some of the best warriors in the whole academy are women— Senndra for instance. I never thought about this until I was in a real battle, but do you agree with women fighting?"

"It's a fact of life," Timothy answered. "I don't see that there's a whole lot I could do to change it even if I didn't agree with it. Besides that, I just don't see anything wrong with it. You yourself said that some of the best warriors at the academy are women, so what problem do you have with them fighting?"

"I don't know," Vladimir said. "It's just that when I was fighting in that battle and I saw a female fighting against those dwarves, I got this feeling that it's not how things should be, you know? Didn't you feel the need to defend those women against the enemy?"

"Actually I think you may be right," Timothy admitted. "Whenever I saw a woman fighting, I always felt the need to help her, even if it put me in danger. I don't know what made me do that. After all, it's not a very logical thing to do."

"What if that is just the way we were created?" Vladimir said. "I think Elohim instills in men the need to defend women. If you look at it that way, what you did was perfectly logical."

"Now that you say that, I'm almost certain you are right," Timothy said. "Maybe Elohim does create men with an instinctive need to defend women, even if it puts them in danger."

"That is why I have a problem with women fighting," Vladimir said. "When you have a mixed army, the men would feel the necessity to defend the women, even if it put the greater good of the army in danger. If the army was only composed of men, however, this wouldn't be a problem. Even very good friends do not feel that strong of a need to protect each other."

"You may be right," Timothy said, "but it doesn't matter. There are women in the army and that's a fact. They have just as much a right to fight for the country as we do. We need to control our own actions; we can't blame others for what we feel or do." That ended the conversation. Neither cadet said another word. When they reached the trees, they lay down on the ground and were asleep in an instant.

******

Senndra sat beside Lemin at the large round table in General Uriah's office. Seeing as how he was now the second highest ranking officer in the city, Lemin had decided that it would not hurt to take up residence in the headquarters while the

225

general was away. Along with Senndra and Lemin, there were a few soldiers from Gatlon and some other cadets as well. They were gathered together, packing the room so tightly that many of them were standing behind the chairs or against the wall. The meeting was not mandatory, so Senndra was surprised at the relatively large turnout. Lemin stood to his feet and waited for the whispering to die down before he began.

"Thank you all for coming today," he said. "I'm sure that most of you already know what this meeting is about, but let me tell you so that we are all on the same page. It has come to my attention that knowledge of Elohim is severely lacking in this country, particularly in the army. Nowadays, people do not believe in what *they* call 'fairy tales for small children.' My purpose today is to prove to you that Elohim is not just another fairy tale, but a real being at work in the world in which we live.

"First let me address the question of whether or not there is a God. Look around and see the world in all of its beauty. Watch the sun set and try to tell yourself that there is not a God who made it. Study wildlife in all its intricacies. Each area contains animals that interact with each other in such a way that they had to have been created by someone. For instance, in any given place, there is an abundance of animals, all of them preying on each other and on various plants in just the correct amounts so that all of the species survive. Then consider how each region interacts with those around it. A system so complex could not have evolved; it had to be created. And if all of this is not enough proof for you, consider this…"

Lemin snapped his fingers and a small flame appeared above his hand. With a flick of his wrist, the flames disappeared. The room was as silent as death, and Lemin continued with his display. He didn't even move his body this time, but a sheet of paper that had been lying on the table slowly began to rise into the air. When it had risen about six inches, the sides of the sheet slowly folded inward until they touched. Finally the paper fell back to the table in exactly the position that it had originally been.

"It's only magic," one of the spectators said.

"Only magic?" Lemin questioned. "Since when can the word *magic* be preceded by the word *only*? The very existence of magic is strong proof of God. After all, can you explain how the paper just did what it did? There is no one here who can explain what I did and how I did it. Actually, I could try to spew out some pseudo-scientific sounding explanation for magic, but only of how I use it and not of what it actually is or what causes it. So then, if no one here can explain the phenomena, not even the one that controlled it, it follows that there must be another force at work, one that does know what just happened and how it happened. A doubter could explain this as a coincidence and say that I am working with a natural force that I do not completely understand. But if that were true, it would be safe to assume that when I attempted to manipulate magic, it would not always work. Every time except for once when I have set out to perform magic, I have succeeded. The one time that I failed, I was disobeying Elohim and fully expected nothing to happen. In conclusion, there is plenty of evidence of the existence of God, and a doubter is only trying to make excuses.

"Now we need to address the question of what Elohim expects from us. If there is indeed a God, then we have an obligation to Him more than anybody else. As soldiers, you know what it is to have an obligation. You hold your oaths to defend Magessa to be of the utmost importance. Part of the reason for this is that you have received so much from the country, and you wish to give back in return. How much more should we want to give back to Elohim? He has given us the whole world in which to live, not to mention that it is only by His grace that the nation of Magessa remains free from the rule of Molkekk. For this and more, we can never repay Elohim. We could go about His work for our entire lives, as some have done, and still never repay Him what He deserves. Thankfully He does not ask too much of us, only that we obey His commands as well as we possibly can. In fact, the extent to which you obey his commands is not as important as the state of your heart. A person who follows His laws perfectly and yet does not do it for the correct reasons is as guilty as a pagan. By the same token, if you are sincere in your desire to obey Elohim, yet fail to keep His commands perfectly, He will delight in you just as much as a person who is able to follow His law more closely. In other words, our duty to Elohim is to truly desire to obey Him and do our best to follow Him. If we do this, we are fulfilling our duty to Him, and He will enable us to obey His laws.

"The final thing that I would like to speak about is the role of Elohim in the world today. Many people who believe in Elohim believe that He created the world and that He was involved here in the past, but now He has withdrawn from His creation. Simply put, these people are wrong; evidence of Elohim's involvement in the world is everywhere. One example, which I have previously mentioned, is the existence of magic. If not for Elohim's work, there would be no magic, period. Another example is the fact that Magessa has been able to successfully stand against the will of Molkekk for so long. The human, elfin, dwarf, orc, and ogre nations to the north have fallen under His power, whether by their own free will or by force. And yet, though he has armies many times larger than those of Magessa, we have been able to repel him each of the three times that he has attacked in the past. You experienced Elohim's help as we held back the dwarf attack until reinforcements could arrive. There is no other explanation for our strength except for Him. It is only by His power that we have remained free for so long, and it is only by His power that we will continue to remain free."

The meeting lasted for more than an hour as Lemin answered questions from various people. As he continued to whittle down the objections to his call to return to Elohim, he could see the resistance of the doubters in the room beginning to wane, until finally they were out of excuses. In the end, only a few clung to their doubts and resisted the call while the majority of those gathered promised to obey Elohim.

After the meeting ended, Senndra followed Lemin out of the headquarters and toward the south gate of the city. Senndra had so much on her mind that she did not say a word, and Lemin seemed content to keep his peace. When they reached the gate, they entered the gatehouse and ascended the staircase to the top of the wall. Lemin went off to speak to the newly appointed watchmen of the city, and Senndra found herself alone. A hand touched her shoulder, and she turned to find Rita standing there.

"Let's go someplace," she said. "Our shift doesn't start until sundown, and I'm really bored."

"I suppose we could go back to our tent," Senndra said, "though I can't think of anything to stave off your boredom."

"Even if it's just talking to someone, I need to do something," Rita said. "If I don't do anything, I have too much time to think, and these days that's a dangerous and depressing prospect."

\*\*\*\*\*\*

The sun had sunk below the horizon more than two hours earlier. Josiah slowed his horse to a near halt as he cast a watchful gaze over his soldiers. He desperately wished that he could give the command to halt, but knew that the army would have to be pushed to their limit in order to overtake the dwarves. The scouts sent to locate the dwarves had not yet returned, so he figured that the enemy was more than a day's march ahead. So far, the march had gone relatively well, covering smooth terrain on a beaten path, but Josiah knew that eventually the path would end. Still, he figured that if they spent long days traveling, they could overtake the dwarves before they reached Belmoth.

For the remainder of the march, Josiah forced himself to search the road before him for enemies. This task became increasingly more difficult as his mind began to wander. He looked back at his men and saw that they were practically dead on their feet and wished, for his men's sake, that the order to halt would be given. It was another half hour before the order came.

The soldiers wasted no time in unrolling their blankets and falling asleep as those unfortunate enough to be chosen for the first shift of sentry duty took their posts.

Josiah unsaddled and unbridled his horse, hobbled it, and turned it out to feed. He unrolled his blankets and tried to sleep, but was unable to do so, even though he had been working hard since daybreak. The soldiers envied the officers for having horses and other amenities, unaware of the other concerns that taxed them. Josiah's mind kept wandering back to the inevitable battle with the dwarves. Even if the army was pressed hard enough to overtake them, he didn't know what chance they stood against the massive army of the enemy. With ogres to bolster their ranks and elves attacking the army head-on, their odds would be better, but he still did not know how good their likelihood of survival was, much less of victory. Their only hope was for dragon support to arrive in time, but that seemed more unlikely than ever before. For Timothy and Vladimir to carry the message for help more than two hundred miles in five days seemed like an impossible feat.

"I know that I shouldn't despair," Josiah prayed aloud to Elohim, "but when I consider the enemy that has pitted himself against us, I cannot help but think that we are doomed. The vastness of the enemy's army is as the sand of the seashore; to hold them back would be like holding the sea back. But with Your power, I know that all things are possible. Please strengthen my men and give them the courage to face their enemy with honor. Help us to gain the victory when the time comes."

His nerves settled by the prayer, Josiah drifted off to sleep. He woke only a few hours later to see the sun peaking over the horizon. He stretched and stood to his feet, not ready for another hard day's march, yet feeling the need to set an example for his men. He had slept with his armor on, and the unnatural position that the suit had caused him to lay in had given him cramps in his neck and back. He tried his best to stretch these out, but failed. With a simple word, he condemned his troops to another day of marching, and in half an hour, they were moving down the road again. They marched west for almost three hours before the path turned to the south and disappeared at the base of a mountain. Josiah received the order to call a halt, and he allowed his men to rest briefly before they began to march again. Following the dwarf trail was simple; the passage of seventy-five thousand warriors had left a great impact on the ground, so the army had only to follow this beaten path. They made excellent time for the next few hours, yet Josiah knew that it would still be difficult to overtake their quarry.

Noon came and went. Men sweated, but the march continued unabated. At about two hours to sunset, the ogre army came in sight, but the army's pace did not slow. The ogres covered the distance between the armies quickly, and by nightfall, they had almost caught up with Josiah's army. As they came within a bow's shot of the army, their scent finally reached the horses that were scattered throughout the column, causing them to prance about nervously. Josiah saw that if they did not stop moving, the horses would end up hurting someone. He called his men to a halt, and the other commanders followed his example. He reined his horse to a stop and slid off of it, not wanting to take it any nearer to the ogres than he had to since the sight of them might spook the beast. Quickly he strode through the ranks of soldiers toward the approaching crowd of ogres. When he reached the rearguard, he stopped. He stood with the soldiers and various officers as the ogres ceased running and came to a stop with their front line only a dozen steps from the humans. One of them stepped out from the rest and crossed the distance to the humans in three giant strides.

"Where can I find General Uriah?" the ogre asked. His voice did not sound thickheaded and stupid as Josiah had expected it to. In fact, if Josiah were going by voice alone, he would guess that this particular ogre was very bright.

"I am Uriah," the general answered and stepped forward out of the crowd to meet the ogre. "And you are?"

"I am Looran, commander of the ogre army," the ogre answered. "My army is here to reinforce you in your attack against the dwarves."

"Your help is greatly appreciated," Uriah said. "When we stop next, I will sit down with you and thoroughly go over the battle plan."

"It is already getting dark," Looran said. "When do you plan on stopping for the night?"

"We need to keep moving or we will never catch the dwarves," Uriah answered. "We will continue to march until the moon is directly overhead. I would be obliged if you would take your men to our flank so as to not upset our horses."

"As you wish," Looran said. "I will speak with you when we stop."

Without another word, the commander turned and walked back to his army. Josiah watched as the ranks of ogres quickly formed again before he hurried back through his soldiers to his horse. He considered climbing into the saddle, but decided against it. Instead he wearily gripped the halter of the stead and, motioning to one of his officers, gave the order for his men to form ranks and march. Slowly the column of soldiers moved out again. By simply looking back, Josiah could tell that his men were exhausted, and he wondered exactly how they were going to be able to engage the dwarves when they caught up with them. The battle was going to be very hard to win, and even if victory was ultimately theirs, they would suffer many losses. After the first half hour of marching, he stopped thinking; it was simply too depressing.

******

Timothy and Vladimir ran full tilt across the open countryside. This second day of their journey was much easier than the first, and since they had covered roughly twenty-five miles on the first day, they planned on covering at least fifty on the second. The ground sloped gently downward, so they increased their speed as they pressed forward. They slowed to a jog when they reached the bottom, hopped a small stream, and continued on their way. Ahead they could see the river blocking their path, so they made an adjustment in order to intercept the bridge that spanned the water. They began to encounter more densely populated country. Now that they had paved roads to follow, their pace increased once again. They alternated regularly between running and jogging and reached the bridge long before midday.

The bridge was crowded, so their pace slackened as they forced their way through the mass of people. Vladimir stayed close behind Timothy the entire way as they weaved a path around carts and through throngs of customers and merchants who were doing business on the bridge. In all the congestion, it took them close to half an hour to cross the river. They stopped on the far side of the bridge, rested for five minutes, and drank some water. After that they were off again running down the road, dodging farmers and merchants. Soon they were out of the heaviest of the crowds and were able to make good time again. The well-built road allowed them to maintain a brisk pace without fear of stumbling and injuring themselves.

They pressed on until an hour past midday, when they rested for ten minutes, ate a quick lunch, and drank some more water. They were off running again soon after they had finished eating, but this time their pace was slower due to their full stomachs. The exercise soon drove the boys too far, and they vomited the contents of their stomachs on the roadside. They didn't let that stop them, however, and they continued running.

******

Josiah relayed the order to halt from the general to his troops. He led his horse to a spot that was a short distance from the main army and turned it loose, allowing it to find what food it could. Josiah sat down to watch the beast, but sleep slowly overcame him. As he drifted between consciousness and sleep, he inadvertently began to speak to Elohim.

"I don't see how we can emerge from this encounter victorious," he said. He looked up and was mildly surprised to see that he was not in the field with his army anymore. Instead, as he rose to his feet and looked around, he saw that he was in a large hall. Golden furniture lined the walls, and light was provided from some strange stones that were embedded in the ceiling. The beauty of the place was almost too much for Josiah to take in, and he sank slowly to the floor. He gazed at his surroundings and, for the first time, noticed that there was the faint sound of music. It seemed to be coming from the far end of the hall where Josiah noticed that a brightly colored curtain was hung over a doorway. Slowly, almost as if he were in a trance, he rose to his feet again and began to walk down the hall. As he moved, the music gradually grew louder until he had reached the curtain-covered doorway. He lifted a hand to draw back the barrier between him and the music but froze, his hand still on the fabric. He knew this was something that he must not do. He let his hand fall back to his side and stood for a long time simply staring at the cloth. He felt a presence behind him, but he did not turn around.

"You would like to go inside?" the person behind him asked eventually. Josiah turned his head to look at the man. He was about Josiah's height, but much more muscular. His closely cropped hair was sandy blond, and when Josiah looked closely, he could not tell if he was a human, elf, dwarf, orc, or ogre. His face bore a resemblance to each of the races, so he didn't look completely like any of them. More amazing, though, were the eyes of the man. When Josiah looked into them, he saw incredible love.

"Do you want to go inside?" the man asked again.

"Yes, I do," Josiah answered, "and yet I know it is something that I am not supposed to do."

"Your feelings serve you well," the man responded. "I would not stop you from going in, yet it is something that would end in grief for you."

"If I am not supposed to enter, why am I here?" Josiah asked.

"You are here because I wish to speak to you," the man answered. "You are a staunch supporter of Elohim, and I know that you would give your life to protect His people. Very soon your courage and commitment will be put to the test. The army of dwarves has turned and, even as we speak, is making its way toward your army."

"What?" Josiah said in astonishment. "But aren't they marching all the way to Belmoth to break through the gap there? Lemin said that was what he figured they were planning on doing."

"The elves are not all-knowing; it was never the intention of the dwarves to attack Belmoth," the man explained. "They knew that the elves were coming and that with their help you would be able to hold Saddun indefinitely. That is why they staged a secret retreat of their forces. They knew that there were magicians among your ranks and expected them to detect the retreat. They knew that the token force they left in the city would almost certainly be defeated, but their original purpose was fulfilled: to draw the bulk of the army out of Saddun. On the plain, it is very unlikely that you will defeat them."

"Then all is lost," Josiah said, shaking his head. "The dwarves may have as many as seventy-five thousand men, and our army has less than fifteen thousand. The only way we had any chance of victory was with dragon support. But if we are to be attacked soon, the dragons will never get here in time."

"All of your intelligence up to this point has been hampered by the magic of the dwarves," the man said. "They have been reinforced on the march and now have close to one hundred and fifty thousand men. Also, you are correct when you say that the dragons will not arrive in time to assist you; however, this is not the time to cower in the sight of your enemies. Elohim is on your side, and He will give you the strength you need to meet your enemies with courage."

"But what is the point?" Josiah asked, despair evident in his voice. "There is absolutely no way that we can defeat the dwarves."

"You're right," the man said. "There is no way that you can defeat them. But isn't that the point?"

Josiah had uncertainty written on his face as he lifted it, but the man had gone. Or, rather, Josiah had gone. He was no longer in a long hall with a curtain covering a doorway on one end. There was no more golden furniture, nor were there angelic voices coming from behind a curtain. Josiah was back on the plain. His horse was a short distance away eating grass, and the sun was just coming above the horizon. Josiah turned away from the sunrise and looked intently across the plain. He thought he might be able to make out some movement, but he couldn't be sure. As he looked, he saw sun glint off of metal. He leaped to his feet and left his horse as he sprinted toward camp. The army was in disarray with soldiers getting ready for the day's march. People were milling around, gathering up their weapons and armor, and no one seemed to be on the lookout for the enemy.

As Josiah burst into camp, a single roar went up from the ogre camp. Pandemonium broke out in the human camp as they also spotted the massive army moving in their direction. Men panicked all around as Josiah stopped to catch his breath. He began to search for General Uriah and quickly found him standing by his horse and staring out at the vast army of the enemy.

"Your orders, sir," Josiah said breathlessly as he came to a stop in front of Uriah. Uriah didn't answer but kept his gaze fixed on the approaching army. He kept mumbling to himself, and Josiah realized that he was in shock. He turned and pushed his way through the soldiers to the front line to where a few dozen of the more seasoned soldiers had formed a shaky line.

"The blasted general has never been in a battle except for the one at Saddun," Josiah muttered to himself. "I guess he just isn't cut out for this sort of thing. Form battle lines!" He bellowed aloud at the panicking soldiers. The sound of his voice over the panic seemed to calm the men down to a certain extent, and many of them turned to look at him.

"Swordsmen in front and archers behind," he shouted. When few soldiers moved to follow his orders, he added, "If you want to live out the day, move!"

The soldiers quickly scrambled to form a more solid line. Even so, they looked pathetic compared to the advancing dwarves, and Josiah knew they didn't stand a chance against the horde. He quickly gave orders to cut the length of the line and increase its depth. The soldiers expertly moved to follow the new order without so much as a pause. Even with the new formation, the army looked too small. Josiah turned to face an approaching ogre.

"What is it?" he asked when the ogre had halted in front of him.

"Commander Looran wants to know what you would have him do," the ogre responded.

"Tell him that if he would split his troops into two groups and position one on each side of our line, I would be obliged."

"Yes sir," the ogre said, but he remained where he was.

"Is there anything else?" Josiah asked.

"To be honest, sir, what can we do against the enemy?" the ogre asked. "They have five times the number of troops that we have."

"Oh, they have a lot more than five times as many men," Josiah said, "but we can still give them one hell of a battle. We can buy time for our army back in Saddun. No, we can't beat them, but we can help save Magessa. And as long as we fight with all of our might that is all Elohim asks."

"Thank you, sir," the ogre said. "I needed to hear that."

"Really," Josiah said with a raised eyebrow. "Most people wouldn't want to hear that there is no hope."

"Not that part, sir—your *reason* for fighting."

The ogre turned and ran back toward his commander to relay the message that Josiah had given. Josiah turned back to his army, casting his gaze over the small group that had rallied under his command. As he looked into the eyes of the men, he saw fear in most of them. He broke away from the army and turned to face them. He had always heard of great generals giving great speeches before battles, and he felt that he should do something like that.

"Soldiers of Magessa," he began. "I know that many of you cannot see victory at the end of this battle. The truth is that we are badly outnumbered, probably worse than many of you are aware. And because of that, I see fear in the eyes of many of you, a fear that would be covering me as well. But I have realized something. Whether we live or die is not important in the grand scheme of things. No, the lives of a few thousand soldiers are not worth much; however, it's what we do with our lives—how they end—that is what is really important. What use is running from this battle to escape death when the very army that we are facing will then go on to destroy our country? At that point, I think many of you will find that you do not have a reason to live. On the other hand, all Elohim asks is that we fight bravely, even if that means giving our lives to defend Magessa. As long as we are faithful in His service, the result of the battle is up to Him, and He will make all things work toward the continuation of His plan. As long as we serve Him faithfully, He will invite us to something much better when we pass on. I don't know about you, but that encourages me to no end."

As Josiah looked into the eyes of the soldiers this time, he saw that while some still held fear, many of them were devoid of that fear, and it had been replaced by peace. They gripped their weapons with steadier hands, and Josiah knew that he could trust them to fight until life left their bodies. He took a place on the front line and watched as the dwarves advanced. They were just out of bow range now, so he made the signal for the archers to nock their arrows. As the dwarves reached the range of the bowmen, they let loose a volley from their crossbows and broke into a run. Josiah motioned for the lines of infantry to raise their shields, and the volley splashed against them, punching through some, but causing only a few casualties. The infantry returned their shields to their former positions and waited as the enemy drew nearer. Josiah gave the signal for the archers to draw their bows. The dwarves pressed even closer. They were only a hundred yards away now, then only fifty. Finally Josiah signaled, and the entire line of archers let loose their arrows, cutting down hundreds of dwarves. Quickly the archers nocked arrows again and drew the bows, letting loose another volley of arrows when the enemy was no more than twenty yards away. They scrambled to get off another volley, which hit the dwarves when they were less than five yards from the front line of the human army. Then, with a mighty crash of metal on metal, the dwarves smashed into the army of Magessa, driving the defenders back a few steps. The fighting was fierce as the dwarves tried to drive their enemy back, but the defenders would not give. The dead soon covered the ground, giving evidence to the resolve of the soldiers. The dwarves surrounded the army, trying to sweep in on the flanks, but the ogres held them off until the humans were able to form a large ring. The ogres fell back to take their places among the defenders, smashing their way through the large crowd of dwarves with their clubs. The fighting was brutal and lasted throughout the day. The ring of defenders slowly contracted as it lost more and more men. The humans and ogres slew their fair share of dwarves, but there seemed to be no end to the horde of enemies. They continued to press the beleaguered humans and ogres until dusk, when they finally fell back for the night.

The first day of fighting was over, but Josiah knew that their numbers had been more than cut in half. Another day like this would certainly result in the total annihilation of their army. They had to find some way to turn the fighting in their favor.

*"I need to talk with the other commanders,"* Josiah said to himself. He turned to look for someone that he trusted to carry out the task for him and saw Cirro and his captains coming across the battlefield. When they reached him, they offered a salute which he returned.

"At ease," he told them. "I need something from you immediately," he continued. "I want you to gather the other officers of this army that are my rank or higher and ask them to meet me at the rear of the army."

"Yes, commander," they answered, and with another salute they were gone.

Josiah made his way to the back of the army and sat on the grass to wait. He didn't know what the meeting would decide, but he did know that if they wanted to survive the next day of fighting, they would have to move to a better location. Perhaps the large group of officers would give General Uriah some ideas to consider. Josiah thought their best chance would be to fall back to the Pelé River. If they made their stand there, they would have the advantage when the dwarves attempted to cross. Of course this plan was not without its difficulties. The dwarves could split their army into several groups and cross the river in multiple places. The army of Magessa would not be able to protect all of these crossing points.

Josiah tried to fill in all of the holes in his plan, but his ponderings were cut short as the officers began to show up. He rose to his feet and greeted each as they arrived. It was half an hour before most of the officers were present, but Generals Uriah and Looran had still not appeared. Finally, after another ten minutes, the ogre general lumbered up, followed shortly by Josiah's Captain Stanslaw.

"Where is General Uriah?" he asked with some urgency in his voice.

"Deserted, sir," Stanslaw answered. "I just heard news that he fled back toward Saddun with several of his officers just as the battle was starting."

"Thank you, Captain," Josiah said. "You are free to go; however, please send me two soldiers to act as my messengers."

"It shall be done, sir," Stanslaw said. He turned to go, and Josiah faced the officers that had gathered at his wish.

"This meeting has suddenly become more vital than I had originally thought," Josiah began. "I had planned on simply advising General Uriah on what to do next; however, the general has turned coward, fleeing to Saddun at the beginning of the battle. Due to this unforeseen difficulty, we need to decide who will lead the army against the dwarves.

"Before you cast your vote, be sure to consider the qualifications this person must have. First, he must be intelligent in the ways of military strategy. He must be someone that the men will follow even to the death; he must be willing to commit all of these soldiers to the defense of Magessa; and above all, he must have the courage to stand with his soldiers, to stay and fight with them until victory is achieved or he has given his life in defense of our country.

"Now I would like for you to nominate the officers that are most likely to fill this position, together with all of the requirements that I have just stated. I myself think that General Looran is the most likely candidate for this position, as he is of the highest rank and has all of these qualities. What say you, general? Do you accept the nomination?"

"Nay, I cannot," Looran answered, rising to his feet. "I am not the one that is able to fill this station. I do not have as good of a mind for military strategy as many humans do, and I am sure that not all of the soldiers here would follow me to the death.

It was not I that stopped the soldiers from retreating and formed them into organized battle lines. No, this position should go to someone who is better suited for it: Commander Josiah. I trust him to pull us through this battle. But even if that is beyond his power, I will follow him to the death. I say this because I know that he is not one to spend the lives of his men lightly, and I feel that he will stand with us to the bitter end, if that be our lot. Therefore, I think that we should give him at least a temporary promotion to the rank of admiral so as to give him the authority to unite these two armies."

"I agree," another of the ogre officers said. "It was Josiah that led our army today, and we survived against insurmountable odds. I move that we give this same power to him in tomorrow's battle."

Sounds of agreement came from all sections of the crowd; it was obvious that this was the choice of the group. The noise gradually resolved itself into a chant, "Josiah! Josiah!" Finally General Looran stood to his feet and raised his hands for silence. The noise finally died down.

"To make this official, I call for a vote," he said. "All who are for the leadership of Commander Josiah, please stand to your feet."

The crowd rose together, giving a cheer as they did so. The sound was deafening, and Josiah briefly wondered what the dwarves were thinking at that moment. He looked at General Looran who approached him and saluted. The entire assembly snapped to attention.

"What are our orders, Admiral?" Looran asked.

"If this is indeed your wish," Josiah said, "then I will do my best to lead this army to victory. Prepare to move your troops, gentlemen. We're falling back to the Pelé River tonight."

******

The road turned sharply to the south, so Timothy left it and cut across a field that stretched for as far as he could see. He looked behind and saw Vladimir staggering up the road. He stopped to wait for his friend, but he didn't sit down since he knew that he would not be able to force himself to get back up. The surrounding country was lit only by the faint light of a small sliver of moon, so Timothy was unable to rely on landmarks to guide his steps. Instead, he was following a spell that he had used the previous day to locate the academy. They had been running three, maybe four days; the constant running had made events blur together. Every muscle in his body ached, but he was not about to stop. His mission was crucial, and he intended to carry it out to the end. Vladimir finally staggered up to where Timothy stood and doubled over, trying to catch his breath. It was a minute before he was even able to stand up again, but when he did, Timothy was able to look into his eyes. They were normally bright, but now had taken on a dull look. Timothy decided that a real rest couldn't hurt.

"No, don't stop," Vladimir gasped. "Don't stop for me. I'll keep going until I drop. Just go as fast as you can until we reach the academy."

"I'm not going to leave you out here in the middle of nowhere," Timothy said suddenly, almost vehemently.

"Don't stop for me," Vladimir said again and gripped Timothy's shoulder. "You have to promise me that you won't stop for me. This message that we carry is more important." When Timothy was silent, Vladimir shouted, "Promise me!"

"Okay, I promise," Timothy said. "I won't wait for you."

"Good," Vladimir said. "I don't think I can make it any farther, but you can. Run as fast as you can. Get the message to the academy."

"I can't leave you here," Timothy said, tears building up in his eyes. "You might die if you stay here."

"Don't be so melodramatic. You'll come back to get me once you reach the academy. You promised you wouldn't wait; now GO!" Vladimir shouted and collapsed onto the ground in a faint.

"Very well," Timothy said as he wiped his eyes with the back of his hand. "I'll leave you the food we have left, as little as it is." He was so exhausted that he had to think aloud to maintain his train of thought. "May Elohim protect you."

Timothy dropped the bag that he had been carrying beside the unconscious Vladimir. What he did was probably the hardest thing he had ever done in his life. It went against everything he had ever learned—to leave a comrade behind—but he knew that it was for the best. Even so, it took all of his willpower to turn his back on Vladimir and begin to run again. To forget the scene that he had just witnessed, he forced himself to run faster. Soon the pain shoved all thoughts from his mind as he flew across the field toward his mission's goal.

\*\*\*\*\*\*

Lemin sat on the northern wall of Saddun, looking out over the plain on the other side. The small portion of moon that hung in the sky did little to illuminate the earth, so it seemed probable that Lemin was not looking at anything. Senndra approached and stood behind him, trying to work up the courage to talk to him about an issue that plagued her.

"Senndra, sit down," Lemin said without turning. Senndra took a seat beside him on the cold stone of the wall and waited for him to speak again.

"Something troubles you," Lemin said, finally looking at Senndra. It was not a question, but a statement.

"It's not something, sir," Senndra responded. "It's someone. Ever since the battle, Rita has been acting strangely."

"Acting strangely? How?" Lemin asked.

"I'm not sure exactly," Senndra answered. "If I had to name one thing, I would say that she has become much less trusting and more cynical. I think that perhaps she is beginning to doubt Elohim."

"That is definitely possible," Lemin said. "That happens to many soldiers after their first battle. When they see the carnage and brutality of war, they wonder if there can possibly be a God. They wonder why God would allow this to happen if He did indeed exist. It might help if I talk to her."

"Maybe, but I have doubts about that," Senndra said. "She came to the first of your talks about Elohim, and while many of the people that attended came away changed for the better, she didn't want to talk about it at all."

"If that is the case," Lemin responded, "the best thing you can do is what you have been doing all along. Encourage her and be a friend to her and continue to show the love of Elohim. Other than that, you can do nothing."

"But there has to be some way that we can make her come to her senses," Senndra argued.

"There is nothing we can do," Lemin answered. "Each person has a free will, either to choose to follow Elohim and believe His promises or to disregard everything He has said and go his or her own way. If Rita chooses to do the latter and will not be influenced by anything, there is no way that you can force her to accept what you know to be true."

"That makes me feel helpless," Senndra said. "So I can't help her at all?"

"As I have said, continue to act as you have been," Lemin answered. "Other than that, you can only ask Elohim to be with Rita in this time. He is the only one that can change her. Of course, be reminded that He is all-powerful, and that no matter what happens, it is for His glory and the good of His people."

"Thank you, Lemin," Senndra said after several minutes of thought. "I needed to hear that."

******

Josiah watched through the rain as his army forded the Pelé River and set up camp on the east side. They wouldn't have a *good* chance of winning even from this side of the water, but they had a *better* chance. Their archers could pepper the dwarves as they tried to cross the river, and their infantry would have an advantage since the dwarves would be coming out of the water. The problems that Josiah had previously found with the plan had mostly been rectified, making this the best chance for the army. The rain had swelled the size of the river to such an extent that there was only one place that could be crossed for miles in either direction. On the east side of the river there was a rock-strewn field that Josiah had not remembered but that would provide excellent cover for archers. Also, the bank of the river had risen to a point where the dwarves would have to go through a narrow pass between two rocks as they came out of the river. In this position, Josiah figured that his men could take on a much larger army. Even with all of the advantages that the defenders had, the battle was sure to be a bitter one.

Josiah turned to his two messengers that Stanslaw had provided from his men. Both were fatigued from the march, but they stood straight, ready to take messages to whoever was necessary.

"Benjamin," Josiah said to the man on the left, "go tell General Looran to move his archers and his infantry to the pass that the dwarves are going to come through. I will meet him there and tell him exactly where I want his men located." He turned to the man on the right. "Jonathan, inform the human officers that I want all of their archers positioned in the boulder field in a spot where they have cover, but where the river is still in range. Also, tell the humans to use a third of their infantry to protect the archers and tell them to send the rest of their infantry to the pass by the river."

The two messengers ran toward the bulk of the army in search of the officers. Soon, the soldiers were moving to their respective positions, so Josiah walked down to the river to meet the officers. When he got there, General Looran was the first to greet him with a salute. The rest of the officers saluted as well, and Josiah returned them all. Then he began to look over the troops that were available.

"General," he said to Looran, "you will position your archers on the tops of the boulders that compose the pass. Make sure they have cover, but I want them to have clear shots at the river and the pass. If there isn't enough room or cover up there, position your men at the head of the pass so that they have a line of sight down to the water's edge. Position your infantry at the mouth of the pass. You will help hold it; however, keep your soldiers ready to move. If the dwarves manage to cross at another spot, you will be the one to counterattack.

"The rest of you will position your men with the ogre infantry. In all scenarios, you will stay at the pass and defend against the dwarves crossing there. Under no circumstances are you to abandon your post. If you do, you will be endangering the rest of the army and the whole country."

Josiah turned from the river and headed toward the archers that were positioned to the east. They had entrenched themselves in the field of boulders, and Josiah saw that they had plenty of cover. A detachment of infantry had already arrived, and the soldiers were creating a perimeter around the archers. They had effectively hidden themselves among the boulders, using the natural defenses to their advantage. It would take a force of at least three or four times their size to defeat them.

As Josiah approached the soldiers, he looked for a way to get to the high ground that they occupied. Two steep and narrow paths had already been blocked up with debris, and the wide path that was the obvious approach was being filled with boulders to make it only wide enough for one or two people to pass through at a time. At the narrow pass, Josiah encountered a sentry who saluted and did not try to stop him. Once he was past, Josiah saw the true extent of the soldiers' activity. A system for moving the large rocks had been developed, and about half of the soldiers were working to enforce their position with the stone. The other soldiers stood with their weapons, ready to fight in an instant should the dwarves manage a swift advance across the river. Josiah spotted a commander that appeared to be in charge of the working men, so he went to talk to him.

"Are you the one who is giving orders up here?" he asked the man.

"No sir," the commander answered. "I'm just in charge of moving the boulders to block the way. You should speak with the officer over there." The man pointed to the pass that Josiah had entered through on the way up."

Josiah thanked the man for the information and headed back the way he had come. As he neared the pass, he began to scan the crowd for the general. His attention was drawn to several soldiers that were standing atop a portion of the barrier that had been finished. Most of these were regular soldiers that were on lookout duty, but Josiah's sharp eyes spotted the rank of general on the uniform of one of the older men. He quickly scaled the pile of boulders and approached the general cautiously, due to his uncertain footing.

"General," Josiah said so as to get the attention of the older man.

The general turned to face Josiah and saluted, even if it were a bit grudgingly.

"What is your position here?" Josiah asked.

"We are well-entrenched," the general answered tersely. "All of the paths to us have been blocked except for the small path over there." He motioned with his head to the path that had been left through the wall of boulders. "We have all of the human archers in the army, but that is still less than a thousand. There are even fewer swordsmen, but we should not need very many of them to hold this location."

"Very good," Josiah answered and considered the information. "I will be here with my two messengers when the battle begins. I would request that if your lookouts spot any unusual movement of the dwarf army, they report it to me. Other than that, I will not attempt to command your men; they are at your disposal."

"Very good, sir," the general answered in a somewhat friendlier tone.

Josiah carefully picked his way to the front edge of the barrier where a lookout was standing. From this new perch, he slowly scanned the river and the field beyond it for any sign of movement, but could detect nothing. He figured that the dwarves would not reach the river until well after dawn, so he settled down to wait.

****** 

Timothy continued to run throughout the night and into the next day. His lips were parched from the lack of water, and his muscles screamed for relief, but he wouldn't—he couldn't—stop. He was beginning to lose his sense of balance so that he staggered as he ran. The exertion was also having effects on his eyesight, causing his vision to come and go, but he still pushed himself onward. His mind began to wander due to his weariness, dredging up events that he had not even considered in years. Finally the whirlwind of thoughts settled on the comrade that he had left behind. He didn't know what would become of him or if he would survive. He had done what he could for him by leaving the food and water behind, but his conscience still troubled him. He would have to have a search party sent out to look for him when he reached the academy.

He came to a stream and saw a ford that was a hundred yards upstream from where he was. After only a moment of thought, he ran into the knee-deep water, ignoring the shallower water at the ford. In no time he was on the other side of the stream and running again. He tried to remind himself of the message that he was supposed to deliver to the people at the academy when he got there, but his brain could not conjure it up. As he concentrated, his pace slowed, and he was able to think more clearly as more oxygen was directed to his brain. In one massive rush, it all came back to him. He remembered the battle at Saddun and the dwarf army; that was his mission, to bring news to the academy. With that question out of the way, he turned his attention once again to his running. He noticed that his pace had slowed, but when he tried to speed up, his legs tangled and he fell to the ground. He tried to rise to his feet, but utter exhaustion prevented him from completing this simple action. With magic, he reached out to the surrounding area to summon anyone near to his aid. To his surprise, he made contact and was able to send out his plea for help.

The use of magic sapped the last of his energy reserves, and he lost consciousness. He slept for a long time, having the weirdest dreams. He was prodded from his unconsciousness by the same mind he had contacted previously, and he slowly and painfully lifted his head. Through his sleep-blurred eyes, he saw a large blue shape dropping toward him from the sky. Two more shapes, one red and the other yellow, circled in the sky above him. His last thought before he lost consciousness again was that these were dragons, though the significance of that fact was lost on him.

****** 

Senndra sat atop a pile of rubble that had once been part of the northern wall of Saddun. She ignored her surroundings as she stared out across the plain to where she could just barely make out the top of a mountain that stood alone beside the Pelé River. "*So this was Mt. Nebal, the dwarf fortress,*" she thought. It didn't look like it could contain the entirety of the dwarf army that had attacked Saddun, but it didn't have to. Senndra had dug several old manuscripts on the subject out of the library, a building that had miraculously not been seriously damaged in the battle. Most of the manuscripts did not contain the information she was trying to locate, as they had been written after the dwarves had alienated themselves from Magessa. There was, however, one scroll that had been written before the dwarves' separation, and though Senndra had trouble reading it due to the old writing style, it was the only source she had. According to this scroll, though Mt. Nebal was a large mountain, it did not have very many natural caverns. And since the dwarves had done little more than connect them together with tunnels, there was not very much room inside the mountain. Though this seemed to indicate that the dwarves could not have come from Mt. Nebal, the manuscript revealed more information that contradicted this theory. The mountain might not have very much room in it, but the ground surrounding it was honeycombed with tunnels. Also, according to rumors, the dwarves had dug a tunnel that stretched all the way from a mountain range to the northeast to Mt. Nebal. Therefore, though the dwarves living in Mt. Nebal had not supplied all of the soldiers for the attacking army, it seemed likely that it was the staging point for the attack.

In reading about the dwarf mountain fortress, Senndra had become engrossed in the topic of dwarves and read several other books about them. Again, the information in the more recent volumes was scant, and she was forced to resort to struggling through the older, harder-to-read scrolls. She was, however, able to extract several interesting facts about dwarves that she had not known before. After she emerged from the library, her brain brimming with the new information, she walked to the northern wall of the city to find a place to sit down and think.

"Hi, Senndra. What are you doing?" a voice behind her asked.

Senndra turned to look at the intruder and was confronted by a beautiful girl with long black hair and green eyes. Her skin was a shade darker than most of the people of Magessa, marking her as the descendant of a foreigner. Senndra knew that she recognized her from somewhere, but was still unsure who she was. Finally it flashed into her mind; her escape from the brooding Rita had crossed her path with the girl that now stood before her. She was, as Senndra recalled, one of the kitchen maids of Saddun, though she could not recall her name.

"Just sitting here looking at the scenery," Senndra replied. "You want to join me?"

"I guess," the girl said and climbed onto the rocks next to Senndra. "What were you thinking about?" she asked when she had gotten herself settled.

"Nothing really," Senndra answered. "I was just contemplating some information that I found in the library—some stuff about dwarves."

"Really?" the girl said. "I just love that building. I'm glad it wasn't destroyed in the battle. Did you find anything interesting there?"

"I found a lot that was interesting, but not much that was of any practical help, I'm afraid," Senndra answered with a short laugh. "For one thing, it seems like no one really knows much of anything about the dwarves."

"Well, they have been rather reclusive for more than a hundred years now," the girl responded. "I'm surprised that you found anything that was of use."

"Well, the only manuscript that I put much stock in was one that was a hundred and fifty years old," Senndra said. "Besides the fact that the language of that period is extremely hard to read, I figure that the information might be a bit out of date. As for the books that were written more recently, they gave only very vague information, and what specifics they contained, I have severe doubts about trusting."

"I'm sorry you didn't find anything more helpful," the girl said. Then she added, "I go there a lot; I might be able to help you find what you're looking for. You know, something that is a little bit more helpful."

"Thank you. That would be very kind," Senndra said. She wondered what to say next, but the girl took care of that.

"I heard that you came from another academy in Magessa," she said.

"The dragon rider academy in Belvárd," Senndra agreed. When she saw the clueless look on the other girl's face, she expounded, "It's located in the Apathy Range up at the top of the district."

"So you live in the mountains?" the girl asked. When Senndra nodded, she continued, "What is it like living up there?"

"The scenery is amazing," Senndra answered. "When the sun is shining and the sky is clear, you can see for miles. The mountain range is especially beautiful from that high up. Even if a storm is moving in, the sight is still breathtaking. The storm clouds with lightning flashing between them as they approach the mountains are stunning to watch. There...there just aren't really any words to explain it."

"What about actually living up there?" the girl asked. "Is it any different from living down here on the plain?"

"Well, for one thing, the air up there is much thinner than it is down here," Senndra said. "That makes exercise much more difficult. But it also prepares us for when we are ready to ride our dragons. Actually, our dragons routinely go quite a bit higher than the academy, but that just emphasizes the need for our exercise in a high altitude.

"Other than that slight difference, I would say that life there is pretty much the same as life in this academy. Of course we have classes every day where we learn to fight, make decisions, and think clearly. That is pretty much what I do all day. But enough about me...what is life as a kitchen maid like? I would imagine it isn't a whole lot like my life."

"No, not much like your life at all," the girl said. "I don't even cook or anything like that; I clean the dishes and floors. My father decided that it would be a good idea for me to learn to be a cook, so he apprenticed me to the head chef here. I don't think it was ever the intention of the chef to teach me how to cook, though, so I guess I will be stuck cleaning my whole life until I get married. If I ever get married, that is." The girl muttered the last part so quietly that Senndra barely heard it.

"Why do you say that?" she asked. "I mean, a whole lot of young men come through here, after all, and you can't be more than sixteen."

"I'm nineteen," the girl stated. "Actually, I'm almost twenty, but it's not the age that makes me say that. It's just that several girls, all my age, were apprenticed at about the same time as me. All of them met boys that they fell in love with and married, but it just hasn't happened for me. I guess it is kind of stupid for me to think that way, but I do anyway."

"Look here," Senndra said, pulling on the girl's chin so that her head turned to face her. "Don't worry about it so much. You haven't found anyone yet because the right person hasn't shown up yet. I know that there is someone out there for you, and you have to be willing to wait until you meet that person. If you try to create that person, and end up marrying someone just so that you can marry someone, you'll never be happy with the situation."

"Granted, I am younger than you," Senndra continued, "but I think the same way you do sometimes. Maybe that's a stage that everyone goes through. I don't know. But what I do know is that if we wait for the right person, all of that waiting will be worth it."

"But what makes you so certain that there is such a person in the world?" the girl asked. "Don't you think there's a possibility there just isn't anyone for me?"

"It's possible I suppose," Senndra answered, "but if that's the case, I don't think you would ever be happy with anyone anyway. In this case, you just need to let go and trust Elohim to guide you. After all, He knows what is best for you, and He'll take care of you the whole way."

"Elohim?" the other girl asked. "I think I've heard about Him. He's supposed to be the god of Magessa, right?"

"Not just the god of Magessa, but *the* God of the whole world," Senndra said.

"But my father told me all of that was just for young children to believe," the girl said.

"I can't convince you, but I know someone who can," Senndra said. "One of my instructors who is here has been having meetings for unbelievers to discuss exactly this sort of thing with them. If anyone can answer your questions, he's the one. You should come to one of his meetings."

"I'll think about it," the girl said and stood to her feet. "It's time for me to get back to work, so I guess I'll see you around?"

Senndra nodded and waved good-bye to the girl. Lydia. That was the girl's name. Why could she never remember these things when she needed to remember them?

# Eight

Josiah crouched behind a large boulder with a handful of soldiers. His two messengers were with him, prepared to carry his orders to the rest of his command if he chose. But at the moment, they had their swords out and were ready to fight. The rain had ceased an hour ago, just in time for the rising of the sun, which shone over their shoulders and into the dwarf army. At least the enemy archers would find it harder to shoot straight. The dwarf army stretched at least fifty across, and their first line alone was almost impressive enough to frighten Josiah into retreat. But he had chosen this place to make the final stand, so this was to be where they would ultimately be victorious or be defeated. The dwarves had apparently not seen their opponents yet and were marching straight for the ford.

Josiah peeked over the boulder again and saw that the first of the enemy was already entering the river, so he made the sign that would set in motion the first phase of a plan that he and his advisors had come up with only an hour earlier. A few dozen soldiers rose from where they were hiding and formed a very thin line between the two rocks where the dwarves would have to pass. Some of the dwarves hesitated at the audacity of the humans, but they kept coming. Logic dictated that there was no way the humans could hold off the attack; however, they stood resolutely in the gap waiting for the dwarves. The dwarves surged over the last few yards between the armies and hit the defending line with all of their might. Josiah had chosen these soldiers so that they would not run and would be able to hold their ground, and he had chosen well. As he watched, the line of humans bowed, but did not break, staving off the dwarves for a moment; however, they would soon be overcome. Josiah raised his hand again and signaled for the second part of his plan to commence. The archers, who had been hiding along the riverbanks and around the ford, rose from their positions and fired a volley of arrows into the dwarf ranks. That cut their numbers back, but not by much. The archers broke for the boulder field on the east side of the river and took cover in it.

The dwarves had fallen back at the volley of arrows, but they were not to be defeated so easily. They quickly formed a more organized line and charged again, bringing the full might of their army to bear against the humans. Though they outnumbered the humans, the narrowness of the ford prevented them from surrounding the defenders and all they could do was push the humans further up onto the river bank. The humans slowly gave way as the members of their line began to drop one by one until the dwarves had forced their way completely out of the river and onto its bank. As the dwarves began to circle around the edges of their line, they broke ranks and sprinted for the boulder field, where the archers were hiding. The dwarves were surprised by the move and were therefore a dozen feet behind the retreating humans when they started their pursuit. Already, the arrows of the defenders were raining down on them, but they kept sprinting. Within seconds they would overtake the archers' position and cut them down. But just as they were nearing their goal, a force of ogre and human infantry rose into view from the boulder field and advanced toward them at a slow walk. Two other squads of ogres and humans appeared from the field and hurried to positions on the right and left sides of the attacking dwarves. Quickly they united their lines with the one in front of the dwarves, forming a half-circle of troops around the dwarves and blocking them from moving any direction except back into the river.

All of this happened so quickly that the dwarves did not have time to take stock of the situation before they hit the line of defenders in front of them. The humans and ogres stubbornly held their ground long enough to hit the sides of the dwarf army. The dwarves were not ready for this kind of complex strategy, and many of them sprinted for the river. Only a few dwarves stayed to fight, and these were quickly overcome. The dwarves jostled each other as they fled into the river, and many slid down the steep banks and into the swiftly flowing current. They struggled against the pull of their heavy armor to no avail and many were drowned.

The humans and ogres followed the dwarves to the edge of the river and shouted taunts after them as they fled. Then they turned back to take their positions for the fight they all knew might very well end in all of their deaths. The archers moved to the edge of the river and rained arrows into the dwarfish ranks, forcing them to fall back out of bow range. The dwarves retaliated with a rain of arrows from their crossbows, but the defenders had excellent cover, and only a few of the archers were injured.

"It's very uncharacteristic of dwarves to panic like that," Benjamin said from his position at Josiah's side. "I wonder what caused them to do it."

"Elohim," Josiah responded. "He has been watching over us. But even so, this battle will be tough. Only a few hundred of the dwarves crossed the river this time, and we would have had trouble holding them back if they had not panicked. I hate to think what will happen when they attack all at once. There is no way that we can hold them off; we'll have to fall back to the high ground where the other archers are if worse comes to worst."

Josiah walked to where his troops had taken up positions by the river and began to inspect their lines. Everyone seemed to have minor injuries, but miraculously, there were no major ones. In fact, the most serious injury had been caused by a soldier cutting himself as he sharpened his sword the night before. Josiah stopped to talk to this particular soldier, crouching down next to him as he did so.

"What's your name, soldier?" he asked.

"Marcus, sir," the soldier replied.

"How is your wound holding up, Marcus?" Josiah asked.

"It's doing fine, sir," Marcus replied holding up his left arm to reveal a nasty-looking gash running down it. "It gave me a little bit of grief when we first started fighting, but the pain was dull, and it went away after a while."

"You think that you're going to be able to hold up for the rest of this battle?" Josiah asked.

"Yes sir, I'll hold up until we defeat these dwarves or until I die," Marcus said. "Either way, I'm not going to let down my fellow soldiers because of my wound."

"Good man," Josiah said as he rose to his full height. He turned to continue down the line, but was confronted by one of his messengers sprinting toward him from the river. As the boy got closer, he saw that it was Jonathan.

"Sir, the dwarves are getting ready for their second attack!" Jonathan said breathlessly.

"Already?" Josiah said in surprise. "I would have thought they would lick their wounds for longer than that. Well, our army is already in position, so let them come. I have new orders for you to carry. First, have most of the infantry pull up to the ford where the enemy will have to pass between those two rocks. If we have any chance of holding them we will do it there. Second, have most of the archers gather near the river. The boulder field is a good defense, but that will be our last stand. That is all."

Jonathan saluted and was off to deliver the messages, leaving Josiah to make his way back to the ford. When he got there, confusion ruled his previously organized troops as they scrambled to form lines. Josiah pushed his way through the crowd and stood on a boulder.

"Silence!" he bellowed to his troops, but it had no effect on them.

"Silence!" he shouted again, even louder, and this time the soldiers closest to him quieted down.

"Line up with five men across this gap," he said, gesturing to the two rocks by the ford. "The dwarves have to come through them, and if we can hold them here, we will take away the advantage of their numbers."

The soldiers seemed to regain their composure and quickly moved into position until there were seven lines of five people. Josiah jumped off of his boulder and strode back to where the majority of the infantry was still in disarray. Grabbing a bugle from one of the soldiers, he blasted a loud, long note until all of the soldiers had quieted down. When he had their attention, he handed the bugle back and turned to address the soldiers.

"This behavior is ridiculous," he began. "You were trained to carry on war in an orderly and organized fashion—not in the state of hysteria that has ruled until now. I know that many of us may die today, but if we are to have any chance of defeating the dwarves and walking away from here alive, it will be because we fight in a calm and orderly fashion. Now, I want you to form organized ranks behind the soldiers that are already in position. If any of them fall or drop back to rest, it is your job to step up and take their place. Do you understand?"

Josiah took the silence as an affirmative reply, and he turned and trotted back to the front of the army. He climbed back onto the boulder that he had vacated only minutes before and watched as the soldiers formed ranks in a semi-orderly fashion. The archers were also finally arriving, so Josiah motioned for his messenger Benjamin to join him. The boy climbed onto the boulder with Josiah and waited for the message to be given.

"Tell the new archers to take position behind the infantry," Josiah said. "Their commander is given full authority over when they will fire; however, tell him to have them conserve their arrows."

Benjamin hopped down from the boulder to carry the message, and Josiah turned back to the dwarf army. The retreating soldiers had fallen to the back of the army to regroup, and a new breed of dwarves now faced Josiah's army. Dwarf giants, the scourge of the dwarf army, now composed the front several lines. These soldiers were all around six feet tall, and they maintained the classic build of a dwarf. Their armor covered their entire bodies, with the exception of their joints, and gruesome helmets sat on their heads. In the way of weapons, each had a battle ax about as big as the two-handed axes that the regular soldiers used; however, the giants carried these weapons as though they were toys. They each also had a massive hand-and-a-half sword that was at least five feet long.

Josiah looked back at the ranks of his army and saw that many of them showed fear in the face of this new enemy. He couldn't think of any encouraging words to say, so he leaped lightly down from the boulder and strode to the front line, where Jonathan was waiting for him. Jonathan had his shield strapped to his back and held on his arm another shield, this one painted pure black.

"This shield is a gift for you from the ogres," Jonathan said when Josiah reached him. He extended the shield toward Josiah who took it carefully. The piece of armor was obviously made for an ogre and was a bit too large for him, but it would work well. Even its weight was well within the capacity of Josiah's strength.

"Commander Looran sends it with his best wishes," Jonathan continued. "He worried that it might be too heavy, but he hopes that you will take it into battle with you."

"Indeed I will," Josiah said and strapped the shield onto his left arm. A few adjustments were needed, but soon the shield fit almost as if it had been created for him.

"I also managed to find this to complete your armor," Jonathan said and held out a helmet that Josiah had not seen before. Josiah took the headpiece and examined it. It was of orc workmanship and covered the entire face with only two eye slits. A row of small spikes ran from the top of the helmet down the back, but other than these, it was entirely unadorned. Josiah placed the helmet on his head, and though the fit was a little tight, he decided that it would work. The range of vision was much better than he had expected, and small holes on the side of the helmet allowed him to hear what was going on around him much better than a human helmet would have.

With his armor properly adjusted, Josiah took his place in the front line, and Jonathan stood next to him. Together they waited for the dwarves to make their charge, and as they watched, a black cloud rose from the rear of the army and arched through the sky toward them.

"Arrows!" someone shouted. "Shields up!"

The soldiers dropped to their knees, and each man tucked himself behind his shield. The first arrows splashed into the river, but soon they began to rain on the army of defenders, slamming into their shields and bouncing off or occasionally sticking into them. The soldiers hid behind their shields for several minutes as the rain of arrows gradually lessened and finally stopped. Josiah stood to his feet along with the rest of his army and looked across the river in defiance of the dwarves. Already the giants were splashing into the river with a crazed battle cry; they would be upon the defenders in moments. Josiah braced himself for the impact of the enemy, but was still forced backward by the sheer force of the dwarf bodies hitting his shield. The soldiers in the front line dug their feet into the ground, but they slid across the soggy earth until they hit the shields of the soldiers behind them. The soldiers in the second line dug in as well and pushed as hard as they could against the might of the dwarves, but they were still not enough to stop the advance of the enemy.

Josiah was getting pressed between his shield and that of the man behind him, and he knew that if something didn't give soon, he would literally get the life crushed out of him. He collected what was left of his breath and gave a strangled command to push, but he didn't know if anyone had heard him. In the following seconds, the pressure on him did not let up, and he was convinced that his life would end here. But then he felt a strong shove from behind that was moving him forward and throwing the dwarf directly in front of him backward. He gulped in a lung of air and almost simultaneously slashed his sword across the neck of the dwarf. With a flick of his wrist, he jerked the blade down and slashed the dwarf across his waist. His blade came away bloody, and he knew that the dwarf was dead even before he collapsed to the ground.

"The armor is weak at the neck and waist!" Josiah shouted. He plunged his sword into the neck of the next dwarf and quickly jerked it free, while blocking a blow from another dwarf's ax with his shield. He swung his sword at the dwarf that was attacking him, but the brute deflected the blade and landed another smashing blow, which Josiah again caught on his shield. He swung with his sword again, this time at waist level, an attack for which the dwarf was not prepared. The blade scraped across the dwarf's armor, but it jumped down into a seam at the last minute, laying open the brute's stomach and dropping him immediately. The minutes blurred together as Josiah continued to receive and deliver blows. Sometimes he was fighting dwarves he was able to easily dispatch, but just as often, his opponent was at least his equal in strength and skill. He was steadily tiring, and there did not appear to be an end to the attack in sight. He relinquished his position to another soldier, an orc, and passed back through the ranks to relative safety.

Now that Josiah was able to take a look at the bigger picture, he saw that his strategy of stopping the dwarves at the narrow pass was working brilliantly. Hundreds of dwarves lay dead on the banks of the river, whereas only a handful of his men had fallen. Even though they continued to hold the line despite the perpetual pounding of the dwarves, Josiah knew that his men required rest. He needed to figure out a way to force the dwarves into a retreat, but he could not see how he was going to do it. After all, even though his men had held the pass with a determination that would put fear into the hearts of most people, the dwarves were a different story. Infused with unshakable courage, they did not know fear on this battlefield and refused to retreat. Josiah wondered what could be more intimidating than men so determined to hold their ground that they killed the dwarves by the dozens. As he glanced around at his army, his gaze locked on the answer to his question. He motioned for Benjamin, who had fallen back with him.

"Tell the ogres that their turn is here," Josiah told his messenger. "I need them to move up to the front line and show the dwarves what they can do. Tell them to be as intimidating as possible."

Benjamin ran to Commander Looran and conveyed the message. The ogre leader gave a deafening roar, and his soldiers, eager to get into the action, bellowed in return. With massive strides they cleared a path through the ranks of humans and broke into the front line with a terrifying battle cry that shook the ground. They had a variety of weapons, from clubs to massive axes and gigantic swords, and everywhere they struck, dwarves were crushed and sent flying. The ogres' legs became weapons as well when the dwarves got too close, and many enemies found that a powerful kick could prove just as fatal as a slash from a sword. The ogres killed scores of dwarves, but even they were not able to inspire the fear that Josiah had so desperately needed.

Whenever a dwarf fell, another would step up to take its place, and now a new weapon threatened the defenders. Dwarves carrying crossbows mingled with the hand-to-hand units and advanced with them. They didn't seem to care about the safety of their own soldiers, and dozens of dwarves dropped from their own arrows. Even so, the effect against the defending army was devastating. The ogres were large and made prime targets for archers.

Ogres have tough skins and can absorb a lot of abuse, but it is still possible to deal them a mortal blow. When this wound is delivered to an ogre, they are far from out of the battle. Sensing that they are about to die, they make the famous "ogre's death charge," smashing through the enemy ranks and killing as many enemies as they are able before they fall. As the dwarf archers began to fire, many ogres took the death charge, killing hundreds of dwarves. But still, not even a dent had been made in the massive numbers of the dwarf army. The remaining ogres were forced to fall back and let the humans take the front line again. However, the dwarf crossbows were just as deadly against humans and orcs as they were against the ogres, and for the first time, Josiah truly realized that his army was going to be totally annihilated.

"Archers, fall back to the hill," Josiah shouted, implementing his plan for the army's last stand. The archers quickly retreated to the hill that had previously been fortified, even as the dwarves chopped their way through the defending swordsmen.

"Commence an orderly retreat," Josiah ordered. "All but the first three lines will fall back to the hill. The rest will hold the dwarves."

The infantry immediately ran to the hill, which was a little too quickly for Josiah's taste. It seemed almost as if they were running away. Josiah turned to where the final section of his army was holding the dwarves in a standstill. He drew his sword, raised his shield, and ran toward the action.

"Fall back toward the hill, but maintain a tight group," Josiah shouted. The soldiers formed a tight ring, with men facing out on all sides, and slowly pulled out of their position. The dwarves immediately pushed around the outer edges of the band and quickly surrounded the little party. Josiah was still in the middle of the group, so he took a position facing the hill that they were trying to reach. This was where the most fighting would take place, and he wanted to be there to lead his men. The dwarves pitted the full weight of their army against the small group of soldiers, trying to make a hole in their line, but Josiah's men stubbornly held their ground. Then the crossbow darts came. The dwarves fired a barrage of the deadly projectiles into the group, cutting down more than half of the soldiers and wounding the rest.

Instinctively the soldiers pulled into a small knot and crouched down so that they would be harder for the crossbows to hit. Josiah ducked behind his shield just as a dwarf swung an ax at him. He peeked out and swung his sword low, cutting the dwarf's feet off at the ankles. The dwarf fell outside of his range and another moved to take its place. As this enemy brought his ax down, Josiah raised his shield and caught the blow. Then he rammed the bottom of the shield into the dwarf's midriff. The dwarf fell away, clutching his stomach. Josiah planted his shield back in front of himself and stabbed and slashed with his sword, taking down anyone who came within reach of his arm.

Another barrage of arrows hit the soldiers, killing two more. Josiah caught a bolt on his shield, but the razor-sharp tip pierced through the metal and dug into his breastplate. Josiah glanced back and saw that only five more soldiers remained. They pulled into a tighter knot and fought for all they were worth, but they knew that it was only a matter of time before they would be slaughtered just like the rest of their comrades. Time seemed to shift into slow motion for Josiah as he watched a nearby dwarf sight in on him with a crossbow. The dwarf's finger applied pressure to the trigger of the weapon, releasing the string, which flung the bolt out of the weapon. Sound faded as the bolt slowly cut through the air, over the shoulder of a dwarf, and straight at Josiah's head.

"Courage, Josiah." The voice was soft yet powerful, and it gave Josiah a new strength. He jerked his shield up in front of his face and the bolt smashed into it, punching through the metal, but coming to a stop before it reached his helmet. Josiah gave a guttural roar and rose to his full height. He swung his sword furiously, clearing an arc around himself and leading his small band toward the hill where the rest of his army waited. The dwarves in front of him fell as they came into his range, their helmets and shields cloven in two by his brutal slashes. He used his shield for a weapon as much as he used it for defense, and many dwarves were hurled back into their comrades by blows from it. Slowly Josiah led his soldiers toward the hill, cutting the distance in half and then in half again. With only a few dozen yards left to go, two dwarves attacked him simultaneously. He hit one with his shield and slashed the other in the stomach, but in doing so, he left himself unprotected. The flailing weapon of the second dwarf slashed the bicep of his left arm, rendering his shield useless.

A shout from behind distracted Josiah; therefore, he was unprepared when the next dwarf attacked. He was forced to stumble backward to avoid the swipe of the dwarf's weapon, and though he attempted to maintain his balance, he was unable to do so and fell to the ground. His left arm and shield flopped onto his chest, and moments later, the ax of the attacking dwarf slammed into it, driving the breath out of Josiah. The inevitable was only prolonged, however, and Josiah watched as the dwarf raised his weapon for the final blow. Just as the ax reached the apex of its swing, an unknown form leaped over Josiah's head and landed between him and the dwarf. The sword of Josiah's rescuer flashed, and the arm of the dwarf flew off. Again the sword flashed and this time the dwarf's head was separated from his body. A shower of red speckles painted Josiah's shield, and the dwarf toppled backward onto the bloodstained ground.

Josiah's rescuer, who Josiah could now identify as an elf, turned and helped him to his feet. Hidden by the massive dwarf army, the elves had arrived from the west and joined the fight. Their arrival was a complete surprise to both armies, and they held the upper hand, though only for a brief amount of time. Josiah allowed himself to be led to the hill, to which the elves had cleared a path. The elves quickly followed him to the high, fortified position.

"Josiah, are you okay?" Josiah turned to see Cirro jogging toward him.

"I just got slashed on the arm," Josiah answered, "which is a lot better than most of the soldiers out there got."

"True," Cirro said as he tore a piece of cloth from his shirt and wrapped it around Josiah's arm. He knotted the cloth and tucked the stray edges of the makeshift bandage under it.

"Do you want some water?" he asked as he handed a canteen to Josiah. Josiah was silent for several long moments as he downed a long draught of water. Finally he handed the canteen back to Cirro and wiped his mouth with the back of his hand.

"Thanks," he told Cirro. "You don't know how much I needed that."

The two friends walked across the hill together and approached a large group of elves. Josiah recognized Wellter, so he forced his way through the elves to him. He saluted and waited for Wellter to return the salute.

"Hello, Josiah," Wellter said after Josiah stood at ease. "I sense that you have a reason for being here."

"Yes, sir," Josiah responded. "As admiral of the combined human and ogre army, I feel that it is my duty to confer with you on what we are to do about our current position."

"Admiral?" Wellter asked with a twinkle in his eye. "I don't recall you having that rank when we set out from the city."

"Things change quickly on the battlefield, sir," Josiah answered.

"Indeed they do," Wellter said in a more serious tone. "I also recall that you had many more soldiers when you set out than you do now. Exactly how many men are under your command?"

"I don't know exactly, sir, but I think there are around five hundred humans and five hundred ogres. I haven't seen any orcs, but that's not surprising considering how few of them there were when we left Saddun."

"I don't see how you survived at all," Wellter said, shaking his head.

"Only by the bravery of my men and the help of Elohim," Josiah answered.

"Indeed…" Wellter began, but was cut off by a cry of warning. Seconds later, a boulder flew over the makeshift battlements and hit a massive rock, turning it into fragments and flinging these into the army of Magessa.

"Get under cover!" Josiah shouted uselessly. Already the soldiers were scrambling for the nearest and safest places they could find. Josiah followed Wellter and his entourage to a position behind two massive boulders.

"Where the hell did the siege machines come from?" Josiah yelled.

"They took it with them when they left Saddun," Wellter yelled back. "We didn't think anything of it because we assumed they were going to siege Belmoth with it."

"We have to attack the dwarves and take out that siege equipment or they will pelt us to death with it!" an elf shouted.

"We can't," Josiah countered. "They have it set up on the far side of the river. Besides that, we'd never get past the dwarf crossbowmen. My guess is that they already have them in position and ready to take out any living thing in this area that provides a target. You're more than welcome to take a peek if you want to test the theory."

"We'll just have to weather the attack then," Wellter commanded. "If we stay behind cover, we might be able to survive until they cease their fire. They have to run out of ammunition eventually."

"That's true, but we'd better bunker down good," Josiah said. "Those boulders they are flinging at us are no joke."

"Of course," Wellter agreed. "That's why I'm staying with you. Because you think of important things like that."

Josiah didn't acknowledge the humor in the statement and the look of concentration never left his face.

"So, how did you end up in this mess?" Wellter tried again. "At the academy, I mean."

"Do you really think this is the time for that?" Josiah asked with a puzzled look at Wellter.

"If you think about the battle too much, you're going to fry your brain," Wellter explained. "You have to take time to relax."

"Well, you've been doing this a lot longer than I have, so if you say so, I'll believe you," Josiah conceded.

"I say so," Wellter said. "Now tell me how you ended up at the academy."

"I'm afraid to say it isn't a very interesting story," Josiah said. "I grew up in a small village that is set off the beaten path. There wasn't much of a future for anyone who stayed there so most of the young men left to join the army. I happened to be smarter than most, I guess, because before long I was sent to the academy. I've been there ever since."

"You were correct, that wasn't very interesting," Wellter quipped.

"So, what about you?" Josiah turned the question back on the elf. "What's your story? I bet it's a lot more interesting than mine."

"It is," Wellter agreed. "I would tell you, but it is a very long story. I wouldn't have time to finish and then you'd be wondering about it when you have to fight. That's how people die."

"Very funny," Josiah said. Clearly he wasn't going to get anything else out of the elf on that subject, but the talking was calming his nerves. "Well, if you don't want to tell me about you, do you have any good jokes?"

******

Vladimir opened his eyes and wondered sleepily where he was. As his consciousness deepened, he took in his surroundings—the walls that surrounded him, the ceiling over him, and the bed beneath him. He recognized this place, but its name was eluding him. Then the memory of the past few days broke over him like a spray of cold water, and he sat up in the bed. He knew where he was: the infirmary at the academy, which could only mean one thing—Timothy had succeeded in his mission and had told those at the academy where he had left Vladimir.

The door to the room opened and Timothy strode in. He did not look particularly happy, and Vladimir suddenly wondered if the mission had actually failed. He held his tongue until Timothy sat down in a chair by his bed.

"So what's happening?" he asked. He was so eager to hear the answer that he was actually leaning toward Timothy.

"Some dragons found me just before I passed out, and they brought me here," Timothy said. "When I regained consciousness, we had just reached the academy, and I wasted no time in telling the grand admiral about the dwarf army. He immediately sent messengers throughout the country to warn about the attack. He also sent a force of seventy dragons to assist in the battle against the dwarves."

"So what's wrong?" Vladimir asked. "It looks like you aren't entirely satisfied with the results of our mission."

"I only wonder whether or not we arrived in time for our dragons to be of assistance. I can't remember how many days it took to get here from Saddun, but I can only hope that it was fast enough."

"We did all that we could, and that is all that anyone can ask of us," Vladimir said. "We will have to leave the rest in the hands of Elohim. All we can do now is pray that He will sustain our armies until the dragons reach them."

"Can we do that now?" Timothy asked.

Vladimir had always looked up to the older cadet as a wiser and more mature person, but right now he had the look of a lost puppy. Vladimir nodded, and together they knelt on the floor and prayed silently. For half an hour not a word was spoken between the two cadets as they prayed. Finally they rose to their feet and without breaking the silence Timothy left the room while Vladimir climbed back into bed to rest.

******

Senndra and Lydia stood in the library of Saddun and gazed up at massive shelves that contained hundreds of books, scrolls, maps, and other pieces of written material. All Senndra could do was stare and wonder how in the world she was going to find what she wanted from this huge compilation of volumes. Lydia, however, went straight to work, running her finger along the spines of the books. She passed several shelves altogether and resumed her search again, moving up the bookcase until she was forced to use a ladder to reach the higher shelves. She finally discovered the section that she was looking for and began to pull out various volumes and browse through them. Whenever she found one that she liked, she handed it down to Senndra. By the time Lydia came down from the ladder, the stack of books in Senndra's hands had grown to perhaps a dozen volumes.

"These are some of the most informative books on dwarves that can be found anywhere in the country," Lydia said as she led Senndra from the shelf and into the main hall of the library. This hall was lined with numerous others which housed even more shelves of books. The number of volumes was staggering, and Senndra wondered again how Lydia was able to find exactly what she wanted. At the front of the building, Lydia led Senndra to a counter where an older lady made a note of each book that was in the pile.

"So you're back into dwarves now, Lydia?" the woman asked.

"No, these are for my friend," Lydia answered.

"Well, I hope she enjoys them," the woman said as she finished putting the book names into her log.

"I'm sure she will," Lydia said.

Senndra followed Lydia out of the library and down the street outside. The sun had sunk behind the mountains, and the sound of people returning from their work was no longer in the air. Since the battle, a great deal of progress had been made toward restoring the city. The debris was being cleared away and many of the buildings as well as the northern wall were being repaired. The wall had obviously been the first priority, and the breaches in it had been barricaded by wooden palisades. Stone was now being brought from a quarry in the mountains to restore the wall to its original strength. During the day everyone helped with the repair efforts, so it was only in the late afternoon, after the work was finished for the day, that Senndra and Lydia were able to visit the library.

The two girls entered the building where the servants slept and climbed the stairs to the second floor. A hall stretched the entire length of the building, and halfway down, they entered a room. Due to a lack of sleeping quarters, they shared this small room with three other girls who were not there at the moment. Five cots covered the majority of the floor, leaving room for only a small path along one wall. Senndra sat on one of the end cots and wedged her books into a small gap between the cot and the wall. She kept one back with the title *Dwarves and Their Habitat* and immediately opened it and began to read. She became engrossed in her reading, only looking up when Lydia tapped her on the shoulder.

"It's dinner time" she said. Senndra put her book aside and followed her friend out of the room. They left the building and headed toward the mess hall. A group of people had gathered in front of the hall, and as the girls were about to pass them, Senndra spotted Lemin standing in the middle. She grabbed Lydia's arm and pulled her into the group until she was close enough that she could hear what was being said.

"The army that left this city had a very small chance of returning, much less defeating the dwarves," Lemin said. "They knew that when they set out, and yet they still went in order to protect their country. They put together a plan that had a chance of defeating the dwarves. But even the best laid plans go amiss, and I fear that their strategy has been brought to naught. Therefore, I have asked you to gather here so that we might pray for our comrades that Elohim will give them strength and uphold them in their trials."

Lemin got on his knees and bowed his head. One by one, the members of the crowd followed suit. Senndra did the same, but as she closed her eyes, an image of Josiah, Cirro and a few other soldiers, both elf and human, crouching behind a boulder, jumped into her mind. The enemy soldiers surrounding them outnumbered them heavily. Senndra snapped her eyes open and found herself in a circle of praying people, so she slowly shut her eyes again. This time she saw nothing but darkness, and she began to pray. If the vision that she just had was anything like reality, the army needed all the prayer they could get.

274

The sun had set by the time the dwarves stopped flinging boulders from their catapults, and torches now lit the ranks of their army. Somehow the darkness made the dwarf army seem more ominous than before, and the remains of the army of Magessa huddled in their natural fortress. Their numbers had been cut greatly by the pounding of the dwarves' catapults, but Josiah knew that their losses could have been much greater. At the onset of the barrage, he had figured that at most a fourth of the army would survive and was therefore greatly encouraged by the number of warriors that were left. He watched as the ranks of the dwarf army moved toward him, but he did not stir or make a sound. He and Wellter had already decided that the best plan of action would be to remain silent and motionless until the dwarves moved in to make sure that they were dead. Then they would kill as many as they could without presenting themselves; however, when they were forced out into the open, they would attack ferociously and stay among the dwarf lines so that their crossbows would be useless. This was why the entire army stood motionless on the hill, hiding among the boulders and waiting.

A group of one hundred dwarves slowly made its way up the hill. They were clearly not expecting to find any survivors, and they held their shields and weapons in a careless manner. As they neared the defenders, the soldiers tensed, ready for the first strike. The dwarves passed the first line of defenders, searching among the boulders. The soldiers caught the unsuspecting dwarves as they came through, covering their mouths and slashing their throats. Neither the muffled cries nor the thud of falling corpses could be heard above the sound of the advancing army, and the dwarves continued their advance until there was no more ground left to take.

Josiah turned to Cirro, who stood beside him, and punched his outstretched fist in triumph. Then he peered around the boulder he stood behind and observed the dwarf army. They had no idea what had just occurred and were waiting for the search party to return. Minutes passed, and after half an hour, it became obvious that they were not coming back. So another party, with twice the number of soldiers, was sent to find the first. Josiah motioned to Cirro that there were two hundred dwarves this time, and the two friends readied themselves for the attack. This time the dwarves carried their weapons and shields at the ready, prepared for anything. Josiah heard a soft moaning to his left and recognized it as a signal. Wellter had decided that the dwarves were well-prepared and that a concentrated attack would be the best course of action. The dwarves were within feet of the first soldiers when the signal to attack came. Humans and elves burst from their hiding places and smashed into the dwarf contingent. The dwarves were heavily outnumbered and didn't stand a chance. The army of Magessa trampled them and continued the frenzied charge down the hill toward the main dwarf army. The dwarves were stunned by the attack, and the crossbowmen barely had time to fire before the humans and elves hit them. With swords flashing, the small army pushed its way through the dwarf lines, killing and trampling anyone who stood before them; however, as they progressed, their momentum steadily diminished until the sheer number of dwarves forced them to a halt. The soldiers formed a circle, but even this did not work. The dwarves crushed in on them, forcing soldiers from the circle and killing them. The crossbowmen began their attack, their first barrage devastating the army.

As Josiah stood with the few remaining defenders, he knew that the end was near. The dwarves were closing in to finish off the last remnants of the army. But just then, they were interrupted by a harsh sound that was music to Josiah's ears. A dragon's roar washed across the armies and distracted the dwarves. Josiah and his small army seized the opportunity and attacked the dwarves, cutting a path through them and out into the plain. Quickly they put as much distance as possible between themselves and the dwarves. Finally they turned and saw one of the most stunning sights in the world. Seventy dragons circled over the dwarves, blasting the army with fire. The dwarves were running in all directions, clearly panicked by this new development. Crossbows were discharged at the beasts, but a flying target is hard to hit. The bolts that did reach the dragons bounced off of their scales, doing nothing but aggravating the beasts. A few of the enemy were manning ballistae, siege equipment that fired large javelins. Three dragons swooped in on a concentration of the machines, spiraling as the weapons discharged their missiles. Two javelins ripped through the wing of one dragon, and the beast hit the ground at full speed, sliding through several of the ballistae. Each of the other two dragons hit one of the machines with its tail and reduced it to matchwood.

The fallen dragon regained its feet and did not appear to be seriously damaged by the fall. The dwarves swarmed the beast, but soon discovered that even a fallen dragon can be extremely dangerous. It torched the dwarves in front of it and cleared out those behind it with its tail. The rider astride it fired arrows into the dwarves, but all of this was to no avail. Finding the blind spots on the dragon's sides, the dwarves fell upon the beast with weapons drawn. The first wave of them was trampled beneath the beast's feet, but not even the mighty beast could hold off thousands of dwarves. In no time, they had pulled the rider from his saddle and killed him. Then they swarmed the dragon, hacking and stabbing at his scales, trying to find a weak spot. The dragon roared and thrashed, but the dwarves continued to pile on top of it. It was only a matter of time before they found a weakness to exploit. The dragon gave one last roar, thrashing his tail and head wildly. His movements became weaker until he collapsed, unmoving, to the ground.

The dwarves gave shouts of triumph, but their elation was short lived. Hearing the calls of the dying dragon, the other riders had come to the rescue, albeit too late. All that remained was for his death to be avenged, and this was easily accomplished. Waves of fire rolled across the ground and over the fallen dragon's body, igniting anyone in its path. The dragon riders shot arrows into the dwarves, killing those who escaped the fire and claws of their mounts.

As Josiah watched, the dragons annihilated the army that had once appeared impossible to defeat. The battle lasted for half an hour, after which time all that could be seen was smoke rising from the battlefield as the dragons circled overhead and gradually began to land. Josiah sank to his knees and raised his hands in victory. Then he bowed his head to give thanks to Elohim who gives all victories.

# Nine

The army that marched into Saddun had a very different feel than the one that had left the city only a few days ago. The soldiers were tired, but the feelings of victory in their hearts showed on their faces and obscured their exhaustion. The group was small, containing only a fraction of the soldiers that had left, but above them circled a battalion of dragons. The soldiers also appeared sure of themselves and more formidable than they had been only days ago.

The makeshift gates of the city were thrown open wide for the army, and all of its inhabitants hurried out to meet the victorious soldiers. The army made its way slowly through the city in a triumphant procession, which ended in the parade fields of the city. The dragons landed and let their riders slide off before leaping into the sky again and flying toward the mountains where they would spend the night. The wounded soldiers were spirited off to the hospital while the rest of the army was led to the mess hall where everyone in the entire city, it seemed, had gathered. Everyone sat down at the tables and settled in to wait for the cooks to throw a meal together. The noise in the hall was deafening as everyone talked at once, the soldiers telling about their experiences and the rest listening and asking questions.

Josiah sat at a table beside Cirro and only partially listened to the stories being told.

"Were you scared when the dwarves attacked?" someone asked Cirro.

"I was scared spitless," Cirro answered with a small laugh.

"*I* wasn't scared," one of the other soldiers boasted. "I said to them 'Come on and we'll see who fights better,' and when they came, I gave them hell."

"Let's think back," Cirro said with a smirk. "You want me to believe that with the lines upon lines of dwarf giants, not to mention the crossbows and the tens of thousands of dwarf regulars, you weren't the least bit afraid? You're saying that, as you were looking out at that massive army, not even the smallest fraction of fear slipped into your heart?"

"Maybe a little bit of fear," the soldier conceded, "but it passed, and I took on those dwarves and beat them."

Up until this statement, Josiah had held his tongue, but he could not stand it any longer.

"Really? Not the least bit of fear and then you took on the entire dwarf army?" Josiah glared at the soldier. "Let me tell you two things. First, neither you nor anyone else beat the dwarf army; the dragons did that. Second, if you were so brave, why weren't you in the front line when the dwarves charged across the river?"

"You think that I wasn't in the front lines?" the soldier retorted.

"Yes, that's what I think," Josiah answered, "and let me tell you why. Every man that was in the front lines died except for him," Josiah pointed to Cirro. "They died holding off the dwarves so that the rest of the army could fall back to safety. If you're going to tell what happened, tell how it really happened. You're a hero in your own right; you don't have to make up things that didn't happen."

The bragging soldier became quiet, and the listeners around him turned to others to hear the tales of the battle. Josiah fell silent again and stayed that way until the food was served. He ate heartily, and after the meal, he retired to a barrack that had been set aside for the returning army. As he unrolled his blankets on one of the bunks, Cirro entered and sat on the bed opposite Josiah's.

"What's the matter?" Cirro asked.

"With me?" Josiah asked. "Nothing; I'm just tired, that's all."

"I can tell when something is bothering you," Cirro said. "Don't lie to me. Something is troubling you big time. I mean, you should be celebrating, not sulking around."

"What do we really have to be celebrating?" Josiah asked. "Sure, we defeated the dwarf army. It was a very large dwarf army at that, but so what? Why would the dwarves attack Magessa? There has to be a bigger reason than they just don't like us."

"So what do you think is happening?" Cirro asked.

"If you ask me, a shadow is spreading over the entire northern country, starting in Volexa Temp," Josiah said.

"So you think that this is the doing of Molkekk," Cirro said.

"Maybe so, but no matter who is behind it, you can be sure of one thing—we may have won a single battle, but the war is far from over."

\*\*\*\*\*\*

Josiah's dreary state of mind had passed by the next morning. He and Cirro were up before sunrise, and by the time the sun peeked over the Apathy mountains, they were already at

281

the practice field facing each other. Once again they had exchanged their deadly weapons for blunted practice swords and were circling each other as they each searched for an opening in the other's defenses. Cirro lunged at Josiah, and the silence of the morning was broken by the ringing of metal on metal. The two friends had fought hundreds of times before, but the feeling of this contest was different. Both used everything they had learned in the recent battle, making this match extremely fierce. One thing remained the same, however; the battle ended with Cirro's sword at Josiah's neck. The two friends fought for a few more rounds before sheathing their weapons and sitting at the edge of the field to catch their breaths. Josiah flopped onto the grass, looked across the field, and spied half a dozen figures coming toward him. They were too far away for their features to be distinguished. As they got closer, Josiah was able to identify them as cadets from the academy in Belvárd. He recognized four of them as Senndra, Timothy, Vladimir, and Rita, but the other two were strangers to him. He and Cirro scrambled to their feet as the cadets approached.

"Good morning," Timothy called out as his group neared Josiah and Cirro.

"That it is," Cirro answered. "Of course, it could be pouring down rain and I would still think it was a good morning because I'm alive."

"We heard about your run to Belvárd," Josiah said. "I just wanted to say thank you because without you, the rest of the army and I would have been crushed by the dwarves. By the way, how did you get here? I thought you were still in Belvárd?"

"We arrived this morning with a huge entourage," Vladimir answered. "Apparently there is going to be some sort of official ceremony here commending everyone involved in the battle for their bravery, so practically the entire academy came with us."

"Rumor is, the elders of Rampön, Belvárd, and Gatlon are coming and should be here in the next couple of days," Senndra said. "It seems like anyone who has any kind of political position at all is going to be here."

"Of course you know what that means," Josiah laughed. "We're going to get kicked out of the buildings to make room for all of the visiting dignitaries. Not that I'm complaining, but it figures that the heroic warriors get stuck outside while the politicians get pampered."

"Isn't that what always happens?" Cirro commented. "After all, if the dignitaries did end up sleeping outside or something like that, they might get a little taste of what it's actually like to be in the military. They like to think that war is all about glory. Heaven forbid that they ever find out what it actually entails."

"So you like to get up early and practice fighting as well," Timothy noted, changing the subject. "I always make it a point to do the same thing. I don't know why, but it seems that my day goes better if I do."

"Actually, he has a terrible memory, so if he doesn't practice at the same time every day, he forgets to do it at all," Rita said.

"So how good are you at hand-to-hand?" Cirro asked Timothy.

"He's spectacular," Vladimir said before Timothy could answer. "He won the sword play competition at the academy this year. Of course, he almost got beat by a girl, but he did end up winning."

"Well, let's see how good you are, Timothy," Cirro said, drawing his sword. He winked at Vladimir. "After all, if you almost lost to a girl, how good can you be?"

"I guess we'll find out," Timothy answered with a good-natured smile. He drew his sword, and the two cadets moved into the practice field.

"I never got to thank you for the way that you commanded the army, Josiah," the young man that Josiah did not recognize said. "If it weren't for you, we would have all died out there."

"First of all, it was Elohim that kept us from being killed," Josiah said. "We were horribly outnumbered, and by all rights we should have died. Second of all, it was just as much the doing of the soldiers as it was my doing." Josiah looked hard at the young man. "Do I know you, or am I just imagining things?"

"Petra Bentinck," the man said. "I believe you were the commander who first met me when I arrived with the message from Gatlon."

"That's right," Josiah said. "You came and said that no one was coming. So, how do you think they are going to cover up that little piece of information?"

"I don't know," Petra said. "But you can be sure that they're going to come up with something. They're politicians—it's what they're good at."

"You seem just a little bit cynical," Josiah stated.

"Remember that I have spent more than a year guarding the door to the chambers where these men meet," Petra answered. "I have heard their councils and the councils of many like them. It seems like they are always trying to cover something up."

"And these are the kind of men that are ruling the country?" Senndra asked with exasperation. "These are the men that are making our laws and commanding our armies?"

"Making laws, yes; commanding armies, it would seem not," Josiah retorted quickly.

"They are not fit for the task of commanding," Petra added. "I would sooner trust a mule with an army than those conniving men."

"So what loyalties do they hold?" Senndra asked. "Do they still claim to serve Elohim?"

"I don't know how it is at the academies, but in the rest of the realm, the popularity of serving Elohim has been on the decline for many years now," Petra answered. "There are still people that seem to serve Him and profess to follow Him, but many do not even pretend anymore."

"And these are the people that we are defending with our lives," Josiah commented. "You have to wonder why Elohim has granted us success in this venture so far. It seems to me that this nation has fallen away from Him so much that perhaps it would be better if it was wiped from the face of the earth."

"You make it sound as if the whole nation has followed the path of the few that govern it," Petra chided. "A larger portion of the population than you would think still follows Elohim, though admittedly it is the minority. All that is required to see this is a visit to the temple of Elohim. It is still in good repair, and the ceremonies that have always occurred there in the past are still in effect, all paid for by tithes from regular people."

"Then why is nothing being done about the corrupt government?" Josiah asked. "If the common people follow Elohim, why do they allow a few evil men to rule them?"

"Many of them probably do not realize what has happened," Petra answered. "Also, a great number of the people do follow Elohim, but there are still many that have turned from Him."

Josiah nodded and turned away to look at the two cadets on the practice field. Cirro made a quick move toward Timothy, but Timothy blocked the sword slash. He reached under the crossed blades, grabbed Cirro's shirt, and threw him on the ground. Cirro hit the ground and bounced, his sword flying from his grip, and Timothy laid his sword's point on the throat of his opponent.

"So what do we do?" Josiah asked as he turned back to Petra. "If we do nothing, we will eventually end up like Cirro..." Josiah brought his fist into the palm of his other hand. "...on our backs with the sword of the enemies of Elohim at our throats."

"You're correct," Petra confirmed. "Doing nothing would be one of the biggest mistakes that we could make. Of course, doing something drastic might also be a mistake, depending on the ramifications of the action. It all depends on what is to be done, and I don't think that I am the one to answer that question."

"You could ask Lemin," Senndra offered. "He knows a lot, especially about the things that you are discussing."

"Are you serious?" Josiah asked. "I didn't think that he was the political type."

"No, he's not political, but he does know a lot about spiritual issues," Senndra answered. "I know that he will give you his opinion if you ask him, and his opinions are always good."

"Thanks for the advice. I think that I will ask him," Josiah said. He turned to Petra and asked, "Do you want to come with me and see what he has to say?"

"I guess so," Petra answered. "When are you planning on going to see him?"

"There's no time like the present, is there?"

******

It was an hour and a half before Josiah and Petra found Lemin. They had asked more than a dozen people if they had seen him, but had no luck. Finally, an older man directed them to the library, where they found the object of their search sitting amidst a pile of dusty volumes and scrolls. He was so absorbed in his reading that he didn't even notice the two young men approach him. Josiah and Petra stood for a few seconds, waiting for the elf to notice them. When he did not, Josiah cleared his throat. Lemin looked up from the scroll that he was reading, and when he saw the soldiers, he motioned them to two chairs that sat opposite his. He rolled his scroll up as Petra and Josiah sat down and placed it on top of a small pyramid of similar-looking scrolls. He looked at his two visitors expectantly and waited for them to open up the conversation.

"Well, I suppose you are wondering why we're here." Josiah started. Lemin nodded, so he continued. "We were having a discussion about the spiritual condition of the nation, but we could not decide what needed to be done about it. One of your students, Senndra by name, mentioned that we should ask you for your opinion, and we took her advice. So we are here to ask you what you think needs to be done about the nation's condition."

"Then you both agree that the nation is not where it needs to be spiritually?" Lemin asked. His listeners nodded, so he continued. "The spiritual condition of the nation is indeed depressing to consider. While very few would deny the existence of Elohim altogether, most people would rather not count Him into their thinking of daily life at all. They follow His commands outwardly by bringing tithes to His temple and praying daily, but their hearts are not in the actions. Instead, they seem to think that strict adherence to the ceremonies is enough. However, what Elohim really wants is for His people to follow Him in their hearts."

"Yes, we agree that the spiritual condition is appalling, but what should we do about it?" Petra asked. "A revolution, either political or military, will not help because the problem lies with the hearts of men rather than their physical state."

"You are correct when you say that no revolution, no matter what kind it is, will help solve this problem," Lemin said. "Since the problem is in the hearts of men, who is our opponent?"

"Anyone who is against Elohim," Josiah answered immediately.

"Those who are against Elohim are not our enemies," Petra quickly countered. "The people who are slaves to sin are not the enemies. Rather, they are the prisoners that we are trying to set free."

"Petra is correct," Lemin interjected. "We should not view mere people as our opponents in this battle. Our battle is not against flesh and blood, but against sin and the powers of darkness."

"So now we know who the enemy is, but how are we supposed to wage this war?" Josiah asked. "I have been trained in military arts for my entire life, and I simply do not know any other way to fight."

"Well, what does it take for the enemy to be victorious?" Lemin asked. "If you can isolate the cause of the enemy's victory, it is easier to determine how to make sure that it never happens again."

"I'm not sure," Josiah said slowly. He turned to Petra and restated the question thoughtfully. "What is the cause of sin's victory?"

"Well, humans are naturally sinful, correct?" Petra began. Lemin nodded, and he continued. "Therefore, it doesn't take anything for sin to be victorious. If nothing is done, the sin nature controls humans and causes them to act in opposition to Elohim."

"You are right," Lemin said. "It is easier for sin to be victorious than for it to be defeated. In fact, all that is required for sin to prosper is for the righteous to do nothing. So then, what is the cure for sin?"

Josiah and Petra looked at each other and shrugged.

"If all that was at work in the body was sin, men would not follow Elohim because their sin nature would urge them to throw off all authority, even that which is good," Lemin said. "If sin was all that was at work in the human mind, there would not even be nations of people under governments, for as I said, sin urges people to not submit to authority. However, there are functional governments, and many people follow Elohim. Therefore, it follows that there must be some other force at work in the human mind."

"The conscience," Josiah stated.

"That is correct," Lemin affirmed. "When Elohim created humans, he instilled in them what we call a conscience. That is, He made a part of the mind that constantly reminds people what is wrong and right. Yet even with this check, sin is still exemplified in the actions of men. Sinful men cannot do anything but sin. Of course, there are occasions in which sinners do things that appear to be selfless; however, they are always done with an ulterior motive in mind. In and of themselves, there is no way that men can ever do anything but sin."

"So that is where Elohim comes in, correct?" Josiah asked.

"No, Elohim does not come in," Lemin answered with a smile. "He has been around since the beginning, so He cannot *come in* as you have put it. However, your thought is correct. It is at this point that it becomes evident that it is only through Elohim that we can do what is right."

"And is there anything we can do to make other people accept Elohim as their master?" Josiah asked.

"No," Lemin said. "We cannot do anything to make people accept Elohim. People were created with a free will, so it is up to them whether or not they will follow Elohim."

"Well then, what can we do?" Josiah asked. "Surely we are not supposed to just sit by and hope that people follow Elohim."

"Of course not," Lemin said. "How can people follow someone they know nothing about? It is our job to tell everyone about Elohim."

"So all we can do is tell them," Josiah said. "Somehow it just doesn't seem to be enough."

"We should first follow Elohim with our actions," Lemin corrected. "If we do this, others will see it and want to know what is different. Then, when we tell them about Elohim, they will want to follow Him."

"You said that we are to tell all people about Elohim," Petra said. "What about the dwarves? Are we to tell them just as we are to tell everyone else?"

"What do you think?" Lemin asked.

"I think they are people, just like everyone else, but they are our enemies," Petra answered. "How are we supposed to tell them about Elohim? They would kill us rather than listen."

"We are not called to decide which people to tell and which not to tell," Lemin said. "Our duty is to tell all people, and the result is left to Elohim. If we die, at least we have died in His service, and there is no nobler cause to give your life for than that."

"But do they deserve to be told about Elohim?" Josiah asked. "They had their chance and turned their backs on Him. Hasn't He turned His back on them as well? Shouldn't we treat them as His enemies?"

"Think about this country, Josiah," Lemin said. "How many of its people still follow Elohim? They have had their chance and turned their backs on Him as well. Are they so much different than the dwarves?"

"No, I guess not," Josiah conceded finally.

"Then you have your answer," Lemin said. "There are people of every race and nation who are sinners and do not follow

Elohim. Their heritage or the location of their home does not make them any different than anyone else in this world. Elohim created the whole world, and that is the extent of our mission. Not until the whole world has been told about Him is our job finished."

Josiah and Petra nodded and got to their feet. With absentminded thanks, they turned and headed out of the library. Lemin smiled and retrieved his scroll from where he had placed it. He had given them a lot to think about, but he was sure they would consider it and arrive at the correct conclusion when their thoughts had run their course.

******

The next few days were a blur to Josiah. Saddun was filled past its limit with people from every corner of the country. Politicians from all three counties, as well as many retired and active military personnel, filled every building in the city to overflowing. In fact, there were so many extra mouths to feed that even with food being brought into the city every day there was still a shortage. This problem was solved by feeding the guests as much as they wanted and leaving the rest for the army and other normal inhabitants of the city. There was never enough food to go around, which Josiah found ironic.

"Apparently," he grumbled to Cirro, "the proper thing to do is congratulate soldiers on how they have heroically saved the country from invasion and at the same time not feed them enough."

"It's probably for the best," Cirro pointed out. "If the politicians find out what it's like to be short on food, as we often are, they might become disillusioned."

"Or make sure we have more food," Josiah countered. Cirro laughed so long and hard that Josiah decided to let the issue go.

Hundreds of additional workmen were also brought to the city to repair its damaged buildings and its wall. They also helped to prepare the city for the fabulous ceremony in which the victorious army was going to be recognized as national heroes. Professional chefs were brought to the city for the occasion, freeing the normal mess hall staff from their duties. During this time, the soldiers and other occupants of the city found that the best way to stay out from under foot of the workmen was often to leave the city altogether. Josiah, Senndra, Cirro, Rita, Petra, Timothy, Vladimir, and Lydia spent a great deal of time hiking in the mountains that surrounded the city. The young people were often accompanied by Lemin, who possessed an incredible amount of knowledge concerning the mountains and the animals that made their homes in them. The elf's appearance had changed greatly since his arrival at Saddun. Whether he did not have access to a razor or simply chose not to use one was unknown; however, his facial hair grew unchecked, at least for the moment.

It was during these relatively carefree days that Josiah really had a chance to get to know the cadets from the academy in Belvárd. Although Timothy and Vladimir were often found together, they had practically nothing in common. Timothy was a very outgoing young man, whereas Vladimir was rather shy. While Timothy was always willing to participate in a conversation with other people, or at the very least put in his two cents, Vladimir was more reserved and would not usually join in unless he held a very strong belief on the subject being discussed. Since Vladimir did not talk a whole lot, when he did speak everyone listened. What he said was always well thought out and wielded a fair amount of influence.

Both Timothy and Vladimir were open to the idea of playing games like chess, but here again they were very different. Both had excellent minds, with Timothy being the more impulsive of the two. Often times, Josiah was able to bait Timothy into making mistakes. But he found that this was not an option with Vladimir, who carefully thought through each move before he made it and was often the winner in contests of the mind. However, his tentative mindset hindered him in physical competitions. While he was not a bad swordsman, he was much more cautious and defensive than Timothy. And since battles cannot be won solely by defense, no matter how good it is, he was not victorious very often. Another difference between the two boys was that Timothy was a man of action and preferred getting physical, while Vladimir would much prefer to read than debate. Despite all of these differences, the boys were still best friends and were very hard to separate.

In contrast to the many differences between the boys, Senndra and Rita were very similar in most aspects. Both girls enjoyed reading and could spend hours at a time devouring books and scrolls. As a result, both had sharp minds and excelled in debates and other contests of the mind. They were also very accomplished with the sword, Senndra particularly so, though it was very obvious that Timothy's near defeat by her had been more her good luck than her equality with him concerning sword-fighting skill. Finally, both girls loved nature and enjoyed to hike through the mountains that surrounded Saddun.

It was because of the hiking that one day Josiah found himself high on the slopes of the mountains of the Apathy range. He stopped and looked back at the city, which they had left early that morning. From this distance, the ruined state of the city was not evident. The wall had been the first thing to be repaired, and it could hardly be discerned where the destroyed section had stood. Even the buildings that had been damaged in the fire that broke out during the fighting had been repaired and repainted, and there was new construction occurring in the middle of the city where the ceremony to honor the soldiers was to take place. Workers looked like ants as they scurried around this area.

"Are you coming, Josiah?" Senndra called from further up the mountain. Josiah turned from the city and climbed up the slope to where she stood. Ahead of her, the other cadets and Lemin were still climbing.

"It's a beautiful view from up here," Josiah commented as he and Senndra resumed the climb. "Is this anything like the view from a dragon's back?" he asked a moment later.

"Well, if you forget that you are standing on a mountain and not riding on a dragon…" Senndra began. Josiah waited for her to finish the sentence.

"No, this is nothing like a dragon," Senndra finally finished. She looked sideways at Josiah and continued. "Dragons normally fly much higher than we are, so the earth appears much smaller. Everything is so small that you can hardly distinguish the people from other features. The sun glints off the rivers as they wind across the ground and finally empty into the sea. You're so high and the earth moves beneath you so slowly that, if it weren't for the wind rushing past at incredible speeds, you can forget that you're moving at all. It's just…incredible," Senndra finished and looked at Josiah. She got the feeling that he had no idea what she was talking about.

The two young people caught up to Lemin and the others, who had stopped to rest on an outcropping of rock. Below them, the mountains sloped down to the plain outside of Magessa. From their vantage point, the dwarf fortress, Mt. Nebal, was just a peak rising out of the desert. The Pelé River passed very close to it and extended through a pass in the Apathy Range and out of sight. The Apathy Mountains extended indefinitely to the east and west, with the city of Saddun filling the only visible gap in the range. From the height that Lemin and the young people were, the city looked like an anthill with barely visible humans scurrying around it.

As they were admiring the view, Timothy made a motion to the east. When the others followed the direction of his outstretched hand, they could barely make out a winding line making its way toward the city.

"What is that?" Rita asked. "Surely the dwarves can't have scraped together another army this quickly."

"No, it is not dwarves," Lemin answered. "Nor is it even an army of our enemies. What you see now is the army from the elfin nations to the east. They have traveled as quickly as possible, but even they are restrained by distance and fatigue and are just now arriving."

"That is the elfin army from the forest across the mountains?" Josiah asked. A look of astonishment covered his face. "How many soldiers are there?"

"I would estimate somewhere between thirty and forty thousand troops," Vladimir spoke up. "Of course, at this distance, it is hard to be certain."

"If they were able to get that many troops here in just a few days, the size of their full army must be staggering," Cirro commented.

"It is not as large as you think," Lemin corrected. "Elves are quick to organize themselves, so what you see before you is probably around a third of their full strength. What makes them such valuable warriors is not their numbers, but the fact that all of them can use magic to a certain degree, and about ten percent of them can use it proficiently. In the army that is approaching Saddun, there are more than likely between three and four thousand powerful magicians who could have defeated the dwarf army by themselves."

"You're being serious?" Cirro asked. When Lemin nodded, he continued, "Then why don't the elves gather their forces and crush Molkekk?"

"The magic of the elves may be strong, but the divination of Molkekk is even stronger," Lemin answered. "Though the whole power of the elves, ogres, and humans attacked the cursed city, it is doubtful whether they would succeed in destroying it. Of course, you must understand that the rifts between the nations are great. It is unlikely that they would be put aside, even for the purpose of destroying Molkekk."

"If Molkekk is actually that powerful, are you saying that it isn't possible to destroy him?" Timothy asked. "I thought you said before that with Elohim anything is possible. If that is true, and magicians use the power of Elohim, how is it that they are not powerful enough to overcome him?"

"You are correct; I have said that with Elohim anything is possible," Lemin answered. "However, I still believe that all of the magicians combined may not be able to overcome Molkekk. This is not as contradictory as it may seem, and there is a rather simple explanation. Magicians do use the power of Elohim; however, this power is limited by their experience, and more importantly by their faith. I have seen the most awesome works done by new magicians who had great faith. As they grew older, however, they grew more cynical and were not able to perform as many great works."

"Then there is no hope for the defeat of the enemy," Timothy said. "If all of the magicians of the elves, ogres, and humans put together cannot defeat him, then there is no way to stand against him."

"First of all, I only said that victory would be doubtful; I did not say that it would be impossible," Lemin corrected. "Second, Elohim can choose whoever He wishes to defeat His enemies, and when He decides that Molkekk's time has run its course, He will raise up someone who can defeat him. Finally, it does not matter whether or not we can successfully defy Molkekk; Elohim simply asks that we stand against His enemies. And if we do that to the best of our abilities, there is nothing more that we can do, and He is pleased with us no matter the outcome."

"So you are saying that our ability to overcome the enemies of Elohim does not enter into the equation?" Senndra asked. "As long as we fight for Him and to the best of our abilities, He will be pleased?"

"That is correct," Lemin answered. "The act of obedience, not our success, is the only thing that matters."

"Well that certainly makes it easier to be brave," Josiah said. "Since Elohim is pleased with us as long as we are doing what He wants us to do, the outcome is only of secondary importance. That means we can do what needs to be done without worrying about what other people think about us or whether or not we will succeed."

"Correct," Lemin agreed. "But enough of this heavy handed talk. The reason that we came up here was to enjoy the exercise and fresh air."

"And we have," Petra said. "Can you keep going, sir, or has your age finally caught up to you?"

Petra had shown a humorous side of late, and Lemin appreciated it. It was amazing how different people were when they were not fighting for their lives.

"I do think that I'll take a while to rest," Lemin said with a twinkle in his eye. "Don't let me slow you down, though. Go off and play patty cake or whatever you young people find fun."

The young people ran off laughing leaving Timothy and Senndra alone with Lemin. The cadets looked at their instructor, but he ignored them as he lay back on the ground and closed his eyes.

"Should we join them?" Timothy asked as he watched his friends romp together.

"I'm not really in the mood," Senndra answered. "Do you want to walk?"

"I guess," Timothy answered.

Senndra sighed inwardly as they began to stroll. Ever since facing Timothy in the sword fight competition she had begun to develop feelings for him. At first it had just been friendship, but it had quickly turned into something more. Besides being attractive, he was also strong, kind, and intelligent. He had even shown interest in her several times over the last few days, but whenever she thought he was indicating something more than friendship, he would say something to make her wonder again. 'I guess' wasn't exactly something that set her heart fluttering. Senndra was so deep in thought that she almost missed Timothy's question.

"Josiah's fine," she answered. "You probably know him better than I do, though."

"Really?" Timothy asked, surprised. "I thought you might be interested in him, you know, romantically."

"Not by a long shot," Senndra said.

"Well, that's good to know," Timothy said. "Is there someone else or is everyone too scared of the dragon riding woman who can kick their butt in a sword fight?"

"Scared, probably," Senndra answered with a smile. "I guess they're just afraid that I can keep them in line."

"You're blowing my mind right now," Timothy said. "As pretty and talented as you are, I thought you would have a hundred guys after you."

"Nope, I'm as free as a bird," Senndra said. What did it take for this guy to get a clue? "I'm not interested in anyone which means I'm free if someone was interested and just hasn't said anything yet."

"Well, that's too bad," Timothy said. "Some guy is really missing out. Hopefully he'll catch on one of these days."

Senndra wanted to scream, but just smiled as they continued to walk. Timothy changed the subject, but she couldn't forget it. Was he interested in her or not? All of the questions about her romantic involvement would suggest that he was, but then he had just blown the whole thing off. Was he actually too scared to express interest? That seemed unlikely; after all, this was Timothy, the fearless magician. Was it possible that he had simply not noticed her interest? That was practically impossible, she decided. With as obvious as she had been, it would take an idiot not to notice. He was confusing, frustrating, and impossible to figure out.

Though she tried not to show it, the thoughts kept bothering Senndra for the rest of the day. All of the way back to the city, through dinner, and even as she climbed into her bed, she kept wondering: What is going on behind Timothy's inscrutable, red eyes?

$$******$$

It was well past noon the next day, and Josiah was glad to break formation and watch his men disperse. He had lost more than half of his men in the battle with the dwarves, but in his mind, the ones that remained were the best of the best. They had just stood in formation for two hours through an extremely boring ceremony in which the soldiers that fought against the dwarves were praised for their valor. Josiah found all of the formalities to be extremely dull, especially since they took place under the blazing midday sun. He also had to struggle to hold his tongue when the elders of Gatlon took credit for sending the reinforcements to Saddun. They all wore the silver cross of Elohim and couldn't appear more patriotic.

The ceremony finally ended and all that remained was a feast to celebrate the victory. Then perhaps life could get back to normal. Josiah saw that workmen were already beginning to set up tables all over the drill field for the feast. He got out of the way and allowed the men to do their job. In next to no time, the task was completed and people began to quickly fill the tables. Looking at the mass of bodies occupying the field, Josiah was seriously considering the idea of leaving and not attending the feast; however, he decided to stay for two reasons. The first was that this was going to be the only dinner that he would receive that day. The second reason was that just as he was deciding what to do, an elder of Gatlon captured his attention.

"Commander," the old man began, "though it was not recognized in the ceremony, we have heard that it was your leadership that facilitated the survival of the army when it was attacked by the dwarves."

"Thank you for the recognition," Josiah said and bowed slightly in respect for the man. "However, I only did what was my duty."

"No, you went beyond the call of duty," the man said. "What you did was a great accomplishment. In fact, you are the hero of the entire war, and I would like to personally invite you to share the table of the council."

"Sir, the offer is very generous," Josiah said trying to make himself sound sincere. "However, considering the circumstances of the invitation, I don't think that I deserve this honor."

"Nonsense," the elder said. "You shall dine with us today."

At those words, Josiah's mood dropped considerably, though he did not let it show on his face. Had he chosen to remain at the feast, he would have much rather spent it in the company of his own men, where loud talking and joking would be accepted. Instead, he found himself at the table of the elders of Gatlon, where the conversation threatened to be dull and full of formalities. With a sigh, he followed the elder toward an area where several tables were set up on a platform. After all, how could he turn down an elder, especially when they seemed to think that their invitation was very generous? Josiah stepped up onto the platform and was directed to a seat at the far left of the table. He sat down and watched as servants brought out hundreds of dishes and placed them on the table. He was completely famished, but rather than immediately start to eat, he watched the people at the tables around him to see how he was supposed to eat politely. He carefully mimicked the motions of the man that sat beside him, even to the detail of where he placed his cup when he was not drinking out of it. To make matters worse, the man sitting beside him felt that it was his duty to ask the most pointless and dull questions of Josiah, and of course Josiah felt obligated to answer them. He sat at the table like that for close to an hour, trying to eat in a polite way, but knowing that he was failing miserably.

Finally there was a lull in the conversation. Apparently the surrounding people had run out of stupid questions to ask, and Josiah was left to eat in peace. He ate as quickly as possible, not wanting anything to tie him to this place longer than was absolutely necessary. After he was finished with the meal, he sat back and began to scan the crowd. It was a lot more fun to people watch with a friend, but doing it solo was still better than listening to whatever droll subjects the council members around him were talking about.

Josiah's eyes settled on a section of tables where the cadets of both academies had congregated for the banquet. They were talking and laughing and, by all appearances, having a much better time than he was. With the events of the past week, he hadn't had much time to think, but it suddenly occurred to him that the young men and women sitting out there were his best friends in the whole world. He had fought side by side with them, trusted his life to them, and come out the other side with them. If fire forged stronger steel, combat forged stronger friendships, ones that words simply couldn't describe.

His eyes scanned the cadets one at a time; and he thought of all of the times over the past several days that he had come to rely on them. Cirro was the first to come to mind because he had fought side by side with Josiah for almost the entirety of the battle or 'war' as it was starting to be called. Every time that he had turned around, Cirro had been there helping him or defending him. Their friendship was certainly stronger than it had ever been.

Besides Cirro, the host of new friends that he had made was astounding. Timothy and Vladimir, Senndra, Rita, even Lemin was, in his mind, counted among his friends. These and countless others had stood with him through thick and thin over the last several days, and what they had accomplished had been amazing. Being victorious against an army of dwarves was impressive in and of itself, especially considering the size of their force, but to defeat them so completely went beyond all expectations. Granted dragons had played a very important role in the victory, but the actions of the soldiers could not be discounted. The event had, however, given Josiah a new respect and appreciation for dragons as assets in a battle.

If there was one thing that Josiah placed above all else, in this encounter, it was the new appreciation and knowledge that he had of Elohim. While most people professed to follow Him, Lemin was one that actually did with all of his being. The elf had been convincing on the subject to say the least and Josiah knew that he would be pursuing it more fully in the weeks to come.

Just as Josiah was getting comfortable, out of nowhere, the questions began again- more stupid questions from people that didn't know a blasted thing. Oh well, perhaps, contrary to his first impressions, they were actually trying to understand some of this so that they could make better decisions in the future. At least, he could only hope. Otherwise all of this talking would become completely useless. With an internal sigh he began answering the questions again, seeing the rest of his night disappearing before his eyes.

******

Timothy was having a great time at the feast, cramming his mouth with food and swapping stories and jokes with the soldiers around him. Though he scarcely realized the transition, many of these people had become his best friends over the past several days. He looked to where Vladimir was seated on the other side of the table and several seats to his right. Shared experience and facing death together seemed to bind people faster than years of training together ever had a chance to do.

Timothy looked down to where Lemin, though he was a Commander, sat among the rank and file of the army, laughing and joking with them. That was an instructor that he would have to pay more attention to and spend more time with in the future. He knew how to take control of his men in battle and maintained their respect for him, but at the same time managed to keep a certain familiarity with them. It was a skill that most officers lacked and yet, one that was almost necessary for a good command presence. Not to mention that the elf was a master magician and could certainly teach Timothy a thing or two.

Timothy also realized with a certain amount of surprise that he considered the elf to be one of his friends. He would still feel awkward exchanging jokes with him and the feeling of respect toward the instructor still remained, but something was different now. Lemin was relatable now, unlike most other instructors at the academy. Lemin had stood with Timothy against hordes of enemies and together they had been victorious. They had watched each other's backs and saved each other's lives on multiple occasions. And they were both magicians, a connection that few shared with the elf. It would be a strange friendship Timothy knew, but it was one that he definitely wanted to continue.

Timothy allowed his eyes to continue to wander, and they came to rest on Senndra, a girl he had gone to school with for several years and yet hadn't really paid much attention to until recently. During the past few weeks, they had become better acquainted, but now, like a blow to the head instantly reorganizing his thoughts, he saw her differently. He hadn't realized this before, probably because he always saw Senndra with Rita, who was admittedly the more attractive of the two, but Senndra *was* quite pretty. Add to that the fact that she had an incredible personality, was smart and funny, and had a million other traits that Timothy appreciated and suddenly he had a funny feeling in his chest.

Timothy had never been in love before, nor did he believe in love at first sight. On the other hand, it wasn't like he was seeing Senndra for the first time, though in a way it felt like that was the case. He told himself that he shouldn't feel anything for her, but the feeling that had appeared only a few moments ago grew stronger as he thought more about her. He had to admit to himself that he liked Senndra, but that didn't mean that she had any feelings for him. As far as he knew, she saw him as nothing more than a friend.

Senndra turned to look in Timothy's direction, and their eyes met. He was flustered, but was determined to not let it show on his face. He raised his glass slightly to acknowledge her and was about to look away when she motioned with her head. The movement was very slight, but somehow he knew what it meant anyway: Let's get out of here.

Timothy was taken aback for a moment, then rationalized it. He was just interpreting it like he wanted to interpret it. But, he didn't even want to see it that way. She was just a friend, he told himself, a friend and nothing more. The way his heart was pounding in his chest seemed to disagree. He squinted in a quizzical fashion and shrugged his shoulders slightly to let her know that he didn't understand what she was trying to convey.

Senndra's motion was again slight, but this time she used her hand. Again the meaning was unmistakable: Let's get out of here. Timothy actually started to sweat. He, who had held his own against legions of dwarves, who had personally dispatched scores of the enemy, who was not frightened in the most dangerous of circumstances, *sweated* at the thought of being alone with Senndra Felling. He gave a slight nod to indicate that he understood what she was conveying and stood up from his place at the table. He had a lame excuse prepared to explain his departure, but no one noticed.

Senndra met him about twenty yards from their table, grabbed his hand, and started through the crowd. They moved north until they had broken out of the drill field and away from the people. Senndra released Timothy's hand, and they walked in silence toward the northern wall of the city. Timothy took Senndra's hand as they climbed a set of newly assembled stairs that led to the top of the wall. They sat on some boxes that were by the parapet and looked to the north. By now the sky had darkened considerably, and the moon was just beginning to rise.

"It's beautiful," Senndra said, motioning to the landscape in front of them. Timothy looked out and saw that the word beautiful was about the only way to describe the scenery before him. The moon bathed the plain and mountains in a pale light that made even the foreboding Mt. Nebal look pretty. Timothy looked at Senndra and said the first thing that jumped into his head.

"Not as beautiful as you."

"How long did it take you to come up with that?" Senndra asked and pulled her hand from his. She gave a small laugh and added, "I mean, I don't want to be cruel, but that was a pretty pathetic attempt at a compliment."

"Then I guess I'll have to make my next one better, won't I?" Timothy said.

"You're a smart person, so I'm sure that you'll be able to," Senndra assured him.

"Well, it's not going to be too hard for me," Timothy said. "I mean, it's actually hard to think of an insult for you."

"You mean you can't think of anything that you don't like about me?" Senndra asked. When Timothy nodded she laughed. "I know you must be talking about someone else because there are lots of things wrong with me."

"Well, you just point them out to me and I'll be sure to insult you with them," Timothy said.

"I think that I would rather you not know what they are," Senndra decided. "You'll just have to figure them out for yourself if you want to know."

"Forget what I just said, I've got one," Timothy said. "You like to be hard to get along with."

"That's very perceptive of you," Senndra laughed. "If I can continue to convince you that that is my worst vice, I'll be doing well."

"I don't know about that," Timothy disagreed. "There are very few things in this world that I hate more than someone who is hard to get along with. I don't know why, but I just can't stand someone like that."

"If you hate me so much, why haven't you left yet?" Senndra asked coyly.

"I don't know," Timothy answered. "I guess I must think that there's a chance of changing you. Also, you actually put up with me, so..."

"You know what I think?" Senndra asked. "I believe that you don't actually hate people that are hard to get along with. I think you like it when I am being difficult."

"Now you are the one who is being very perceptive," Timothy said. "I don't know if I can handle a woman with as much insight as you have."

Senndra gave a small laugh and leaned her head on Timothy's shoulder. They sat there together for a long time, talking about nothing and at the same time talking about everything. The moon was almost straight above them when they climbed down from the wall and walked across the city to the south wall. They exchanged a word with the soldiers who were guarding it and passed through to the area that contained the military camp. When they reached Senndra's tent, they said goodnight, and Senndra entered the cloth dwelling. She quickly prepared for bed and slid between her blankets, all the while thinking about Timothy. He was not like the other boys her age; rather he seemed to be more mature and courteous. She fell asleep thinking about him.

Timothy strolled back to his tent. When he reached it, he looked one last time at the moon before passing inside. In no time he was rolled up in his blankets and drifting off to sleep very rapidly. That night he dreamed about Senndra Felling.

******

Those days were some of the happiest for the cadets of both academies at Saddun; however, all things must come to an end, even those that are the best of this life. The dignitaries left Saddun and were followed shortly by the cadets of the Academy of Belvárd. The ogres stayed longer to prevent a repeat attack; however, none was forthcoming, and they returned to their forest in short order. A portion of the elves stayed after all the others had left, convinced that there would soon be a threat to the security of Magessa. They waited for half a year and more, but their vigilance appeared to be unnecessary. Eventually, even they returned to their home in the forest across the mountains.

Peace had returned to Magessa by all outward appearances; however, Mt. Nebal, the dwarf fortress, still stood ominously to the north of Saddun while to the west, the black shadow of Volexa Temp marred the landscape. At the center of Volexa Temp stood a black tower that pointed to the heavens before branching off near its summit. In this tower resided Molkekk, bane of Magessa, who was loath to see any free nation. To be sure, he wanted nothing more than to cast his shadow over the nation to the south of him, but he knew full well that the dwarves had been foiled in their attempt to capture it. Therefore, he determined to wait and watch for the time when he would be able to complete the task that they had started.

# Epilogue

Darkness engulfed the room. The wizard swept across the only illuminated section of floor toward a large glass orb resting on a massively ornamented pedestal. Although his face normally boasted a look of smug satisfaction, it showed only fear now. Sweat stood out on his bald head and even his expansive robes seemed diminished somehow. News of the "Dwarven Failure" as it was already being referred to had just arrived and it was the wizard's job to deliver it to the dark lord. Given the nature of the news, this would probably be the last time he brought any news, and he knew it. His hand shook as he placed it on the orb as if to scry some distant location.

"Why are you here?" a deafening voice boomed from every corner of the room at once.

"My lord Molkekk, I am afraid I have some bad news," the wizard said. His face had gone completely pale now, and he waited for Molkekk to respond. When there was nothing but silence, he continued. "The dwarf army that you sent to breach the northern defenses of Magessa has failed."

There was a blanket of silence for a moment.

"And what of the magicians?" Molkekk finally asked. "Were they harmed in the process?"

"No my lord," the wizard answered. "*He* did an excellent job of making sure that they were not."

"I know that he would like nothing more than to run away from all of this and yet he stays," Molkekk said. "Apparently the leverage is working. They are still in good health, are they not?"

"Yes my lord," the wizard answered.

"With the dwarves' defeat, our position has become more tenuous," Molkekk said. "We will need to remove some of our assets from this place. You know where to take them?"

"Yes my lord," the wizard said. After a moment he added, "Will I be moving *his* family?"

"Yes," Molkekk said. "Anything that is not a direct military asset will be moved."

"Understood, my lord," the wizard said, bowing. "Is there anything else that you require?"

"It was your counsel that convinced me to hire the dwarves," Molkekk boomed. "You have failed me, but are too great of an asset to wipe away for one mistake. Nevertheless, I do not wish to see you again. You will accompany the assets and stay with them to protect them."

"Yes, my lord," the wizard said, happy to escape with his life.

"And wizard," Molkekk said, stopping his underling in his tracks.

"Yes, lord Molkekk," the wizard responded, slowly turning around.

"I would not kill you for a single failure, but do not make a habit of it," Molkekk said. "Fail me again and I will dispose of you."

---

If you enjoyed this book and would like to help others make an informed decision, please go to Amazon and/ or Goodreads and post a review.

Amazon Review

Goodreads
Review

You could also Tweet about it

Tweet

If social media and other technology has changed to the point where none of these exist you'll have to just modify and use your brain. If you live a post-apocalyptic world, please spray paint a review on a dilapidated building. Thanks so much.

# About the Author

Peter Last was very nearly born in an elevator and has continued to be unconventional ever since. He is the sixth child in a large family and has had a conservative upbringing by Yankee parents living in the south. Despite having been homeschooled from kindergarten until twelfth grade, Peter has an expansive social life and has never been locked in a closet. He began writing his first novel, *Guardians of Magessa*, at the age of eleven, receiving great encouragement from his family in the form of compliments such as "Your book is actually not that bad!" Now, eleven years and several massive rewrites later, Peter is finally ready to release his brilliant work to the world. He is currently slogging his way through his fourth year in college, doggedly working toward a degree in Civil Engineering and promising himself he will have more time next semester. In the little spare time he has, Peter writes a blog ([www.peterlast.com](www.peterlast.com)) where he posts short stories, reviews books and movies, and addresses a mixture of serious and absurd topics, from global warming to pencil sharpeners. Peter's other hobbies include drawing, dabbling in amateur film directing, and discharging powerful firearms at shooting ranges. Between school, his social life, and his hobbies, Peter has been forced to cut back on unnecessary activities such as sleeping. At present, he is busy with his series, *The Birthright Chronicles*, of which *Guardians of Magessa* is the first volume.

 The Archives of Magessa contains exclusive members' only content. Members have access to the forum, some of the concept art for my book series, and more. Join the club today to receive access!